TO ONCE AND FUTURE KINGDOMS—

Castles are the citadels of the fantasy realm, just as their real world equivalents are the ultimate representation of power and protection. But not all castles are alike, as the sixteen original stories included in this volume make very clear indeed. So get ready to take a one-of-a-kind castle tour without even leaving home, a tour that will make Europe's most impressive medieval structures seem tame by comparison. . . .

"The Garrison"—They had appeared on Earth without warning, swiftly building their castles on opposite sides of the planet. Perhaps they'd come to defend Earth in some interstellar war, perhaps this was just a convenient stopping-off point, but whatever their reasons for being there, their very presence would change the world forever. . . .

"Concrete Example"—Everyone in the neighborhood thought Mrs. Rizzo was crazy for turning her home into a fortress. But sometimes crazy is the only way to survive. . . .

"Death Swatch"—When the Grim Lord took an elfin princess captive, determined to claim her for his bride, he had no idea how dangerous a move he was making . . . at least not until the dragon interior decorator arrived!

"Swimming the Moat"—They were trapped in the castle, weekend guests whose host had been unexpectedly murdered, and the only way they'd ever win free was to catch the killer before they followed their host down the path of no return. . . .

CASTLE FANTASTIC

Edited by
JOHN DeCHANCIE &
MARTIN H. GREENBERG

DAW BOOKS, INC.
DONALD A. WOLLHEIM, FOUNDER
375 Hudson Street, New York, NY 10014

ELIZABETH R. WOLLHEIM
SHEILA E. GILBERT
PUBLISHERS

First Printing, March 1996
1 2 3 4 5 6 7 8 9

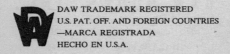

DAW TRADEMARK REGISTERED
U.S. PAT. OFF. AND FOREIGN COUNTRIES
—MARCA REGISTRADA
HECHO EN U.S.A.

PRINTED IN THE U.S.A.

ACKNOWLEDGMENTS

Introduction © 1996 by John DeChancie.
Hall of Mirrors © 1996 by Roger Zelazny.
The Garrison © 1996 by Lawrence Watt-Evans.
Castle Collapse © 1996 by Jane Yolen.
Broomworms and Nosewigs © 1996 by John DeChancie.
Concrete Example © 1996 by Nancy Springer.
Death Swatch © 1996 by Esther Friesner.
Brigbuffoon © 1996 by David Bischoff.
Gie Me Somethin' Ta Eat © 1996 by John Alfred Taylor.
Gwythurn the Slayer © 1996 by Lawrence C. Connolly.
Collectors © 1996 by Pamela Sargent.
Getting Real © 1996 by Raul Cabeza de Vaca.
Merdinus © 1996 by Mike Resnick and Linda Dunn.
Knight Squadron © 1996 by S. N. Dyer.
Swimming the Moat © 1996 by Barbara Paul.
The Soft Terrible Music © 1996 by George Zebrowski.
Held Safe by Moonlight and Vines © 1996 by Charles de Lint.

CONTENTS

INTRODUCTION

by John DeChancie

The reader should be forewarned that this book, despite its title and editor, is *not* an anthology of stories about John DeChancie's "Castle Perilous." That volume may arrive in its time; but for the present, *Castle Fantastic* is, simply put, stories about any and all castles that have something fantastic lurking about them, or built into them. Although the theme readily lends itself to the genre of fantasy, herein contained are some tales people will point to and say, "That's science fiction!" All to the good, for we don't want to restrict any castle's realm. Perhaps one or two of these pieces will take the theme and fashion it into a structure that stands on the genre borderline.

All the same, the bulk of this volume's stories are fantasy, and that's fine, too. There is fantasy of every stripe and kind: dark fantasy, light fantasy, high fantasy, epic fantasy, antic fantasy—again, the more variety the better. There are traditional castles aplenty here, set in various times and places that favor or have favored the growing of castles—Wales, Ireland, England, and various European settings. But not all are set in historical periods or in some fairy-tale kingdom. For instance, we find one stronghold in the midst of the inner city, today; another stands at the South Pole, in the future. You will find within these pages extraterrestrial castles, feminist castles (for who would these days gainsay that a woman's home is her castle?), and a few that are virtual (in the modern, electronic sense). You will find contemporary castles that make their presence felt in the lives of the baby boomers next door.

Merlin's castle, Arthur's castle, castles out of time, castles in cyberspace—we explore many structures, varying the theme as much as possible. *Castle Fantastic* will take you places. We'll put you up in our keep; sometimes we'll scare the hell out of you—but you can take it.

Above all, we have castles that will entertain. The drawbridge descends, the portcullis begins to rise. . . .

Do step inside.

HALL OF MIRRORS

by Roger Zelazny

The last time I talked to Roger Zelazny was on June 6, 1995, when he phoned about some editorial trivia concerning the story below. We had a pleasant conversation, but I noticed something amiss. His voice was thick, and he seemed to be having trouble concentrating. Suspecting nothing serious, I didn't inquire as to his health. I should have. Eight days later, he died of cancer. I couldn't have known; Roger chose not to tell anyone but family about his illness, which he had been fighting for over a year. Looking back on the call, I can see it for the tacit farewell it was. The SF community was shocked and saddened by the loss of one of its most able practitioners. I am disconsolate, for although Roger was a friend, we had seen each other only a few times over the past few years at conventions, and during that time I had passed through his part of the country many times without dropping in to see him. As consolation, I have the honor to present another Amber story by Roger Zelazny. Sadly, it is the last.

Neither of us realized there had been a change until a half-dozen guys tried an ambush.

We had spent the night in the Dancing Mountains, Shask and I, where I'd witnessed a bizarre game between Dworkin and Suhuy. I'd heard strange tales about things that happened to people who spent the night there, but I hadn't had a hell of a lot of choice in the matter. It had been storming, I was tired, and my mount had become a statue. I don't know how that game turned out, though I was mentioned obliquely as a participant and I'm still wondering.

The next morning my blue horse Shask and I had crossed the Shadow Divide 'twixt Amber and Chaos. Shask was a Shadow mount my son Merlin had found for me in the royal stables of the Courts. At the moment, Shask was traveling under the guise of a giant blue lizard, and we were singing songs from various times and places.

Two men rose on either side of the trail from amid rocky cover, pointing crossbows at us. Two more stepped out before us—one with a bow, the other bearing a rather beautiful-looking blade, doubtless stolen, considering the guy's obvious profession.

"Halt! and no harm'll happen," said the swordsman.

I drew rein.

"When it comes to money, I'm pretty much broke right now," I said, "and I doubt any of you could ride my mount, or would care to."

"Well now, maybe and maybe not," said the leader, "but it's a rough way to make a living, so we take whatever we can."

"It's not a good idea to leave a man with nothing," I said. "Some people hold grudges."

"Most of them can't walk out of here."

"Sounds like a death sentence to me."

He shrugged.

"That sword of yours looks pretty fancy," he said. "Let's see it."

"I don't think that's a good idea," I said.

"Why not?"

"If I draw it, I may wind up killing you," I said.

He laughed.

"We can take it off your body," he said, glancing to his right and left.

"Maybe," I said.

"Let's see it."

"If you insist."

I drew Grayswandir with a singing note. It persisted, and the eyes of the swordsman before me widened as it went on to describe an arc calculated to intersect with his neck. His own weapon came out as mine passed through his neck and continued. His cut toward Shask and passed through the animal's shoulder. Neither blow did any damage whatsoever.

"You a sorcerer?" he asked as I swung again, delivering a blow that might have removed his arm. Instead, it passed harmlessly by.

"Not the kind who does things like this. You?"

"No," he answered, striking again. "What's going on?"

I slammed Grayswandir back into the scabbard.

"Nothing," I said. "Go bother someone else."

I shook the reins, and Shask moved forward.

"Shoot him down!" the man cried.

The men on either side of the trail released their crossbow bolts, as did the other man before me. All four bolts from the sides passed through Shask, three of the men injuring or killing their opposite numbers. The one from ahead passed through me without pain or discomfort. An attempted sword blow achieved nothing for my first assailant.

"Ride on," I said.

Shask did so and we ignored their swearing as we went.

"We seem to have come into a strange situation," I observed.

The beast nodded.

"At least it kept us out of some trouble," I said.

"Funny. I'd a feeling you would have welcomed trouble," Shask said.

I chuckled.

"Perhaps, perhaps not," I replied. "I wonder how long the spell lasts?"

"Maybe it has to be lifted."

"Shit! That's always a pain."

"Beats being insubstantial."

"True."

"Surely someone back at Amber will know what to do."

"Hope so."

We rode on, and we encountered no one else that day. I felt the rocks beneath me when I wrapped myself in my cloak to sleep that night. Why did I feel them when I didn't feel a sword or a crossbow bolt? Too late to ask Shask whether he had felt anything, for he had turned to stone for the night.

I yawned and stretched. A partly unsheathed Grayswandir felt normal beneath my fingers. I pushed it back in and went to sleep.

Following my morning ablutions, we rode again. Shask was taking well to hellrides, as well as most Amber mounts did. Better, in some ways. We raced through a wildly changing landscape. I thought ahead to Amber, and I thought back to the time I'd spent imprisoned in the Courts. I had honed my sensitivity to a very high degree through meditation, and I began to wonder whether that, coupled with other strange disciplines I'd undertaken, could have led to my intangibility. I supposed it might have contributed, but I'd a feeling the Dancing Mountains were the largest donor.

"I wonder what it represents and where it came from?" I said aloud.

"Your homeland, I'd bet," Shask replied, "left especially for you."

"Why did you read it that way?"

"You've been telling me about your family as we rode along. I wouldn't trust them."

"Those days are past."

"Who knows what might have happened while you were away? Old habits return easily."

"One would need a reason for something like that."

"For all you know, one of them has a very good one."

"Possibly. But it doesn't seem likely. I've been away for some time, and few know I'm free at last."

"Then question those few."

"We'll see."

"Just trying to be helpful."

"Don't stop. Say, what do you want to do after we get to Amber?"

"Haven't made up my mind yet. I've been something of a wanderer."

I laughed.

"You're a beast after my own heart. In that your sentiments are most unbeastlike, how can I repay you for this transport?"

"Wait. I've a feeling the Fates will take care of that."

"So be it. In the meantime, though, if you happen to think of something special, let me know."

"It's a privilege to help you, Lord Corwin. Let it go at that."

"All right. Thanks."

We passed through shadow after shadow. Suns ran backward and storms assailed us out of beautiful skies. We toyed with night, which might have trapped a less adroit pair than us, found a twilight, and took our rations there. Shortly thereafter, Shask turned back to stone. Nothing attacked us that night, and my dreams were hardly worth dreaming.

Next day we were on our way early, and I used every trick I knew to shortcut us through Shadow on our way home. Home.... It did feel good to be headed back, despite Shask's comments on my relatives. I'd no idea I would miss Amber as much as I had. I'd been away far longer on countless occasions, but usually I had at least a rough idea as to when I might be heading back. A prison in the Courts, though, was not a place from which one might make such estimates.

So we tore on, wind across a plain, fire in the mountains, water down a steep ravine. That evening I felt the resistance begin, the resistance which comes when one enters that area of Shadow near to Amber. I tried to make it all the way but failed. We spent that night at a place near to where the Black Road used to run. There was no trace of it now.

The next day the going was slower, but, more and more, familiar shadows cropped up. That night we slept in Arden, but Julian did not find us. I either dreamed his hunting horn or heard it in the distance as I slept; and though it is often prelude to death and destruction, it merely made me feel nostalgic. I was finally near to home.

The next morning I woke before sunup. Shask, of course, was still a blue lizard curled at the base of a giant tree. So I made tea and ate an apple afterward. We were low on provisions but should soon be in the land of plenty.

Shask slowly unwound as the sun came up. I fed him the rest of the apples and gathered my possessions.

We were riding before too long, slow and easy, since there would be some hard climbing up the back route I favored. During our first break I asked him to become once more a horse, and he obliged. It didn't seem to make that much difference, and I requested he maintain it. I wanted to display his beauty in that form.

"Will you be heading right back after you've seen me here?" I asked.

"I've been meaning to talk to you about that," he

responded. "Things have been slow back in the Courts, and I'm no one's assigned mount."

"Oh?"

"You're going to need a good mount, Lord Corwin."

"Yes, I'm sure."

"I'd like to apply for the job, for an indefinite period."

"I'd be honored," I said. "You're very special."

"Yes, I am."

We were atop Kolvir that afternoon and onto the grounds of Amber Palace within hours after that. I found Shask a good stall, groomed him, fed him, and left him to turn to stone at his leisure. I found a nameplate, scratched Shasko's name and my own upon it, and tacked it to his door.

"See you later," I said.

"Whatever, Lord. Whatever."

I departed the stables and headed for the palace. It was a damp, cloudy day, with a chill breeze from the direction of the sea. So far, no one had spotted me.

I entered by way of the kitchen, where there was new help on duty. None of them recognized me, though they obviously realized that I belonged. At least, they returned my greeting with due respect and did not object to some fruit I pocketed. They did ask whether I cared to have something sent to one of the rooms, and I answered "yes" and told them to send a bottle of wine and a chicken along with it. The afternoon head chef—a red-haired lady named Clare—began studying me more closely, and more than once her gaze drifted toward the silver rose on my cloak. 'I did not want to announce my identity just then, and I thought they'd be a little afraid to guess ahead at it, at least for a few hours. I did want the time to rest a bit and just enjoy the pleasure of being back. So,

"Thanks," I said, and I went on my way to my quarters.

I started up the back stairs the servants use for being unobtrusive and the rest of us for being sneaky.

Partway up, I realized that the way was blocked by sawhorses. Tools lay scattered about the stairs—though there were no workmen in sight—and I couldn't tell whether a section of old stair had simply given way or whether some other force had been brought to bear upon it.

I returned, cut around to the front, and took the big stairway up. As I made my way, I saw signs of exterior repair work, including entire walls and sections of flooring. Any number of apartments were open to viewing. I hurried to make sure that mine was not among their number.

Fortunately, it was not. I was about to let myself in when a big red-haired fellow turned a corner and headed toward me. I shrugged. Some visiting dignitary, no doubt. . . .

"Corwin!" he called out. "What are you doing here?"

As he drew nearer, I saw that he was studying me most intently. I gave him the same treatment.

"I don't believe I've had the pleasure," I said.

"Aw, come on, Corwin," he said. "You surprised me. Thought you were off by your Pattern and the '57 Chevy."

I shook my head.

"Not sure what you're talking about," I said.

He narrowed his eyes.

"You're not a Pattern ghost?" he said.

"Merlin told me something about them," I said, "after he effected my release at the Courts. But I don't believe I've ever met one."

I rolled up my left sleeve.

"Cut me. I bleed," I said.

As he studied my arm, his gaze appeared more than a little serious. For a moment, I thought he'd actually take me up on it.

"All right," he said then. "Just a nick. For security purposes."

"I still don't know who I'm talking to," I said.

He bowed.

"Sorry. I am Luke of Kashfa, sometimes known as Rinaldo I, its king. If you are who you say you are, I am your nephew. My dad was your brother Brand."

Studying him, I saw the resemblance. I thrust my arm farther forward.

"Do it," I said.

"You're serious."

"Dead right."

He drew a Bowie knife from his belt then and looked into my eyes. I nodded. He moved to touch my forearm with its tip and nothing happened. That is to say, something happened, but it was neither desired nor wholly anticipated.

The point of his blade seemed to sink a half-inch or so into my arm. It kept going then, finally passing all the way through. But no blood came.

He tried again. Nothing.

"Damn!" he said. "I don't understand. If you were a Pattern ghost, we'd at least get a flare. But there's not even a mark on you."

"May I borrow the blade?" I asked.

"Sure."

He passed it to me. I took it in my hand and studied it. I pushed it into my arm and drew it along for perhaps three-quarters of an inch. Blood oozed.

"I'll be damned!" Luke said. "What's going on?"

"I'd say it's a spell I picked up when I spent a night in the Dancing Mountains recently," I replied.

"Hm," Luke mused. "I've never had the pleasure, but I've heard stories of the place. I don't know any simple ways to break its spells. My room's off toward the front." He gestured southward. "If you'd care to stop by, I'll see what I can figure out about it. I studied Chaos magic with my dad, and with my mother, Jasra."

I shrugged.

"This is my room right here," I said, "and I've a chicken and a bottle of wine on the way up. Let's do the diagnosis in here, and I'll split the meal with you."

He smiled.

"Best offer I've had all day," he said. "But let me stop back at my room for some tools of the trade."

"All right. I'll walk you back, so I'll know the way in case I need it."

He nodded and turned. We headed up the hall.

Turning the corner, we moved from west to east, passing Flora's apartments and moving in the direction of some of the better visitors' quarters. Luke halted before one room and reached into his pocket, presumably after the key. Then he halted.

"Uh, Corwin?" he said.

"What?" I responded.

"Those two big cobra-shaped candle holders," he said, gesturing up the hall. "Bronze, I believe."

"Most likely. What of them?"

"I thought they were just hall decorations."

"That's what they are."

"The last time I looked at them, they kind of bracketed a small painting or tapestry," he said.

"My recollection, too," I said.

"Well, there seems to be a corridor between them now."

"No, that can't be. There's a proper hallway just a little beyond—" I began.

Then I shut up because I knew. I began walking toward it.

"What's going on?" Luke asked.

"It's calling me," I said. "I've got to go and see what it wants."

"What is it?"

"The Hall of Mirrors. It comes and goes. It brings sometimes useful, sometimes ambiguous messages to the one it calls."

"Is it calling us both, or just you?" Luke said.

"Dunno," I replied. "I feel it calling me, as it has in the past. You're welcome to come with me. Maybe it has some goodies for you, too."

"You ever hear of two people taking it at once?"

"No, but there's a first time for everything," I said. Luke nodded slowly.

"What the hell!" he said. "I'm game."

He followed me to the place of the snakes, and we peered up it. Candles flared along its walls, at either hand. And the walls glittered from the countless mirrors which hung upon them. I stepped forward. Luke followed, at my left.

The mirror frames were of every shape imaginable. I walked very slowly, observing the contents of each one. I told Luke to do the same. For several paces, the mirrors seemed simply to be giving back what was before them. Then Luke stiffened and halted, head turning to the left.

"Mom!" he said explosively.

The reflection of an attractive red-haired woman occupied a mirror framed in green-tinged copper in the shape of an Ouroboros serpent.

She smiled.

"So glad you did the right thing, taking the throne," she said.

"You really mean that?" he asked.

"Of course," she replied.

"Thought you might be mad. Thought *you* wanted it," he said.

"I did once, but those damned Kashfans never appreciated me. I've got the Keep now, though, and I feel like doing a few years' research here—and it's full of sentimental values as well. So as long as Kashfa stays in the family, I wanted you to know I was pleased."

"Why—uh—glad to hear that, Mom. Very glad. I'll hang onto it."

"Do," she said, and vanished.

He turned to me, a small ironic smile flickering across his lips.

"That's one of the rare times in my life when she's approved of something I've done," he said. "Doubtless for all the wrong reasons, but still. . . . How real are these things? What exactly did we see? Was that a conscious communication on her part? Was—"

"They're real," I said. "I don't know how or why or what part of the other is actually present. They may be stylized, surreal, may even suck you in. But in some way they're really real. That's all I know. Holy cow!"

From the huge gold-framed mirror, ahead and to my right, the grim visage of my father Oberon peered forth. I advanced a pace.

"Corwin," he said. "You were my chosen, but you always had a way of disappointing me."

"That's the breaks," I said.

"True. And one should not speak of you as a child after all these years. You've made your choices. Of some I have been proud. You have been valiant."

"Why, thank you—sir."

"I bid you do something immediately."

"What?"

"Draw your dagger and stab Luke."

I stared.

"No," I said.

"Corwin," Luke said. "It could be something like your proving you're not a Pattern ghost."

"But I don't give a damn whether you're a Pattern ghost," I said. "It's nothing to me."

"Not that," Oberon interjected. "This is of a different order."

"What, then?" I asked.

"Easier to show than to tell," Oberon replied.

Luke shrugged.

"So nick my arm," he said. "Big deal."

"All right. Let's see how the show beats the tell."

I drew a stiletto from my boot sheath. He pulled back his sleeve and extended his arm. I stabbed lightly.

My blade passed through his arm as if the limb were made of smoke.

"Shit!" Luke said. "It's contagious!"

"No," Oberon responded. "It is a thing of very special scope."

"That is to say?" Luke asked.

"Would you draw your sword, please?"

Luke nodded and drew a familiar-looking golden blade. It emitted a high keening sound, causing all of the candle flames in the vicinity to flicker. Then I knew it for what it was—my brother Brand's blade, Werewindle.

"Haven't seen that in a long while," I said, as the keening continued.

"Luke, would you cut Corwin with your blade, please?"

Luke raised his eyes, met my gaze. I nodded. He moved the blade, scored my arm with its point. I bled.

"Corwin— If you would. . . ?" Oberon said.

I drew Grayswandir and it, too, ventured into fighting song—as I had only heard it do on great battlefields in the past. The two tones joined together into a devastating duet.

"Cut Luke."

Luke nodded and I sliced the back of his hand with

Grayswandir. An incision line occurred, reddening immediately. The sounds from our blades rose and fell. I sheathed Grayswandir to shut her up. Luke did the same with Werewindle.

"There's a lesson there somewhere," Luke said. "Damned if I can see what it is, though."

"They're brother and sister weapons, you know, with a certain magic in common. In fact, they've a powerful secret in common," Oberon said. "Tell him, Corwin."

"It's a dangerous secret, sir."

"The time has come for it to be known. You may tell him."

"All right," I said. "Back in the early days of creation, the gods had a series of rings their champions used in the stabilization of Shadow."

"I know of them," Luke said. "Merlin wears a spikard."

"Really," I said. "They each have the power to draw on many sources in many shadows. They're all different."

"So Merlin said."

"Ours were turned into swords, and so they remain."

"Oh?" Luke said. "What do you know?"

"What do you deduce from the fact that they can do you harm when another weapon cannot?"

"Looks as if they're somehow involved in our enchantments," I ventured.

"That's right," Oberon said. "In whatever conflict lies ahead—no matter what side you are on—you will need exotic protection against the oddball power of someone like Jurt."

"Jurt?" I said.

"Later," Luke told me. "I'll fill you in."

I nodded.

"Just how is this protection to be employed. How do we get back to full permeability?" I asked.

"I will not say," he replied, "but someone along the way here should be able to tell you. And whatever happens, my blessing—which is probably no longer worth much—lies on both of you."

We bowed and said thanks. When we looked up again, he was gone.

"Great," I said. "Back for less than an hour and involved in Amber ambiguity."

Luke nodded.

"Chaos and Kashfa seem just as bad, though," he said. "Maybe the state's highest function is to grind out insoluble problems."

I chuckled as we moved on, regarding ourselves in dozens of pools of light. For several paces nothing happened, then a familiar face appeared in a red-framed oval to my left.

"Corwin, what a pleasure," she said.

"Dara!"

"It seems that my unconscious will must be stronger than that of anyone else who wishes you ill," she said. "So I get to deliver the best piece of news of all."

"Yes?" I said.

"I see one of you lying pierced by the blade of the other. What joy!"

"I've no intention of killing this guy," I told her.

"Goes both ways," Luke said.

"Ah, but that is the deadly beauty of it," she said. "One of you must be run through by the other for the survivor to regain that element of permeability he has lost."

"Thanks, but I'll find another way," Luke said. "My mom, Jasra, is a pretty good sorceress."

Her laughter sounded like the breaking of one of the mirrors.

"Jasra! She was one of my maids," she said. "She

picked up whatever she knows of the Art by eaves-
dropping on my work. Not without talent, but she
never received full training."

"My dad completed her training," Luke said.

As she studied Luke, the merriment went out of
her face.

"All right," she said. "I'll level with you, son of
Brand. I can't see any way to resolve it other than the
way I stated. As I have nothing against you, I hope
to see you victorious."

"Thanks," he said, "but I've no intention of fighting
my uncle. Someone must be able to lift this thing."

"The tools themselves have drawn you into this,"
she said. "They will force you to fight. They are
stronger than mortal sorcery."

"Thanks for the advice," he said. "Some of it may
come in handy," and he winked at her. She blushed,
hardly a response I'd have anticipated, then she was
gone.

"I don't like the tenor this has acquired," I said.

"Me neither. Can't we just turn around and go
back?"

I shook my head.

"It sucks you in," I told him. "Just get everything
you can out of it—that's the best advice I ever got on
the thing."

We walked on for perhaps ten feet, past some absolutely lovely examples of mirror making as well as
some battered old looking glasses.

A yellow-lacquered one on Luke's side, embossed
with Chinese characters and chipped here and there,
froze us in our tracks as the booming voice of my late
brother Eric rang out:

"I see your fates," he said with a rumbling laugh,
"And I can see the killing ground where you are des-
tined to enact them. It will be interesting, brother. If
you hear laughter as you lie dying, it will be mine."

"You always were a great kidder," I said. "By the way, rest in peace. You're a hero, you know."

He studied my face.

"Crazy brother," he said, and he turned his head away and was gone.

"That was Eric, who reigned briefly as king here?" Luke asked.

I nodded. "Crazy brother," I said.

We moved forward and a slim hand emerged from a steel-framed mirror patterned with roses of rust.

I halted, then turned quickly, somehow knowing even before I saw her who I would behold.

"Deirdre ..." I said.

"Corwin," she replied softly.

"Do you know what's been going on as we walked along?"

She nodded.

"How much is bullshit and how much is true?" I asked.

"I don't know, but I don't think any of the others do either—not for sure."

"Thanks. I'll take all the reassurances I can get. What now?"

"If you will take hold of the other's arm, it will make the transport easier."

"What transport?"

"You may not leave this hall on your own motion. You will be taken direct to the killing ground."

"By you, love?"

"I've no choice in the matter."

I nodded. I took hold of Luke's arm.

"What do you think?" I asked him.

"I think we should go," he said, "offering no resistance—and when we find out who's behind this, we take him apart with hot irons."

"I like the way you think," I said. "Deirdre, show us the way."

"I've bad feelings about this one, Corwin."

"If, as you said, we've no choice in the matter, what difference does it make? Lead on, lady. Lead on."

She took my hand. The world began to spin around us.

Somebody owed me a chicken and a bottle of wine. I would collect.

I awoke lying in what seemed a glade under a moonlit sky. I kept my eyes half-lidded and did not move. No sense in giving away my wakefulness.

Very slowly, I moved my eyes. Deirdre was nowhere in sight. My right-side peripheral vision informed me that there might be a bonfire in that direction, with some folks seated around it.

I rolled my eyes to the left and got a glimpse of Luke. No one else seemed to be nearby.

"You awake?" I whispered.

"Yeah," he replied.

"No one near," I said, rising, "except maybe for a few around a fire off to the right. We might be able to find a way out and take it—Trumps, Shadowalk—and thus break the ritual. Or we might be trapped."

Luke put a finger into his mouth, removed it, and raised it, as if testing the wind.

"We're caught up in a sequence I think we need," he said.

"To the death?" I said.

"I don't know. But I don't really think we can escape this one," he replied.

He rose to his feet.

"Ain't the fighting, it's the familiarity," I said. "I begrudge knowing you."

"Me, too. Want to flip a coin?" he asked.

"Heads, we walk away. Tails, we go over and see what the story is."

"Fine with me." He plunged his hand into a pocket, brought out a quarter.

"Do the honors," I said.

He flipped it. We both dropped to our knees.

"Tails," he said. "Best two out of three?"

"Naw," I said. "Let's go."

Luke pocketed his quarter, and we turned and walked toward the fire.

"Only a dozen people or so. We can take them," Luke said softly.

"They don't look particularly hostile," I said.

"True."

I nodded as we approached and addressed them in Thari:

"Hello," I said. "I'm Corwin of Amber and this is Rinaldo I, King of Kashfa, also known as Luke. Are we by any chance expected here?"

An older man, who had been seated before the fire and poking at it with a stick, rose to his feet and bowed.

"My name is Reis," he said, "and we are witnesses."

"For whom?" Luke said.

"We do not know their names, There were two and they wore hoods. One, I think, was a woman. —We may offer you food and drink before things begin...."

"Yeah," I said. "I'm out a meal because of this. Feed me."

"Me, too," Luke added, and the man and a couple of his cohorts brought meat, apples, cheese, bread, and cups of red wine.

As we ate, I asked Reis, "Can you tell me how this thing works?"

"Of course," he said. "They told me. When you're finished eating, if you two will move to the other side of the fire, the cues will come to you."

I laughed and then I shrugged.

"All right," I said.

Finished dining, I looked at Luke. He smiled.

"If we've got to sing for our supper," Luke said, "let's give them a ten-minute demonstration and call it a draw."

I nodded.

"Sounds good to me."

We put aside our plates, rose, moved to the fire, and passed behind it.

"Ready?" I said.

"Sure. Why not?"

We drew our weapons, stepped back, and saluted. We both laughed when the music began. Suddenly, I found myself attacking, though I had decided to await the attack and put my first energies into its counter. The movement had been thoughtless, though quite deft and speedy.

"Luke," I said as he parried, "it got away from me. Be careful. There's something odd going on."

"I know," he said as he delivered a formidable attack. "I wasn't planning that."

I parried it and came back even faster. He retreated.

"Not bad," he said, as I felt something loosened in my arm. Suddenly I was fencing on my own again, voluntarily, with no apparent control but with fear that it might be reasserted at any moment.

Suddenly, I knew that we were fairly free and it scared me. If I weren't sufficiently vicious, I might be taken over again. If I were, someone might slip in an unsolicited move at the wrong moment. I grew somewhat afraid.

"Luke, if what's happening to you is similar to what's been happening to me, I don't like this show a bit," I told him.

"Me neither," he said.

I glanced back across the fire. A pair of hooded individuals stood among the others. They were not overlarge and there was a certain whiteness within the cowl of the nearer.

"We've more audience," I said.

Luke glanced back; it was only with great difficulty that I halted a cowardly attack as he turned away. When we returned to hard combat, he shook his head.

"Couldn't recognize either of them," he said. "This seems a little more serious than I thought."

"Yeah."

"We can both take quite a beating and recover."

"True."

Our blades rattled on. Occasionally, one or the other of us received a cheer.

"What say we injure each other," Luke said, "then throw ourselves down and wait for their judgment on whatever's been accomplished. If either of them come near enough, we take them out just for laughs."

"Okay," I said. "If you can expose your left shoulder a bit, I'm willing to take a midline cut. Let's give them lots of gore before we flop, though. Head and forearm cuts. Anything easy."

"Okay. And 'simultaneity' is the word."

So we fought. I stood off a bit, going faster and faster. Why not? It was kind of a game.

Suddenly, my body executed a move I had not ordered it to. Luke's eyes widened as the blood spurted and Grayswandir passed entirely through his shoulder. Moments later, Werewindle pierced my vitals.

"Sorry," Luke said. "Listen, Corwin. If you live and I don't, you'd better know that there's too much crazy stuff involving mirrors going on around the castle. The night before you came back, Flora and I fought a creature that came out of a mirror. And there's an odd sorcerer involved—has a crush on Flora. Nobody knows his name. Has something to do with Chaos, though, I'd judge. Could it be that for the first time Amber is starting to reflect Shadow, rather than the other way around?"

"Hello," said a familiar voice. "The deed is done."

"Indeed," said another.

It was the two cowled figures who had spoken. One was Fiona, the other Mandor.

"However it be resolved, good night, sweet prince," said Fiona.

I tried to rise. So did Luke. Tried also to raise my blade. Could not. Again, the world grew dim, and this time I was leaking precious bodily fluids.

"I'm going to live—and come after you," I said.

"Corwin," I heard her say faintly. "We are not as culpable as you may think. This was—"

"—all for my own good, I'll bet," I muttered before the world went dark, growling with the realization that I hadn't gotten to use my death curse. One of these days. . . .

I woke up in the dispensary in Amber, Luke in the next bed. We both had IVs dripping into us.

"You're going to live," Flora said, lowering my wrist from taking my pulse. "Care to tell me your story now?"

"They just found us in the hall?" Luke asked. "The Hall of Mirrors was nowhere in sight?"

"That's right."

"I don't want to mention any names yet," I said.

"Corwin," Luke said. "Did the Hall of Mirrors show up a lot when you were a kid?"

"No," I said.

"Hardly ever, when I was growing up either," Flora said. "It's only in recent years that it's become this active. Almost as if the place were waking up."

"The place?" Luke said.

"Almost as if there's another player in the game," she responded.

"Who?" I demanded, causing a pain in my gut.

"Why, the castle itself, of course," she said.

THE GARRISON

by Lawrence Watt-Evans

Lawrence Watt-Evans, author of many novels and stories, won the Hugo in 1988 for "Why I Left Harry's All-Night Hamburgers." Here he explores the unsettling notion that our planet may be regarded, by a far-flung interstellar empire, as a remote outpost, worthy of a military presence but little else.

Billy stuffed his turnpike receipt in his back pocket and stepped on the power, heading out of the tollgate and straight up I-576. He wasn't trying to beat out anyone or give the state cops a challenge, but his foot was pretty heavy on the pedal, purely out of enthusiasm—and nerves. Another hour's drive and he'd be there.

This load was gonna do it. This was the one that was gonna make him rich. He just knew it. It *had* to. He'd been looking at who did best selling stuff to the aliens and who went broke, and while he wasn't one of those egghead professors or anything, he thought he had it doped out.

He *knew* he'd doped it out, because if he hadn't, he was ruined, broke—he'd put every penny he had into this.

The aliens were gonna *love* what he had filling his van. They had to!

He charged past Spring Run and Dry Run and Doylesburg at sixty, slowed a bit for the traffic at the Waterloo-Blairs Mills exit and the long curve to the left, then floored it to get his load up the slope and across the ridge without losing speed.

At the top, as he crested the ridge, he took his foot off the power and stared. He'd been here half a dozen times before, as a tourist, as someone else's roadie, and on his own, but it still got to him every time.

The alien fortress. The castle. The Black Log Mountain garrison.

The whole structure was gleaming white, shining brightly in the midday sun. The outer walls curved up gracefully—he couldn't see the base, the surrounding buildings clustered too closely, but Billy had seen them close up, and he knew that they started out flat to the ground and swooped upward in smooth soaring organic curves that were made up of thousands of narrow ribs, ranging from the thickness of threads to the size of century-old tree trunks, weaving and interweaving to form a solid wall. Billy had had a coral paperweight once, and the way those walls were put together reminded him of coral somehow.

And at the top those curves ended in upthrust spikes and pinnacles that looked like some sort of gigantic bleached-out spun-sugar thistle.

And then inside the ring of the outer walls stood the main structure, with its spiral towers and twining buttresses, like a wild hybrid of Cinderella's Castle at Disney World and some science fictional city of the future run amok, all glowing softly—it didn't really show by daylight, but at night the whole thing was lit up like one of those Christmas lawn displays, white speckled with dots and lines of red and green.

And at the center of the whole thing, that central tower, what some people called the Keep, rose up and up and up, half a mile into the sky, bristling with spines like some impossible pale cactus.

That was the actual ship—at least, that's what everyone said. Billy hadn't seen the place before the castle was built. Hell, he'd still been in diapers when the aliens first landed and settled in on Black Log Mountain—plastic diapers, not the modern live ones. No one had figured out back then how to use the alien's sludge-eaters to make diapers. No one had ever *seen* the alien's sludge-eaters.

Billy supposed it must've been one hell of a surprise when that half-mile-long starship dropped down out of nowhere like that, and started growing a castle here in the middle of Pennsylvania. The one in New South Wales had caught everyone off-guard, too, but Billy'd never seen that one up close. He'd never been to Australia. From the pictures, the castle there looked exactly like the one here; the only difference was in the surroundings.

Billy remembered when he'd first seen the castle. He'd been about six, and his parents had driven up here with him and his sisters, all of them jammed into an old gas-burner. I-576 hadn't been built yet, they'd come up the old roads through Orbisonia.

When they first saw the castle, his father had stopped the car and they'd all gotten out to look at it.

His father had stood there saying, "Oh, my God," over and over. His mother had stared silently, but Billy had thought she looked scared.

And his kid sister Susanna had been openly terrified; she'd started shrieking, "Too big! Too big!" Then she'd climbed back in the car and hidden her face, refusing to look at the castle again.

His older sister Lita hadn't been scared, and neither had Billy. It wasn't fear he'd felt.

It was greed. He'd wanted a piece of it.

And now he was going to get one, as much as any human could.

He was over the top of the ridge now, and headed down the western slope, down toward the foot of Black Log Mountain.

The city of Black Log reached from the castle walls at the top of the slope all the way down to the valley floor, and the sides of the interstate were lined with signs advertising power stations, motels, and short-term storage. It seemed as if there were even more than there had been on his last run.

Well, that was no surprise. Black Log had been growing constantly ever since the government first put up a couple of tents outside the castle gates. Back then the towns like Waterloo and Doylesburg had been tiny, half-forgotten villages reachable only by winding back roads, and Black Log Mountain itself had been nothing but woods—but then the aliens arrived. As long as the aliens were here and willing to do business, Billy figured people would be coming here to do business with them.

'Course, he'd heard a rumor when he was loading up that they weren't buying much lately. His cousin Al had said he'd heard that the aliens had got real busy with something inside the castle, no one was sure what—or if anyone was sure, whoever it was wasn't talking about it. The aliens were pretty careful about who they let in and where Earthpeople went while they were in there.

Billy smiled. What really drove the eggheads batshit was that the aliens preferred generals and admirals to professors when it came to picking houseguests.

They liked artists, too, but they had their own ideas of what was art—Billy was counting on that. Maybe they'd got busy, but they'd still be interested in what he was carrying, he was sure of it.

He was into the city now and cutting diagonally up the side of Black Log Mountain, passing the run-down apartments where many of the less successful traders lived.

Billy had heard plenty of folks saying that the way to get rich off the aliens wasn't to trade with 'em directly at all, it was to come in here and open a restaurant or a motel or something to make money off the actual traders—like in the gold rush days, when most of the prospectors wound up broke, and the merchants who sold the prospectors their supplies wound up rich. That might have been true when the castle first went up, but after almost twenty years the competition in the service industries was pretty fierce; it looked to him like the only way to make a real killing was off the aliens. Twenty years they'd been here—well, nineteen and a half—and they still didn't have a good handle on what Earth money was worth.

Or maybe they just didn't care. They hadn't come here for money, after all—the trading that went on was just a sideline, something to keep the natives happy and to keep from getting bored.

Billy didn't remember when the truth had come out; he'd been about four when the aliens had finally admitted why they were on Earth, and why they'd built two castles on opposite sides of the planet. It had been big news for a long time, but hadn't meant much to a four-year-old.

Billy figured the Earthpeople back then must've been pretty damn stupid to have not figured it out for themselves—or maybe they had figured it out, and it had just taken a while to get the aliens to admit it. He wasn't clear on that, and it didn't much matter. He didn't remember not knowing, and couldn't really imagine it.

He passed the Warehouse Row exit and slowed up a little. The castle towered over him now; he was close enough that he couldn't see it all any more. The view had been far better from the ridgetop across the valley.

A castle like that, what had they *thought* it was for? What was a castle *ever* for?

A castle was a war machine, a defensive system—

everyone knew that. And with one on each side of the globe, they could defend the whole planet.

That's what they were doing; they were guarding Earth, keeping everyone safe. To Billy, that soaring central spire was a promise of protection—and now, a promise of wealth.

What had really worried the eggheads and the generals, though, was who were the aliens guarding against?

The aliens had never explained that very well—but then, how could they, beyond the obvious? *Their* bunch of aliens was at war with *another* bunch of aliens, and neither side had a name that would translate into English. Big surprise.

Billy took the Market Square exit and made the three-quarters-of-a-circle turn onto Market Street.

As long as the war wasn't *here,* Billy didn't really give a damn who was fighting, or why. It wasn't any of his business. Earth wasn't involved. The aliens in the two castles had assured everybody that Earth wasn't involved, that they were just here to keep an eye on this part of the galaxy to make sure the other side wasn't trying to sneak anything past them.

And they'd been here almost twenty years without any enemy fleets showing up, so Billy figured they'd told the truth. This wasn't some frontline unit here; this was a backwater garrison in the middle of nowhere, with nothing to do but pass the time trading with the natives.

And Billy, as one of those natives, was eager to trade—*desperate* to trade. He'd always felt drawn to the castle, ever since he first saw it, as if he knew that his entire life was tied to it, for better or for worse. He'd dropped out of high school to hire on as a roadie for Jack Chu, helping old Jack load and unload pinball machines, when Jack had decided that the aliens would love pinball machines—it had been a way to get close to the castle, and Billy hadn't hesitated an instant.

The aliens hadn't been all that impressed. They'd bought just one machine, then lost interest. Billy figured it was because pinball machines were too big and heavy. Jack had lost a bundle, and Billy had been out of work, as well as out of school—but he was hooked more than ever. He'd been inside the castle, hauling that old pinball machine, and he wanted to get in there again.

There was money to be made, trading with the aliens—and Billy *liked* the aliens. Jack never really had *liked* them; he'd just seen the chance for a quick buck.

Most people just saw a chance for a quick buck.

The market square was crowded—jammed, in fact. Billy saw that he wasn't going to find any on-street parking. In fact, he wouldn't be surprised if he had to double all the way back down to Warehouse Row and take a shuttle back up. He decided to try the Northeast Garage first, though.

A chance for a quick buck, all right. Fortunes had been made trading with the aliens. The guy who'd traded a Swiss army knife for a jar of sludge-eaters, the company that had swapped an antique steam engine for instruction in building portable fusion plants, the belly dancer who'd gotten the secret of fixed-field levitation for her performance, they were all unspeakably rich now.

And the aliens were rich, too—they collected royalties on the fusion plants and levitation fields. A few lawyers had gotten unspeakably rich off *that*.

They used their royalties to buy things that interested them, often paying outrageous prices—but not as outrageous as what those lucky few had received. Nobody had gotten any really valuable secrets out of the aliens in years now.

Billy's onboard computer reported four parking spaces still vacant in the Northeast Garage; he stepped on the power to get one of them while he still could.

The aliens' computers made Earth's best look like alphabet blocks, and that wasn't even mentioning the nanomachines, like the ones that had built most of the castle, but the aliens insisted they couldn't teach anyone how to make those. Most people didn't believe them; most people assumed the aliens just didn't trust Earthpeople with secrets that powerful.

Not Billy; he believed the aliens. After all, these weren't some hotshot scientists sent to Earth to teach Earthpeople alien technology; these were soldiers. If you put an ordinary American soldier on some South Seas island, he'd be able to show the natives how to do *some* stuff—build a water wheel, say—but what if one of them asked how to make a radio? That soldier could show them how to *work* a radio, maybe how to *fix* one, but not how to *build* one.

So Billy was perfectly willing to believe the alien soldiers when they said they couldn't explain their computers or other molecular machinery. He sympathized with them. They were doing their job, guarding Earth against the enemy; teaching the natives wasn't what they were here for.

The four parking slots were on the top level, and two of them were gone when Billy got there, but he snagged the third one. He maneuvered the van in and cut the power.

As the field collapsed and the vehicle settled slowly to the pavement, he pulled the big portfolio out of the back. This held his sample. He thought he'd only need the one, though you could never be sure with the aliens. They didn't always think like Earthpeople.

They sure didn't always agree with Earthpeople about what was valuable. Billy was counting on that. If the aliens didn't buy his cargo, he was ruined. He was out the twelve grand he'd put together from his own savings and all the money he could borrow, because no one else was going to pay for what he was hauling.

For lots of people twelve grand would be nothing much; for Billy it was everything.

It was a good thing, he thought, that the aliens didn't have the same standards humans did.

That was something a lot of the traders didn't understand. They figured the aliens would appreciate quality, like human millionaires. They'd show up on the aliens' doorstep with truckloads of top-of-the-line electronics or first-quality gemstones or fine art from the galleries in New York, and go into shock at how little the aliens offered. Billy had seen it.

And then there were other traders who thought the aliens were the ultimate rubes. They'd show up with velvet paintings of matadors or big-eyed kittens, or with cheap kids' toys, and sometimes the aliens bought and sometimes they didn't.

Billy jogged down the sidewalk with the portfolio swinging. He thought he'd come up with something the aliens would buy. He'd listened to the older traders talking, he'd listened to the government officials who were constantly holding meaningless meetings with the aliens, he'd even listened to the professors who came to study the aliens and never seemed to realize that the aliens didn't *want* to be studied, and he thought he'd figured it out.

He thought probably plenty of other folks had figured it out before him, but they'd kept their mouths shut and made their money and gone home to live in luxury. That was what *he* intended to do. He wasn't going to find out how the nanomachines were made, or how to build a faster-than-light drive, but Billy was willing to settle for a few million dollars from the aliens' royalty money.

He didn't bother with the market square, where the crowds milled about, buying from each other and selling to each other while two of the aliens stalked curiously about, looking down at the humans. Those aliens weren't going to be shelling out real money; they were just low-ranking grunts with pocket change. Instead he marched straight up to the castle gate.

A dozen pairs of eyes turned to watch him as he did.

"Hey, kid," someone called, "forget it. They're not letting anyone in any more."

Billy didn't hesitate; he wasn't falling for that. He walked up to the human guards at the security point and pulled out his wallet.

"William Rodriquez," he said. "I've got a pass." He opened the wallet and showed the nearer guard the glittering little token that an alien had given him the year before, the token that meant the aliens liked him and that mere humans shouldn't keep him out.

Of course, it didn't mean the aliens would let him in this time; people with tokens got turned away all the time. The tokens all looked the same to Earthpeople, but the aliens could read them somehow; if the alien who had given a particular token was busy, or out of favor, or simply gone, the token would not be honored and no admittance would be given.

"Won't do you any good, son," the guard said. His manner was friendly enough, so Billy listened politely. "That fellow out there wasn't just giving you a hard time; they haven't let *anyone* in for the past three weeks. No traders, no brass, nobody. Hell, those two out in the market are just about the only ones who've been outside the walls since last month."

Billy blinked. Now, *that* hadn't been in his plans. He'd heard they weren't buying much, but he hadn't realized it was *that* bad.

"Anyone know why?" he asked.

The guard shook his head. "Lots of guesses, of course, but they're not talking. They just say they're busy."

Billy didn't like that. When soldiers were busy, that was a real bad sign.

"Mind if I try anyway?" he asked.

The guard shrugged. "Fine by me. You've got the pass, you go on in. You know the rules, right?"

"Sure."

And of course he did. No knives, no guns, no explosives, and for some reason the aliens had never explained, no phones, no eyeglasses, and no fingernail polish. Never touch an alien. Never kick anything, though pushing with your hands was okay, and keep your shoes on at all times, even if you had to wade through one of the streams of water that sometimes ran through parts of the castle. Don't cover your nose or mouth if you have to cough or sneeze.

He didn't understand all the rules, but he knew them. And he didn't have to understand them; he was a human, and the rules were alien. He only had to obey them.

He walked through the metal detector and the bioscanner without setting off any alarms, and then his feet were on the edge of the castle walls. Ahead of him the tracery of white fibers curved gradually upward; if he were to walk straight ahead, in twenty meters he'd have to get down on hands and knees to climb the slope, and in thirty he'd be stopped when the walls reached vertical.

He didn't expect to go that far.

And sure enough, before he'd gone a dozen steps the wall opened before him.

And it wasn't the high narrow opening with the blue light in it that meant "go away"; instead it was the regular gate, the big door and smooth gray path that would lead him into the castle.

Billy grinned with relief. Behind him, he heard the guard mutter, "Well, I'll be damned."

He strolled on down the path and through the doorway, into the familiar gray-and-white waiting room. Two aliens were waiting there for him.

These were the usual sort, not any of the exotic varieties—they were humanoid, eight or nine feet tall, very thin, with bluish-gray skin. They wore white overalls decorated with odd patterns of short lines in bright colors. Some Earthpeople theorized that those lines were insignia of rank, or clan designations, or controls for devices built into the overalls; Billy had no idea what they were, and didn't much care. He lowered his portfolio and did the formal arms-spread, knees-spread gesture of greeting.

The aliens responded in kind, but quickly and sloppily.

Billy didn't think he'd met either of these two before. The ordinary aliens weren't always easy to tell apart, but these two didn't look quite right to be anyone he'd dealt with before.

Of course, some aliens were completely different—there were aliens that looked like walking sea anemones or exploding turtles or plumbers' nightmares. But ordinarily, humans didn't see those aliens. Dealing with the natives was generally left to the eight-foot blue-gray humanoids, and those all looked more or less alike. And they wouldn't give names, which made identification more difficult.

Nobody knew whether the other kinds were different species, or other parts of some complex life cycle, or artificial creations; for that matter, a good many scientists thought the blue-gray humanoids were robots built specifically to deal with humans. That was just one of many subjects where the aliens weren't talking.

"Hello," Billy said. "I'm a trader. I'm called Billy."

"Hello, Billy," the nearer alien replied. "We will consider your wares. And we have news for your people."

"What news?" He'd never heard that before.

"Let us trade first. What have you brought?"

Billy smiled. He lifted the portfolio, and a platform rose from the floor to accommodate it. He zipped it open to display the painting inside.

The aliens bent over it for a few seconds; then one of them asked, "Have we not seen images of this image before? Have we not been told that this is a cultural treasure? Our laws forbid the acquisition of any item you people consider to be a cultural treasure."

Billy shook his head. "Nope," he said. "This isn't the original. Let me explain."

The two aliens turned to listen to him, and Billy launched into his prepared speech.

"The original painting, Van Gogh's 'Starry Night,' is indeed one of our great cultural treasures. My people value it above all other handmade images. So greatly do we value it that many of our young artists strive to recreate it, so that their hands may learn the skills that can make such a thing. I had heard how one of your people admired this image, and how greatly you regretted that you could not acquire it without harming us, so I thought of those young artists. Ordinarily, their recreations are stored away or even destroyed, for they are not the original and may not be displayed, but if they were instead to be given to you, in appreciation of your long service in guarding our planet from all enemies, would that not be a good thing for everyone?"

"This is a copy?"

Billy started to nod, then remembered that the aliens interpreted nodding as indicating boredom, rather than agreement. "Yes, this is a copy, made by a skilled young artist."

"This is not itself a cultural treasure?"

"No."

"And you have other copies?"

"Yes. In my vehicle I have one hundred forty-three more copies of this image, each handmade by one of our finest artists."

The aliens looked at one another and murmured quietly in their own language. Billy stood, watching, trying not to show how nervous he was.

He thought he had it figured right.

He'd known about the cultural treasure rule; plenty of would-be traders didn't, and ruined themselves as a result. The aliens were fascinated by human arts and crafts, but had strict rules about what they could acquire.

Photographs didn't interest them, not even photographs of famous artworks, or photos that were art in themselves; Billy wasn't sure why this was so, but he'd seen it for himself, and he supposed it was because the aliens' own recording devices were so superior to anything humans could do that buying human-made photos would be like a man with a good camera buying a child's stick-figure sketch instead of snapping his own picture.

And Billy had observed, in his visits, that the aliens weren't much interested in humans as subjects. They didn't like portraits of any kind, or figure studies. He supposed that was natural enough; he wouldn't have wanted to buy himself a painting of an alien. Let alone several paintings.

After all, they all looked alike.

The aliens weren't much interested in anything else on Earth, either—paintings of dogs or horses or landscapes didn't excite them.

And they didn't think much of pure abstraction—

or photorealism. They liked paintings that looked like paintings.

And the aliens *were* interested in things relating to themselves, to some extent. Humans had never been able to produce portraits of the aliens that the aliens appreciated—something indefinable was missing—but human paintings of the castle on Black Log Mountain had been popular for a while.

And the aliens came from the stars.

Billy had put that all together, and had taken his savings and hired a bunch of art students to copy the Van Gogh, and here he was, trying not to sweat or tremble.

He even thought he knew *why* the aliens were interested in human art. It wasn't as art for its own sake; it was as souvenirs. Quality didn't matter. It was like tourists buying local arts and crafts. They didn't care how good a piece was; they just wanted something that would show they'd been someplace unusual, something that would look interesting on a shelf or a wall back home.

And tourists *wanted* their souvenirs to look a little primitive, a little strange, but recognizable.

That fit the Van Gogh perfectly.

One of the aliens turned to him. "What price are you asking for each image?"

This was it. This was the crucial moment.

"These were made by the finest artists. I must ask five hundred thousand dollars for each painting."

The alien hesitated.

The other alien murmured something—probably the equivalent of, "They expect you to haggle. They don't respect you if you don't."

"That seems a high price," the first alien said.

Billy nodded.

The two aliens conferred.

"Surely one hundred thousand each would be enough?" one of them suggested.

Billy suppressed a grin. If they took them all, that would be more than fourteen million dollars, and even if they only bought the single sample, he'd have a healthy profit—and that was their *starting bid*! He'd done it!

"The artists will be shamed," he said, "that you could offer so little."

The dickering took about twenty minutes, and settled on buying the entire batch at a quarter million each—thirty-six million dollars for a vanload of cheap copies! Billy was ecstatic.

"I will bring my vehicle to the gate for delivery," he said.

"Yes," the alien said, "but first, the news for your people."

"Oh, yeah," Billy said. He waited politely, expecting something trivial or incomprehensible.

"We are leaving," the alien said. "The garrison is being withdrawn."

Billy's jaw dropped. In an instant, his world shifted beneath him.

The aliens had always been here, as long as he could remember, guarding Earth; how could they leave?

"Your paintings are a fine parting gift for our soldiers here. We thank you for that, but we will not be trading anything more with your people. We are prepared for our departure and will launch in seven hours. We strongly advise everyone to leave the area."

"But . . . what about the one in Australia?"

"That garrison is also withdrawn. We are leaving your planet entirely."

"Why? Is the war over?"

The alien made an ugly little noise that Billy couldn't interpret—a laugh, perhaps? "No," it said.

"But then why?" He tried not to sound as panicky as he felt.

"We are needed elsewhere."

And that was all the answer Billy could coax from them; a moment later he was deposited back outside the gate.

A line had formed at the security checkpoint—people had seen Billy go in, and they assumed that meant a return to business as usual.

A few had already been turned away, though, from the dejected look of a group clustered to one side.

Billy's appearance created something of a stir.

"Are they buying?" someone called. "What'd you sell 'em?"

Billy ignored the question. He hesitated, unsure what to do.

He had to bring his van around, of course, and get his money—the aliens would pay him with a check drawn on their accounts here on Earth.

Would that check still be good when they were gone? He'd have to get it certified or something.

But he also had to tell everyone the news. And he didn't know how.

At last he stepped up to the nearer of the two guards at the checkpoint. "I have to talk to you," he whispered.

Startled, the guard glanced around, then stepped back past the bioscanner to Billy's side.

"What is it?" he asked.

"They told me to tell everyone," Billy said. "They're leaving. In seven hours. And they said something about people should be clear of the area when they launch—I guess it won't be safe."

"What?" The guard blinked at him. "Are you serious?"

"Damn right I am," Billy said.

"This . . . you aren't trying some sort of scam, are

you, buddy? Because I swear, if you are, I'll see your ass rot in jail."

Billy shook his head. "Nope," he said. "I swear right back at you, I'm telling you what they told me. If anyone's lying, it's them."

"Oh, shit." The guard looked up at the wall that towered over them. Then he turned and headed for his phone.

"Hey," Billy called, "I got a delivery to make—they're buying my cargo for souvenirs. When they open up for it, you can ask them yourself."

The guard looked up from the phone with a slightly dazed expression; it took a few seconds for Billy's words to penetrate. "Right," he said at last.

Billy threw him a mock salute and headed for his van.

By the time he maneuvered the vehicle into the market square, soldiers and police were forcing the crowds back, ordering everyone away. A soldier came up to the van window and said, "You'll have to back this right out of here, mister—square's closed to traffic."

"Not me," Billy said. "Ask the gate guard—I've got a delivery." He flashed the alien token in his wallet.

The soldier hesitated. "Wait here," he said.

"Sure thing."

By the time the soldier returned and waved Billy through a cluster of brass was forming at the security checkpoint. By the time he maneuvered the van backward through the heavy vehicle gate, he was driving through a solid wall of officers and bureaucrats.

The castle wall opened, and three men in fancy uniforms marched through before Billy could even get the van's rear doors open.

Billy watched them go, then shrugged and lifted a stack of paintings up onto one shoulder.

Once inside, an alien directed him down one passage, but he could see that the generals had taken another. He could hear their voices—they were already starting to shout.

That wouldn't get them anywhere. Billy smiled at the alien, put down the paintings, and went back for more.

When he had transferred his entire cargo into the castle, he smiled and said, "You pay me now, right?"

The alien handed him a slip of paper. Billy looked at it; sure enough, a check for thirty-six million dollars, made out to William Rodriquez.

His hand trembled.

Thirty-six million dollars.

And it was *already* certified, he saw.

No one had ever said the aliens were stupid. If there were things about Earth they didn't seem to understand, it wasn't because they were stupid, it was because they hadn't bothered to learn them.

"Thank you," Billy said.

He felt as if he should shake the alien's hand, or even give it a big hug, but he knew the rules. He turned to go, holding the precious check out before him. Then he paused.

"Hey—good-bye, to all of you," he said. "And good luck. I hope you guys win your war." He waved, and walked out.

The alien didn't respond to his farewell; it simply stood and watched him go.

Billy climbed into his van and tucked the check securely into a dashboard compartment; then he slammed the door and turned on the power.

It was time to get the hell out of here, and to never look back.

He wondered whether the brass would figure it out, and what they would do if they did. Would they pick through the wreckage, trying to rebuild the outer defenses? Would they try to build their own castles, their own starships? Would there be enough of the alien technology left to be any help?

Billy doubted it. He imagined South Sea islanders trying to build jeeps and radios from leftover spare parts.

The aliens said they were leaving because they were needed elsewhere.

That meant they were losing the war. Billy was sure of it. Why else would their commanders be desperate enough to withdraw a little backwater garrison like this?

And their enemy, whatever it was, might well hunt down and destroy every outpost it could find, even abandoned ones, just to make sure that victory was secure.

And when that enemy found Earth, Pennsylvania was going to become a very unhealthy place. Maybe not tomorrow, or next week, or next year—maybe never, really. Maybe the enemy would never bother with a place like this.

But Billy knew, as he joined the honking angry crowd of vehicles trying to crowd onto I-576 and get out of Black Log, that he was never coming back here. He was going to take his beads and trinkets, his thirty-six million dollars, and go as far away as he could get—California, maybe, or Europe. And he was going to enjoy life while he could.

Because any day, any time, the enemy could show up, and find the garrison gone, the castle walls undefended, the area unguarded against rapine and pillage.

And whoever was out there that would justify a castle like *that* was probably pretty damn good at rapine and pillage. They might well take out the entire planet. There might be nowhere to hide—but Billy was going to try.

The traffic was unbelievable. He was only a hundred miles away and headed west when the ship's launch lit up the night sky behind him, and the castle keep rose toward the stars.

CASTLE COLLAPSE

by Jane Yolen

Over a long career, Jane Yolen has written many a marvelous fantasy for adults and young people. Here she beguiles us with a witty, postmodern comment on the classic fairy tale, a form of literature about which she is an expert.

At 1700 hours the castle decided to shut itself down. That meant the moat could not be drained, which meant the dragons would have to get their gills rootered out, and Cook would have to do the kitchen spits by hand. Again.

"If we weren't behind on the payments, I'd raze the damned thing," King said.

"There, there, dear," said Queen. It was all she said these days, her brain box having short-circuited in the last shutdown. "There, there." As it was appropriate to King's mood, he hadn't yet noticed the problem.

Herald walked into the room doing a hesitation step which had more to do with the shutdown than parade mode. *This* King noticed.

"Get your walker fixed!" he shouted.

"Sir!" Herald snapped, turned, and went out again, even more slowly.

"I don't know what I have done to deserve this," King said. He would have wept but had somehow misplaced the royal handkerchief.

"There, there, dear," said Queen, absently patting

his hand and missing by three whole inches. "There, there." Her hand stroked the arm of the throne.

King started to get up when the candle flames flickered, dimmed, went out.

King turned to Queen. "Do we have extra matches?"

"There, there," Queen answered.

"Where?" King asked. "Where?"

"There, there," Queen repeated. Her hand, meaning to pat his, missed by five inches and he mistook it in the gloom for a gesture.

"Oh, there," he said, standing and heading toward the spot to which Queen had pointed.

It was the open window.

He glanced at the sky.

One by one, the stars were going out, too.

"Bother," said King. "And just when I thought I'd got it debugged. Well, there it is."

"There, there," said Queen.

It was not the greatest of epitaphs, but at least it had resonance.

BROOMWORMS AND NOSEWIGS

by John DeChancie

A castle, after all, is a residence. Most castles today are empty of inhabitants and have become museums, mere tourist attractions. The one featured in this story is both a museum and residence. But you might not want the guided tour. You could find out something you don't want to know.

Little did I know then, last Tuesday night, very late, that a broom left out on the patio would initiate my association with Castle Sondergaard and its collection of zoological exotica, which would lead to my impending demise. I sit at my word processor as the funnel cloud and its resident housegobbler approaches. The eaves shiver, the walls vibrate, the roof shakes. Soon the housegobbler will blow its cover, so to speak, flush from its whirling column of dust and vapor, and strike. The housegobbler does not gobble houses so much as it smashes them to flinders, to root among the ruins for a toothsome bite—a succulent shard of wooden joist, perhaps, or a tasty fluff of fiberglass ... but I get ahead of myself.

Better to backtrack a bit to last Tuesday night, when I had an Honors Seminar in classical ethics the next day, and had not yet graded papers to hand back. This happens often. I am by nature an indolent procrastinator; but then again the cretinous scribblings of my students were hardly inducement. They attested sadly to the sorry state of the contemporary undergraduate. Some of these papers were barely literate. Spelling and punctuation? "Abysmal" does not adequately say it, but would that those were the only problems. However, there is nothing to be done. In recent years the halls of Academe have been flung open to everyone and anyone, regardless of talent, brains, or preparation. I am as egalitarian as the next social critic— but there are limits to how much remedial instruction can be done at an institution of higher learning. Oh, hell ... I'm not getting to the point, am I?

Enough. To delay the struggle with the papers even further, I wanted to sweep out the kitchen and couldn't find the broom, and chanced to look out on the patio of my garden apartment, which backs on lawn bordered by a stand of timber. There stood the broom against the outside wall. I went out and fetched it back to the kitchen, where I hit the straw against the smudged linoleum a few times, whereupon, to my chagrin, out from the broom scurried a swarm of resident insects. Earwigs, mostly, curious rear pincers flailing. I stamped a few of them to death, but the rest dashed for cover among the cracks of the cabinets, never to be seen again. I turned the broom upside down and peered into the tattered straw. Any more in there? I was on the verge of deciding that the last of the squatters was out when I noticed something: a fat, moist, dark brown mass nestled, and I mean *nestled,* comfortably, right at home there, among the yellow stalks of straw. I thumped the brook against the floor again to try to shake it out. At first I mistook it for a cocoon, but, seeing it writhe and burrow itself down again, I couldn't imagine what it was. A slug? No, it was sluglike, but much too active, too quick in its movements, to be a garden slug. A larva? Of what, then? Whatever, it was a thick brown vermiform ... thing. A wormlet. Maybe it was a fat night crawler.

The phone rang, and I went to pick it up, broom still inverted and in hand.

It was my ex-wife, but I won't go into the gruesome details of the conversation. Every conversation with Aline is at least a skirmish, if not a pitched battle. She and her lawyer had perfected the fine art of flensing a man, of separating him from his fatty layer of comfort. I had lost my house, and most of my salary. Now she was going after the capital of my trust fund. She deserved the lion's share of it, she and her legal goon reasoned. Never mind that gutting it would reduce its quarterly dividends to practically nothing and force me into either bankruptcy or moonlighting to meet my monthly expenses, which, recently fattened by alimony payments, were formidable to say the least. And that was before taxes levied against a single person with no dependents. Sans Aline and her worthless brother, I was now ensconced in that tax category. Her worthless brother. The ne'er-do-well brother-in-law: a cliché in drawing-room drama, but I had a real-life one, Brent, by name. Brent Rhys Osborne, of the Boston Osbornes, from which Back Bay Brahmin tribe, naturally, Aline also derived. Like many contemporary scions of blue-blooded families, he had taken to causes. He fancied himself an environmental and animal rights "activist." He loved the birds, he loved the bees. He cared not much for human beings, freely admitting that he regarded human beings as congenitally flawed and unworthy of concern. Humans, in fact, according to his curious *Weltanschauung,* were "viruses" invading the ravaged body of Mother Earth.

"Who's going to do the job of antisepsis, Brent?" I asked him once. "You and your tree-hugger friends? You're the *good* viruses, I take it?"

Brent would sneer. "Fred, did you get that from Rush Limbaugh's newsletter? Or the National Review?"

To which I said, "Eh? Get what?"

"The 'good viruses' thing. Look, Fred, if you restrict your input on environmentalism to what drips out of quasi-Nazi rags—"

"Who said it dripped from quasi-Nazis? Fact is, I wrung it out of something on your bookshelf, Brent. A very sympathetic swatch of cloth indeed. It came from a quoted interview with one of your ideological buddies."

"Uh-huh. Well, people say all sorts of crazy things. No, I don't consider myself a good virus. I don't want to wipe out the human race. What if I were to quote some of the more extreme racist and anti-Semitic positions on your side of the spectrum and hold you accountable? Fair is fair."

"Good rejoinder. But there are racists and anti-Semites on your end, too. So, where does that leave you?"

It left him, most of the time, broke. I know what you are thinking: Back Bay Brahmins aren't usually broke. Nevertheless, Brent Rhys Osborne was, and he was simply because, for all his egalitarian and eleemosynary leanings, he liked to spend money on himself, the more money and the faster he spent it, the better. Naturally enough, he refused to "go into trade" to make up the shortfalls. He was above working for his living. American aristocrats get their habits from their British cousins. His family had settled money on him long ago, but the capital had been gutted over the years, victim of Brent's high living habits. However, Brent felt someone still owed him a living, so he came to College Green to sponge off his sister and her stock portfolio, and when that was consumed, he began slavering for his sister's husband's trust fund. He'd lived off and on with us for over two years before I'd left, all the while scheming to get Aline and me to separate. My money, in trust, was invulnerable except through court action. Now I was well rid of his raging sneer of a mouth but not of the gaping maw of his constant economic need, into which my ex-wife was perfectly willing to throw the greater part of my money. She couldn't very well let him give up his berth at the Salem Yacht Club, could she?

What was it I said about getting to the point? Forgive me.

The worm in the broom didn't exactly bother me, but the question of what it was nagged at me from the musty back storage shed of my brain all week. It was no pressing need. Skeptical rationalist that I am, I simply don't like the unexplained. I wanted things like strange broom-dwelling worms explained to me, preferably in simple terms. What was that damned thing I had seen?

I had no friends in the university's Life Sciences department, but there was one acquaintance, John Bruckner, the chairman, who might be willing to help. Trouble was, I didn't know which specialized reservoir of biological expertise I wanted to tap.

"You're probably wanting an entomologist, Fred," Dr. Bruckner told me. "A bug man. Professor Sondergaard sounds like the specialist you need."

"Sondergaard? Never ran into him."

"He's eccentric, keeps to himself. Rare bird. When he does come in, he sometimes wears a surgical mask."

"So do some Orientals, out of concern for spreading flu microbes. Are you saying he has a phobia?" I ventured.

"Don't know, really. He's in a strange field. Specializes in discovering and naming new species of crawly things. Has several discoveries to his credit."

"Okay, Dr. Sondergaard sounds as though he's right up my alley. Sondergaard. Scandinavian?"

"Norwegian. Born there, came here as a young man shortly before the Second World War."

Bruckner gave me his number and his College Green address. So I dialed the number and got on the other end a lightly accented voice that answered to my "Professor Sondergaard?" Getting an affirmative, I introduced myself, and asked him straightaway about the strange broom interloper.

"You have a specimen?"

"Eh? Uh, no. It got away. Could you tell me what it was?"

"Young man, you do not want to know."

And he hung up.

Undaunted and implacable, I called him right back.

"See here, Professor Sondergaard. You and I are tenured professors at the same university. We are colleagues. If you had one shred of an idea of what professional courtesy is—"

"Say no more," Sondergaard said wearily. "I am sorry for hanging up. If you only knew, you would forgive."

"Knew what?"

"Ah, that is what you should not be asking."

"I am simply asking for your professional opinion on an unusual species of ... well, insect life, I think, though it could have been a worm."

"It was, and worms are not insects. Insects are of another family completely."

"Of course. But could you tell me what that thing was in the broom?"

"It was a broomworm."

"I see. Interesting."

"Does that help you?"

"Are they rare?"

"Extremely. There are in a sense almost nonexistent, except under certain circumstances."

"Which are?"

"In the circumstances of someone observing them."

"Oh."

"I am afraid I haven't been much help."

"Not a lot, true. Could you tell me why—?"

"Young man . . . excuse me, what is your name again?"

"Frederick Mallory. Dr. Frederick Mallory, Department of Philosophy and Symbolic Logic."

"Ah, then you can appreciate the philosophical import of what I'm about to say. I have been for years investigating the field of cryptozoology. Strange and unknown forms of life."

"I thought that pertained to life on other planets, or something like that."

"That is xenobiology. Dr. Mallory, do you know the total number of different forms of life on this planet—the total number of individual species?"

"Oh, I've heard guesses."

"They are shots in the dark. The answer is that no one knows. Not a month goes by that some entomologist somewhere doesn't discover a new species of insect."

"Yes, but insects—"

"The plethora of species does not confine itself to the insect realm. True, very few new types of large mammal have been found recently."

"I should think."

"But have you heard of the microbes that live only in the vicinity of volcanic vents in the ocean floor? They thrive in water that is boiling hot and in the complete absence of sunlight."

"Yes, I've seen any number of nature documentaries. But what I'm asking is—"

"What you see in the TV documentaries is not even the tip of the iceberg of what I'm talking about. I'm talking about biological exotica that live right under our noses, but which practically no one notices. For instance, your broomworm. It is related to the night-crawler, but it does not live in the ground. It makes its home among the stalks of thick patches of bulrush or other aquatic grasses. Occasionally, it stumbles into human territory and finds a happy environment in a kitchen broom."

"Fascinating, Doctor." I flinched at sounding like Spock of *Star Trek*. "That's really interesting. So this thing does exist, eh?"

"Most assuredly. But they are rare. That is why I asked if you had captured a specimen. I would be very interested in obtaining one."

"I'll keep an eye out. Or a broom, actually."

"Yes. But sightings have been exceedingly few. You are only the second person to report one directly to me."

"How do you know the broomworm actually exists?"

"A colleague in Hungary claims she has one. I have never seen it, though."

"What did you mean by that business of its existing only in the circumstances of someone observing it?"

"This is a touchy philosophical issue. Cryptozoology, in the sense of studying unknown forms of life, is not a recognized field of investigation, you know, at least not in the West. We have no professional journal, no international conferences are funded. We are a laughing stock in some circles of the biological sciences. 'Tabloid stuff,' they say. Like Bigfoot, and the beast that lives in the Scottish loch."

"But if you have specimens ... ?"

"They are few and far between. I have indeed established the existence of a few new species, with specimens to back up my claims. But these are paltry, and of no especial interest. For you see, Dr. Mallory, there are hundreds, if not thousands of totally unknown species of life, insect and otherwise, wriggling under our feet. Some are quite amazing."

"You haven't explained about the philosophical part."

"Out of our despair of ever becoming respected ... after mountains of rejected papers on the possible existence of this or that exoticum, with data admittedly based on fleeting observations and hearsay—some of us have advanced the theory that something else is going on. It may be that not everyone can observe these creatures. Some human beings may be endowed with certain gifts of perceptual ability. The reason that these life-forms are almost completely unknown may be that the vast majority of mankind simply cannot perceive them."

"I can see how all this dovetails into Bigfoot and UFOs," I said. "Sounds very familiar."

"If only our task was merely to establish things as mundane as UFOs! Millions of people have seen a UFO. Practically no one has ever observed or documented any true exotica. Some of these life-forms are truly astounding. You would not believe half of them. Some are even quite dangerous."

"Dangerous? Could you give me a for instance?"

"The nosewig."

"Nosewig?"

"Yes. By chance have you ever been walking along, say on a bright summer day, and have something fly up your nose?"

I laughed. "Yes. A gnat, surely."

"What do you do in that circumstance?"

"Well, you root your finger around in there to try and dig the bugger out. Or you blow your nose."

"Have you ever succeeded in killing or capturing the thing?"

I chuckled. "No, can't say that I ever did. It's happened rarely. Surely the thing flies out by itself."

"How are you sure? How do you know that the creature did not crawl up the nasal passage and up in the sinus cavity? For that is exactly what it did."

"I can't say that I ever suffered any dire consequences from it."

"Have you ever had a bout of migraine headaches?"

"Of course, but that doesn't establish—"

"Nosewig infestation can be fatal. The thing, which is exceedingly small, by the way, insinuates its way through the blood-brain barrier and on up into the cranial cavity, where it causes no end of damage. The process can take years, but the result is always death."

"Ridiculous."

"Oh, you think so? Then I think there can be an end to this conversation."

He hung up, and this time I did not call back.

A true crackpot, I thought. A rarity in academic circles, but not completely unknown.

At least that's what I thought until Friday afternoon, when I was making my way across the Quadrangle and saw stocky, ill-dressed John Bruckner shuffling in the other direction.

"Fred! Ever connect up with Sondergaard?"

"I did."

"And he helped you?"

"Immensely. He informed me that if you have a worm in your broom, it's a broomworm."

John cackled. "Sorry he couldn't be of more value."

"Don't apologize for him. He's one rare species himself. And that accent of his sounds like a parody of an Ingmar Bergman film—"

"What's wrong, Fred?"

I had doubled over, both hands over my nose, one finger frantically trying to prize out the tickly, buzzing thing that had flown up into my left nostril.

Reacting quickly, I tore a swatch of tissue paper out of my pocket—it just so happened that I had suffered an attack of sniffles that very morning (I'm allergic to house dust and some forms of pollen). I thrust the ragged mass over my face and blew my nose, hard. Very hard. In fact, I sounded like a goose in heat.

"Whoa," John said, backing away. "Your allergies again?"

I couldn't talk, for I had something, I thought. I had caught some wriggling critter between my index finger and thumb. It was small, but hard. I stuffed it into the tissue and squeezed as hard as I could, trying to crush it. Bruckner looked on uneasily.

I looked up and grinned sheepishly. "Sorry. Some damned thing flew up my nose."

"Ewwww, I *hate* when that happens."

I felt a sudden pang of acute embarrassment. There I was, blowing my nose and clutching God knew what unmentionable nostril product in my fists. Hoping the little bugger was truly dead, I pocketed the clump of damp tissue.

My nose started to bleed.

I won't go into further unpleasant descriptions. Suffice it to say that I made haste from that place and came straight home, my embarrassment giving way to intense curiosity about what I had caught in the sodden clump of tissue.

As soon as I got into the apartment, I went to the kitchen, found a wooden salad bowl, and set it down over the tissue on the dining room table. Then I searched for the reading lens that had come with my copy of the compact edition of the Oxford English Dictionary. I located it, then searched the bathroom for tweezers. Finding one, I brought it to the dining nook and, after carefully lifting the salad bowl, began a painstaking search of the soggy, bloodstained clump.

This was not a pleasant task, but my efforts were ultimately rewarded. There, caught in the tweezers, was a tiny, tiny hard black bit of something. Carefully, I looked at it through the glass. My God, it was small, but it was definitely an insect of some sort. A dead insect, I'm glad to say. It didn't move.

In another five minutes I was on my way to Professor Sondergaard's address with the carcass of the whatever-it-was imprisoned in an empty plastic drugstore pill bottle, safe in my coat pocket.

Sondergaard's house was a castle. Not real, of course, but one of those neo-Gothic knockoffs of which some nineteenth century architects were inordinately fond. The place had turrets, battlements, the whole bit. Suitably eccentric, even kooky.

I touched the front doorbell button and heard bonging inside. The tune was familiar, but I couldn't place it.

Waiting patiently, I watched ravens wheel in the sky over the house. Wind whipped through the sycamore trees in the side yard, making dead branches rattle and tick. Cinematically, this whole affair was quickly going from Bergman to Corman.

It was some time before the door opened, and there stood Sondergaard, tall and gaunt and white-haired. Thick spectacles covered his eyes.

"Dr. Mallory, I presume?" he said.

"How did you know?"

"I expected you would show up sooner or later. Come in, if you must. And I suppose you must."

I went in. The front room was a foyer lit dimly by stained glass clerestory windows. He led me through the gloom to an Edwardian parlor.

"Welcome to Castle Sondergaard," my host said, gesturing me to a carved rosewood armchair. It looked comfortable, so I sat down.

After refusing the offer of a drink, I got to business.

"I have something. I caught it. I want you to look at it."

"I see. What is it?"

"I want you to tell me," I said, trying not to sound too cagey.

"Very well. Come into my laboratory."

I had never in all my life imagined that anyone

would ever say "Come into my laboratory" to me. But there it was.

I followed Sondergaard into his laboratory, which turned out not to be such a spooky place. I can't say as much for the house itself, for along the way I noticed the place was also a museum. Insect specimens were on display everywhere, in wooden and glass cases. They lined the walls and occupied space on many pieces of furniture. Here and there were standing cases, and all these exhibits featured the carcasses of insects, pinned and labeled: butterflies, moths, beetles, flies, gnats, grasshoppers, bees, wasps, locusts, and more.

My host ushered me into the laboratory—more insect cases, a few stuffed and mounted fur-bearing animals (these were hard to identify), and a long bench with some ordinary lab equipment on it—a Bunsen burner, some flasks and a retort or two. An antique microscope sat on a desk by the window.

"Well, my friend, let's see what you have."

I handed him the drug bottle. "It's inside."

He held it up to the light and peered inside, saw nothing, of course—and then seated himself at the desk. He took out a glass slide, set it on the desktop, and carefully upturned the pill bottle. The little black thing slid out. He eye-droppered a drop of clear liquid onto the thing, ostensibly affixing it to the slide.

After waiting a moment, he placed the glass slide under the lens of the microscope and looked into the eyepiece.

Looking up again, he gave me a broad smile of satisfaction.

"A nosewig."

"So it is one!" I shook my head in wonderment.

"You are very lucky to have captured it. Otherwise, you would have ended your life in misery and pain.

May I ask, do you intend on keeping this specimen? If not, I would be happy to—"

"By all means, Professor, keep the thing. I have no intention of starting a collection of buggy curiosities."

"Thank you very much, Dr. Mallory. I have been wanting one for years. Decades."

I looked around at the endless insect cases. "Do you have any other rarities?"

"Many. I have undertaken several expeditions to tropical locales to collect specimens."

"Tropical bugs? What about these other life-forms you were talking about, like the nosewig?"

"Long ago I gave up the notion of collecting any evidence to substantiate a claim that would be rejected out of hand, specimen or none. You must understand, this entire field has been a pastime for me and for many of my colleagues. You can't get funding for it."

"Tell me more about these strange and unknown forms of life. Please."

"I have no qualms about doing that now, because you seem to have the knack for finding them. For seeing them. It's a special talent, as I said. I have it as well, and I rue the day that this gift was bestowed."

"Why so?" I asked.

"Because things like this begin happening to you. Nosewigs seek you out and fly up your nose. Your house becomes home to creatures whose existence you never suspected. Tunnel ants make holes in the basement walls—"

"Tunnel ants?"

"Tunnel ants. Frightful creatures, huge things about an inch long. They will honeycomb under your house, and your foundations eventually collapse. Great expense to undo the damage."

"They used to call that mine subsidence, or sinkholes."

"Nonsense! Tunnel ants."

"I see."

"Only you will see them. You will invite the exterminator into your basement. He will see the loose foundation block, but he will not think of tunnel ants. He does not know of tunnel ants. You will tell him that you have seen these creatures, and he will think you mad."

"Will I see anything else interesting?"

"You will see many things. You have the gift."

"Are there any other life-forms to which my house will be vulnerable?"

"I hesitate to tell you."

"Why?"

"For fear that you might actually see one."

"Please tell me. I'm not afraid."

"Very well. The biggest threat is the housegobbler."

"And what might that be, beyond the obvious?"

"I detect a note of skepticism."

"Not at all. Please continue."

"Very well. The housegobbler is an insectoid form of life, but very large. The wingspan sometimes exceeds twenty feet. They lie dormant most of the time, until certain weather conditions come about: high heat, high humidity, a sudden drop in air pressure, and electrical activity."

"Thunderstorms?"

"Tornado conditions. Under these conditions the housegobbler comes out of hibernation and takes wing. If it sees a funnel cloud, it hides inside it, and comes out again only to demolish a house and consume parts of it."

"It hides inside funnel clouds. But, Professor . . . isn't that rather questionable logic? Of course tornadoes cause lots of damage, but do you really think—?"

"I KNOW, Dr. Mallory. I do not think. I have seen them. They work blindingly fast, reducing a structure to toothpicks in a matter of seconds."

I couldn't resist chuckling. "Professor Sondergaard, I'm afraid. . . . My apologies, sir, really, but you strain my credulity."

Sondergaard shrugged his narrow shoulders. "I am truly sorry."

"Do you still want to maintain that the observer is somehow part of the process that brings these things into existence?"

"As I said, Dr. Mallory, this is a thorny philosophical issue. I avoid it gladly. Besides, that is *your* field, is it not?"

"You're absolutely right."

I'd heard enough. At that moment, I had no fear of tunnel ants or housegobblers, and was ready to consign Professor Sondergaard and his maverick science to the same daffy realm inhabited by supermarket tabloids and sensational talk shows.

The professor showed me out, and I walked home, but not without wondering why I had never before seen a certain variety of green leaping insect that looked more like a praying mantis than a grasshopper. They leaped out of the grass along the curb, lawns were alive with them. The park chirped and twittered and clicked.

As I approached my house, I saw more apparitions. Purple flies buzzed me, flitted, and flew everywhere. Odd, multilegged things scurried across the sidewalk. A pink snake, almost three feet long, slithered through some azaleas in the neighbor's front yard.

When I got inside the house, I went straight to the basement. Sure enough, some loose foundation blocks in the far rear corner. I was hard-pressed to explain why I didn't notice them before. I had cleaned out that corner only last week. The whole wall was sagging and bulging.

"Fred! What brings you here?"

Aline's eyes were suspicious, but she was trying

hard to be friendly. Her face was still gorgeous. She could have been a supermodel.

"Just thought I'd drop over to chat."

"Well, come in. Why is the sky so dark?"

"Storm warning on the TV. Tornado watch until five p.m."

"What's to worry? When was the last time a tornado touched down around here?"

"Nineteen fifty-six. Twenty people were killed."

"You have some memory."

"I did some research. Is Brent around?"

"He's upstairs napping. Have a seat. What did you want to talk about?"

"The settlement. I want you to call off your legal jackals."

That did not start the conversation off on a pleasant note, I will admit. But Aline didn't help any. We ended up shouting at each other, and I stormed out.

Meanwhile, the storm outside had been brewing up, too. The sky darkened more, and then turned a sickly shade of yellow-green. My ears popped as the pressure dropped. I took a station well away from the house but still in the yard, among a copse of silver maples to the side.

Well, upcoming was an empirical test of a philosophical theory. Would my mere presence induce a sighting of the feared housegobbler? Would my wanting to see one set up preconditions for the formation of a funnel cloud?

True, the storm was not of my doing, and this was the Middle West, where tornadoes are a daily occurrence. But a funnel-cloud touchdown in these parts had been rare in the past. If one whirled up now, I'd take it as something just short of absolute proof of Professor Sondergaard's nutty theory.

And, by God, one did come along eventually. My jaw dropped. I'd never seen a tornado before, not in person. My instinct was to run, but if Sondergaard was right, I had nothing to fear. Housegobblers gobbled houses, not humans.

The wind whipped up fiercely, and for a moment I had my doubts about this crazy experiment—however, if the theory was true, the whirlwind did no damage whatsoever. So I was safe.

Ah, but flying debris? What of that? Hadn't thought this through quite as thoroughly as I should have. I fell to the ground and stretched out and pulled my raincoat over my head.

Rain began to beat against the wide maple leaves. And I heard the tornado's steam-locomotive chugging, like a runaway train. Terrifying, if I hadn't known better. Still, I was afraid some. This seemed a crazy thing to do. It *was* a crazy thing to do.

The funnel cloud was heading straight for Aline's house, but the house next door, the Beckers' place, was in the way. Hadn't bargained on that. I watched in horror until, at the last second, the tornado veered off.

But that did not save the Beckers. I saw something—but it was so fast I couldn't be sure of what it was. The suggestion of great double wings, multiple legs, a long conical body, and numerous sets of pincers in the region of the head—something like a dragonfly but a trifle fatter, crossbred with a crab. Over the din of the wind I heard a buzz like a gigantic circular saw. The creature left the funnel cloud in a rush and fell upon the house. Shards of the house flew off as in an explosion. The beast worked with lightning speed, as lightning itself crackled through the mass of dark clouds above. In moments half the neighbors' home was reduced to splinters. The other half was, inexplicably, intact.

Perhaps the Beckers' place was not a tasty enough morsel?

Very well, go next door.

By that time, I was up on my feet, instant camera in hand. I had to get a picture of it, to show to Sondergaard, and to shore up my own sanity. I had to have some objective proof that this enigma existed.

I stepped out from the trees just in time to catch on film the destruction of what had been my house. The place flew into a million pieces.

I snapped the shutter, not knowing whether I had caught anything at all. The picture slid out of its slot and just as quickly was safe in my pocket to work its arcane, semimiraculous, image-producing chemistry.

With a short, loud buzz, the beast ducked back into the funnel cloud and the cloud moved on. The wind died a bit, and the rain abated some.

I left the cover of the trees, but did not move toward Aline and the house. Instead I crossed through a hedgerow of wisteria, entered the Beckers' back-yard, and walked cautiously through the house shards that littered the back lawn.

As I neared the house, the shattered patio door slid back and out came Sam Becker.

"Fred? Thought you moved out. How did you—?"

But then he saw the remains of the cataclysm next door.

"Man, you're luckier than we were! How did you survive that? It just so happened that the kids were in the basement, and Jen and I ran down as soon as the sky turned. My God, if we'd had one less minute's warning!"

I was relieved, of course. I told Sam I'd been caught outside, and after asking if he needed any help, which he declined, I recrossed the wisteria and made as if to see to my own house.

I did no such thing, going directly to Castle Sondergaard, which had come through the storm unscathed. I rang the bell and waited.

Sondergaard opened the door, took one look at me, and said, "You brought the tornado."

Walking in, I nodded. "Not only that, Professor." I took the photograph from my pocket. On it was the image of the housegobbler. I held it up proudly. "Look."

He took the photograph and examined it with great interest.

"Remarkable. Absolutely remarkable. You have reached an astonishing level of talent, Dr. Mallory. Or you were born with it, I should say. This is truly unprecedented. No one before has even come close— But come, come."

We repaired to the laboratory, where he subjected the photograph to a strong light and a reading glass. The detail was not great, but there could be no doubt that the creature existed. Cameras do not lie. I looked over his shoulder and noticed that I had captured a good shot of the head. The pincers were frightfully multijointed and looked capable of doing a demolition job on anything short of a skyscraper. And above that ragged, horrible mouth—a single almost mammalian eye. No half-blind faceted eye for this insect. I had been elated up to that point, but now a faint shudder went through me.

And when Sondergaard finally looked up and spoke the words that cast a pall over my life, the shudder turned into a cold, electric jolt of terror.

Aline and her brother had died, and her legal machinations came to an end. In fact, I benefited directly from her death. Ironically, she had neglected to delete my name on the beneficiary line of her life insurance. I collected $100,000 without a murmur from the insurance company or her lawyers.

But Castle Sondergaard extracted other costs from me. For the last year I have not been able to leave the house without a surgical mask. My nights have come alive with the chittering and chirping of unnameable things. I cannot sit in my backyard without seeing the lawn writhe with all manner of snakes and reptiles. The tunnel ants have undermined the entire house. One more day, I keep thinking, and it will collapse in on itself.

Broomworms have taken up residence in all sorts of cleaning implements, from the kitchen broom, to the big push broom in the garage, to the whisk broom in the linen closet.

But I could live with all of that. What I cannot live with—and it looks now like I have but seconds more to go—is what Sondergaard informed me was in store for the rest of my natural life.

"I am afraid you and the creature are locked into one reality. You did not start out that way. You began life in the mundane world of everyday experience—but the sighting of the broomworm began an inexorable process of interperceptual cross-fertilization. You could have gone on with that process indefinitely. Being aware of the other world, taking an occasional peek into it. I have been at that stage of development for years. But with your talent, you have crossed over into the ultimate phase. Look here, my poor friend. Do you understand?"

I leaned forward. The creature's single eye stared out from the photograph like a bloated poached egg, emotionless and inhuman, but possessed of the sharpest, most discriminating acuity.

"For you see, Dr. Mallory," Sondergaard said, "not only did you see the creature. The creature saw you."

CONCRETE EXAMPLE

by Nancy Springer

As we said in our introduction, who today would deny that a woman's home is her castle? Nancy Springer, a fantasy writer of great distinction, claims to believe that there are some good men, which makes the editor feel a lot better. But sometimes a woman needs more protection than a man can or is willing to give, as we see in this story of victimization and healing.

The way I got to know her was I'd see her over there building her forms. She had a big pile of scrap lumber, skids and two-by-fours and yellow pine planks, and all day every day she'd be out there in her little-old-lady cardigan sweater and her polyester pants and her rubber rain boots, pounding away until she got some kind of walls up—not always four, and not always square; I never saw her use a level or a square or a plumb bob—and then besides wood she used all kinds of stuff. She brought in junk furniture—she would haul a junk sofa in her old pickup truck and stand it on end to prop up the insides. Some lawn-service guy brought her big piles of grass clippings, and she would build arches and curves. If she didn't have grass clippings, she would use salvage-yard auto hoods to make her curves, or you would see her out there digging dirt and piling it in her forms and shaping it like clay. Then she'd slip chicken wire into the form like for reinforcement. Then she'd cover everything with wet

77

burlap and you'd think she'd be worn out by this time, but she wasn't done yet. She'd bring funky stuff, like pocket mirrors and pieces of tile and big old junk jewelry and flat plastic flamingos, and she'd lay it out facedown on top of the burlap. And then every evening just like some sort of natural cycle the mixer truck would drive in spinning like fate and pour her new room. Floor, walls, ceiling, they were all concrete. I think she had some kind of deal with Sandmaster Concrete that they would bring her their leftovers at the end of each day, because the concrete didn't always match the previous batch. Like, sometimes it was pebbled, or sometimes it was tinted, like pink. Every day a new room got added on, but there didn't seem to be no sort of plan or architecture. It was more like a seventy-year-old kid building a sand castle.

Then a couple of days later, in between building new forms, she would rip off one of the older ones and have a look-see. And then, often as not, in a day or two she'd be out there with her jackhammer tearing it down. Or maybe she'd leave it standing for a week or two, maybe get glass in the puny windows placed high up in the walls like this really was a fortress, maybe even build onto it, and then all of a sudden she'd be out there with a jackhammer and an acetylene torch to cut through the metal reinforcement, destroying it. The neighbors said she was crazy, wheels wobbly on her wagon, lead loose in her pencil, several fries short of a Happy Meal, goofy. But I didn't care. I couldn't stand it. When she came out and took her jackhammer to a big pink room, I marched on over there.

"Mrs. Rizzo, what are you doing that for?" I yelled at her. This must have been back almost four years ago. I know it was, because I was pregnant but still working at the beauty shop part-time in the evenings. She turned and beamed at me through her bad glasses like I'd paid her a compliment. "Why, Harold tells me to," she said.

I just stood there trying to see past her glasses to tell what she was like, but I couldn't. She wore those horrible old-lady bifocals shaped like Christmas-tree-angel wings with rhinestones at the tips—I don't know where the old ladies can still find those things to buy them, but they do. She had a poodle perm, too.

"You're my neighbor, I believe, aren't you, dear?" she said brightly.

I realized I was being rude. "Um, yeah," I mumbled. "I'm Joleen." I don't think any of the other neighbors had talked with her yet, because they were pissed off because she had bought four lots and was building her weird all-concrete house, which was stupid, being pissed off I mean, because it wasn't like the neighborhood was losing any class. Had none to start with. It was just your generic no-trees dirt-lawn sun-punished trailers-and-prefabs housing development.

"Nice to meet you, Joleen." She offered a hand that might as well have been a land turtle's claw, all the wrinkles filled with grit.

Shaking hands with her made me feel entitled to ask, "Uh, who's Harold?"

"My spirit," she said cheerfully. She put her jack-hammer down. "Please come in."

"Your spirit? Uh, as in, uh, spirit?"

"My spiritual adviser." She led the way inside. There were lots of rooms but only one door, a big metal one, and the minute I stepped into that chilly damp dim concrete place I understood about Harold, because he was in there. I could feel him. The ceiling curved up like a rotunda with circular pieces of mirror and foil pinwheels and those candy-store holograph rings stuck in the concrete, and all those shiny circles were his eyes. I could feel him in the air. I was walking through Harold, breathing Harold. It weirded me out a little, but I kept my face under control, because I have pride about showing my feelings. It didn't really scare me, anyway, and the reason was, right away I didn't like Harold much. So it wasn't like God or an angel or something. It was just this annoying Harold. I mean, I've always been kind of open to new experiences. Life is boring enough without being careful. But if I had known then what Harold dear was capable of, I would have been good and scared.

"He always promised me a castle," Mrs. Rizzo sang, her voice echoing in her arched hallways. "Now I get to build myself one. This is the great hall." Actually it was several of her do-it-yourself rooms honeycombed together, with built-in concrete coffee tables and concrete slabs—were those meant for sitting on? No cushions, but I figured she wasn't done yet. "This is the kitchen." Nothing but a concrete countertop, a fridge and a microwave. The john was awesome, though, as big as the great hall, with a fountain and a shower and a tub like a swimming pool and a bidet which is really just another kind of fountain and a jacuzzi and rows of yellow plastic bug-eyed fish heads like for fishing lures stuck everywhere.

"Where'd you get those?" I asked.

"Bins of them down at the plastic extrusion plant. Harold told me. Harold tells me everything." She led the way to the next room. "Every morning I consult him."

"And sometimes he tells you to tear down what you just built?"

"Harold wants everything to be very, very safe."

Didn't look all that safe to me. I saw cracks in the concrete some places, and I had seen her pulverize good solid walls and leave ones that never set up right. "So aside from being a spirit, who is Harold, anyway?" Did this guy have any qualifications? He sure had ordered her a dud kitchen. I guess my attitude seeped into my voice, and I didn't care that he was listening—I could feel him listening.

Mrs. Rizzo seemed not to have heard me. But right at that moment I felt something squirm like a fish inside me. Right inside me. I stopped breathing for a moment, but then I realized—the baby, it was my baby. It was the first time I had felt the baby move. I'd never been pregnant before. It startled me.

"This is the bedroom," Mrs. Rizzo said.

There were more Harold-eyes embedded in the concrete walls and ceiling, white hollow circles that I think might have been insulators like for stringing electric fence. Them and bicycle reflectors. White and red eyes looking down. But I didn't see any bed, just a big concrete slab.

"Oh." I got it. "You're going to put a mattress on that?"

"No! No mattress." All of a sudden she wasn't a cheerful, beaming lady anymore. She got agitated. Her claws shook. Her voice shook and went real high as she said, "Nobody can set fire to concrete."

When I got home, Bruce was there flopped in a living room chair. We'd been married about a year, living in this tacky little so-called starter home. "Hi," I said, heading over to give him a kiss. "The baby moved today."

"Where you been?" He sounded mad, but he was usually crabby when he got home. He was a rookie cop, which in the first place is not easy and in the second place tended to make him testosterone-prone. I stopped where I was. Cancel that kiss.

"Talking with Mrs. Rizzo," I said.

"Who?"

"The castle lady."

"I don't want you talking with her!" Right away he

sat up all dicky. "You got no business over there. Aincha got nothing better to do?"

I kept my face from showing it, but my heart hurt in my chest because I was still so young I didn't know any better, just a kid of twenty, we were both just kids and once upon a time not so very long ago we had been lovers and I sure hadn't minded it then that he had wanted me to spend all my time with him and nobody else. What with all the kissing and cuddling, being possessed had seemed real sweet. But now we were married, it seemed like love had turned into a sex cure and besides wham-bam all that was left was the jealousy. Bruce never wanted me to talk with anybody. Didn't even want me to work. He hated my job. I liked it. I liked doing hair and having some money of my own.

"It's not like I'm out flirting with construction workers," I said, though Mrs. Rizzo was kind of a construction worker, come to think of it. "What is this, I'm not supposed to talk to the neighbors now?"

"She's a nut."

"So maybe I enjoy talking with nuts."

"Not when this place is a pigsty and supper ain't ready!"

"*Ex*cuse me. I forgot your mommy used to have the milk and cookies waiting on the table."

"Shut up," he said, and his voice got that low, ugly tone, and I shut up and went to hustle some dinner together. Joleen, I told myself, you've got a big mouth. If I would learn not to answer back so much, he wouldn't get so mad. Later, around bedtime, he would start to get affectionate, and it would be okay, sort of. I loved him. He was so handsome. A gorgeous young hunk of a husband. And brave. Not afraid to get involved. I remembered the way we had met, which was the one and only time I had tried Rollerblading and I had wiped out and he had stopped his car to help me and drove me to the emergency room and hung around while I got treated and drove me home. That was Bruce, he wanted to do good in the world, make a difference, and I was proud of him for being a cop, and I knew it put him through a lot of stress. I was lucky to be Bruce's wife, real lucky. I just had to learn to keep my big mouth shut and do better at keeping up with the housework and stuff. I had to get it together so he wouldn't be mad at me so much.

Dinner was spaghetti and I asked Bruce how was work, but he wasn't talking to me. I never did tell him that there was a spirit named Harold residing in and supervising the construction of the castle next door.

The baby moved again during supper. I didn't say anything to Bruce, but I thought, *what's it going to be like when the baby comes?* We would be more of a family, so he would like me better, wouldn't he? I mean, having a baby was a big accomplishment. He would have to like me better once the baby came.

Being pregnant got to be pretty much of a bore, what with Bruce working more and more hours and then going out to drink with his cop buddies afterward. He needed to unwind, he said. Well, I needed a life. I went over to see Mrs. Rizzo every time I got a chance, at first just to be contrary because Bruce wouldn't like it if he knew (which he didn't know, because as well as being proud and contrary, I am a complete coward), and later because I got genuinely interested in her and her weird concrete castle. It took me a while to get used to the idea that she was living in there with no cushions, no drapes, no carpeting, no blankets, no fabric or softness of any kind. Not to speak of no closets. I kept trying to assume that she slept somewhere else, some nice comfortable motel room maybe, and came to work on her castle in the daytime. But then I started noticing lights on at night, dim, probably she was skimping like a lot of old people do and trying to save on the electricity, but it made me feel like I had a ghost for a neighbor. And in the morning I would see her come out, so it was no use kidding myself; that woman slept on concrete, maybe in her clothes. Maybe not. Maybe she was afraid somebody would sneak in while she was sleeping and set her clothes on fire.

She really was terrified of fire. I flicked my Bic to light a cigarette one day and she jumped back like I had cocked a gun at her and her face went sweaty-white. I said, "Sorry," and put it away, but it was a while after that before she started to act friendly to me again. I never took a cigarette near her after that. Which made it real weird, considering her phobia, that the way she communicated with Harold dear was with fire.

I got to see her report in to Harold one morning when me and my big belly went over to try to borrow some milk for breakfast because Bruce had sold my car since I quit at the beauty shop and I couldn't just run and get some. Bruce wanted me home when he wasn't around. "It's not safe out there for a woman by herself," he said, which was kind of sweet but showed what kind of strain being a cop was putting him under. So he went and sold my car. Anyway, Mrs. Rizzo let me in when I knocked at her big metal door, but she was in a tumult. "Harold hates to be kept waiting," she gasped, and she ran for the so-called kitchen. Me, I am in certain ways not shy. I followed and stopped in the doorway and watched. There she sat at her built-in square of concrete kitchen table, and in the exact center of it stood a lit candle like a slim little yellow-headed person in a white suit.

Mrs. Rizzo sat staring into the flame and nodding nervously and wetting her lips with her tongue. I guess the candle was Harold. I couldn't tell. Since that first time I couldn't feel Harold in the castle. It was like he was a smell and once you get used to it you can't smell it even though you know it's there.

"Yes," Mrs. Rizzo whispered to the candle, nodding. "Yes, of course. That's exactly what I'll do. Yes, dear." She called me "dear" sometimes, too. "All right. I'll take care of it."

She was nodding so hard that she was like bowing down to the candle. Then it looked like her briefing session was over because she got up. But she never turned her back on that candle or blew it out. She grabbed it like it was a snake and rushed it over and dropped it into a whole sinkful of water, holder and all. It made a spitting noise like a cat, then went out, of course. I came into the kitchen and looked. Like, what did I expect to see, Harold lying there? Under all that water the candle lay drowned and soaking like a white corpse in a lake.

"That was the good Harold," Mrs. Rizzo said earnestly to me, though I had never mentioned any opinion of Harold to her. "There is a good Harold, you know."

"Sure," I told her.

It was better than the soap operas, trying to figure out what it was with her and Harold. She seemed like such a with-it old lady, all the things she was able to do, pound nails and build forms and boss the guy who brought the concrete and live by herself in the middle of her fortress—she even ran the wiring herself, and the plumbing—what did she need Harold for? Not any of the things I needed a man for, that was for sure. She was past all that. Or at least I was so young I figured she was.

So why didn't she just tell Harold to go take a flying leap? I mean, there are ways to get rid of spirits. At least I had heard there were.

And she didn't always seem to feel like there was

a good Harold either. "Look what he's making me do," she said one time, her little round chin jerking like she was going to cry as she took the jackhammer and torch to a really pretty rosy-concrete room decorated with hundreds of glass marbles.

"Why are you letting him make you do things?" I said. Yeah, right, I was a fine one to talk, but I kept right on going. "Don't do it if you don't want to."

"But I've got to! I've got to do what he says." She turned off her jackhammer and grabbed the acetylene torch, holding it far away from her body—the way she felt about fire, she had to be terrified of it, yet she handled it. "Bolt cutters aren't good enough, no, I've got to use this thing, and I've got to do it because he says so." The torch melted right through an iron bar like it was chocolate candy. Mrs. Rizzo shut it off and threw it down, then turned to me in a wild whispering way. "He'll get me if I don't."

"How?" What could Harold do to her? It wasn't like he could pull back his fist and punch her.

"I don't know. Somehow." She lifted her jackhammer and got going, smashing all her pretty work to bits. When it was all just a mess lying on the concrete slab of a floor she stood there looking at it. The silence was pretty strong after the racket of the jackhammer, so I wasn't saying anything, but Mrs. Rizzo said under her breath, "You're right. I don't know why I bother. He'll get me anyway. He'll get me somehow. Eventually."

"Why, for God's sake?"

She jumped, startled, like she had forgotten I was there. Then she laughed nervously. "Because I've got all his money," she said.

"Good," I said, I don't know why, and she laughed like she was going to cry, and all of a sudden she hugged me like I was her daughter.

*   *   *

Maybe because of Harold or maybe in spite of Harold, Mrs. Rizzo's castle got to looking more and more like a castle and less like a bizarre concrete house. It kept gradually getting bigger and more complicated. A central courtyard kind of developed, with flights of concrete stairs to nowhere, like to heaven. But then she went up on her flat concrete roof and started putting more weird concrete rooms on top of the ones that were already there, with a derrick thingamabob handing the big buckets of sludgy concrete up to her. She never seemed to take a day off, even when winter blew in and the weather got nasty. About the time I went in the hospital to have my baby, she had started building towers, tall sawtoothed things made out of, you guessed it, concrete. Concrete block. When I came home with Emily, she was pouring footers for a wall. That's how I remember things, by whether Emily was born yet or whether she was a baby or how old she was. Having Emily around didn't change things with Bruce as much as I had hoped. I mean, he was real sweet with the baby sometimes, but then other times he screamed at her when she hadn't done nothing except just be herself. Kind of like he was with me. But when he got like that, I just took myself and the baby into another room and I didn't care anymore, I loved little Emily so much. She was the most beautiful baby. I mean, I know they all are, but she really was. Like a storybook child. Must have got her good looks from her daddy because she sure didn't from me. She had the most perfect delicate pale angel face and loads of golden hair and big wide gazing eyes so dark they were almost black. She stopped people on the street with her looks, those huge midnight eyes in that starlight face under that sunshine hair.

About the time Emily was sitting up, Mrs. Rizzo had her wall built all around her place, so tall she needed stairs inside and a kind of catwalk thingy to see over the top. About the time Emily was crawling, Mrs. Rizzo was working on a gatehouse decorated with all colors of glass bottle bottoms. It's funny that I keep calling her Mrs. Rizzo because I spent a lot of time over at her place and I really started to like her even though she was crazy. I would take Emily and go visit with her while she was working. I hardly ever got to see my own family because Bruce didn't like them and he pretty much kept me away from them by controlling the car, but he couldn't keep me away from Mrs. Rizzo. I got to thinking of her like a mom even though she never gave me any advice, it wasn't like she knew about babies or stuff, it was just that she was always glad to see me, which made me feel special because in general she kept to herself. I think I was about the only person she ever spoke to aside from the cement truck man and people like that.

"It's been just about a year, hasn't it?" Mrs. Rizzo says to me one day when summer had come back again. She straightened up from the footer she was digging and took a good look through those God-awful glasses of hers at everything she had done and she smiled like glory under those rhinestoned wings. "There," she said. "He always promised me a castle, and now I've got one." Then she turns to me like I matter. "That means he really does love me, don't it? He really does love me even though he's dead."

"Sure," I said.

I knew by then, because I'd brought her mail to her one day and there was a letter in it addressed to Mrs. Harold Rizzo. I didn't say nothing or ask nothing. It's rude to ask personal questions and I wouldn't want her doing it to me. I have pride to keep my personal concerns to myself and let others keep theirs. I don't like nosy people and I am not gonna be one. Taking an interest, now, that's different.

About the time Emily was walking, Mrs. Rizzo had

got a backhoe in to dig a big ditch all around her place, which I might as well go ahead and call a moat. And she was working on rigging up a metal drawbridge.

This was also about the time that I finally admitted to myself that Emily was just not right, no matter what the doctor said.

"Calm down, mama," the kiddie doctor had been telling me when I asked. "Don't be in a rush." Some little ones were quicker to talk than others. Emily was developing normally, and she would talk when she was good and ready.

But it wasn't just that she wasn't talking. If she would have smiled—but she looked straight at me a hundred times a day and never smiled. Not once. My angel-faced child, I had never seen her smile. She cried sometimes, but not like she wanted me to comfort her—I tried to cuddle her and comfort her, but she raged, she whacked me with her fists. "She's throwing tantrums," the doctor said. "That's normal, mama. Stop worrying." But it wasn't normal. I didn't know enough about kids to be sure, but she didn't seem like a regular kid to me. She didn't seem to want me.

She didn't seem to love me at all.

The day I finally faced it, Mrs. Rizzo was trying to rig up some sort of guillotine gate that whanged down in sync with her drawbridge pulling up. That woman really was turning her place into a fort. I wondered what she wanted to shut out, besides fire. I guess mostly just fire. It was no use trying to shut out Harold; he was in there with her. Emily and I weren't out with Mrs. Rizzo while she rigged up her gate because it was half raining, but Emily had climbed up on the sofa and was watching through the window. She never played with the toys I got her. All she wanted to do was watch Mrs. Rizzo. Staring with no more expression than if her sweet baby eyes were black marbles. She would stay like that for hours.

Like hell.

What happened was, I went to change the sheets on the beds. Always doing some damn house thing, trying to keep Bruce happy, even though in my heart I already knew that the house was just his excuse to put me down, it was as clean as any normal person's, but for some lamebrained reason I kept trying anyway. I changed Emily's crib and was halfway through the bed when I smelled something burning.

I ran back out into the living room and there was Emily with the kitchen matches, setting the sofa on fire.

It wasn't just that she was playing with matches. Somehow she already knew how to use them. Here was this kid barely a toddler, not out of diapers yet, but her hands moved like an adult person's, and she had a strategy. Kneeling on the floor, she had matches stuck in rows in the cracks of the sofa cushions and she was working her way from the far matches to the near ones lighting up the sofa like a big birthday cake.

"Emily!" I snatched the matches away from her, then her away from them, then grabbed the fire extinguisher—being a cop's wife does have some advantages; Bruce got stuff like that for next to nothing. I doused the sofa—it was only charred a little around the edges. Emily sat watching like one of those mini ceramic masks you hang on your wall. She wasn't scared and she didn't seem to care what she had done except that I had come in and wrecked her fun. "Emily," I screamed at her, "you could have burned the house down! You could have killed yourself!" Or me. But she just looked at me with those no-look black eyes. She either didn't know or didn't care what she had done. So I grabbed her and held her against my leg and pushed her diaper down and spanked her.

I spanked her until my hand hurt, but she didn't cry. I was the one who started to cry. "Emily," I said, and I picked her up and tried to hold her and cuddle her, but she went stiff as stone and pushed me away with fists that were stronger than they ought to be.

I carried her to her crib and put her in, and she stood there glowering at me with eyes no more human than polished circles of coal. I turned away and closed the door on her. Couldn't stand to look at her. Couldn't stand what I was thinking. I wandered around the house until I saw the half-made bed and then I went to finish it. My hands were shaking. I couldn't remember which way the sheets went. I heard Bruce's car come in and stood there trying to think what I was doing. I heard the door as he came in. "What the hell happened!" he yelled when he saw the sofa. *"Joleen!"*

I dropped pillowcases on the floor and hurried in there. "Emily," I blurted.

"Where were you?"

"Emily set fire to—"

"Can't you keep an eye on that kid?" he yelled.

I was so upset about Emily that I yelled back at him. I don't even remember what I said. Nothing terrible. It didn't matter. Because I was yelling at him, he pulled back his fist and punched me in the eye. And because he was a cop, he knew how to punch pretty damn hard.

I slammed back against the wall, and I screamed, and then I started to cry. I should have had more pride, I should have told him where to go, but I felt so horrible about Emily and everything I couldn't help it. And at first Bruce just stood there, but then he started saying, "Joleen, babe, never mind, it's okay," and I felt his arms around me. "It's no big deal," he said. "We can get a new sofa." He thought this was about a sofa? "Just don't yell at me, okay? I'm sorry,

baby, I'm sorry. Did I hurt you?" Noooo, of course
not—but I couldn't find any pride, I couldn't stay away
from him, because he was kissing my face. He was
really sweet. This was the good Bruce. And I bawled
on his shoulder and let him cuddle me, I needed so
bad for somebody to love me. Emily didn't love me.
Not at all.

"There's—something—wrong with her," I sobbed.

"Nah. C'mon, hon, kids get into trouble all the time.
Did I hurt your eye?" Of course he hurt my damn
eye. He hooked a couple of fingers under my chin and
lifted my face to look, but next thing his mouth was
on my mouth, opening me up so passionately that I
let it happen. We had sex whenever he wanted, but it
had been a long time since he had really made love
to me like he did the next couple of hours. It was
weird, it was like hitting me or the tears or something
had opened up his heart, like he didn't know how to
connect with me any other way.

So I had to forgive him, didn't I? I had to forgive
him for hitting me if he loved me so much.

"She's artistic or something." I had to talk to somebody, so I was talking to Mrs. Rizzo. The minute I
walked over there I could tell from her face that she
saw the black eye under the makeup, but she didn't
say anything, like to ask how I got it, so I knew she
understood. And if she understood that, no need for
pride, I could tell her anything. "She don't talk. She
don't smile. She don't cry."

"Autistic, you mean?" The way Mrs. Rizzo corrected me didn't make me feel bad. She was as gentle
as a mom. I felt like she was kind of a mom to me
but with none of the negative stuff that kept me from
calling my own mom. Mrs. Rizzo wouldn't treat me
like a child or try to tell me what to do. "And your
fool doctor keeps saying there's nothing wrong?"

"He thinks I'm just being silly. So does Bruce."

"Men," Mrs. Rizzo said, like all the troubles in the world were caused by men, which seemed about right to me at the time. "Some men from the township were here, wanting me to fill in my moat." She was pounding a framework together, getting ready to pour a new slab for another tower or something, and she pounded a little harder with each word. "Said some kid might drown in it. I told them get out. The whole reason I built here is no stupid rules about what I can or can't put on my property, and the whole point of a moat is to keep people out, and kids are people." She finished up and stopped pounding. "Where's Emily right now?"

"Locked in her room." It sounded heartless, but I knew Mrs. Rizzo would understand, and she did. She nodded.

"Bring her over here sometime if I can help out," she said.

I knew she wouldn't want to stop building her castle long enough to watch a kid, but it was a nice thing to say, and maybe sometime I would. There wouldn't be anything at Mrs. Rizzo's place for Emily to set on fire. I went home and let Emily out of her room and kept an eye on her while I looked in the blue pages of the phone book where all the human services numbers are. Emily settled on the slightly toasted sofa looking out the window at Mrs. Rizzo, and I started dialing. A dozen phone calls later I had a referral from the child crisis intervention people with a doctor who specialized in artistic, uh, autistic children.

Then Bruce came home and growled at me as usual because the house wasn't a pristine palace. Then after I had given him his dinner and he should have been in a better mood, I told him about the appointment I had made for Emily.

"She don't need no appointment," he said.

"The insurance'll pay for it," I said. "Look, all I'm telling you is that I need the car on Thursday, so ask somebody to give you a ride."

"Don't you try to tell me what to do! You're not going running off to some doctor—"

"She needs a doctor! Would you look at her, for God's sake? Just look at her!" Any other kid would have been bawling because we were shouting, or babbling or grinning or dropping food on the floor or *something,* but Emily sat there in her high chair like an old man on a park bench just watching us. What made it worse was that I knew she was not stupid. I got the feeling she understood exactly what was going on. I got the feeling she followed every word.

Bruce said, "For God's sake, Joleen, you're making a mountain out of a molehill."

It took a whole evening of arguing for me to get him to promise me the car. I wouldn't give in. When he finally said okay, he slammed off to bed early and in an ugly mood. Fine. Whatever. I turned on the TV.

All of which is to explain why I was watching "America's Most Wanted" by myself the night the Mrs. Rizzo segment was on. Only her name wasn't Mrs. Rizzo, of course. Actually, it was halfway through the segment before I recognized her, and then it was only because I was kind of blipped out and sleepy and drifting and all of a sudden I sat up like I'd been jabbed because it was her. Mrs. Rizzo. Though I doubt anybody else would have recognized her. The wanted woman, the pictures they were showing of her, she was all polished to a country club shine—Liz Claiborne clothes, manicured nails, foundation on her face like a mask, lipstick with liner, false eyelashes, perm like a red wig, the works. No glasses. Probably wore contacts. But I'm a beautician, I'm used to noticing the shapes of people's faces and I know how a woman without her hair and makeup is like a different person, and I saw. It was her.

And I just sat there with my mouth open, because she was wanted for the murder of her husband, Harold something-or-other. Yes, his first name really was Harold, and they had been married for forty-three years, and he had burned to death. In his bed. At first it was supposed to have been an accident. He was smoking and the mattress caught fire, so the widow inherited all his estate, which was a bundle. Then somebody said something that made the police get suspicious and some evidence came together and the district attorney wanted to question Mrs. Rizzo, only her name wasn't Rizzo, but she wasn't there. She had made like a tree and left. So now there was pretty strong evidence that she was "mentally unstable" and had torched him while he was asleep and there was a warrant out for her arrest.

I knew what I should do. I was a good citizen, knew right from wrong and all that, I should head straight for the phone and call the cops. Turn her in. Maybe get some sort of reward.

I sat there. I thought about what it was going to be like to be married to Bruce for forty-three years. I whispered to the tube, "Probably the son of a bitch deserved it."

The first thing I thought when I woke up in the morning was, what was I going to say to Mrs. Rizzo when I saw her? Was I going to pretend I didn't know anything? Or tell her I knew who she was? I probably ought to, for her sake, so she could get out in case anybody else had recognized her from the show—but what if she really was psycho? What if instead of leaving her castle she stayed and tried to get rid of me? I didn't think she would—but how did I really know? How did anybody ever really know about anybody? I had thought I knew about Bruce, I had thought he loved me, and now—

No. I wasn't going to think about it.

I wasn't going to think about Mrs. Rizzo either. I stayed inside all day, staying away from her, so I wouldn't have to deal with her.

That was the day Bruce didn't come home at the end of his shift, and didn't call.

That was also the day Emily ran away.

Night, rather. She waited for dark. She was too small and short to open the door herself, but she waited until I had it hanging open while I took the garbage out. She must have slipped out behind me and around the corner. I never saw her. I was back inside for a couple of minutes before I noticed she wasn't in front of the TV where I'd left her. Then I thought maybe she was hiding from me. It must have been fifteen minutes before I realized she wasn't in the house. Then I panicked and wasted more time trying to call Bruce, tracking him down to a bar, talking to him. "She knows," I babbled to him, sobbing. "She heard me on the phone. She shouldn't understand, but she does. Now she's gone."

"God's sake, Joleen, she's just strayed off." He sounded half drunk, and stupid. "Don't shit a brick. Just go out and find her."

"How, for God's sake? She doesn't want me to find her! Bruce, you've got to come home. Hurry!"

"I don't gotta do nothing!" He was drunk. "I been catching people all day. You catch her." Then the son of a bitch hung up on me.

So much for Bruce the cop who wanted to help people. It sure looked like I didn't qualify as people. Just his wife. But I didn't have time to think about it. Had to find Emily. Funny how I could still love her so much even though she didn't love me. Out the door, I ran for the castle. Maybe Mrs. Rizzo would help me.

Luckily she hadn't got her drawbridge working yet; it was just a metal slab lying across the moat. I ran over it and across the rubbly yard past a tower Mrs. Rizzo was tearing down because Harold didn't like it. I banged on the metal front door.

Where was she? "Mrs. Rizzo," I called, tears in my voice, "Mrs. Rizzo, please, I need somebody to help me!"

Through one of the little slitty windows I saw a light go on. Finally the door opened. She had been in bed, that was what had taken so long. Or on bed, in her case. On concrete. Even though it was summertime she stood there in a flannel nightgown that reached to her bare yellowish feet.

She stood with the door wide open, peering at me. "What's the matter, Joleen?" I couldn't talk, I was sobbing so hard. "Come here, dear." She let go of the door and took my hand, tugging me gently toward her so she could hug me.

"Thank you," said a man's sarcastic voice. "You've saved me having to cut my way in."

Mrs. Rizzo gasped harder than I did, because she knew that voice. But then I screamed and started to shake, because the voice came from Emily.

There she stood holding the acetylene torch like an Uzi in her dainty little hands. "Back," she ordered, the man's deep voice crawling like a snake out of that angel face, that cherub body. The yellow flame flared.

"Harold, no!" Mrs. Rizzo stumbled back from the door, and I knew she was physically strong enough to take most men let alone a one-year-old girl, but she was quivering all over. "Don't! Don't hurt me. I tried, I really did, I tried to do everything you said—"

"Stupid bitch," Harold said.

"—but it was never enough. You hurt me—" All

of a sudden she was talking to me like she knew I knew she had killed him. "He hurt me and hurt me till I couldn't take it anymore. I didn't have any choice."

"Tell her about the cigarette burns," Harold said with zest that was almost affectionate, like he was saying, tell her about our good times. But then his voice turned hard and harsh again. "Get to the bed."

"No! Please—"

"Yes." He triggered the torch to flare higher as he came in, trundling the dolly and tanks behind him. Emily's little body was just big enough to handle everything. Probably he would have preferred to wait until she was older, but he was afraid I would stick her in a hospital. Probably he hated me, too, though not as much as he hated his wife. He had only been with me for one year, but he had been with her for forty-three.

"Dumb slut," he said to her. "Move!"

Somebody screamed—probably me, as I darted behind the acetylene tanks and ran out the door. I ran like a crazy person, home, home, but home was not safe anymore. I locked all the doors and windows, turned out the lights and went down and crouched under the stairs in the basement, trying to listen, but I couldn't hear a thing because I couldn't stop sobbing.

Footsteps—coming—down the stairs—

It was Bruce. He pulled me to my feet and put his arms around me, and he seemed sober now. "All right," he said, hugging me; this was the good Bruce. "Okay, what's the matter?"

I just cried.

"Did you find Emily okay?"

I shook my head and cried harder.

"No?" He stopped hugging me and grabbed me by the shoulders instead. Pushed me to arm's length and started shaking me. "You dumb slut, where is she?" You dumb slut, he called me.

* * *

There's so much I can't tell anybody, it's a wonder I'm not in the mental hospital. But I'm not. I'm fine now. It turns out I'm a survivor. It turns out Mrs. Rizzo helped me.

Mrs. Rizzo is dead, of course. They found her body when they searched her castle looking for Emily. She was so crisped they never did identify her right. They never put it together, who she was and what she had done and what that had to do with what had been done to her. And they never found the murderer. Not that they would have found him anyway.

So they were looking for this murderer, and they were looking for this missing little girl, and they thought they were two different people, and they thought that maybe he, the murderer, had taken her, the little girl, and in a way they were right.

They never found Emily. Bruce blamed me. It was a lot easier on him that way. He was grieving, too, probably worse than I was, and he wanted to live in a logical world where a person could find a culprit and inflict justice and restore the order of the universe.

I went to pieces after what had happened to Emily, and it took me a while to get myself back together. And it took me a while to leave Bruce. We would have a fight, and he would hit me, and I would pack my things, but then he would cry and beg me to stay and get down on his knees and love me so sweet I turned to jelly, all I wanted was for him to love me, I couldn't seem to care about myself anymore. What finally gave me strength to leave was thinking about Mrs. Rizzo. She was, like, an example of what might happen, caught in this same kind of lovey-go-round with Harold till it got so bad she killed him. Then still caught in it after he was dead. Building a castle to keep harm out and to shrine him in at the same time. Hating him and wanting him to love her. No goddamn logic. Thinking she could have him and be safe from him at the same time.

Men, she had said like it was all their fault. Bull. She went right along with him.

So I got out. I may be a coward, but I am not stupid. I called a cab and got out one day while Bruce was at work. Went home to my mom and dad for a while. Got myself a job doing hair. Found an apartment. Started over. For a couple of years now I've been dating a guy and he doesn't seem to mind when I say what I think or work or want to go someplace by myself or any of the weird stuff I do. He's not exciting like Bruce was, but I think maybe I've had enough excitement. He hasn't mentioned getting married, but that's okay.

I talk with Bruce sometimes, just for old times' sake and because I don't want to be the sort of person who holds a grudge. Bruce is terrific as long as you're not married to him. He got cop of the year last year, and he's kind of like one of those drop-dead-good-looking moody-broody guys on TV because he's got a sorrow, he's never quit looking for Emily. But I hope he never finds her.

See, I'm a survivor, and I figure Harold is a survivor, too. Maybe the greatest survivor of all time. I figure once he had got his revenge on his wife, he didn't just give up that baby-girl body he had stolen and go back to being a spirit blowing in the wind. I figure he kept that body and started walking and found a home somewhere. I figure he's clever enough to hide in that body until it's big enough to really use. I figure Emily's body is about three years old now.

I figure she'll be back some day.

So I'm building my fortifications. I'm not like Mrs. Rizzo. I've got my place all planned out on paper and when I put up a wall it stays there and it's not going to be big and fancy, just strong. Moat, concrete block outer wall with artillery mounted along the top, court-yard, inner wall, and concrete block living quarters with gun slots. I've got no money, so I'm doing it all myself, on land Dad gave me, and I work on it all the time when I'm not in the beauty shop, all my evenings and weekends and vacations. My boss at the beauty shop is starting to get after me about my rough hands and my hair. I haven't had time to get my hair done and sometimes I come in without makeup, but they're just going to have to deal with it. If they fire me, I'll get a job at RPS being a package gorilla. I just need enough money to buy mortar and concrete blocks. So far I've only got the moat dug and part of the outer wall up. I'm going to have to start getting up a couple of hours earlier to spend more time on the castle. I've got to get it done. Got to. Mrs. Rizzo says. I talk to Mrs. Rizzo every morning, and she tells me what to do.

DEATH SWATCH

by *Esther M. Friesner*

Esther Friesner is a deranged woman living in Connecticut. In her more lucid moments she is a perfectly conventional hausfrau and mother of two children. When the wolfbane blooms, however, she produces outrageously funny stories, such as the following one of a serial decorator run amok.

Jorc the orc shifted his warty bulk from paw to paw and lugubriously announced, "I don't like it," to his companion on guard duty. "I don't like bein' held r'sponsible fer what's behind this door. Gives me the willies, it does."

"Two questions," the troll replied through his tusks. "One: What's not to like? And two: If you think the Grim Lord cares whether us poor menial slaves like his doings or not, you're crazy, even for an orc."

Jorc blinked slowly, his thick eyelids making an audible *thunk* every time they met. "Tha's not a question. I know. I can tell. Hasn't got one o' them twizzly rune-thingies at the end o't to tell you that yer voice's gotta go *up*. What makes it sound more interrogative-like."

"Ahhh," the troll said, his face showing as much innocence as possible, given its aesthetic limitations. "So it's things that make your voice go *up* that makes it a question?" And to be honest, his own voice did lift a bit at the end of that sentence, giving a creditable imitation of a rusty door hinge.

Jorc nodded vigorously and leaned back against the jamb of the monstrous door that he and the troll had been set to guard. It was a post of honor, being as it was the sturdiest portal in the Grim Lord's castle, the gateway to the tower rooms where His Awfulness lodged only those "guests" of the highest rank or the most amusing pain thresholds.

None of which had much bearing on the matter presently under discussion between these two minions.

" 'Sright," Jorc said. "If it makes yer voice go up, then s'a question-rune."

"Oh," said the troll, and he took his mace and bashed Jorc squarely between the legs.

"eee!" Jorc trilled, folding over double.

"Well, I'll be," the troll said, regarding his mace with a false expression of maiden startlement. "And all this time I've been toting a question-rune into battle and I never knew it! If that doesn't beat all!"

"That does not beat all," came a deep voice from the shadows of the stairwell. "I do."

A figure stepped out of the stairwell, into the light cast by the twin torches flanking the great portal. The troll saw and trembled, then fell to his knees. Jorc the orc was already on his knees, but one look at this dread caller knocked him all the way down onto his belly. Both guards groveled in terror.

"My—my lord!" the troll gasped.

"Is this how you ward my prisoner?" the Grim Lord thundered. "Nutting one another?"

"N–now my lord, strictly speaking I did not 'nut' Jorc. In the first place, the term 'nutting' refers to a severe blow to the head, and in the second place, orcs do not have—"

A bolt of pure red power arced from the Grim Lord's fingertips and barbecued the troll where he stood. Even his sturdy mace was reduced to a pitiful puddle of slag. The Grim Lord casually blew the smoke from his nails. "Mmm. A shame. Now I'll never know what it is that orcs do not have. Unless you can tell me?" He bent the gaze of his awful Eye upon the still-writhing Jorc.

"Job security!" Jorc blurted, and scuttled down the stairwell and out of the castle without so much as a note of resignation left behind on his captain's desk.

The Grim Lord sighed. "I lose more Level G-7 personnel that way." A sphere of Faroverthereseeing materialized in his hand. "Captain Slugwallow! Dispatch two fresh guards to the Tower Ruthless. I am going to visit the princess. They had better be on post by the time I leave her apartments. Do I make myself clear?"

The face of a much-harried orc appeared in the sphere. The whims of optics distorted his features in the crystal so that he looked like a cross between a true orc and a hamster with fully-stuffed cheek pouches. *Then again,* the Grim Lord mused, *considering the barrack-room gossip about Captain Slugwallow's mother and her sexual inclinations. . . .*

"Aye, Dread One," Captain Slugwallow said wearily. "It shall be as you command."

"It always is," the Grim Lord replied affably (for a magical megalomaniac). "By the way, give your mother my regards." He tossed the sphere into the stairwell and smiled to hear it smash. "Plenty more where that came from," he told the shadows. Turning, he regarded the heavy portal. It was secured by a large oaken bar, a crisscross of iron chains, and a combination lock threaded through a hasp in the upper right-hand corner. The Grim Lord merely gave it a pointed glance with his Eye and the whole thing turned to raspberry gelatin.

As he stepped through the swiftly melting mess, the Grim Lord yanked a pixie out of his tunic pocket and squeezed it until the sprite's eyes bugged out of their sockets. "Memo to Captain Slugwallow:" he said. "Send the royal carpenter up here along with those guards." Then he lobbed the pixie over his shoulder and went on his way.

Beyond the now-liquefied portal stood the twisty narrow stairway that scaled the dark heights of the Tower Ruthless. Even though this was the highest point in all Dire Garde, the Grim Lord's fortress, it was still as dank and moldy as the lowest dungeon. Not so much as the glimmer of a candle flame broke the pitchy blackness of this dismal aerie. Even the scuttling vermin seemed to go about their filthy lives with constant squeals and chitterings of misery. The Grim Lord set his lipless mouth in a grimace of satisfaction. Could he build 'em or could he build 'em?

At the top of the stair stood another door. This one was not locked or barred. Why bother? Anyone who could breach the lower portal clearly knew his business. Setting a second barricade in his path would accomplish nothing and merely serve to irk him. Even the Grim Lord, who could number his living enemies on the fingers of one tomato, knew better than to irk a worthy opponent. On principle, anyway.

The Grim Lord paused at the second portal and harked. No sound reached him from the other side. "Perhaps she is asleep," he murmured, and for an instant his mind—normally preoccupied with a thousand plans of conquest, world domination, and the enslavement and torture of anyone whose face he didn't like—strayed to gentler images. In his imagination he saw the wide, silk-hung bed which he had provided for his captive. Upon it slept the princess, a maiden of transcendent beauty, even for an elf of the blood royal. He sighed wistfully as he imagined her milk-white eyelids closed in blissful dreams, her diaphanous wings chastely folded over the scented curves of her lithe yet voluptuous body, her full, ripe bosom glimpsed beneath the golden veil of her hair, her slender legs inexorably drawing the beholder's eye up, up, up to rest at last upon the exquisitely tempting sight of her—

"Yipe!" cried the Grim Lord as the door spontaneously burst into flames. His musings upon the princess' many charms had caused him to inadvertently confuse the controls governing his mind's eye with his mind's Eye and the inevitable had happened. A mystic gesture turned on the castle sprinkler system, dousing the blaze. He stepped over the smoldering timbers and into the princess' chamber.

"Knock, knock," he said sheepishly.

She was not asleep. She was fully awake and dressed. (*Dang!* thought the Grim Lord.) Attended by her two handmaidens, the Princess Minuriel stood before the sole window of her tower prison, all her regal dignity upon her. She wore the gown in which she had been captured by the Grim Lord's minions, although since her imprisonment he had sent her a hundred lavish robes, each more dazzling than the last. The princess scornfully cut them up and used them for unmentionable purposes, in spite of the fact that all those sequins had to hurt.

Elves! the Grim Lord thought bitterly. *Proud creatures! If I had it my way, I'd scour them from the face of this world. Except the cute ones.* He stared at the princess, and for all his dark powers he could not conceal how he hungered for her.

"What do you want?" the princess demanded.

"The same thing I always want," the Grim Lord replied. "Your consent to be my bride."

"That you shall never have while I live, while yet there is justice in the world, hope in my heart, or breath in my body," she shot back. "So buzz off."

The Grim Lord's mouth turned up at the corners,

an uncanny expression that made him look like a soup tureen (if soup tureens could smile with an air of hovering menace). "I do not think so," he said. "My lady, the time for trifling has passed. You know, do you not, the reason why I ordered your capture, abduction, and imprisonment?"

Princess Minuriel's huge blue eyes opened even wider. "You mean it's not just because you're a squidhead?"

The Grim Lord's chuckle was deep, false, and patronizing. "I am afraid not. Although I am flattered that you noticed." He tucked a stray tentacle back into place behind his left ear. "No, my lady; charming though the, ah, charms of your body are, there is more than mere raw physical lust behind my actions."

"According to what they say about you in the elfin court, mere raw physical lust is *never* behind your actions." The princess gave him a nasty, knowing grin. "If you release me, I'll use my magic to whip you up a batch of Uncle Oriel's Quick Fix Elixir, guaranteed to put a little lift in your driftwood."

The Grim Lord's smile blinked away. Small thunderheads gathered themselves over his brow. "I do not have that problem!" he snapped. "As you will be the first to know after you give your consent to our marriage!"

"Which I will never do," Minuriel returned haughtily. "Nor is there any way for you to force your loathsome attentions upon me. Truly it is written that an elf maiden of royal blood, so long as she keep herself virgin and pure, may never be possessed in body or spirit by a pig like you unless she gives her express consent. Fat chance."

"Then you leave me no alternative. I tire of the waiting game. Behold!" The Grim Lord snapped his fingers and a fresh sphere of Faroverthereseeing materialized. This was the larger model, a crystal taller than the Grim Lord himself. It took up most of the floor space in the princess' tower cell and almost nudged one of her handmaidens out the window.

Princess Minuriel and her attendants gazed into the vision that swam out of the crystal's depths. All three of them gasped. There, before their eyes, they saw the full complement of the Grim Lord's forces massed on the borders of the elfin homeland. Ravening orcs, repulsive trolls, host upon host of the living dead, ghastly wraiths, and really ugly dogs stood poised and ready for the invasion. But this was not the deepest horror.

"Picnic baskets!" the princess whispered.

"Yes!" The Grim Lord was never famous for being able to suppress that nasty habit of gloating. "Packed full with all manner of noxious edibles, for my loyal forces' delectation: Limburger cheese! Garlic bagels! Lutefisk! Poi! Kim chee! Sauerkraut! Quiescently frozen artificial chocolate flavored extruded dessert product! *And there's more where that came from!"* He clapped his hands together over his head and the panorama of the dark hordes, on pleasure bent, vanished from the sphere. It was replaced by a vision of the forest elves falling like autumn leaves before the onslaught of having to watch sentient beings happily devouring foodstuffs that looked and smelled like landfill.

How can they put stuff like that in their mouths? *Eeeeeeewwwww!* The dying cries of hapless elves echoed mercilessly within Princess Minuriel's brain as she watched her people perish. And of course there was the matter of litter.

"Enough!" The elfin princess threw out her hands, her own considerable magic shattering the sphere into a billion pieces. Her wings drooped and she bowed her head. "No more. I cannot stand by and allow my subjects to suffer so. I will give my consent to wed you, Grim Lord. And well I know that you do not seek to possess me for my beauty alone, nor for the sake of true love, and positively not because you lust for my fair young body, I don't care what you say, you *do* have that problem. No, I know that the real reason you would have my hand in marriage is so that you might conquer my father's lands through his only child. You stink."

"Not as much as lutefisk," the Grim Lord said, that old contented-soup-tureen look back on his face. "You are as wise as you are beautiful, my lady. I will give orders that the wedding preparations begin at once." He turned on his heel and strode from the room.

"Ow! Owowowowowowowow!" The Grim Lord hopped from foot to foot, pulling slivers of the shattered Faroverthereseeing sphere from his soles. With a single poisonous glance of his Eye, he caused the rest of the shards to melt and fuse into a glassy carpet. Then he departed, very much on his dignity. The elfin maidens heard him clump down the tower stairs and slam the brand-new door at the bottom shut behind him.

"Well, *someone's* in a pissy mood," said Shikagoel, the princess' right-hand handmaiden. She sneered at the now-empty doorway through which the Grim Lord had so recently passed.

"He'll get over it," said her companion, Shiksael as she fussed over her mistress' wings. "Just as soon as he remembers that he's going to get his own way with our lady."

"No, he's not," said Minuriel. Her mouth was set in a taut, determined line that might have given even His Abominability pause.

"But, my lady, you gave your consent!"

"So I did. And by the same enchantment that seals the marriage bond between a highborn elfin virgin and her chosen mate, now it is his turn to give *me* something."

Shiksael was puzzled. "I heard he couldn't."

Shikagoel gave her a sharp poke with her elbow. "Not *that*. Her Highness speaks of the Gift."

"Gift?" Shiksael's usually vacant face lit up at the mention of this Word of Power.

"It is the requirement of all who would wed a daughter of the elfin royal house to grant the bride one Gift, of her own asking, before the wedding may take place," Minuriel intoned. "Unless this condition be fulfilled, the maiden is freed of her promise and must be returned to her father's house, lest a great evil befall."

"Oh, like *that's* going to scare the Grim Lord." Shikagoel snorted. "He lives with evil. He lives *for* evil. Evil is just so much diaper rash to him."

"This is a really, really, *really* great evil," Minuriel reproved her skeptical attendant. "And he knows it." A scary little half-smile touched her lips. "That's why he'll do anything to fulfill my request for a Gift ... and that is why my Gift shall spell his doom."

"Ooh! Ooh! I get it now!" Shiksael jumped up and down, clapping her hands together excitedly. "You're going to ask him for something impossible, right?"

Shikagoel sighed. "*Not* the decimal equivalent of *pi*. It's been done to death."

"No," the princess replied. "By the laws governing all magic, I am forbidden to demand the impossible for my Gift. But not—" there was that nerve-scraping smile again, "—the unpleasant."

The great hall of the Grim Lord's castle was being decked out in finery suitable for the celebration of His Atrocity's nuptials. Gray garlands of swamp-blooming bug-in-the-coleslaw dripped from the rafters, nosegays of smuksmuk flowers were set out on the banquet tables, and orange crepe paper had been strewn about with a hand that understood the meaning of "lavish" but hadn't a clue to the implications of "tacky."

A raised platform had been set up directly beneath the minstrels' gallery, mercilessly out of sight of that selfsame gallery's decor. (The Grim Lord had ordered that the stone balcony be adorned with the severed heads of minstrels who refused to believe that their dread patron's *Absolutely No Polkas!* rule meant them.) It was draped with costly black silks and carpets of the finest weave. Pearls and diamonds had been scattered hither and yon to sparkle at the feet of bride and groom. The attar of rare blossoms drenched the fabrics underfoot, filling the air with their heady fragrance, although not heady enough to overcome the lingering aroma of yogurt. A bower constructed entirely of wrought silver and gold rose from the center of the platform, crowned by a single sapphire whose worth in lives and souls could not be calculated by mortal men. A honeycomb paper wedding bell dangled from the center of the pavilion.

Minuriel's expression was unreadable as her handmaidens led her into the great hall and her eyes first lit upon her future husband's decorating efforts.

"This is going to serve him right," she gritted.

The Grim Lord stood awaiting her upon the platform. He offered her a hand to help her climb the stairs, which were made entirely of the prone bodies of troll cadets who had proved themselves unable to master the making of hospital corners on their cots. There was a brief pause when one of the cadets tried to sneak a peek up the elf-maiden's wedding gown and needed to be beheaded and replaced. At last the princess stood upon the dais, facing the Grim Lord in the shadow of the paper wedding bell.

Due to religious differences, the ceremony could be performed by neither a Singer of the Light (bride's side, Orthodox) nor a Howling Priest of Slaughter (Groom's side, Reformed). As a compromise, the Grim Lord's minions trundled a heavy pulpit onto the platform, set upon it the Great Book of Intonations for All Occasions, and placed on the open pages the Grim Lord's pet chipmunk, Skully. Being the Grim Lord's pet chipmunk had transformed the simple forest creature into a green, slavering, one-eyed killing machine, as many a foolhardy servant had learned who crossed paths with the mad rodent in the castle's endless corridors. And yet, being a chipmunk, Skully still managed to retain that quality which the elves prized above all others:

"Oooooooh! He's sooooo cuuuuuuute!" cried Shiksael. She tried to pet the beast. It snapped off one of her fingers.

"Bad Skully!" said the Grim Lord severely. "No eating the attendants until after the wedding."

The chipmunk stuffed the severed digit into his cheek pouch and tried to look remorseful.

"And now," the Grim Lord announced to the massed congregation—his own warriors to an orc, the bride's family not having been notified of the impending ceremony—"Skully will scamper back and forth over the text, chittering after the fashion of his kind. When he pauses, the fair Princess Minuriel will give her spoken consent before you all to be my submissive, obedient, totally subservient spouse and I will say more or less the same thing, excluding adjectives."

"I don't understand this," Shikagoel whispered in her mistress' ear. "How can a chipmunk perform the holy ceremony of marriage?"

"In my father's court, when the Singers of the Light offer up their paeans in the High Tongue of the Somewhat Misplaced Elves, do you understand what they're saying?"

"Not a word. I don't speak High Tongue."

"Do you understand fluent Mutant Chipmunk?"

"Not a chitter."

"Then by the rule of mutual ignorance—very big in most marriage ceremonies—the Grim Lord's pet is just as qualified to unite us as any cleric in the land."

"Do you *mind*?" The Grim Lord glowered at the elfin maidens. "We are trying to conduct a wedding here. There'll be lots of time for gossiping with your girlfriends on the honeymoon."

"So I suspected," Minuriel muttered. Aloud, in a voice that carried to the farthest reaches of the great hall, she cried, "Halt! Grim Lord, I charge thee, stay thy chipmunk!"

"What's this?" The Grim Lord frowned. "Are you trying to back out of our agreement? Do so and you shall be condemned by the highest bonds of magic that rule our realms! I understand it hurts."

"I am backing out of nothing, my lord," the princess returned smoothly. "But by those same bonds of magic, whose power not even you dare to challenge, I call to mind the fact that we can not be wed until you have satisfied the one condition of a royal elf-maid's marriage."

"I had the blood test," the Grim Lord snarled.

"Not that. I mean ... the Gift!"

There came a slowly swelling murmur of expository affirmation from the assembled throng below the dais:

"Ah, yes, the Gift!"

"The Gift, of course, the Gift!"

"Well, naturally, the *Gift*."

"How could we have forgotten about the Gift?"

"Does this mean we've got to return the steak knives? Me an' t'other orcs in Company C chipped in an'—"

"Shut up, bonehead, we're talking about the *Gift*."

"Oh. I gets yer," said the young orc, who didn't.

"The Gift," the Grim Lord hissed—no easy task

when uttering words devoid of sibilants. "You speak the truth, my lady, for which I thank you. Verily it is written in volumes as old as time and monstrously overdue at the library that unless all conditions governing the marriage of royal elf-maidens are met, grievous are then the ills which shall befall he who did not heed them. Name what it is you would have! I swear by all the dark and awesome powers at my command, it shall be done!" He thrust his mail-sheathed fists heavenward and an earthshaking peal of thunder shook the castle to its very foundations. Orcs trembled and trolls fled. Wraiths paled to mere specters of their former selves, and the Grim Lord's mortal servants left the hall to change their underwear.

And when the last reverberations of that unholy thunderclap had faded from the hall, the princess Minuriel spoke:

"I want to redecorate."

"What?"

Acting as if she had just heard the most eloquent of blessings (as opposed to the monosyllable of blankest confusion) Minuriel flung her arms around the Grim Lord's neck and exclaimed, "Oh, *thank* you, darling! You won't regret this. And it'll be no trouble to you, absolutely no trouble at all. All I need from you is your cooperation; I'll handle everything else. Just wait, you'll be *so* pleased with the results, you won't know *what* to think!"

With a light laugh on her lips, she danced a few steps away from her intended spouse and began to wave her slim hands sinuously before her face, weaving invisible patterns on the air. At the same time, she recited an eldritch elfin chant of great power and antiquity.

In the front ranks, one wraith nudged another in

the intangible short ribs and inquired, "What means this 'Eeny meeny chili beenee'?"

The second wraith shrugged misty shoulders. "Elves. Go figure."

As Minuriel's chant rose in intensity, a lozenge of dappled golden light took shape between her and the Grim Lord. It grew until it was man-high, then the watery curtains of brilliance parted and a tall, masterful, mighty-limbed, keen-eyed specimen stepped forth. His chin was cleft, his shoulders monumental, his hair a froth of gold, his eyes of a blue lambence to dim the great sapphire of the wedding bower with shame. He wore naught save a loincloth, a cape, and sandals laced to the knee. They were very attractive knees. Needless to add, his thews were of steel, and his very presence seemed to proclaim that he possessed the brilliance of mind to know what *thews* meant without having to go look it up in the dictionary.

His cool gaze swept the room, coming at last to rest upon the Grim Lord who, despite himself, felt distinctly uneasy under that silent evaluation. One perfectly arched eyebrow raised in inquiry. The stranger spoke:

"You are the owner of these premises?" His voice caused Shiksael to collapse in an ecstatic faint (or maybe it was just the loss of blood from where Skully had bitten off her finger) and sent Shikagoel staggering under an assault of suddenly unleashed elfin hormones.

The Grim Lord moistened the edges of his mouth. "Uh, why, yes. Yes, I am."

"Then take *this*!" cried the stranger. His hand dropped to his belt. A slender shape flashed straight for the Grim Lord's heart. Instinctively the Grim Lord launched the spell for shattering dagger blades, but to no avail. He reeled backward as the object struck him full in the chest.

"That's my standard contract," the stranger said, still holding one end of the scroll. "Go on, read it; you'll find it entirely reasonable."

Wordlessly, trying to beat back all outward sign of the heebie-jeebies, the Grim Lord accepted the scroll. As he unrolled it, the stranger turned his back to him and contemplated the great hall. "You didn't summon me a moment too soon," he pronounced. "This is all wrong, wrong, *wrong*. Whatever were you thinking of? I mean, did you decorate in the dark? Black. Oh, dear, why does it always have to be black? It's sooooo depressing." The stranger strolled across the dais, making frequent tsk-tsk sounds. From time to time he would give the trolls in the front row a sideways glance that sent them into a self-conscious frenzy, running their paws through their greasy thatches and sucking telltale bits of bone marrow out from under their yellowed fingernails.

The Grim Lord made a heroic effort and wrenched back his self-possession. "It's supposed to be depressing," he boomed. "It's a stronghold of evil. *The* stronghold of evil!"

"*Do* tell." The stranger pivoted on tiptoe to confront his employer. "And where is it carved in stone that evil has got to be done in black? I mean, evil is supposed to be an attitude, not a color scheme. Why can't evil be, oh, *que voulez-vous* ... green? I don't know about you, but when it comes to evil incarnate, creamed spinach gets my vote."

"*Who in the nineteen netherworlds* are *you, you lizard-hipped blatherer?*" the Grim Lord bellowed. "And what's all this prattle of evil and spinach and voting?"

The stranger took a single, small step backward and waggled a reproving finger at him. "Temper, temper," he said. "It's all there in the contract. I am Selvagio Napp of the Borders, whom the dwarf-folk call Dado and the elven races name Velour. I'm from the Interior Decorators' Guild, and I'm here to help you."

"I'll help you to your death, you threadbare remnant of a—" The Grim Lord's stream of invective was abruptly dammed by a gentle tap on his shoulder.

"You promised," Princess Minuriel reminded him.

The Grim Lord put his head down on his desk and screamed.

"Beg pardon, m'lud?" his living-dead manservant inquired. "I didn't quite hear that. All this racket, donchaknow."

He was right: The sound of saws, drills, and hammers reverberating through the castle made a ruckus over which not even the Grim Lord's loudest shriek might be heard. There was also the slop-slip-slap of an army of glue-and-paintbrush wielding dwarves to add to the cacaphony.

The Grim Lord raised his head slowly from the desktop. "I think I shall go mad," he told the world.

"Very good, m'lud," said the zombie. "Will you be wanting to change your shirt first?"

From somewhere in the castle's innumerable suites of rooms came the sound of Selvagio bullying trolls. "No, no, *no*! *Much* too dark, *much* too gloomy! I tell you, that dungeon simply screams for pastels!"

And the hapless troll's meek reply came creeping to the Grim Lord's ear: "Surr, 'tis a dungeon. O' *course* it screams."

The Grim Lord's hand reached out to seize a statuette that stood upon his desktop. It was not a very attractive object—no doubt Selvagio would banish it to the nethermost recesses of the castle basement once he got a look at it. It might pass for the bust of a man, although such a lantern-jawed, pop-eyed, unnaturally elongated physiognomy made this a difficult call. No matter. The Grim Lord crushed it in his fist as readily as though it had been the very acme of artistic beauty. "Barkwell, bar the door," he gritted.

"Yes, m'lud," said the zombie, doing so with his own gray-green arm. "Will there be anything else, m'lud?"

"Yes, Barkwell. Stand brave. Maintain your post. *No pasaran.* That—that *creature* has been prowling my castle for months, mucking up an interior scheme it took me aeons to perfect. When the folk of these realms speak of my stronghold, they speak in tones of awe and mortal terror. The mere mention of Dire Garde is enough to make strong men faint and send lovely women into a tizzy. But now—!" He shuddered. "Now *he* is afoot. He has thrown away all the nice, thick, blocky uncomfortable furniture which I accumulated by unbending force of will and attending many, many garage sales. Cushions, Barkwell! There are now *comfy cushions* within the precincts of Dire Garde! Is there no end to the fellow's degeneracies?"

"No, m'lud," said Barkwell from his post at the door. "It would appear not."

"Have you seen what he has done with the barracks?" the Dark Lord demanded in piteous tones. "Floral wallpaper. Pleated blinds. *Ferns,* Barkwell!"

"Yes, m'lud. Ferns, as you say."

The Dark Lord let his head sink to the desktop once more, where he cradled it in his arms. His words emerged badly muffled, but still audible: "You know, Barkwell, I used to be a happy fellow. And do you know why I was happy?" Barkwell allowed that he was unaware of the cause. "I had orcs. It's a point that's been proven time and time again: Unhappiness is practically an impossibility if a fellow's got enough orcs on hand. When it comes to following orders for pillage and rapine, nothing beats an orc, that's what I always say." He looked up, and his Eye held a suspicious moisture. "Barkwell, do you know why I am no longer a happy fellow?"

"No, m'lud. That is not my place to say."

"Guess."

"Very well, m'lud, in that case I should venture to surmise that your present unhappiness stems from the fact that you no longer have orcs."

"Gone!" the Grim Lord wailed. "Expelled from my sanctuary, evicted under my very Eye! And do you know why? *Because he said they didn't go with the drapes in the great hall!*"

Barkwell knit his rotting brow. "Begging your ludship's pardon for the liberty of an unsolicited observation, but there are no drapes in the great hall."

"There are now." The Grim Lord's fingers dug trenches an inch deep in the desktop. "Pink ones. He says the color's something called Shire Sunset, but I know pink when I see it and those drapes are damn well *pink*!"

"Aye, m'lud," Barkwell agreed. "Pink, as you say." The zombie sighed loudly, launching a squadron of maggots into free fall from his ashy lips. As one of the Grim Lord's living-dead servants, there were many things he wanted very badly to remark which were Not His Place To Say. Given the choice this very moment of bringing up just one of those *verboten* topics—with instant, *permanent* death to follow, naturally—he knew precisely which one he'd choose:

"Goddamit, m'lud, if you can't stand the way that crepe-kisser's screwing up your castle, why don't you just drop the silly bugger off the Tower Ruthless and be done with it?"

There was a moment of silence as Barkwell realized that he had inadvertently spoken his thoughts aloud. "Oh, poop," he commented. With another sigh he disengaged his arm from the door and said, "My apologies, m'lud. I forgot myself. I'll just be toddling down to the Executioner's office to have myself burned at the stake. Might I bring you a nice cup of tea before I perish utterly?"

"Sit down," the Grim Lord directed, motioning the zombie into a hardbacked chair near the desk. Barkwell sat. "I don't blame you for this uncharacteristic outburst, Barkwell," the Grim Lord said. "None of us can be held responsible for our actions while our dear, familiar little world of torture and mayhem and elvish harassment is being set on ear by that—that—"

"Teacup twiddler?" Barkwell suggested.

"Oooooh, that's a good one!" The Grim Lord gave his servant a thumbs-up. Four times. All at once. "Now Barkwell, you've been a good and loyal servant. You posed a fair question and you're entitled to a straight answer without fear of reprisal or incineration. The reason I don't just boot Selvagio into the moat— and don't think the image doesn't taunt me damply in my dreams—is that I can't."

"Can't, m'lud?" It was not a word frequently heard from the Grim Lord, unless one counted the number of times he'd said: *No, honestly, I just* can't *eat another bite of stewed halfling!*

"Not if I ever want to make the Princess Minuriel my own. And her father's kingdom with her. If I evict her chosen champion—I mean, interior decorator— then not only do I forfeit all claim to the maiden's hand, but by the bonds of magic that invest this realm, I will be cast down from my position of power and reduced to the status of a—a—*a common archetype of evil!*" The strain was too much. The Grim Lord broke down in tears. Those corrosive drops shed by his Eye had the expected effect on the desk, which disintegrated into chunks of acid-washed wood.

The Grim Lord staunched his tears and regarded their handiwork. "Damn. And I really liked that desk," he said.

"Very true, m'lud," said Barkwell. "However, perhaps it is better thus. You have no guarantee that Selvagio would have liked it, nor that he would have allowed you to keep it."

"*Allowed* me to keep it?" The Grim Lord's words crackled through the air, leaving little puffs of ozone in their wake. "*Allowed*, say you? This is my private study! This is my refuge from the demands of absolute sorcerous omnipotence! This, Barkwell, is my *thinking corner*! I like it the way it is. Dust bunnies are our friends. Would the rascal dare to take liberties with even this, my most personal space?"

"Begging your pardon, m'lud, but you seemed to be under that impression not too long ago. When you instructed me to bar the door against him, m'lud," Barkwell elucidated.

"Oh, *that*." The Grim Lord waved away the zombie's words with a nervous laugh. "I just didn't want to be bothered by any of my underlings bursting in upon me with yet another complaint against that awful man. Since I'm not in a position to do anything to stop him, I'd only have to kill all the complainers. I've lost enough of my fighting force as it is."

"Ah, yes." Barkwell nodded. "Orcs. Drapes. Quite so."

"Do you think I *enjoy* feeling this helpless, Barkwell?" the Grim Lord implored. "It's not something I'm accustomed to, believe me. I tell you, lord-to-lich, that if someone can come up with a way for me to be rid of this meddlesome beast, I will—I will—well, I'll do my level best to keep from killing him in an offhanded manner in future."

"An offer both magnanimous and tempting, m'lud," said Barkwell. "Who could ask for anything more?" The zombie lapsed into a profound and significant silence.

"What are you thinking, Barkwell?" the Grim Lord asked.

"I, m'lud?" Barkwell returned innocently. "Thinking is not part of my job description."

"You are too thinking!" The Grim Lord smashed his fist onto his desktop. He had forgotten that he no longer had a desktop, overbalanced himself and sprawled at the zombie's feet. "Don't toy with me, Barkwell. I am a desperate locus of unfathomable evil."

"I admit, m'lud, that I did have an idea. However, I do not think you are going to like it."

"At this point, I'm ready to like *anything*. Except those goddamn pink drapes."

"In that case, m'lud, I do have a suggestion: Dump her."

"What?"

"The princess, m'lud. Disentangle yourself from any alliances, domestic or otherwise, with the lady in question. Concede the match and allow her to return unharmed to the bosom of her family. Give her the royal kiss-off and get the hell out now."

"What?" This time the Grim Lord said it more vehemently, with a lot of veinage showing in his Eye.

Barkwell shrugged. "There comes a time in every man's life when he must examine his priorities and ask himself whether the game is worth the candle. In this case, our artistic guest will very likely adorn the niches of the Tower Ruthless with hand-dipped, patchouli-scented beeswax candles set in candelabra shaped like unicorns. He may even use *bobeches*."

"What?" Now the word was used in its purely information-seeking sense. The Grim Lord got to his feet and dusted himself off.

"Those little collars you put around the bases of candles so you don't get wax drips on the floor," Barkwell provided.

The Grim Lord shivered at the horror of it. "You're right, Barkwell. It will be hard for me to admit defeat, but better surrender and save what's left of my sanity than put up with one more day of Selvagio."

"Yoo hoo!" came a familiar voice from the far side of the study door. "I just wanted to let you know that I haven't forgotten you! I'll be coming in tomorrow to give you the high concept for a completely new vision of your study. I've found some corduroy swatches that—"

"Not a moment too soon, m'lud," Barkwell murmured.

"Corduroy . . ." The Grim Lord mouthed the word as charily as if it were a live lizard. More charily; he liked keeping live lizards in his mouth. "Is the fiend a living cornucopia of cruelties and perversions?"

"Let us fervently hope we need never learn the answer to that, m'lud," said Barkwell. Ever the considerate servant, he provided his master with a set of earplugs while on the far side of the door Selvagio continued to rhapsodize over the many uses of terra cotta and chintz.

"Would it help if I said I'm sorry?" the princess Minuriel asked. She was mounted on a fine steed, ready to depart Dire Garde. Her handmaidens had already passed beneath the portcullis and awaited her on the road.

"It would help if you said you're taking him with you," the Grim Lord replied. He held the bridle of her horse in a death grip. Despite all he had done to her, the expression of panic and desperation now on his face called up pity in the elf-maiden's heart-of-hearts.

"But I can't," she replied. "My father banned him from the elfin lands—"

"Your father is one smart elf."

"—and besides, you signed the contract. You can't

get rid of him until he's finished the job; otherwise he'll file a grievance and the Guild of Interior Decorators will investigate."

"What do I care if—"

"Sixty-eight more Selvagios?"

The Grim Lord began to weep. This time he was able to keep his Eye out of it, so the tears that fell did not melt anything save Minuriel's heart. To her surprise, she found herself leaning over in the saddle to stroke the Grim Lord's hair—which was a very nice shade of brown if you could manage to catch sight of it between the tentacles.

"There, there," she said. "I feel just awful about this, especially since you've been so nice about letting me out of my marriage agreement with you."

"I thought you'd take him away with you!" the Grim Lord wailed. "That's the only reason I let you go free!"

"Nevertheless—" The princess didn't like to be corrected when she was riding the crest of an altruistic moment. "I feel a certain obligation to you. I must rescue you from this plight. I feel responsible. *Noblesse oblige.*"

"Is that anything like *bobeches*?" the Grim Lord asked suspiciously.

The elf-maiden dismounted. "Wait here," she instructed the Grim Lord. "I'm going to ask Selvagio to let you out of your contract as a personal favor to me."

The Grim Lord held her horse's bridle with one hand while with the other he pressed her fingertips to his mouth. "Oh, thank you, thank you!" he enthused between grateful smooches. "I know he'll listen to you! How could anyone resist granting you anything your heart might desire?"

Despite having no lips, he was a surprisingly capable kisser. (It is a little known fact that the predominating elvish erogenous zone resides in the fingers. This accounts for the preponderance of pickpockets in the population, as well as why most elves don rubber gloves before shaking hands with orcs.) The princess felt an unwonted flush rising to her cheeks at his attentions. Almost reluctantly she disengaged her hand. "Please, there—there's no need to thank me," she stammered. Flustered, she fled into the castle.

She emerged a short time later, much changed. No longer did she blush or flutter. She was in full command of herself. She was every inch the royal virgin elf-maiden. She was nursing a slow-burning rage the size of a yak.

"That miserable little *grub!*" she bellowed, stamping her foot. One of the forecourt paving stones cracked right up the middle. The Grim Lord jumped at the sound and dropped the bridle; Minuriel's mount bolted.

"Oh! Uh ... oops. Sorry. I'll have my men fetch you another one in just a—".

"Forget the frammin' horse!" the princess swore. "I don't *want* a horse. I want *blood!*"

"Er. ... You do?" The Grim Lord teetered between shock and hospitality. "What—what vintage?"

"*His* blood," Minuriel specified. "The thin, worthless, probably pastel blood of Selvagio Napp!"

"He—he turned you down? He refused to cancel my contract?"

"Worse!" She began to pace up and down before the Grim Lord, working herself up into a royal snit. "Just because it was my magic that summoned him to Dire Garde, he presented *me* with a bill for his travel expenses. The gall!"

"But if your magic brought him here, he *had* no travel expenses." The Grim Lord was well and truly ferhoodled.

"Well, he did have to send for his clothing and a few personal toiletry articles," Minuriel admitted. "But you'd think a real businessman would write off things like that."

The Grim Lord gazed shyly at the elfin maid. "I'd—I'd be honored to pay the bill for you," he said.

"Would you?"

The Grim Lord nodded.

"No strings attached?"

He shook his head.

Princess Minuriel looked at him—really *looked* at him—for the first time. "Why—why Your Infernality, in a certain light you're—you're—why, you're *cute!*"

"*Shhhhhh!*" The Grim Lord hushed her desperately. "You already ruined my home. Are you trying to ruin my reputation, too?"

Minuriel smiled and patted his cheek. "It'll be our little secret . . . Grimmy."

At this tender moment, Shiksael came trotting back into the castle forecourt. "What's the holdup, Your Highness?" she demanded. "Shikagoel and I thought you maybe stopped to powder your nose and fell in."

"Ah, the elegance of high elfin court training," Minuriel muttered. More audibly she said, "Come on back in and bring Shikagoel with you. We're not leaving."

"What? Why not?"

"You'll see," she said meaningfully.

The scene in the great hall was almost identical to the first time the Grim Lord attempted to espouse the Princess Minuriel. True, the severed heads on the minstrels' gallery had been replaced by plaster cherubs, the black draperies on the dais were now saffron, apricot, and gold, a thick layer of aquamarine stucco coated the walls, the drapes were unarguably pink, and someone had tied a white lace bow around

Skully's neck. Other than that, everything was the same.

Her eyes luminous with devotion, the princess Minuriel spoke the wedding vows of her people: "I, Minuriel, highborn elfin virgin, which nobody can deny, do pledge to thee my heart, my hand, and my dowry, freely and of my own will, so may these witnesses attest!"

The Grim Lord then gave the proper response according to his own beliefs, namely: "Her: *Mine*!" But to do him credit, he had the good grace to look embarrassed. The massed troops cheered.

"*What* is going on here?" Selvagio came tromping into the great hall, bolts of baize and seersucker trailing behind him. "You can't marry him!" He dropped the cloth and produced his copy of the contract. "It says right here that the wedding may not take place until such time as I have been paid for my services."

Coolly Minuriel regarded the obstreperous decorator. "And how much do you expect to be paid, pray?"

Selvagio named a sum that made trolls quail and wraiths give up the ghost. Even the Grim Lord went a little chalky around the gills. The decorator was unmoved by this display. He folded his arms across his chest and said, "I don't know what all the fuss is about. Did you think monogrammed towels for a castle that has fifty-eight bathrooms were going to come cheap? Have you seen the price of terry cloth on the open market lately? I have honored my part of the contract. I expect to be paid. And furthermore, there's the matter of my travel expenses—"

"Well, it says here—" Minuriel whipped a copy of the contract from the bosom of her wedding gown, "—that you don't get paid until you've finished the job!"

"But I have!" Selvagio objected. "I've only just finished his study." He pointed at the Grim Lord.

"My study!" His Atrocity echoed. "Why didn't Barkwell stop you?"

"Barkwell?" Selvagio's brows knit in perplexity.

"My zombie manservant."

"Ohhhhh." The decorator was enlightened. "I mistook him for a stubborn mildew stain. A little lemon-scented cleanser, a little elbow grease, a half dozen bunny-shaped air fresheners, and he was gone."

The Grim Lord groaned. "He was my best servant! Do you know how hard it is to dig up good help nowadays?"

"I thought he was rather outspoken for mildew," Selvagio admitted. Then he shrugged. "I'll deduct the cost of the air fresheners from your final bill, but that's the best I can do."

"You'll have to do better than that," said the princess. "Or this contract is null and void. You agreed to redecorate every interior on the premises."

"But I have!" Selvagio asserted.

Minuriel's lips curved up ever so slightly at the corners. "Not quite. There is one you missed."

By now the decorator was growing irate. "I suppose you're talking about a secret chamber or some such tired old gimmick. Well, you don't get out of paying me that easily. The contract specifies that you've got to show me any interior I might have missed."

"Would you like me to show it to you now?" Minuriel asked sweetly.

"Yes, I would!" The veins on Selvagio's neck stood out in an alarming manner when he shouted like that.

"All right. If you insist." The elfin princess raised her hands and gestured in a style familiar to mystics and hooch-dancers everywhere. There was a thrumming, a flash of green, and the air between herself and the decorator gelled into a conveniently compact indoor-sized dragon. It tilted its head quizzically at the quaking Selvagio and, without any fuss worth mentioning, devoured him.

The princess produced a memo pad and well-chewed pencil stub. With a fine flourish she ticked an item off a list known but to herself. "That's the last interior," she announced cheerfully. "I'd say Selvagio's redecorating it just fine. Of course, as for his bill—"

The dragon gave a short, polite little cough and hawked up the former decorator's paperwork, along with half a bolt of seersucker. Ignoring the fabric, Minuriel picked up the partially digested bill and duly marked it VOID. This done, she noticed the groundswell of terror currently pervading the congregation, all of whom were regarding the dragon askance. "Oh, calm down," she directed. "He's just my dowry."

"Your dowry?" the Grim Lord echoed. "A dragon's your dowry?"

"It's an elf thing. Royal virgins receive the power to command dragons as soon as we're married; it's sort of like practice for handling husbands. Or do you think I'd have stood for being locked away in that tacky old tower of yours for so long if I could've summoned up something like *him* anytime I wanted?" The lady shrugged. "Besides, I already have a blender."

The Grim Lord regarded his bride with renewed respect. "Why, darling, in a certain light you're—you're—why, you're completely merciless!"

Minuriel blushed becomingly. "This old personality trait? I've had it for years!"

Tenderly he took her into his arms, and to the cheers of his subjects and the insane chittering of Skully, they embraced.

Jorc the orc peered around the great hall doorway. "I got fired off me paper route. Any chance o' me gettin' m'old job ba—?" He paused, awestruck by the spectacle he now beheld. "D'I miss anythin'?" he asked, hesitantly creeping to the head of the assemblage.

The dragon, who had digested Selvagio's sense of style along with the rest of the decorator, ate him. He didn't match the drapes.

BRIGBUFFOON

by David Bischoff

David Bischoff, a prolific writer, is the author of over 50 books. He has also written successfully for television, collaborating on two scripts for Star Trek: The Next Generation. *He has also collaborated on two SF novels with the editor. As one reviewer commented, in some countries they shoot collaborators.... Here he blends wistful fantasy with local Pacific Northwest color in a tale of a floating castle that must find a kingdom.*

Batman has his Batsignal.

Lowly E-Mail must suffice for this particular superhero.

I'd finished up my work for the night on my book, *Constructing The Middle Ages: The Shifting Signifier in Fifteenth Century Discourse,* and logged onto the University BBS. Waiting for me in my box was a single message.

GET DOWN TO THE LOFT BY MIDNIGHT IF YOU CAN. THERE'S A GUY HERE YOU'VE GOT TO MEET. SOMETHING SPOOKY, SOMETHING CREEPY. SOMETHING FUN. —JURGEN.

I looked at the clock. A little before eleven p.m. It was Thursday night. Thursday nights at Larry's Loft they served shots of Yeagermeister, cheap. The slackers would be there in droves, and the cigarette smoke would be thick and blue. I tend to avoid the bar at such times; I prefer hanging out there during afternoons and early evenings, or early in the weekend, when the noise volume is low and it looks more like a bar than a mosh pit.

However, Jurgen only summons me when he really needs me, or if there is truly something special happening.

I needed something special, that was for sure. I'd been burdened with three classes to teach this quarter, and my students tended to fall asleep in the middle of class. My book wasn't going well, and I honestly wondered if I had been anywhere near sanity when I'd launched myself into medieval literature. Tenure seemed a distant dream, but the very idea of not having to wade through medieval Latin and fusty manuscripts any more and submit papers to anal retentives with advanced degrees did not trouble me greatly. The distance between me and the Middle Ages seemed far greater than simple centuries could explain.

I put on my dark, cracked, and faded leather coat, petted the cats good-bye, and exited my apartment.

Autumn was just settling over Eugene, and the cooling air had the pleasant smell of a multitude of leaves passing on to their earthy rewards. I strode through the night over pavement and sidewalk, past half-bare trees, and the thought of some new adventure awaiting me was as invigorating as the touch of coolness in the air and the ice of stars and moon in a clear blue night. Professing English, Old and otherwise at the University has its rewards, but I was still young enough to appreciate more scintillating pursuits.

And Larry's Loft has had its scintillating moments.

As I approached it, I realized it was unprepossessing enough: a boxy tacky Chinese restaurant, with a boxy tacky Siamese twin bar neighbor. Too much neon and stucco to be anywhere near respectable. A parking lot crowded with cars.

Inside, the tables were full of young people with old hair. Said young people had lots of pierced noses and eyebrows and ears and, no doubt, lots of tattoos beneath their loose and lumberjacky clothing. There was the smell of peanuts and laughter and serious debate and the blood of Kurt Cobain.

The tables were full, and that was fine, because Jurgen, my E-mail correspondent, was a bartender, which meant he was at the bar. I assumed that the person he wanted me to meet sat there now as well.

I wended my way through the smoke and the buzz of conversation, noting MTV on one television dangling from chains above the bar, and ESPN on the other: strabismic eyeballs strobing Generation X with mutating radiation.

The bar is long and walnutty, and I went to one end, where Jurgen was busy pouring Tequila Sunrises and shots of Yeager.

He noticed me immediately.

"Hey, Ted. Got my message, huh?"

"Right."

"Give me a sec."

He finished his pouring, delivered the drinks to a waiting waitress, then came back.

He leaned over and tapped a burly man on the shoulder.

The man burled around and looked at me.

"You're interested in castles?" he said without preamble.

"Why . . . yes. Of course."

"Ted's a medievalist at the University. That's where castles come from."

"Medievalists at universities?" I said.

"No, no. Medieval times!" said Jurgen.

"I think I'm aware of that," said the man.

He had long black and gray hair and round glasses. A chin strap beard. Beneath a voluminous black jacket, he wore a Megadeth T-shirt, featuring a leering skull. He looked a little too old for a headbanger. But then, this is Eugene.

I held out a hand and he shook it. "Anyway, I'm interested in many things, particularly the odd."

"Then you've come to the right person at the right time," said the man. "The name is Robertson. Bob Robertson. I am the owner of Little Universe Science Fiction Books, at the corner of Fifth and Willammette."

"Right. Across from the post office."

"That's the place. I had an interesting person come into my shop today, and I am entertaining him this evening. Allow me to introduce you."

He stepped away, and I saw that his bulky form has been hiding an equally tall, much skinnier man. Bent like a vulture, this man wore a tattered blue windbreaker and Ben Franklin glasses. A T-shirt peeked up from beneath an old Izod shirt, above worn black Chinos. Around his neck he wore a Catholic style crucifix. His hair was short but uncombed. It looked like a ruffled toupee, badly fitted.

"Ted, this is Dafydd Jenkins from Aberystwyth, Wales."

"Hello," said the man.

He offered a slender hand for me to shake, but somehow a drink got in the way in the process and he spilled beer on the bar.

"Oh, dear," said the man.

"Not to worry. I'll buy another. Nice to meet you."

"Yes, and the same."

Our hands finally clasped. His palm was cool, his wrist limp.

He looked tentative and dismayed by the world, but old fires glimmered in his eyes behind thick hornrimmed glasses. His accent had a definite Welsh lilt. He looked slight and more than slightly eccentric. He appeared to be a whimsical cipher in search of rare moths, carrying a butterfly net with a ragged hole in the bottom. I felt in the presence of a character from those British *Carry On* movies, ripped from celluloid, literature, and stereotype, yet inarguably alive and before me.

"I met Dafydd at a Science Fiction Convention on the East Coast. He's on a budget, so he's staying with me at my house while in Eugene," explained Bob Robertson. "SF fans tend to extend such hospitalities."

"Wait till you hear what's brought him here, Ted," said Jurgen.

"Wait a moment," said the Welshman. "I know you are a medievalist, and I sense a man of curiosity. Jurgen assures me you are a man who has seen some fascinating things and enjoyed some significant adventures in this most charming city. I have one question, before I'm sure you're the man I need."

"Sure thing. Fair enough. Shoot."

He blinked at my triad of Americanisms, but then smiled softly. "Ah, yes. Well, it is this. Can you rise, as our Scots cousins might say, in the wee, *wee* hours?"

I often do, actually. For a wee wee, as a matter of fact. But he was intensely serious, and I returned the answer in kind.

"I prefer to sleep late, but I can get up early and function well enough, given enough coffee."

He nodded soberly. "Good. Then here's the proposition, should you indeed know something of castles."

"I do, and have, in fact, toured many in Europe."

"Good," he said. "And are you ready to tour one in Eugene?"

A castle in Eugene?

Battlements and moat and drawbridge and whatnot in the Pacific Northwest?

I thought I'd toured most of the interesting places already here. The biggest places I knew of were the Hult Center and the Hilton, and the largest old houses are Victorian—barely old and barely Victorian.

Naturally, I was most intrigued.

"A castle in Eugene?" I said. "Where?"

Robertson smiled smugly. "Oh, it's not here. Not now."

I shook my head, baffled. "I don't understand."

"No, nor I, fully," said Dafydd Jenkins, looking stone cold serious. "However, I have made a study of this subject for some time indeed, and I am absolutely certain that there *will* be a castle here in Eugene. To-morrow. Dawn."

Now, if there were any time for a castle to appear in Eugene, dawn, it seemed to me, would be the most unlikely of times. The dead of night, maybe, after too much microbrew. On the other hand, I thought, Eugene dawns could be full of clouds and mist, and cas-tles seemed at home in such, so I decided that this was a definite possibility, especially in the Eugene Fantastique I had come to know.

However, that didn't mean I intended to believe the man entirely. I'd met my share of crackpots here, whose wild stories had not panned out.

Still, it was worth listening to the fellow.

"You must understand, I am a scientist of the amaz-ing," said Dafydd Jenkins. "An archivist of the unique. I know the folklore and legends of Europe, and have developed systems for tracking their reso-nance in the quivering dimensions of transrealities. A dash of astrology, a soupçon of alchemy. Astral as-tronomy, scientology, divination, and the secret cross-world puzzles of the ancients. All contribute to the microscopic mapping of time/space cyberstitching of eventuality, prediction, and legendary geography.

Enough for my credentials: take my word, I am a master of my tools at hand."

"He also plays a mean game of ping pong," said Robertson, nodding with approval.

"Are you, Mr. Medievalist, aware of the legend of Castle Brigbuffoon."

I lifted an eyebrow. Well, yes, of course. There was a famous manuscript called *The Book Of Ten Dead And Smelly Priests* from fifteenth century Scotland. Its principal fame amongst scholars was for its use of medieval Latin for Word Jumbles. However, I *did* remember some silly efforts in its pages at an attempt of a wholly facetious mythos.

Nothing specific.

I shrugged and mumbled something scholarly. The standard academic ploy when in mental difficulty, or when one just plain doesn't know.

Dafydd Jenkins seemed pleased at the opportunity to show off his knowledge and the depths of his research.

"There is the tale that winds through the *ty bachs*—outhouses—of Welsh fable. It is, of course, the tale of peoples lost in time and space, who appear only at certain times. . . ."

"What? Brigadoon?"

"That's an American musical, ja?" said Jurgen, cheerfully juggling a couple of Buds.

"No. No. Sentimental trifle. This is the real stuff, I assure you. The hallowed tale of Brigbuffoon!"

I raised the other eyebrow. "I don't believe, in all my studies of medieval literature, I've ever heard of that story."

"I am not surprised. Actually, it is neither fable nor fairy tale. It is history." He raised his finger authoritatively. "History which I will eventually attempt to relate."

"First, I believe he's going to make a profound statement," said Bob Robertson.

"Yes. Profound indeed. For this aforesaid Castle Brigbuffoon, lost in time and space, is scheduled to materialize tomorrow morning at 6:11 sharp, on top of Skinner's Butte for a total of one hour and fifty-five minutes. And it is my aim to rescue its denizens, or at the very least, discover some of the deep and baffling mysteries. Because of the time constraints, I shall need some help to get through the castle. Which is why I need the assistance of someone who is acquainted with the structure of castles!"

"You could check a book out of the library," I said.

"I'd rather have an expert for consultation than a bulky book. The light, after all, will not be the best. Besides, this fine strapping fellow Jurgen—who by the way has agreed to go along in the way of muscle—told me that you enjoyed wild mysteries."

"Well, I seem to keep on bumping into them—or they into me."

"Excellent. Then you'll come along?"

I was no *expert* on castles. However, I'd done some studies on them, and I knew a crenellation from a portcullis.

"Okay. Sure. Why not?"

"Terrific! Jurgen! A round of single malt whiskey. Peatmulch, I think!" he said exuberantly.

I demurred, explaining that I don't drink anymore. And while I do sniff the occasional beer for enjoyment, sniffing a single malt scotch was considerably deadlier.

Besides, I was going to have to get up pretty early in the morning tomorrow, it would seem.

I don't call the bump we climbed the next morning Skinner's Butte. I call it "Skinner's Butt."

It's just a big hill really, right next to the Willamette

River. When Eugene Skinner emigrated to the area
in 1850 or so, this was where he first settled. Now it's
an official park, with a radio antenna and a reservoir
and winding road that goes to its top, with a parking
lot that has a nice view of the town. Just short of six
a.m. we drove up that road in Bob Robertson's Dodge
van: Bob, Dafydd, Jurgen, and, of course, me.

"Kind of creepy this time of day, isn't it?" said Jurgen, breaking the sleepy silence in the group.

"I wouldn't call it creepy. Eerie's more the word, I
believe," I said.

The Willamette Valley gets a lot of clouds, and in
the mornings it also gets misty. Somehow, there
seemed to be a cloud perched on top of Skinner's
Butte, even as the forest and the whole river was
steaming off cool phantoms of mist. The result was an
atmospheric fog, thin enough to make out trees, thick
enough to swathe everything in mystery.

The headlights cut through easily enough, and Bob
was a good driver and it wasn't as though the road
was long. Still, by the time we got to the top, I felt
quite a bit more nervous than I had when we'd met
at Larry's Loft's parking lot just minutes before.

We got out, and the chill in the air seemed to slide
into me, piercingly. I shivered. It was maybe in the
upper thirties, but it felt colder, somehow.

Dafydd Jenkins stepped through the van door,
wearing a cardigan and a cap and a plaid scarf. His
cheeks were rosy, but he seemed not cold at all. In
his hand was a device that seemed a mutant cross
between a sextant, an astrolabe, and a surveyor's
plumb, covered with odd scribblings of ancient dead
languages. He walked a ways on the gravel lot and
put a lens to an eye.

Beyond stretched the top of the butte: a grassy field
edged with trees. The place smelled of the river and
damp and that peculiar but invigorating Pacific North-

west forest smell, particularly odd so near to a city of over a hundred thousand souls.

Dafydd Jenkins slowly panned the device back and forth, then steadied it toward the dead center of the field.

"There. Brigbuffoon castle will appear there." He pulled a stopwatch up from a pocket, examined it. "And it will arrive in precisely eight minutes and thirty seconds."

Jurgen shivered. "Glad we didn't get here any earlier. It's *cold.*"

"I'll say," said Bob. "I myself suggest we wait for this appearance in the van."

"No, no. Dear me, that won't do at all."

"Why?" said Bob, clearly uncomfortable.

"Metal and glass between appearing object and ourselves may interfere with the bonding spell I've established."

"What?" said Jurgen.

"I think what he's saying is that if we're in the car, we might not be able to see the castle appearing," I said.

Jurgen scratched his head. "I think if a great big castle were to appear in front of me, I'd be able to see it."

"Just take his word for it, please," said Bob, exasperated.

"Yes. The wait will not be long and the cold is, after all, quite bearable, don't you think?"

It wasn't the cold per se, as much as it was the *quality* of the cold. I racked my brain for sensory memories, and finally I had it. I had visited Wales once in the winter, and on a particularly cold, damp day I had taken a walk along a secluded valley.

This was the kind of cold that had been in that valley that day: a wraparound, second-skin, I-won't-ever-be-warm-again-cold.

A *haunting* cold.

I stood there, focused on the field with the rest of the group, thinking about the sight of the castle that we were supposed to witness, and its story that Dafydd Jenkins had told the night before.

Castle Brigbuffoon had been built by renegade Celts after a movement in the fifteenth century to a mountain beside a Welsh river—Brigbuffoon Avon. It was meant to monitor the traffic on the river and prevent the incursion of the English further into Welsh lands. However, just after it was finished, after a record number of crushed and moat-drowned workers, drought hit the land. The river dried up permanently. The result: one beached castle, in the middle of nowhere, with absolutely no purpose.

Initially, the builder and owner, and lord of the area—one Hywel ap Madawg—tried to build a village around it. However, with no particular purpose nor stock in trade, no one came. The only denizens were the knights and peasants and builders under Lord Hywel's employ. One night, depressed Hywel Madawg drank far too much and decided to dive in for a swim in the castle's moat. Unfortunately, he'd forgotten that there was no water in the moat, and broke his neck.

His son, Madawg ap Hywel ap Madawg, inherited the castle and his lands. Alas, he also inherited his father's problems. What, oh what to do with Castle Brigbuffoon? The workers and knights there were slowly drifting away. There wasn't a great deal to do, except play board games like *gwyddbwyll* and ride back and forth the forty miles between the castle and supplies.

Now, the entirety of Europe had just undergone a number of inquisitions. This resulted in a great many wizards and magical sorts being stoned or burned. Those who escaped were homeless. Madawg ap Hywel ap Madawg heard this, and had an idea. He offered sanctuary to these homeless men of sorcery and such. About thirty of them straggled in, and were fed and clothed and taken care of.

Madawg's idea was this: There was no physical solution to his dilemma. Castle Brigbuffoon had to be either deserted or moved, and moving it was a physical and financial impossibility. So why not enlist the aid of magic?

Fortunately, the wizards and magicians were very grateful for this sanctuary.

Unfortunately, they had all been stoned or injured in some ways, and were not the wizards they had once been. In fact, they were rather incompetent. For while they indeed devised a magical method for moving the castle, and indeed transported it through a dimensional gate, they neglected to figure out the proper destination spells.

Thus was Castle Brigbuffoon lost in time and space, appearing hither and thither, looking for a proper home. Alas, they often found such: however, the problem was that the wizards could not come up with the proper "sticking spell." Hours after appearances, the castle would disappear again, carrying its citizens off to some other unknown destination.

And this morning, just a tad after six a.m. it would make Skinner's Butte in Eugene, Oregon, a temporary home.

According to Dafydd Jenkins, that is.

Who was now consulting his timepiece.

"... eight ... seven ... six ..." he counted down. "... one. ... Now."

He looked up expectantly.

Dawn was just peeking up through the Cascade Mountains to the East, struggling soddenly through mist and clouds and fog. The grassy field just sat there, empty, as grassy fields are wont to do.

"Hmmm. Perhaps a miscalculation? A minor one, I hope."

I shuddered, and not entirely from the cold.

A *major* miscalculation actually would not be so bad. I was feeling a teensy bit skeptical anyway. I felt like going home, having some breakfast, then going back to bed. Besides, I was feeling the wrong kind of adrenaline.

"I don't think it would hurt for us to wait a while," said Bob Robertson gruffly. "In fact, I've got a large thermos of coffee in the van, prepared for just such a possibility."

He opened the door and pushed his big frame through.

"Ja," said Jurgen. "I could use some coffee. Did you bring any milk? I really prefer milk with—"

Jurgen suddenly shut up, which was unusual.

I began to see why.

At first I thought it was just the mist rising up from the grass: a kind of slow waver of intermingled light and dark.

But the shadows darkened, solidified, grew, extending upward to the sky. I realized, abruptly, that I was looking at walls. Walls rising up and connecting into an enclosure.

There was just enough light in the mist to make it out quite well, now.

A castle.

A definite castle.

"Oh, my God," I said. "A *true* shifting signifier!"

"Yes indeed. Yes *indeed*!" said Dafydd. "There is! Castle Brigbuffoon!"

Most castles are old now, and have that roughness and age about them. This one, however, had the sheen of fairly recently hewn rock. It was not a particularly large castle, as castles go, nor was it particularly tiny. It looked like a splendid example of a generic fifteenth-century castle, all the way from batters to battlements. Which is to say, from the exterior it seemed to have castle-type requirements: huge thick walls, topped with wall walks and turrets, merlons with finials on the embrasured battlements; arrow loops through which archers could shoot at invaders; and a flag flying from the top of its central tower. It featured a large griffin, and it looked quite new and unweathered.

"Amazing," I said.

Bob Robertson and Jurgen could only nod their heads, looking stunned. It's one thing to go looking for a castle. It's entirely another thing to have one materialize before you, solid and misty, ripped from an earlier, more dangerous time.

Dafydd Jenkins looked to be in a trance. He wandered over toward a wall, reaching out his hand to touch it, to make sure it was real. His hand touched the stone, the rubble, feeling it, caressing it.

"Uhmm ... Mr. Jenkins ... I wouldn't advise standing where you are if ..."

"What?" he turned around.

My warning was too late.

A large dollop of mess dropped down from a bulgy apartment extending from the top of the wall. It plopped directly onto Dafydd Jenkins' head, splatting messily.

He stepped back from the wall, disgusted.

"Shit!" he said.

"Yes," I agreed. "You were standing under the garderobe."

"Garderobe?" said Jurgen.

"Latrine, I believe," said Bob Robertson, his nose cringing at the stench wafting from Dafydd Jenkins. "I've got some towels in the van. Let's clean you up."

With water and the towels, Bob did the best he could with his friend. I was certain that Mr. Jenkins would be more circumspect about where he stood in the future.

"The good news," I said, "is that there is no doubt now that the castle is populated. Looks like you're right, Mr. Jenkins. Any ideas about what comes next?"

"I am beginning to understand a castle's method of repelling the enemy," said Dafydd Jenkins. "Hopefully in this case by mistake. No, my intention here is to communicate. And, since the drawbridge seems to be up, we shall have to get it down to enter. And since we must enter to see what's inside, it would appear we must first communicate. Who amongst us has the loudest voice?"

"That," I said, remembering Jurgen screaming cheers at a University of Oregon football game, "would be our German friend here."

Jurgen grinned. "I am glad to be useful."

"Only I would suggest," said Bob Robertson, "given historical considerations, that you drop the Hunnish accent."

"Ja," said Jurgen.

"Hello!" bellowed Jurgen, hands cupped to his lips. "Hello! Welcome to Eugene. We want to be friends!"

This, of course, not spoken in Eugenian. Or even American, for that matter.

Between us, Jenkins and myself had cobbled together what we reckoned to be something similar to what would have been spoken by fifteenth century Welsh. At first, Jenkins had suggested that I use straight medieval Latin. However, I noted that if indeed there were persecuted wizards inside, we might be mistaken for priests and riddled with arrows.

At first, only silence and mist, the sense of cold and mystery.

"Do it again," I instructed. "Only add: 'Hic est . . .

llyma ... amici ... Su mae?' " I gave that to him in an obscure dialect of middle English used by outsiders—kind of a lingua franca, as it were, generally accepted as being a language of the accepted underclass in the area. (My pronunciation was possibly total rubbish, since there were no tape recorders about to actually transcribe the dialect—I gleaned it mostly from the messy manuscripts of a drunken monk.)

Jurgen cupped his hands again, and called out the message, with surprising lack of Germanic accent.

His words seemed to echo against the walls, and then through the great halls of the castle.

Dawn was brightening, somewhat, so we could see the outline of a man as he stood up from behind a parapet and called down to us.

I was surprised that I was able to understand him quite well.

"Howdy down there. Where the hell did you say we were?"

A strong voice. A robust voice.

A puzzled voice.

"Eugene," said Jurgen. "You're in Eugene, Oregon!"

"Hey," said Bob Robertson. "I understood that, too!"

"Yes. Plain old current-day English. If there are indeed wizards inside, they must have concocted some kind of Magical Universal Translator."

"Like on *Star Trek*!" said Jurgen.

"Yes," I said. "Maybe that's where they got the idea from."

The notion of being doomed to a limbo between dimensions with nothing much else to do but watch *Star Trek* repeats was a bit too hellishly Boschian for me to take, so I quickly discarded it and moved on.

"Some kind of magical kingdom," called the voice. "And by the way ... what year is it?"

This was a problem. Eugene is not strictly a magical kingdom per se, even though I have witnessed what can pass for magic in it—including this current appearance of a fifteenth century castle on top of Skinner's Butte.

"I'll speak here," I said, stepping forward. "You are on terra firma," I said. "You are in the year 1995, Anno Domini."

"Oh, shit!" said the man. I heard the slap of a palm hitting a forehead. "Paracelsus! Did you hear that!"

"Yes, my lord," boomed a voice nearby.

"Well, this beats all. Look, I don't want to get into the next *millennium,* for Chrissakes!"

"No, my lord!"

The voice pitched up to a near scream. "So, do you think it would be at all possible to fix it so that we can find a goddammed *home*?"

"Pardon, my lord, but from all indications, this is rather murky territory. Perhaps we should ascertain the actual nature of this place upon which we have landed. There well may be demons and monsters waiting to pounce upon us and rend us to teensy weensy pieces should we venture too far without."

"Is this actually an issue? Are you telling me that you've finally figured out a way to allow us to anchor and stick for more than two hours?"

A short silence. "Alas, no, my lord."

"I thought not." There was a vast sigh that we could hear quite distinctly, even down here. "Well, we'd better let the welcome wagon in, Paracelsus."

"Yes, my lord."

There were indistinct orders and the shuffling of feet.

We looked at one another, shrugged, and waited.

From the consternated look in Dafydd Jenkins' eyes, I could tell that this was not exactly what he had in mind.

An excited yell could be heard, muffled, through the wood of the gatehouse:

"No! Not that lever, you idiot!"

The drawbridge slammed down across a nonexistent moat. It managed to flatten a great deal of grass in the process.

The portcullis went up.

A tentative voice spoke from the dimness within. "Uhm—you can come in, if you like. But be forewarned. We're quite well armed and—uhmm . . . fearsome warriors . . . and . . . ah . . ."

". . . Terrifying warlocks!" whispered another voice.

"Ah, yes. Truly terrifying warlocks, with fire bolts at our fingertips and thunderbolts and nasty poxes and stuff like— Ouch! That's my shin!"

"Lay down any weapons!" called another voice.

"We have no weapons!" said Dafydd Jenkins. "Of that we may assure you. We wish to be friends. We wish only to help you!"

"Damn. You mean you're not at all interested in buying a castle?"

"Well, I suppose we could discuss that," said Jenkins. "But that's not precisely what we had in mind."

He gestured at the rest of us, and together we followed him (albeit with some trepidation) up onto the wooden drawbridge and through the gate.

We stepped, finally, into a courtyard, slowly filling with light, but even now predominantly filled with shadows, and that ever-present companion, mist.

Standing there before us, looking just as nervous as we were, were several men dressed in simple kilts, and at least a dozen more dressed in robes, with hoods off. On the heads of the men were bandages. Their hands were raised in absurd, crooked-finger imitation of spell-casting. Two of the men held drawn bows notched with arrows. The others held drawn swords.

"We come in peace!" reassured Dafydd Jenkins.

"Ja!" said Jurgen.

The swords were raised higher. The bows tightened.

"Jurgen!" said Bob. "Nix the German."

"Oh. Sorry. Got any rarebit or ale, guys?"

"We're looking at fifteenth-century sorts here, Jurgen. I'm not sure about ale, but rarebit hadn't been invented yet," I pointed out.

"Phew. I'm glad *I* didn't live there then!" said Jurgen.

"Be that as it may," said the man who apparently was the leader. "My name is Madawg ap Hywel ap Madawg, and I am the lord here, for what *that's* worth. Welcome to my manse, temporary as it may be ... for, as you may surmise ... and well may know if you've divined our arrival ... we have a short time to stay, unless we can figure something out!"

We introduced ourselves, and received a bow from the wizards and men-at-arms—whose arms, fortunately, had been lowered.

As the light grew and the shadows withdrew, we got a better look at our hosts.

Madawg was a strapping lad with a shock of black hair and a wispy beard. He had dark blue, troubled eyes and a weak chin. All in all it looked to me as though he'd much rather be playing harps than in a lost castle traipsing across space, time, and Eugene. The wizards in their coarse, itching robes (and they scratched often, in rather embarrassing places) were stunted, with broken noses, or chewed-upon ears and scabrous faces, with expressions that somehow managed to be simultaneously glazed and anxious. It made me wonder if this supposed wizard-purge had occurred in some low-rent countries.

Then again, I well knew that things such as health, beauty, and most particularly height, to say nothing of life spans, had improved markedly since those generally dismal days of plague, Holy Mother Churches, and indoor outdoor plumbing.

"And now, may I present our head wizard, Paracelsus," said Madawg.

One of the robed fellows shuffled forward, looking much the same as the others: damaged, dirty, tentative, and smelly. However, this one's face seemed a little more delicate and well-made than the others, and in his eyes some semblance of intelligence showed.

That and happiness to see us . . .

And perhaps, even hope.

"Dafydd Jenkins," said Paracelsus. "I sense that you are the one who has sought us out. You perceive our difficulty. First, may I inquire: is this place worthy to stop at?"

Dafydd Jenkins looked thoughtful at this, but did not take long to respond. "As good as any, and better than most."

"Good enough, good enough!" cried Madawg. "Oh, this is good news . . . Good news indeed." He clapped his hands together joyfully. "In truth, I am getting awfully tired hopping from one place to another, with a whole lot of nothing in between."

"Then we will attempt to linger," said Paracelsus. "You know of our history and our plight?"

"Yes. It is a fable written in many manuscripts across time and place," responded Jenkins brightly.

"Good! And you know something of magic."

"This and that."

"Excellent. In that case, have you figured out the solution to our plight?"

"Well . . . er . . . no . . ."

"Damn all," said Madawg.

"Not precisely . . . however, I would not be here if I did not have some quite constructive ideas." Dafydd looked around the courtyard. "By the way, lovely place you've got here."

And it was.

Dawn's light had seeped in enough by now to get a good look at the place. For all of its silly name, the castle was a sturdily-made affair, its architecture bespeaking not merely different minds, but different spirits. *Medieval* spirits, with a beauty unique in history.

The inner ward, which was where we stood, was filled with testaments to life. Carts and pots and little huts composed of wattle. All this surrounded by the stony beauty of towers and walls: safety, community. I suddenly had a true sense of the Middle Ages: not merely looking back to it, in an analyzing fashion, but experiencing it, being in the *nowness* of it, no sense of the future, just pure medieval *awareness*. It explained much that my manuscripts could not.

"What *is* it?" said Paracelsus eagerly. "Even ideas might give us a clue. Alas, my colleagues and I are in a complete muddle."

His sincerity shone through the dirt and the grime, and my heart went out to him.

"Yes, well, that's where some of the fable comes in, along with the emotional dimensions of the magical ripping of the fabrication of space/time you've undergone," said Jenkins.

"Yes? Yes?"

"This is all well and good, but unlikely to help," said Madawg. "Besides I have been much amiss in my hostly duties. It is morning and we must offer you breakfast!"

"There is hardly time!" said Jenkins.

"True, true, but think—it is unlikely that we shall have more than two hours together. Let us have a little joy in that time. And what better joy than the breaking of bread between new friends."

"Yes, well," said Bob Robertson. "I must admit I

haven't had a chance to eat this morning, and my stomach's been rumbling quite a bit."

Madawg bellowed out, and we were led through foyers and hallways into a great hall, where a long wooden table had already been set up. Bread and beakers of ale were available, along with savory cooked chicken and cabbage. It seemed more like a Sunday feast than a breakfast; but then, I guess the wizards and people of the castle didn't get many guests. So when they did, they celebrated. I declined the ale, of course; however, I did eat some bread and smoked bacon, which was good and quite filling. We listened as Madawg recounted the wondrous visits they had made throughout the world and the times. He indicated that there were trophies of these visits throughout the storage rooms of the castle—from chastity belts to grimoires to Betty Page posters. To say nothing of the history and experience they had procured.

I asked if I could see some of these artifacts.

"No time for that," said Madawg, seeing that we had been properly supplied with food and drink. "Now then, Dafydd Jenkins. What is this solution that you've been speaking of?" He leaned over his plate, totally ignoring its contents.

I could see his eagerness to find some mooring in the universe; I understood his feeling, and felt for the plight of him and his people.

Dafydd Jenkins chewed a piece of bread thoughtfully, then chose his words carefully:

"It is said that in the matrices of thaumaturgy there exist threads of a binding nature. A large portion of the content of these bindings consist of that odd substance known as emotion. The emotions of humankind haunt the interstices of the multiverses, and form its very nature, long after the emoters are gone.

"However, to be precise and succinct:

"The answer is love."

Bob Robertson scratched his head, a piece of chicken hanging in his beard. "Sounds like a Beatles song."

"Actually, it makes magical sense. Tell me if it doesn't, Paracelsus: the fable goes like this—if an individual from the land in which Castle Brigbuffoon finds itself loves one of its occupants, then that tie will anchor it as long as that love continues. I suspect that it would help if you occupants of said Castle Brigbuffoon love the place you find yourself. But then, I'm sure you'll find Eugene quite lovable."

Lord Madawg looked at his wizards.

His wizards looked at Lord Madawg.

They all looked toward us.

"Well, we're really pretty normal men," said Paracelsus. "But I suppose we can adjust." He fidgeted his robes in apparent discomfort.

"No, no, that's not exactly what I meant," said Madawg, his face growing a little red. "I think we can look at this in a more spiritual, ethereal manner. In fact—"

However, before he could finish, Madawg was already up and hurrying about, a look of excitement on his face. He sped off to some anteroom, jabbering.

"What's he doing?" said Jurgen, mouth full of food.

"Don't know," said Robertson. "Hope he can figure a way to keep this place around. Something about this food is quite interesting."

I knew what he meant. It had some kind of simple, extra zest. In truth, I felt it was all a part of the whole in this amazing castle: A treasure trove of experience and truth here ... packed in this delightful building! Oh, the manuscripts it must hold—but more, the thinking people behind those manuscripts.

Madawg returned.

"Gentlemen, may I introduce to you some other

members of our assembly . . . our ladies in waiting, as it were."

Bob Robertson's eyebrows shot up. "Well, you know I was wondering where the women are. You know, I am not presently encumbered with a relationship. Perhaps this is a good idea indeed!"

In fact, Robertson was quite a connoisseur of women—albeit the type he watched were in the nude dancing bars of Eugene and Portland. I could see it in his eyes: ah, yes—a buxom medieval wench.

Five women walked out, wearing various modes of medieval clothing.

They were short, dumpy, ugly, and they smelled every bit as bad as their male counterparts.

I cringed. I could feel the others of Eugene cringe.

"Here you are, dear maidens. Are these not valiant-looking gentlemen? As I said, they would very much like to court you."

Terror filled my heart.

I expected giggles.

Instead I heard several "Yucks!"

The women turned their backs and hurried away. One paused beside Madawg and grabbed his arm emphatically.

"How could you think of attempting to burden us with such *ugly, smelly* men? Or much less love them."

"Yes, I know," said Madawg. "But they could roll around in the courtyard a while . . . and I'm sure a little magic from the wizards might put a beauty spell on them."

"I'd rather be doomed to limbo with you clods than have one of those barbarians touch me!"

The trollish lady flounced away, trailing her muddy garment, nose stuck in the air.

Robertson and Jurgen looked incredibly relieved. "Well, love, after all, is not a simple thing," said Robertson. He continued to eat happily.

However, Madawg shook his head sadly, obviously crestfallen.

"Where, oh, where, is love when you need it!" He sighed, but then essayed a wisp of a smile. "Ah, well. Eat hearty, gentle friends. And then, in the time remaining, I shall show you our home ... away from home."

Well-stuffed, we set out and were shown about. Rooms with tapestries. Courtyards with odds and ends and games. Children playing. The rooms of charts and thaumaturgy. The smells, the sights, the sounds, the tastes: all were of a different world, and yet still just different shades of human.

In one of the upper rooms, I was introduced to monks, sitting over their works, painstakingly writing and illuminating their lovely manuscripts. Monks in a castle? Their monastery had burned, Dafydd explained, and they were given a home here before the change. The monks were full of questions, however not as full as me: and I knew there was no time for either.

We were ushered around by friendly, accepting Madawg.

"Ah, but I wish that there were time for us to see *your* homes," said the lord. "However, we have plenty of supplies, and the fact that you were waiting for us bespeaks much for your interest in us."

Indeed, time had passed far too quickly, and the less-than-two hour limit on the castle's stay had drawn near.

"If you do not leave, you will be doomed to go with us on our search for an anchoring land, and while we are not unhappy here—" A haunted look entered his eyes. "We are most definitely lost."

Sadly, we allowed ourselves to be escorted through the gates and back outside.

Woeful wizards, looking guilty as much as anything, waved us farewell.

"I shall determine where and when you next set down!" called Dafydd Jenkins. "And if I am alive, I shall endeavor to be at the place upon which you land!"

Madawg and the others seemed moved. I saw a few dabbings at tears. A couple of noses were honked.

As I stood upon the top of Skinner's Butte, the day well advanced, looking at the expanse of the castle, I thought to myself that every good hill deserved a castle, and that Eugene really did deserve to have one, every bit as much as any other odd, albeit European, city did.

Slowly, sadly, Madawg and company pulled the drawbridge back into its place. After all, we didn't want any joggers to end up inside accidentally.

I felt a deep sadness, a wretched loneliness.

Here was something that, I felt, had come here to this strange town uniquely for me—and yet, it could stay so briefly.

Better it should never have come.

Better this town should have been just a pathetic unimportant small town in the middle of nowhere.

Dreams are so much better when you don't have to wake up.

"Well, there it goes," said Jenkins, looking down at his timepiece. "That's it."

He looked up.

I had not stopped looking at the majestic and solid testimony to the power of man, lest I lose one moment of its experience.

Nothing, however, had happened.

A yellow Saab pulled up in the parking lot. A man in a heavy blue windbreaker stepped out and walked up, gawking. Typical Eugenian male. Eyeglasses, balding. Holding a cup of coffee. Liberal stoop to his shoulders.

"Say. That's a castle, isn't it?" he said.

"Actually, it's a flying saucer," said Robertson. "Only it's the medieval type."

The man nodded. "Well, well. Always thought this place needed something like that."

He turned and went back to his car.

"That's particularly odd," said Jenkins. "It should be gone by now." He checked his watch again.

"Well, it did get here late ..." said Jurgen.

"No, no, there's no difference ..." He scrutinized the German bartender carefully. "Jurgen ... did you fall in love with one of those women?"

"Nein! Nein," said Jurgen. "I swear!"

Nor had any of us.

However, the castle stayed here, solid and real, refusing to disappear back into transdimensional limbo.

A couple of weeks later, I ran into Madawg at Larry's Loft, tackling a pitcher of Bridgeport Bitter ale with great gusto.

When he saw me, he hailed me, and motioned me to the bar.

"Well, well," he said. "The professor! My fondest wish now would be to share some beer with you."

"And mine would be to drink some with you."

"The improved spells you've given the wizards have helped our intercommunication with your Eugenians," he said, face flushed with drink. "Everything is working very well."

I only wished such a spell would work for me.

I patted him on the back and ordered a cup of coffee.

With the help of some old Latin texts I'd dug up, the wizards had also figured out how to make the castle, for all intents and purposes, invisible to Eugenians. Oddness was one thing; however, how were you to explain the sudden appearance of a citadel to the Park Service, much less visitors and the nation at large?

Madawg and his people were gradually exploring this new land, learning its strange ways and integrating fairly well—but still, always repairing to their home and living their normal lives ... only infinitely more happily.

"Just on my way up to go over some texts with Brother Gwilym," I said. "I tell you, this is going to make my academic career."

"I am so very happy, my friend. But now you must excuse me. I am sampling this new distilled stuff called Scotch whiskey, and I am hoping to speak to several of these beautiful women here tonight. It was thoughtful of you to provide us with local currency in exchange for some of the useless trinkets and manuscripts we have picked up through the ages."

"No problem. I was just stopping off to fill up my thermos. Brother William and I are going to be going over a manuscript this afternoon, as a matter of fact."

We said good-bye. I got my thermos filled with good fresh coffee (not a specialty at the Loft, but they pulled out the stops for me) and got into my fading Dodge Colt.

It was a typical Eugene day, fleecy clouds in a blue sky, green all around, with a slightly uneasy juxtaposition of civilization and landscape. I drove up to the top of Skinner's Butte and parked above the view.

I was all alone.

There was no castle in view.

I stepped out of my car, thinking about the last two weeks at the University. Somehow, my students were suddenly taking part in class. They seemed to be paying attention to what I said. Somehow, I'd even gotten time to put some excellent work into my book. I burned with enthusiasm for it now. Doors were opening for me now, into the past ... into the future.

I uttered the Latin words of the spell.

The great and majestic Castle Brigbuffoon wavered into view.

I hailed the guard, and got a cheerful response. "Hallo, friend! Brother Gwilym awaits you."

The drawbridge opened, the portcullis was raised.

Through the opening, I could see the new flag.

Instead of a snarling griffin, Donald Duck was squawking through a silly college "U of O."

I stepped into a building—and a time—that I loved.

GIE ME SOMETHIN' TA EAT AFORE I DEE

by John Alfred Taylor

John Alfred Taylor, Ph.D., is a professor of English at a small but prestigious college in western Pennsylvania. A graduate of the University of Iowa Writers' Workshop, his poetry has appeared in The Paris Review *and other distinguished publications. His short fiction has been published in* Asimov's Science Fiction *and elsewhere. In this story he weaves a tale of supernatural terror in a highland castle dour enough to gladden the heart of any Scot.*

"Guid as a MacDonalds'?" asked the counterman.

Alex Latimer had wondered if there was a good meal to be found anywhere in Scotland. "Much better. A real American hamburger."

Alex meant it, too, though he'd have said so even if the hamburger had been a disappointment—always tell people what they want to hear. But it was good to have something that tasted like home after the things he'd eaten since his flight from London.

"I was worried, 'cause I had a twosome of the Big Macs when I was up to Glasgow, and liked them fine."

"Oh, Big Macs are all right." Alex grinned. "Shouldn't say anything against them since I'm a Mac-Donald myself, at least on my mother's side. Though likely no relation to the fast food MacDonalds."

"And now you're here to track down your ancestors?"

"One of them." After another bite: "This the right way to Kilmarnock?"

"Aye. Just keep going down the A77. There's one place to beware of," he warned. "Don't get off on the B7061 just before Fenwick. There's little chance of doing such, it's so clearly marked—but I've heard of people doing that. Just a word to the wise, sir."

Alex had known he was on the right road already, but he'd asked because locals liked to show off their local knowledge, whether in Scotland or Carnegie, Pa. That made them easier to con.

The counterman wished him "Guid luck" when he left. Alex hoped the wish came true, because he *was* looking for an ancestor, Malcolm MacDonald. Or more accurately, looking for what Malcolm was supposed to have been carrying.

Malcolm's wife and son died in a raid led by the Campbell Earl of Argyle, so when Malcolm MacDonald joined Montrose and his Irishmen, he bore the only wealth left to him wrapped in rags under his buff coat, a great circular Highland brooch all gold and jewels. So Alex's mother had said.

The later part of her tale had been even stranger. Though wounded in the debacle at Philliphaugh, Malcolm escaped on his horse as Graham of Montrose sailed into exile. Luckier than the murdered camp followers or the Irish soldiers lined up and shot, Malcolm MacDonald rode west toward Kilmarnock, where his cousin and his cousin's wife would give him shelter for a night or two.

MacDonald was near starving by the time he reached Drumtrodden Castle. "Gie me somethin' ta eat afore I dee." His cousin's wife gave him a stoup of wine to stay him till she brought bread and beef, but never brought the beef.

The wine was laced with laudanum.

Because she was an ardent Covenanter, and her less-ardent husband wanted no involvement with a dangerous fugitive, she persuaded him to help drag Malcolm MacDonald to the entrance of the castle's pit prison—the Scottish equivalent of an oubliette— as soon as Malcolm was unconscious.

They dropped him in, lowered the stone flag that closed it, and attempted to forget he'd ever been, never knowing whether he died of his wounds or hunger or thirst, since the pit prison's ventilating shaft went all the way to the roof. And except for the woman's deathbed confession years after her husband's burial no one would have known a thing concerning Malcolm's fate.

But according to Alex's mother, neither the cousin nor his wife had known of the great golden brooch concealed under MacDonald's buff coat. Which meant the brooch might still be with his remains in the pit prison.

"I ken no castle of that name," said Mrs. Ramsay, the widow who ran the bed and breakfast. "But Hugh Gifford, one of the dominies of the Middle School, kens all about auld times. I could ring him up and see if he'll be free to talk after dinner."

He was, and eager to talk, too, after Alex spun him a yarn about wanting to write a family history for the MacDonalds of Canada and the United States. Not only was the schoolmaster knowledgeable, but it was a relief for Alex not to have to translate from deep Scots—though there was still a burr in Gifford's pronunciation, he used few dialect words. "What happened to your ancestor is a sad story, but those were bloody times. The great Montrose himself danced on air when he came back from the Continent a few years later."

"There was a man," Alex agreed, "whether right or wrong. Graham dressed for his hanging like it was his wedding."

"Aye. *Noblesse oblige* and all that. But back to your quest. Though a word to the wise—I'd certainly wait till morning before trying to find the place—it's hilly and overgrown with gorse. No pleasure to walk through at twilight. Besides that, the locals say the place is cursed." The schoolmaster laughed. "Perhaps another reason to wait till morning. Let me draw you a map."

Next morning Alex was glad he'd taken Hugh Gifford's advice to wait: The ruins of Drumtrodden were hard to find, even with Gifford's map, and tangles of gorse were everywhere. At least the gorse was in bloom, yellow flowers spangling the green thorns. On the way up he scouted a few paths that might make things easier once it was dark.

Judging from what remained, like so many 16th-century Scottish buildings called castles, Drumtrodden must have been a tower house, a z-plan with towers placed at diagonally opposite corners of the central block so each could cover two sides with their defensive fire.

It took Alex an hour to be sure he'd found the slab over the pit prison. The iron staple that had been used to lift it was rusted away, but he had crowbars in the boot of his rental car, and one corner of the stone was broken away by frost and would give him a place to start. Though he'd need some lengths of lumber to brace it while he levered the slab up step by step. Lumber he'd better buy somewhere else than Kilmarnock, if he wanted to cover his tracks.

Alex got on all fours and peered into the dark crevice, but couldn't make out a thing. "See you tonight, Malcolm," he chuckled, "though maybe you're lucky you didn't get your meal. Scottish cooking can kill you."

Alex would swear to that. One component of the breakfast served at his hotel in Glasgow had been a circular slab looking like cranberry jelly made from powdered coal. The waiter explained it was black pudding. One taste and he'd decided black pudding wasn't for him—almost as characterless as tofu, though with a flavor of sorts, if salt and used motor oil was a flavor. His breakfast next day had featured black pudding again. And this morning Mrs. Ramsey had put black pudding before him with a loving smile.

Though the worst had been the chicken supremes stuffed with haggis in a Glasgow restaurant whose decor and seating came from a razed church. He'd heard of haggis, and ordered it out of curiosity, automatically assuming haggis meant a bomb-shaped pudding in a sheep's stomach. (Bobbie Burns had a lot to answer for.) But haggis also meant organ meats, Alex discovered, and the chicken supremes were delicious, though terribly greasy. Greasy enough to loosen his bowels to the point where he had to remain in Glasgow an extra day. Bombs didn't have to be bomb-shaped.

From his experience the amazing thing about Scottish cooking was how your stomach could be bloated and griping with hunger at the same time. Probably some secret culinary revenge aimed at the Sassanach.

Just before Alex stood up, he thought he heard a faint sound from below. Only an echo.

Once out of the gorse the path down to the car was easy. But a hundred yards away Alex noticed he was no longer alone: two road workers were filling a hole near the car. The one with iron-colored hair lifted his head as Alex descended, then beckoned. Alex cursed under his breath, then realized being noticed didn't matter now, because he'd already drawn attention to himself locally.

The old guy pushed his cap back and gave Alex a long look before speaking. His eyes were pale blue and bleak, as if the sky was looking through the weathered pink mask of his face, with one eye disconcertingly unfocused, staring up and to the left. "You the Yank?"

"I'm American, yes."

"Been up to the castle? To Drumtrodden?"

"To what's left of it. Why?"

"It's no a canny place. Specially after sundown."

Alex used a joke to override his alarm at being questioned, pointing back over his shoulder at the gorse and asking, "Do you think I'd try to go through that tangle at night? Even if I'm American, I'm not a total fool."

The old road worker cackled and touched his cap. "You're no fool, sir. Even if you're a Yank. Just a word to the wise, sir, though you dinna seem to need it."

Did every one of these sheep-loving yokels want to give a word to the wise?

That morning Alex had told Mrs. Ramsey he'd be driving up to Edinburgh to do research in the University library, and wouldn't be back till next afternoon.

"No breakfast? Then I'll take some shillings off your bill."

"Not at all. Just knowing I can come back to such a hospitable place is worth more than you charge."

Though if he found the brooch tonight he'd never be back, and Mrs. Ramsey could "whistle o'er the lave o' it." And he'd never have to swallow her murderous scones again.

He spent the day in Glasgow like a proper tourist, looking at the Burrell Collection, and then checking out the Necropolis to get himself in the mood for the night's work.

Alex ate a late dinner. The Black Angus steak was overdone—perhaps Scottish cooks could be trusted with oatmeal, if nothing else—but two shots of The Famous Grouse made up for it. He didn't turn back down the A77 till it was fully dark, then drove fast, passing and being passed by hurtling lorries.

It was eleven when Alex pulled the rental car off the narrow road under the remains of Drumtrodden and drove the vehicle up into the gorse to hide it. Rather than use his flashlight, he let his eyes get used to the dark and opened the trunk by the hint of sky glow from Kilmarnock, putting the bundle of crowbars and lumber over one shoulder and the pack with his climbing equipment over the other.

He was glad he'd scouted the paths by daylight, though still he ended up caught by the gorse more than once, and even had to backtrack to find the right path. But finally he was inside what was left of the walls, and felt he could risk the flashlight, keeping the beam low, and turning it on only a few seconds at a time till he found his way to the slab.

Alex laid the flashlight down, one lonely horizontal beam against the darkness, and glanced around a second before setting to work. The walls around reared up in shadow, lidded with the dark clouds rushing overhead. It was like being at the bottom of a well, except he wasn't at the bottom of a well. But Malcolm MacDonald was. All Alex had to do was take the lid off the place.

"Here I come, Malcolm," he whispered into the

cleft at the corner, unable to resist the impulse. "Hope you don't have any black pudding down there."

Alex listened for a second. No echo this time.

He cut the tape on his bundle, and got the long crowbar under the weathered corner of the stone, levering it up as far as possible and straining to slide a length of lumber under on a diagonal. He rested a moment, and slipped another crowbar in at the side once he was breathing normally.

Ten minutes' work with the crowbars and the timber braces, and the slab thudded upside down beside the pit it had covered for three and a half centuries.

Alex had saved a miniature of The Famous Grouse for this moment.

The whiskey finished, he opened his pack and put on his climbing harness. Tape slings went around two different blocks of masonry, and he clipped the tapes together at the other end with a carabiner, threaded the rope through, and hooked the ends into his descender.

Ready to go now, except for the flashlight—he didn't want to lose that on the way down, so he tied a cord around just behind the flare at the head, then another loop near the back, and attached it to the waistband of his harness.

Alex took a quick look into the pit before he descended: the bleached light showed nothing but the rough sides of the shaft and the almost-featureless floor beyond. His ancestor must have survived long enough to crawl away from where he fell.

"Hope you have a present for me, Malcolm," Alex giggled, and then lowered himself backward over the edge, bending his knees and tucking his neck into his chest so he wouldn't hit his head on the far wall of the shaft while he walked himself down.

After a second he realized the length and width of the shaft allowed him to chimney. Still he'd need the rope. No other way to come up once the cell opened out below. It was dark with the dangling flash pointed down, but reflected light allowed him to see enough to continue.

Alex's boots scraped off the bottom of the shaft, and he let his legs dangle, hanging and resting on the end of the rope before he descended farther. He gasped for breath as he turned there, realizing how out of shape he was.

He thought he heard a scraping below, tried to hold his breath to listen. Then he felt a faint current of air on his trouser leg, definitely heard a soft thudding afterward. That was no illusion.

Had some burrowing animal found a way into the cell through a gap opened by a tree root?

There was the scraping again; a second later a grip like a mantrap snapped onto his right ankle. A great weight dragged him down.

The flashlight pendulumed and strobed, but the middle of each swing showed him all he needed to see: long yellow teeth and sunken eyes in a tangle of red hair and red beard. What was left of the buff coat gave off the stink of mildewed leather.

Then the other bony hand clamped on his knee, and Malcolm MacDonald, starved more than three hundred years, ripped a bite from Alex's calf.

Alex screamed in agony, jerking and setting the two of them swinging wildly.

The grip on his ankle loosened, but a moment later he felt Malcolm clawing at his waist, fastening on the belt of his climbing harness. Alex could only whimper as the ancestor whose body he had planned to loot climbed him like a ladder.

All the time MacDonald had been chewing his first bite. He swallowed with a gulp as he hugged Alex's shoulders.

Alex saw his face come nearer in a terrible parody

of a lover seeking a kiss. Leather over bone, with teeth in the middle and hair blooming everywhere. The revenant's breath was horrible: dry, hot, and putrid.

Alex fainted when the yellow teeth met in his cheek, but was unfortunate enough to regain consciousness more than once before it was over.

GWYTHURN THE SLAYER

by Lawrence C. Connolly

Lawrence Connolly has published numerous short stories in anthologies and magazines. One of them, "Echoes," was made into a short dramatic film by a Hollywood production company. This story of healing and remembrance is at once therapeutic and disturbing.

The beast's tower stood on the horizon, cutting like a blackened tusk into the dusk-red lip of the sky. Gwythurn sat on the shivering back of her bone-white mare. Mist rose from the horse's nostrils as a chilling wind hissed through the boughs of autumn-thinned pines. Gwythurn shifted her sore thighs on the creaking saddle, tightened her grip on the reins, and gave a fast kick with her booted heels. Horse and rider thundered forward, out of the forest, onto the wasteland of rock and scorched weeds, and toward the horizon where the lip of night bled behind the horn of medieval stone.

As she rode, the wind whistled in her ears. The whistling became a voice. The voice spoke a name. "Gwyn."

Gwythurn reined hard. Hooves rattled to a stop on the brittle ground. The horse turned in place, stirring a cloud of dust as Gwythurn scanned the barren landscape. She saw no one. But the voice was there, riding the wind like the whisper of a demon.

"Slow down," said the voice in the wind.

"Who's there?" asked Gwythurn. She reached for the sword that hung at her back. Bronze hissed from the leather scabbard as the blade slid free. Honed metal glowed with the blood of the setting sun as she swung the sword through a circle of humming air. She couldn't see the demon, but at least she could show it that she was willing to fight.

And then the wind whispered, "Virg."

She gripped the reins. The wind brushed icy fingers across her face, and with that touch she sensed the nearness of another reality. For a disorienting second, though she remained in the saddle, she felt as though she were lying on cushions. The wind touched her again. This time it squeezed her hand. "You're talking too fast, Gwyn. Who is Virg?"

The darkening sky crackled with distant thunder.

The blood-red evening vanished behind the swirled plaster of an off-white ceiling. Gwyn turned her head. A leather cushion creaked beneath the back of her head as she looked up into the tired gray eyes of Carol Langland.

"You all right?" asked Carol.

Gwyn placed a hand across her face. She stretched her palm over her eyes and gripped her head with splayed fingers. Thoughts raced beneath her hand. "Another one," she said. "It just happened again."

"The daydream?" asked Carol.

Gwyn nodded. "But it's really not a daydream. It's too strong. Too real." She gazed up across the dark horizon of her hand. Her thumb was a dark tower rising from a fleshy plane. Carol's face looked down like a concerned moon. "What have I have been doing?" asked Gwyn. "Have I been talking?"

"Yes," said Carol. "Don't you remember?"

"No," said Gwyn. "I was zoned. Totally gone."

Carol stared. Wrinkles deepened around her eyes.

She lifted a raised finger to her pursed lips and said, "Gone?" The word lingered in the silent office. "What do you mean gone? Where did you go?"

Gwyn shifted on the creaking cushions. She remembered entering Carol's office, but she had only the vaguest recollection of lying on the couch. She remembered saying, "Should I lie down?" To which Carol said, "Do whatever's comfortable." But beyond that Gwyn remembered nothing. "Have I been talking a long time?"

"About ten minutes."

Gwyn swallowed. Her throat felt dry.

"You talked about a lot of things," said Carol. "You talked about Drake. He's your ex-husband, right?"

"Sort of," said Gwyn. "The divorce is on hold. His idea." She rubbed her eyes. "What did I say about him?"

"You said he's putting you through school."

"That's his idea, too," said Gwyn. "It's his way of possessing me from a distance, keeping me too busy to find someone else while he's free to do as he pleases."

"You sound angry."

"That's because—" She swallowed. "Because I am," she said. "I'm angry that he's still calling my shots. He might be fifty miles away, but he's still sitting on my life."

"Are there things you'd rather be doing?"

"Yes."

"Why don't you do them?"

"I don't know," said Gwyn. "I don't mind being back in school. I like the program. Medieval studies was my major before I married Drake. I could be happy spending my life buried in books ... if it weren't for—" she hesitated. Her head throbbed. In her ears, she heard the drumming of hooves.

"If it weren't for Virg?" asked Carol.

The name washed over Gwyn like a gust of wind. "I talked about him, too?"

"Yes."

"What did I say?"

"A lot," said Carol. "But you were talking so fast I didn't catch it all. I asked you to slow down, but you didn't. You kept on talking. I think you said you love him. You said he asked you to visit him in Philadelphia. You said part of you wants to break away and go."

"But I can't," said Gwyn. "I've been burned once. I haven't the courage to risk it again." Gwyn rubbed her throbbing head. She wondered if she were making a mistake sharing her problems with a woman who was little more than a campus counselor—a clinical psychologist who spent most of her time talking to college kids. Carol probably didn't get too many middle-aged graduate assistants who suffered from runaway daydreams. "So what else did I say?"

"That's about it," said Carol. "Why don't you tell me about your dreams."

Gwyn sighed. The breath rasped in her tired throat. "The dreams are about a woman," she said. "The woman's on a horse. She's searching."

"Searching for what? Do you know?"

Gwyn sighed. A dull cramp pinched the muscles of her left thigh. She flexed her leg. The couch creaked like a leather saddle. "She's searching for someone," she said. "She's searching for a woman who's been locked away by a dragon."

"Tell me about the dream, Gwyn."

"I'll try," she said. She stared at the ceiling. Patterns in the swirled plaster seemed to drift like dust across the wall of a stone tower. "She's riding," said Gwyn. "A moment ago she stopped because she thought she heard voices on the wind, but now she's riding again . . . riding toward a castle."

* * *

The tower loomed before her, thrusting upward into a crepuscular tangle of blood-red clouds. Dirt clung to the chinks and mortared seams of the rounded walls. The base fanned outward, as if bulging from the weight of the worm that lived within. Gwythurn tugged the reins. The horse cantered to a stop. Gwythurn dismounted. She walked to the swollen foundation, extended a hand, hesitated, and then pressed her fingers to the wall. The stone felt warm. She flattened her hand. The stone hissed beneath her palm. "I feel you," she said to the worm behind the stone.

Beside her, the horse snorted and lowered its head to search for grass among the weeds.

"Can you feel me?" Gwythurn whispered to the thing behind the stones.

The bulging stones creaked. Gwythurn felt the weight of twitching coils as the worm shifted in its dungeon lair.

"Yes. You feel me," said Gwythurn. "You know I'm here. Do you know why I've come?"

This time a low rumble shook the stones. Gwythurn withdrew her hand. She stepped back, studying the wall, trying to picture the thing that stirred the darkness less than an arm's length away. But the thing was beyond imagining, and Gwythurn saw only the curved seam of a stone door that the beast had bolted from the inside. She backed up another step and looked up along the tapering wall of the lone tower. No windows. Fortunately, there was another way in.

She stepped back to the wall, raised her hand high, and ran her fingers along the mortared seam at the top of a protruding stone. The dried mixture of sand and lime flaked away. Her fingers wiggled into the gap; she held on and pulled, lifting her feet from the parched ground. Finding a toehold with the point of her boot, she started to climb. . . .

The wind stirred.

"Gwyn," said the wind. "Come on, honey—you've zoned out again."

This time Gwyn sat up. She leaned her shoulders against the stiff back of the couch. She set her feet on the cushions and brought her knees to her chest. "Jesus!" she said. She pressed the back of her head against the wall. "It's getting stronger." She ran her hands along the faded knees of her jeans, trying to rub from her fingers the gritty feel of the wall. "It's still in my hands. I can feel the tower in my hands." Gwyn shifted, trying to get comfortable as her limbs twitched with phantom motion. Sitting on the padded couch with her legs folded and her feet a scant eighteen inches from the carpeted floor, Gwyn feared falling to her death. Afraid to look down, keeping her gaze on Carol's dusky eyes, she said, "She's climbing the tower."

"Who is?"

"Gwythurn," said Gwyn. "The woman in the dream." Her legs twitched. Her foot slipped from the couch. She glanced down. Her foot dangled over the teal carpet. For a moment, before she drew the foot back and returned her gaze to Carol's face, the carpet's fibers looked like stones strewn across a distant desert.

"She's climbing the outside of the tower," said Gwyn. "I can feel her hands digging between the stones. I can feel her legs lifting her upward."

"You're feeling this now?"

"Yes. Now."

Someone knocked at the office door. Carol ignored the sound, keeping her eyes on Gwyn as she asked, "How long have you been zoning out like this?"

"I don't know," said Gwyn. "Maybe a few days. Maybe a week." She looked at the deepening knots around Carol's eyes. "You know what scares me?" she said. "You know what the worst part of all this is? It's that I've probably been doing things that I can't remember. I'll be zoned out, and I'll do things, and later I won't remember what I've done."

Again, someone knocked at the door. Carol turned to the noise. "One minute!" She turned back to Gwyn. "It's probably my son. He borrowed the car. I told him to drop off the keys." She stood. "This'll only take a minute." Carol turned, crossed the room, and opened the door.

Cool wind struck Gwythurn's face. She stood on the top of the tower, perched on the splintered end of a broken beam that must have once supported the structure's roof—a roof that had long since crashed down into the bowels of the tower. Beneath the beam, the world dropped away into a stone-rimmed abyss—full of vertigo and darkness.

The worm was down there. Coiled. Waiting. She could smell its stink on the rising air. She could hear the low drone of its segmented heart echoing up through the darkness. But she still couldn't see it. Her gaze spiraled down along a wall-hugging staircase of stone that gradually vanished into a pool of stagnant shadows. She inched back along the beam, climbed onto the stone stairs, and began her descent.

Thirty feet down, she reached a ring of splintered planks—all that remained of the floor of the tower's uppermost chamber. Shadows deepened. She drew her sword and continued on, descending slowly as her eyes adjusted to the deepening gloom. She continued her descent until the stairs ran out and she stepped onto the tower's rocky floor. She glanced up. Stone walls tapered above her like the lining of a well. Beyond the broken beams and corbels that had once supported the roof, the sky hovered like a circle of blood.

She lowered her gaze. In front of her, darkness churned. "See me?" said the worm.

"Barely."

The beast inhaled. A moaning wind spiraled through the tower as the monster sucked down a draught of dungeon air. Then, with an echoing roar, the worm exhaled. Flames exploded from flared nostrils. The beast looked skyward, exposing the ridges of its segmented neck as it raised its head like a flaming torch. And then the fire went out.

"Now?" it said. "See me now?"

Yes. She saw it. The fiery burst had burned the beast's image into her vision. Standing in the darkness, trying not to choke on the hot fumes that lingered in the scorched air, Gwythurn studied the afterimage that waxed and waned as she blinked her eyes. She saw the forked flames and the flared nostrils. She saw smoke billowing from massive jaws. She saw teeth as long as swords and a blistered tongue covered with barbs and bristles. She saw the endless folds of the beast's coiled body. And she saw the trapdoor in the ground. The image faded with each blink, and as it faded the inky darkness returned. Cautiously, holding her sword in front of her, she felt her way to the trapdoor.

"You're wasting your time," said the worm. "She doesn't want out. She wants to be locked away with her books and papers. She's safe and happy. Trust me."

Gwythurn kept walking. Her boots rustled through the rotting fragments of the tower's fallen roof and collapsed flooring. She knelt and brushed away the debris until her fingers found the curved handle of the trapdoor. And it was then, as she gripped the handle, that she sensed the shifting of the worm's coils. She heard the dark air whisper around the monster's head as its jaws raced toward her. She turned. Looking up, she saw the worm's gaping jaws blurred against the

rusty glow of the distant sky. She raised her sword.
The beast's neck twitched to avoid the blade. Gwythurn jumped aside. The triangular head jerked
toward her. She swung, driving the blade deep into
the segmented neck. The beast jerked away. Too late.
Its head slammed the ground and rolled. Its mouth
gaped in a breathless gasp. Vomit and blood spewed
from the headless neck as writhing coils beat against
the darkness.

Gwythurn scrambled away, cowering by the steps
until the worm's black body collapsed into stillness.
Then, feeling her way with the tip of her sword, she
advanced again to the door in the floor.

Gwyn was home, back in her tiny apartment—the
bohemian niche in the ground floor of University
Towers. She had only the vaguest recollections of leaving Carol's office. She remembered standing to leave
while Carol's son was still at the door. She remembered saying, "I have to go. Really, I'll be fine. I
shouldn't have bothered you with any of this." Those
words echoed in her now as she stood in her cramped
living room. She had no recollection of returning
home. But here she was. And she wasn't alone. Someone stood beside her.

Gwyn turned and realized that she was standing beside her living-room mirror. But the woman reflected
in the mirror wasn't her ... and the reflected room
was certainly not part of Gwyn's apartment.

Gwyn stumbled forward, catching herself on the
edge of her desk. Her hand skidded, scattering the
pages of the first draft of her dissertation. The pages
rattled to the floor as the figure in the mirror stared
at Gwyn. Gwyn studied the face—green eyes, slender
nose, high cheeks, tapered jaw. The mousy face was
her own ... but the resolute stare of the eyes was
straight out of her dreams. She realized she was look-

ing into the face of Gwythurn, and with this realization her attention turned again to the strange room in the mirror. She saw stone walls and a staircase that spiraled up through the splintered halo of a shattered floor. She saw the dead coils of a monstrous serpent lying on the remains of a fallen roof. She saw the rectangular darkness of an uncovered trapdoor. And on the bloody ground she saw footprints stretching from the trapdoor to the edge of the mirror.

Someone knocked on her apartment door. Gwyn coughed, found her voice, and yelled, "Who is it?"

A muffled voice answered with a single word that sounded like, "Scab!"

"What?" she yelled back.

The muffled voice came again. This time it seemed to say, "Scab for hurt."

"I can't hear you," she called back. "Hold on a second!" Then she turned back to face the mirror.

The woman in the mirror was dressed in leather and bronze. Her hair lay across her shoulder in a dusty braid. She held a sword; black blood stained the blade with a crusty glaze. "You're free," said the woman.

Once again, the fist hammered the apartment door. Gwyn turned, crossed the room, stumbled over something dark that lay in her path, and opened the door.

"Miss Hurt?" It was a man in a denim vest and a plaid shirt. A short cigar lay tucked like a smouldering canker in the corner of his mouth. "You Miss Hurt? I got a time call for a Gwyn Hurt. That you?"

Behind the man, a yellow taxi rumbled at the curb.

" 'Cause if it ain't you," said the man, "I'm outta here. I can't blow rush hour waiting for no-shows."

Gwyn looked back into her tiny apartment. In the mirror, the last rays of evening spilled through an open door in the castle wall. Beyond the castle's door, the leather and bronze woman heaved herself onto the back of a waiting mare.

"So you Miss Hurt, or what?" the driver asked again.

Gwyn turned back to him. *He doesn't see it,* she thought. *He doesn't see what's in the mirror.* "Yes," said Gwyn, surprised at the calmness in her voice. "I'm Gwyn Hurt."

"Good thing," said the man.

"But when did I call for a cab?"

"Jeez, lady. I dunno. It's a time order. Scheduled through dispatch. Could've been yesterday for all I know." He pointed through the door. "You want me to get that?"

Gwyn glanced back into the room. For a moment, it seemed as if the driver's finger were pointing at the serpent's severed head in the mirror. But then her gaze snagged on a packed suitcase—the dark thing that she had tripped over while walking toward the door.

"No," she said. "I'll get it myself." The memories came flooding back. Everything fell together. "Give me a minute, okay?"

"Yeah, sure! But the meter's running." He turned and followed the cobbled path to his rumbling cab.

Gwyn closed the door. She turned. The mirror was back to normal. She watched herself as she moved to the center of the room and picked up her suitcase. She remembered packing it now. She had done it yesterday, after receiving the letter from Virg and before calling the cab. She crossed to her desk where the scattered pages of her unfinished dissertation stretched across the floor like the cast-off skin of a snake. In her desk's top drawer she found the plane ticket to Philadelphia.

*   *   *

Gwyn looked out of the cab's side window as the door of her apartment receded into the deepening night. Her vision shifted, and she found herself staring at her reflection in the backseat window. The face was strong, resolute. "Stay close," she said to the face.

"Wassat?" asked the driver.

"Nothing," she said. "Just talking to myself."

Tires clattered like hooves over the cobbles of Academic Drive.

COLLECTORS

by Pamela Sargent

Pamela Sargent's thoughtful novels and stories are grounded in a rationalistic approach to life and the universe; which is not surprising, given that she taught classical philosophy for some time at the State University of New York at Binghamton. This new story of hers concerns a series of seemingly inexplicable happenings centering on one of the most resplendent cha-teaux on the River Loire.

Alberto had bypassed Orléans, where the traffic heading toward that city was as heavy as it had been around Paris. People had flooded into Paris after the announcement, maybe because so much of French life had always been centered there. Whatever happened now, a lot of people obviously wanted to be in Paris when it did.

To have so many coming into Paris had made it easier for us to leave. The traffic had been heavy on the roads leading to the city, but almost nonexistent on the lanes going out. Alberto had filled the tank of his Fiat right after our arrival and hadn't driven the car since, so we had enough gas. The concierge at the hotel had let us check out without paying, maybe because by then the exchange rates were fluctuating from one hour to the next and there was no way of knowing how much any currency would be worth in time. We even had a bag of canned food and bottled water. Making my way back to the hotel, I had been caught in a crowd of looters, and somebody had thrust a canvas bag of food at me. The owners of the shops and stores didn't seem to mind the looting. By then, some of them were standing by the doors of their establishments shouting *"Prenez-en"* and *"Prenez-les tous,"* telling people to help themselves to everything inside.

We left the main highway, then had to detour around a small town. The cobblestone streets leading into the town were blocked by vans. The traffic was thinning rapidly. Soon ours was the only car I could see on the road.

We followed the Loire along a two-lane highway nearly as straight as the line on a graph. On the other side of the river, I spotted the distinctive dome and stacks of a nuclear power plant.

"I hope they've shut that thing down," I said.

Alberto was silent as he drove over a bridge and past the plant, then turned right. He hadn't said anything since leaving Paris. After dropping off my bag of food in our room, I had found him in the hotel bar, sitting with a middle-aged Canadian couple and a young woman in a University of Minnesota sweatshirt. The middle-aged man was saying, "We were on our second honeymoon." The young woman said, "This was my first trip to Europe." Alberto sighed, then said, "We were going to look at some of the châteaux along the Loire before starting back to Italy." It struck me then that everyone was using the past tense, as if their earlier lives were over.

I had let Alberto decide what to do. He seemed to think that the place to be was outside the major cities. Whatever happened now was likely to affect the cities first, so it was better to get out of Paris and then consider what to do next. His thinking had seemed reasonable to me when we were sitting in our room, with the TV tuned in to CNN International for the latest news—or non-news—and the sounds of cars, honking horns, and tolling bells outside growing louder by the minute. Now I wasn't so sure. Alberto had decided to head toward the Loire Valley because that was where we had originally planned to go. I was beginning to think that he simply didn't know what to do, that he preferred to pretend that there was some purpose to his actions rather than sit around in our room or the hotel bar speculating about what might happen and freaking himself out. Probably all the people crowding into Paris and other cities didn't know what to do either. Maybe they just wanted to be in a crowd while they waited instead of getting terrified all alone somewhere.

Alberto turned on to another road. A high stone wall at our left surrounded forested land. I gazed absently at the map on my lap, on which the roads were not very clearly marked, then thrust it into the glove compartment. "Where are we now?" I asked.

"Near Chambord," he replied, speaking at last. "You remember, Lois—we were going to stop there first. It is considered one of the most spectacular of the châteaux, perhaps the grandest. It was the project of François the First—"

"I know all of that," I muttered, wondering why he was mentioning it now.

"—who was a great admirer of Renaissance art, particularly Italian art. Leonardo da Vinci has been credited with drawing up some of the plans for Chambord." Alberto sounded like a tour guide. Hearing him speak in such a flat, matter-of-fact manner made me even more apprehensive. I realized then that he was probably just trying to distract himself from any fears he might be harboring with this pretense of normality. By then, I was wishing that we had stayed in Paris.

My lord and master. I had called Alberto that in

jest during the early days of our relationship, even though I was never sure if he caught my sarcasm or sensed that the phrase was my little joke. Now those terms seemed only too accurate. He was always in charge; there was never any doubt of that. He didn't have to go out of his way to demonstrate it, either; his dominance was simply assumed, without question. A lot of American men might make noises about being in control, but in practice many of them were willing to share some authority, even cede some of their traditional territory. There was an almost appealing insecurity in American men that I hadn't properly appreciated before getting involved with Alberto, whose behavior seemed part of an earlier age.

"We could try to drive back to Rome," I said.

"No. It's much too far. The hotels along the way might be full by now, with no one to attend to anyone, and the service stations will probably be closed." Then his voice got more strained, his accent thicker. "Would you want to pass your time now running a service station or attending to hotel guests?"

"I guess not." I didn't want to pass the time looking at châteaux, either, trying to pretend everything was still normal. There wasn't even any way at the moment to find out what was happening in the rest of the world, since Alberto's car radio had died during the drive from Lyon to Paris. I was about to suggest that we head back to Orléans and take our chances there when the sky suddenly turned white.

Alberto hit the brakes. I covered my face with my hands, thinking wildly of laser beams and advanced weapons, then peered between my fingers. The sky was still white; the stone wall along the road rippled, as if I were seeing it through water, and the forest beyond was black under the piercing light.

I don't know how long it lasted. There was no sound of explosions, no heat, no firestorms, quakes, or other signs of destruction, only the bright whiteness of the sky and the blackness of the trees on the other side of the rippling wall. I glanced to my right and saw that the sky to the west was still blue, the flat land green. I turned back. The white light vanished abruptly; the black leaves of the trees on the other side of the wall were once again green.

Alberto crossed himself. We sat there for a while, and then he started the car again.

They were scanning us, I thought. They would satisfy their curiosity about us and then go on their way. I was so busy trying to reassure myself that we were through a gate and on the road leading to Chambord's parking lot and visitors' entrance before I noticed our surroundings again.

Alberto sucked in his breath; I looked up. That was when I saw the traffic ahead.

Cars and buses were speeding straight at us along both lanes of the road. Horns beeped and wailed, warning us to get out of the way. Alberto slowed, then quickly drove onto the shoulder and into the grass. Vehicles raced past us, heading toward the gate. The cars sped ahead of the buses, but even the buses were barreling along, pebbles flying from under their wheels.

I stared after them until the long procession was out of sight. "If they're all in such a hurry to get out of here," I said, "maybe we'd better follow them."

Alberto rested his hands on the wheel. "To where?"

"Anywhere."

"And what will we do when we run out of gasoline? Staying here is as reasonable as going somewhere else. Think, Lois—where could we be completely safe now?"

I was silent.

"And I must confess to being curious about why all those people were driving away so rapidly."

Of course, I thought. Alberto would never admit to being afraid of anything, even when there was good reason to be fearful. But I didn't feel like arguing with him, and everything looked peaceful now. In the distance, pale stone towers seemed to be floating against the sky, a magical place apart from this world; that had to be the château. Maybe all the people in the cars and buses had simply panicked after seeing the sky brighten. They would come back when they came to their senses.

Alberto drove back onto the road. The parking lot was empty when we reached it. So were the walkways near the souvenir shops and cafés of the tiny town. Alberto parked near an ice cream counter. We got out and wandered along the street in the direction of the château.

Beyond the rows of trees up ahead, the ticket booth was empty, its door open. I could see the château clearly now. Chambord loomed over a vast plain of cropped grass. The pale stone facade was crowned by four large towers and several smaller towers and turrets. One slender tower topped by a dome, taller than the others, stood in the center. It was hard to accept the structure's size, its hugeness; only a megalomaniac could have built such a castle. But Chambord's massiveness and solidity were also reassuring. We would be safe here after all, I told myself. The château would protect us.

The sky was growing gray, the autumn air colder. A voice behind me shouted, "Hey!"

I spun around. A tall lanky white-haired man stood in an open doorway. "Hey!" the man called out again. "You speak English? *Anglais*?"

"Yes," Alberto replied, "I do."

"Everybody just took off—didn't even wait for us."

The stranger had a flat Midwestern accent and looked harmless enough. Alberto strode toward him;

I followed. "We saw them," Alberto said. "They ran us off the road."

"Scared, that's what they were. We were walking to the castle there, ahead of all the others on our bus. Couldn't get back in time." The man motioned with one hand. "Better come inside."

We entered the building. Wooden tables and chairs stood against one wall; a bar ran along the other side of the room. A stocky woman with short curly gray hair was perched on one of the stools. Like the man, she was wearing a windbreaker, sweatshirt, loose jeans, and athletic shoes.

"You're Americans," I said as we sat down. "So am I."

"Well, I'll be," the man said. "You don't look American."

"I've been living in Italy." I wondered if I would ever see my own country again.

Alberto introduced us. The couple's names, they told us, were Edna and Jim Haworth, and they came from a suburb of Kansas City. Jim had been in France with the army toward the end of World War II and had brought his wife there on a trip with several other retired people, all of whom had apparently fled on one of the buses with their tour guide.

"Didn't even wait for us," Edna Haworth said, shaking her head.

"Just took off like a bat outa hell," Jim Haworth muttered, "right after the light changed and the air got all thick. Heard this sound, like a big giant heart beating, and by then my hair was standing up. It went on and on, that sound and the rippling air and all, till I like to be sick. Folks were running out of the castle there, trying to make it to the parking lot—damn near trampled us. Edna was hanging onto my arm like a little kid, and then we started for the bus, but by the time we got to here, they were already driving off."

"We saw something strange," I said, "The sky going white, and—"

"Didn't just see it, young lady. Felt it, right in my guts. I was scared. Edna felt it, too."

"We didn't feel anything like that," I said.

"It's them." Edna gestured toward the ceiling. "Has to be."

She didn't have to say what she meant. I thought of how quickly everything had changed in just three days. Three days ago, I was trying to figure out how to tell Alberto I was going to leave him and go back to New York. Three days ago, nobody had even suspected that visitors from outer space were suddenly going to show up. A physicist interviewed on CNN had said something about the alien vessel stitching its way through spacetime, which was his way of trying to explain how it had appeared near Earth so abruptly, without any warning.

The aliens had come here in a spherical ship the size of an asteroid—if that alien globe could be called a ship. They had sent no messages, no envoys, no signs of hostile intent, no signals, no greetings at all. The Russians had two cosmonauts in orbit, and the United States had begun a space shuttle mission several days early, replacing the scheduled crew with members of the armed forces; they now had some footage of the vessel from a distance, and the aliens still had not reacted. No one was even sure if there were any aliens inside the ship; one theory was that it housed an artificial intelligence, a computer mind of sorts. Nobody knew why it was here, or what the aliens—or the artificial intelligence—wanted.

No wonder people were starting to get unhinged. Anyone could understand malevolent aliens attacking the world, or kindly aliens arriving to solve all our problems. But this ship was just sitting out there, inside the orbit of the moon, and we didn't know anything more about it than we had three days ago. Waiting without knowing anything—that was the worst of it.

Alberto took out his cigarettes, lit one, then slipped his leather case back into his pocket. I had long since given up what he called my puritanical American habit of chiding him about his smoking, and the Haworths didn't object; maybe they were thinking we had more important things to worry about now.

I noticed the TV over the bar. "There must be some news on," I said. That was a safe bet; there hadn't been anything except news on TV ever since the alien ship had appeared. "We haven't heard anything since leaving Paris."

"We tried it," Jim said. "Set's not working."

We sat there for a while. I suppose we were all thinking that some of the people who had left might come back. At last Jim said, "Well, what do we do now?"

We searched through the souvenir shops and cafés. That was Alberto's idea. The doors were unlocked, the rooms empty; it seemed that everyone had fled. Edna and Jim weren't surprised; they remembered how terrified they had been, how the impulse to get away from the terror they had felt had overwhelmed them. Occasionally, we tried one of the radios or TVs we found in a few of the buildings, trying to pick up some news, but none of them worked. A power failure couldn't be the cause; the lights were still working. Maybe the government had ordered an end to the broadcasts. A couple of ministers had been claiming that several reporters were only adding to the panic with their speculations.

"Didn't look like too many people were here to begin with," Edna said as she and I sat down at one of the tables under the trees lining the walkway.

"There wouldn't have been as many at this time of year."

"I know. We wanted to avoid the big crowds. That's why we came in October—it was cheaper, too." Edna gazed toward Alberto and Jim, who were walking toward the empty ticket booth. "Funny. I don't feel scared at all now. I almost feel glad to be here."

I knew what she meant. I was feeling the same way. Under the circumstances, I should have been feeling anxious, jumpy, afraid, despairing, or depressed, all of which were common enough mental states for me anyway. Instead, I was feeling almost reassured; that bothered me.

We got up and joined the men. Alberto and Jim were standing by the booth, staring at the château. The sky still looked gray and overcast, but Chambord's pale walls and cupola-topped towers glowed with a golden light. A few horses, dwarfed by the massive château, were grazing on the groomed grass near the moat.

"Where'd the horses come from?" I heard Jim ask.

"They use them for the carriage rides," Edna replied. "That's what our guide said, remember? Patrick was telling us about how most of the woods around this castle is a big game park where tourists aren't allowed, and then he said that the horses—"

"Someone is with them," Alberto said. I squinted and glimpsed a tiny human form before it disappeared around the far tower. "Perhaps we should investigate."

I was thinking that we should leave, but the château drew me. It was strange to feel so drawn to it, especially when a small part of my mind was insistently telling me that we should get out of here and head somewhere else. I would be safe here. The rest of my mind was insisting on that, drowning out my fears.

*   *   *

Alberto drove along a walkway to the château. He and Jim Haworth sat in the front of the car; Edna and I were wedged into the back.

"So you've been living in Italy," Edna said.

"In Rome, for about a year."

"Is that where you two met?" She smiled. "*Three Coins in the Fountain* is one of my favorite movies—so romantic."

Older American women often seemed to find my situation romantic. I had once thought of it as romantic myself. My taste for romance was probably why none of my relationships had lasted very long; the romance always wore off in the end.

"Actually, we met in New York," I said, "trying to hail a cab on the same corner. Alberto was there on business—his firm imports a lot of American products. We ended up going to dinner, and one thing led to another, and a couple of months later, I was living in Rome."

"How adventurous."

I had never been adventurous; it only sounded that way. However great my longing for romance and a break from my everyday life, I always covered my bets. My job was safe at the ad agency because my best friend owned the agency; Karen had faxed only last week to say I could come back any time. My apartment had been sublet, so I would still have a place to live if I returned to New York. It wasn't my style either to burn my bridges behind me or to commit myself completely by abandoning my previous life. I had read that François I, Chambord's builder, had needed thousands of horses to bring his luggage, servants, and courtiers to this château just for short visits. I could sympathize with that. I took all my baggage with me, psychologically at least.

All of my past caution might not make any difference now, I reminded myself. At the moment, there might be little security for anyone. That thought should have brought on another wave of despair and fear. Instead, I found myself placidly looking forward to a closer look at the magnificent château. Something's wrong, my inner voice told me; I ignored it.

The great château was even larger than I realized. We could have walked around it, following the wide pathway that led around the moat to the entrance on the other side, but it would have been a long walk. If any visitors were still inside, I had the feeling we could wander through the château for days without ever finding them. Chambord was a world in itself; I no longer feared what might be happening elsewhere.

The main entrance was in the center of a wall; the doors and the gate of the arched entryway were open. The towers of the keep rose behind the wall, still golden even under the overcast sky. We got out and went through the entrance to the pebbled courtyard in front of the keep.

"How strange," Alberto said softly. "I feel as if I belong here." In the past, I would have teased him about his arrogance, but the same feeling of belonging here had stolen over me. Perhaps it was the strangeness of our situation, of being alone in this monument to Renaissance architecture while the world outside waited—for what?

"Know what you mean, son," Jim was saying to Alberto. "I feel kind of easy here, too. Almost seems like we got all scared for nothing."

Across the courtyard, the two doors leading into the keep were also open. We walked toward the steps that led to them. "It's almost as if someone wants us to come inside," I said.

"Probably the folks trying to get away just didn't bother to close up," Edna said.

We climbed the steps and entered the keep. In the center of a large bare hall, square, massive pale pillars

supported a winding stairway. From the entrance, it
looked as though there was only one staircase, but I
knew there were two, entwined around each other. A
slight dark-haired woman stood on a lower step, leaning against the marble bannister.

"Vous parlez français?" the woman called out.

"Oui," Alberto shouted back, his voice echoing in
the empty hall.

She hurried to us. There was no tension in her face
and no fearfulness in her brown eyes as she introduced
herself. Her name was Ariane, and she was staying at
St-Michel, the inn across from the château. She had
been over by the canal, speaking to one of the estate's
gamekeepers, when the white light had filled the sky
and the terror had seized her. She and the gamekeeper
were running toward the inn when Ariane saw her
sister, who had traveled there with her, speeding away
in their car. By then, other vehicles were racing
toward the road. Alberto waited until the French-
woman was finished, then translated for the rest of us.

"She must be furious with her sister," I murmured.

Edna shook her head. "Maybe not. Everybody just
ran. You don't know how it was. You couldn't think
of anything else except getting out of here."

Jim nodded. "Might of even left Edna behind if she
hadn't been hanging on to me."

Ariane didn't look frightened now. She said something about being content to stay here for the moment;
I knew enough French to catch that much. Alberto
translated the rest. Jean, the gamekeeper, had gone to
let the horses out of the stables; she would wait here
for him and then return to the inn.

She sounded awfully calm under the circumstances.
I would have found her serenity eerie except that I
was finding it increasingly hard to work up any real
fear myself. I almost felt drugged. Maybe we were all
too stunned by our situation to react to anything. Our

psychological defenses must be kicking in, I thought absently.

The Haworths decided to wait with Ariane, then walk to the inn with her and Jean. Alberto was saying something else to Ariane as I wandered toward the staircase, suddenly wanting to be by myself. Inside this magnificent château, I could pretend, for a while, that there was nothing to worry about.

It struck me then that, no matter what the intentions of the interstellar visitor, our world would never be the same. Even if the alien ship left without revealing its purpose, we would all know that other beings were out there, and that their civilization was obviously technologically far in advance of our own. What would that do to us? No wonder I wanted to remain here, near one of humankind's wonders, thinking back to a time when most people had assumed that beings on other worlds did not exist.

A stocky brown-haired man had come inside the château; I assumed he was Jean the gamekeeper. Alberto said something to him, and then the man led the others toward the entrance.

I leaned against the stone railing. My feet were beginning to hurt. Ankle-high leather boots with pointed toes and narrow heels weren't good for walking very far. That was probably why Jim Haworth was surprised to find out I was an American, because I was wearing a pin-striped pantsuit and chic boots instead of jeans and athletic shoes. Alberto didn't like it when I looked too American.

Things had not been right between Alberto and me for a while. I wasn't sure of exactly when I had begun to notice that. Maybe it was the morning when I stood by our apartment window and realized that Rome no longer looked as it had to me, as though fragments of the past were slipping into the present, or as if the present were just an illusion superimposed on something more ancient. The present had finally overtaken my view of the city. All I saw now was the chaotic traffic, and all I could hear was the constant noise of the streets.

Once, I had been entranced by the city and its layers of history, and then I was longing to get away. The same was true of my feelings toward Alberto. Everything that had drawn me—his expressiveness, his ardent professions of love, his determination to enjoy whatever he wanted to do regardless of the cost, his inability to keep to any schedule for long, his erratic moods—were exactly the same characteristics that had finally convinced me that our relationship couldn't work. His unquestioned assumption that I was the lady of the house and that he was in charge of everything else hadn't helped either.

Everything had come to a head after yet another hair-raising ride through Roman traffic in the Fiat that he would never allow me to drive. I started screaming at him about his recklessness and the motorcyclist he had narrowly missed and the amount of wine he had drunk. He was retaliating with his usual tirade about my constipated American ways when he abruptly fell silent, then said, "You wanted to spend some time in France. We'll go, in September or October. We can drive there, stop along the way. The business will not collapse if I leave it in Giancarlo's hands for three weeks." He had taken me completely by surprise, so I had gone along with his proposal. Maybe I was also thinking that I might as well see some more of Italy and France before walking out on him. I had known that he wouldn't come after me if I left, that the break would be final; he was too proud to beg, however wounded he might feel. How irrelevant and unimportant all of that seemed now.

I looked down. Alberto was below, following me up the staircase. I stopped to work my sore toes inside my boots, and he disappeared behind the central pillar. "Lois!" he called out. He was now above me on the stairway that intertwined with this one.

"Maybe you shouldn't have left the Haworths without an interpreter," I shouted back.

"Jean knows some English. I want to explore the château with you."

I hurried up the stairs after him, through a vast hall, and caught up with him in a room paneled in pale wood, with a large canopied bed against one wall. "This room once housed a king of Poland," he said. "Perhaps we should stay here tonight."

I found myself laughing. We clasped hands and hurried through large bare rooms, smaller rooms tucked away in corners, and narrow corridors. It was difficult, even in the cozier spaces, to imagine anyone, even the arrogant monarchs and nobles of France's past, actually living in the vastness of this château. Chambord was a place for spectacle and display, for the mighty to show off their wealth and power. I thought of the servants that must have once stood in the doorways that led from small alcoves, rooms, and passages into the staterooms and bedchambers, how they must have marveled at the glittering and careless aristocrats who might as well have come from another world.

We scurried up stairs, heedless of where we were going. I was suddenly relieved that I had never told Alberto that I was thinking of leaving him, and deeply regretting that I had ever planned to go back to New York. We would lose ourselves inside Chambord, and never find our way out again. What happened outside could not touch us.

We had climbed to the roof terrace before a stray thought intruded on my contented mood. All of the rooms, even the small alcoves and chambers that lacked the huge windows of the biggest rooms, had glowed with a soft light. I had assumed that daylight was providing much of the illumination, but the overcast sky had not cleared, and evening was approaching. I recalled seeing lighting in some of Chambord's rooms, but not in the small passages where the walls had also glowed.

"The walls here," I said. "It's almost as if they were lighted from inside."

Alberto didn't say anything. On the terrace, we were amid a forest of towers and chimneys, as if an entire town of spires and steeples had been placed on top of the château. I slipped my arm through his as we walked toward the north wall. The air had grown sharper, colder. It had been warmer inside, in spite of the size of the rooms and the lack of fires in the fireplaces.

We came to the railing. I had a clear view of the moat and the canal that ran through the grounds nearest the château. Near a small bridge over the canal, a flock of ducks rested on the bank. I lifted my head, then noticed something else. In the distance, at the western edge of the forest and the groomed field alongside it, a low wall of thick gray mist seemed to mark a boundary.

"That fog," I said. "There's something odd about it."

"I know." Alberto frowned as he rubbed his dark beard. "Perhaps we should leave now, all of us. We would have to squeeze the others into the auto, but—" His voice trailed off. It was obvious that he didn't want to leave. I didn't either, but the voice inside my head was growing more insistent, saying that there was something the matter with my being so serene, with our willingness to linger in a place where people had nearly run us down in their fear to get away, who had been so determined to flee the area that they hadn't cared what was in their path.

"Look there." Alberto pointed. Four tiny shapes

had emerged from the wall of fog. I narrowed my eyes, but some time passed before I could see them more clearly. They were cyclists, pedaling up the road we had taken. "Perhaps we should find out what they want."

We left the terrace. It never occurred to me to worry about whether the new arrivals might be dangerous.

The bicyclists arrived at the inn shortly after Alberto had parked our car near the entrance. One look at their wholesome, clean-featured faces told me that they were no threat to us. They were equipped with maps, backpacks, and other gear; one of them told us that he had visited Chambord before.

His name was Erland; he had startlingly blue eyes, spoke perfect English, and was a medical student from Sweden. He and his friends, another blond young man and two fair-haired slender young women, had been staying at a hostel near Blois when the announcement came, and had left it only that morning. Later, they had seen a large bright flash of light in the distance, in the direction of Cour-Cheverny.

"We listened over the radio," Erland said. We were all sitting in the empty dining room of the refurbished country house that was the inn. "Knut has a shortwave with him. We thought they might be attacking. There were reports from Meung-sur-Loire and Chenonceaux, of people fleeing from the châteaux there, seeing the sky go white, feeling terrified. Then it was over. There were a few auto accidents, collisions, and some people being hit by cars, but nothing more serious."

"Happened here, too," Jim Haworth said, "that business with the sky lighting up. My wife and me saw it."

"Have you heard any news since then?" Erland asked.

Jim shook his head. "Tried a lot of televisions here. None of them worked. Neither did the radios."

"I was thinking the government might have ordered a stop to news broadcasts," I said, "to keep people from getting more frightened."

Erland shook his head. "How could they stop the news, even if they wanted to do so? They can't shut down satellites and the Internet. There are too many ways to spread the news now." He motioned at Knut. The other young man rummaged in his backpack and took out a small radio. We all huddled around it and heard nothing. No static, weak signals, white noise— nothing but absolute silence.

"This radio was working before," Knut muttered in English much more heavily accented than his friend's. "There is nothing wrong with it." Astrid and Dorotea, the two young women, glanced at each other.

The Swedes were on their feet in a few seconds. They swept through the inn, searching for other radios and TVs, but discovered that none of them worked either.

They were coming back into the dining room when I heard Ariane murmur something to Jean about the lights. Alberto leaned forward, then glanced at the Haworths. "She is saying that the lights in this room do not look the same," he said. "When she was having dinner here last night, they weren't as bright."

Erland and his friends sat down at a nearby table. "There is something very odd here," the young Swede said. "When we saw on our maps that we were near Chambord, we decided to stop here for the night. There was this fog—"

"I saw it," Alberto interrupted, "from the roof of the château. It looked almost like a wall."

"It is hanging outside the wall that surrounds these grounds," Erland went on. "We had to ride through it. It felt like a warm soft mass, but dry and not damp.

I could feel it pressing around me. A strange feeling
went through me, like a small electric shock, and I
thought of turning back, but by then we were
through it."

"We all felt it," Knut added. "But then—" He
leaned back in his chair. "I am glad we found this
place. We all found ourselves glad to be here when
we were closer to this inn. There is probably some
food in the kitchen. We should make supper and then
get some rest." He smiled. "Perhaps we should stay
for a few days. We will surely be comfortable enough.
I feared that we might have to camp out in the forest."

Everyone seemed eerily relaxed. Edna's arm rested
on that of her husband; Alberto had the sleepy-eyed
contented look I usually saw after he had drunk a
couple of glasses of wine.

"I think we should leave," I said, having to force
the words from my lips. Even as I said it, the rest
of me was thinking of supper and then some sleep.
"Something's wrong here. I think—" But I couldn't
bring myself to say anything else, and no one was
paying any attention to me.

Knut and Dorotea cooked lamb chops, potatoes,
and carrots for our supper, and served the meal with
wine from the inn's cellar. We found room keys behind
the desk in the lobby and drifted off to St-Michel's
guest rooms. I slept in my shirt and underpants, too
tired even to go to the car and bring in my overnight bag.

A dream came to me. I was standing on the steps
of Chambord's double stairway, gazing down at the
people in the hall below. The hall was ablaze with
light, and four people stood near the staircase beck-
oning to me. I recognized Erland and his companions;
they seemed to want me to join them. Looking up, I
saw Alberto above me; I hurried up the stairs, lifting

the skirt of my long blue silk gown. I left the stairway and came to a room where Edna and Jim Haworth sat in two small wooden chairs, warming themselves near the fire that blazed in the fireplace. Ariane entered the room, clothed in a long red gown. Faces appeared in the embroidery on the walls near the window and smiled at me. I was on the staircase again, with stone dragons writhing on the pilasters above me and stone salamanders flicking their tails as they crawled along the walls. I came to the terrace and found Alberto by the railing, looking out over the forest. He held out his arm and I rested my hand against it, but something about my gesture felt false, as if I hadn't quite performed it correctly. On the other side of the canal, Jean was riding out of the woods on horseback with a deer slung across his mount. It was all ours, this magical place. No one could take it from us.

I woke and lay in bed without moving. I was used to waking in the middle of the night, when all my self-doubt and neuroses were working at full strength to convince me that my life was empty and useless. Even when I slept through until morning, I often had to lie there wrestling with lassitude and despair before facing the day. The hollow, stunned feeling of hopelessness with which I was so familiar was gone; I wasn't quite sure what I was feeling instead. Anticipation? Happiness? I hadn't been truly happy for so long that happiness would be hard to recognize.

I sat up. Our overnight bag sat near the window. The door opened; Alberto entered with a tray holding a pot of coffee and two cups. In all our time together, he had never once brought me coffee in the morning. He had forgotten to bring milk, or else hadn't found any; I drank the coffee black.

"I dreamed about you," I said as he sat down on the edge of the bed. "We were in the château, all of us, Ariane and the Haworths and the Swedes. I found you on the terrace. Jean was riding out of the forest with a deer carcass on his horse. It was as if—"

"—it belonged to us," Alberto finished. "I had the same dream, Lois, or one much like it. I stood on the terrace, and you came to me, and then I saw Jean come out of the forest. Before that, I was standing on the central staircase, and you were there, and the young Swedes were calling out to us. Then I was in another room, with the Haworths and Ariane."

"Isn't that kind of strange, both of us dreaming the same thing?" I poured myself more coffee. "There's something else. My dream didn't feel like one of my dreams. For one thing, mine usually aren't that coherent. For another—" I tried to think of how to explain it. "I felt as if I was playing a part in a way, almost as if someone were trying to cast me, but I wasn't quite right for the role. And yet—"

Alberto said, "I felt I was where I belonged."

"I felt that you were, too. You know, when I was a kid, I used to imagine that I'd meet a prince some day, or a nobleman anyway, and end up living in a palace. It's a common enough fantasy, almost a cliché, but—"

"One of my mother's ancestors was a count," he said. "This was several generations back, but she was quite proud of her great-great-grandfather the count."

I said, "That explains a few things about you," and touched his arm lightly.

"Oh, I considered her pride in him an affectation, but she must have passed on some of that pride to me. There have been a few times, even recently, when I would tell myself while in a bad situation to behave as the count might have."

My dream had seemed familiar, as if I'd dreamed it before, and yet parts of it seemed to come from outside my own memories and imagination. I recalled the feeling that I had been playing a part, that something had forced the role on me. I was about to say that we should go to our car and drive away now, but couldn't bring myself to speak.

Somehow I got up and got dressed. Alberto was uncharacteristically subdued. We left the room together and found the others sitting on the terrace, gazing at the château across the way.

Chambord was unearthly in the early morning light. Despite its size, it had an ethereal air. As I moved across the terrace, my arm looped through Alberto's, I could imagine the great castle ascending to the sky to rest among clouds.

Everyone was staring at us. I was about to greet the Haworths when Jean and Ariane rose to their feet. The blond cyclists stood up then, followed by the Haworths.

Edna came toward us, her husband just behind her. "You were in my dream," she said in a soft voice unlike the heartier one I recalled from the day before, "you and Alberto both. We were over there, in the castle, all of us. We—"

Jim made a sound, almost like a moan. He seemed to be struggling to say something. His thin face contorted, then relaxed. I had the strange sensation that Ariane, Jean, and the Swedes were about to curtsy and bow to us.

No one else spoke. We left the terrace together, in silence. Jean and Ariane led the way, followed by the Haworths. They moved at a stately pace, their backs stiff, their footsteps slow and deliberate. The young Swedes were behind us, bringing up the rear. When I tried to speak, to turn around and go back to my room, my body refused to obey me.

We walked toward the château. It seemed to rise from the ground as we approached it. The horses were grazing nearby; they lifted their heads and whinnied.

A deer was standing at the edge of the forest, unafraid.

We passed through the still-open entrance and went inside the keep. I found myself on the double staircase, feeling as though I was trapped inside last night's dream. I looked down to see Erland and his friends gazing up at me.

I was on the terrace, with no memory of having climbed that far. Alberto was at my side, surveying the woods below. How familiar it all seemed. I had imagined such a scene as a child, when dreaming of a prince who would take me away from my ordinary life and carry me to his fairy-tale realm.

"Alberto," I said, and his name sounded as if someone else had spoken it.

The wall of fog was still visible, but higher now, almost obscuring the distant road. A long line of cars waited beyond the gray mist. It looked as though people were returning to Chambord. I wondered why they had stopped there instead of continuing on their way.

The cars didn't move. A few tiny human figures were walking among the vehicles, waving and motioning with their arms. I continued to watch the misty wall rise until I could no longer see the line of cars. The sun had risen, the sky was a sharp blue, and it came to me then that the air was much warmer than it had been the day before, almost too warm for this time of year.

"Alberto," I said, and the word tore itself from me. "We have to get out of here."

"You are wrong," he said. "Chambord belongs to us now."

I struggled to hold on to my thoughts. The fog was still rising; it would wall us in, cut us off from the outside. What did I care about the rest of the world? I could be happy here as the lady of the castle, my lord at my side. Hadn't that always been a favorite fantasy of mine?

He took my arm. I felt entranced, unable to resist the dreamlike state stealing over me. I drifted across the terrace and down another staircase, clinging to Alberto's arm. We came to a room where the heads of deer and other animals hung on the walls. Jean the gamekeeper was there, standing in front of a tapestry depicting a hunting party.

Jean said something in French. I didn't catch his words. "What did he say?" I whispered. It was an effort to speak; my words sounded as though they were on a tape being played at too slow a speed.

"That he was a gamekeeper," Alberto replied, "and that now he will be a hunter."

I dug my fingers into Alberto's arm and led him out of the room. To speak, even to think of what to say, was becoming increasingly difficult. I could be safe here. Alberto would be transformed into the romantic figure for whom I had always longed, and we would have our castle. Something was drawing those thoughts from me, playing them, making them resonate within me. That was when I knew we had to get out.

I would not try to talk. I would hang on to Alberto and try to guide him away from this place. I looked into his dark eyes and saw the fear that lay beneath the spell that had been cast on him. He understood what I was trying to do, even if part of him was resisting it. Maybe we could escape.

We made it to the double staircase and descended to the floor below. I heard voices echoing through the hall, and followed the sound to a red-walled room hung with portraits. Edna and Jim Haworth stood in the center of the room, speaking in English to Ariane, who was responding in French. Edna was muttering incoherently about a garden, while Jim was saying something about his army days. I couldn't understand what Ariane was saying. One look at their slack-jawed, happy faces and empty eyes told me that they were completely under the château's spell.

"Come with me." I gasped for breath as I spoke, knowing it was futile, that they would not be able to leave. We went through another room, where Dorotea, one of the Swedes, was lying unconscious on a bed. I gazed at her composed face and thought of Sleeping Beauty, then tried to drag her from the bed. She slipped from my grip and fell back.

I had to save my strength. Alberto and I shuffled back to the staircase. The farther down the stairs we went, the harder it was to make our feet move.

We came to the ground floor and left the staircase. Erland was standing by one of the doors that led out of the keep. He seemed to be miles away, a small figure across the vast polished wood plain of the floor. I wondered how we could cross that floor, how we could ever get out of the château.

We struggled over the floor. With every step, I thought of how much easier it would be to stay. I remembered the contentment that had filled me inside these walls, of how much I wanted to remain here. I clutched at Alberto more tightly, knowing that if I gave up now, he wouldn't have the strength to get out alone. His hand found mine and hung on tightly, and I knew that I wouldn't get out without him.

Erland's lips moved, but I couldn't understand what he was saying. I think he was begging us to stay. We pushed past him and went outside. Knut and Astrid were in the courtyard, leaning against each other as they staggered toward the gate.

All four of us got to the walkway. I kept my eyes on the ground, thinking only of getting as far as the inn. Once we made it there, we could get into the car and drive away. I concentrated on that thought. Alberto was muttering in Italian. I kept my hand in his, determined not to let go.

Knut and Astrid were several feet ahead of us, struggling toward the distant inn. The forested land behind the inn seemed beyond our reach. Knut stumbled and fell; Astrid helped him up. We had to get to the car. Maybe by then Alberto and I would have enough strength to help the other two into the vehicle.

"Get to the car," I murmured, "keep going," and then noticed that a misty gray wall was rising behind the trees. For a while, I didn't know what I was seeing as the mist continued to rise, obscuring the cloudless blue expanse. Slowly, I forced my head to my right. Another mass of fog was rising toward the sun.

Astrid and Knut had come to a halt. The young blonde woman turned around slowly. Knut was tugging at her arm. Astrid gazed past me. A smile spread slowly across her face, and I knew that she was looking back at the château.

She sank to the ground, Knut at her side. They were both smiling when we reached them, and I thought of how Chambord must look now, the perfect castle with its crown of towers pointing toward the sky. I remembered how happy I had felt while standing at Alberto's side on Chambord's terrace.

"Don't look back," I managed to whisper as we dragged ourselves around the couple sitting on the ground. They had given up the struggle; the château's spell had claimed them.

I don't know how long it took us to get to the inn and our car. By the time we spotted the Fiat, the sun had disappeared. Most of the sky was obscured by the fog, a gray iris slowly contracting around the blue disk of sky that remained.

Alberto fumbled through his pockets for the keys. It seemed to take forever for him to find them. I heard him whisper in Italian.

"Don't talk." My throat was tight and dry, my voice almost gone.

"We would be happy here," he said.

"No."

"Get me away from here," he gasped, and I knew his strength was almost gone.

He had left the car unlocked. I opened the door on the right and shoved him inside, then staggered around to the driver's side. I got in and started the car.

The engine choked before I could get the motor running. The Fiat weaved as I steered it away from the inn. I clung to the wheel, which kept threatening to twist itself from my hands.

I found my way to a road. If I kept going, I would have to reach an exit sooner or later. The car swerved from side to side as I accelerated. The speedometer was reading fifty kilometers per hour; it felt more like a crawl. Then the motor suddenly died. The car slowed to a stop, throwing me toward the windshield.

"We have to walk." My voice seemed very far away. "Open the door and get out." Somehow Alberto got the door open. He got out and dragged me out after him.

We had our arms around each other, holding ourselves up as we stumbled along the road. I could see the fog ahead of us, a thick curtain hiding everything on the other side. It was foolish to go on struggling when we could stay here. I thought of the contentment I had felt with Alberto inside the château, how we both belonged there, our fantasies fulfilled. Then I recalled the mindless looks on the faces of the Haworths and Erland's vacant blue eyes.

"Don't look back." My mind chanted the words: Don't look back, keep going. We came to the fog. The gray mist enveloped us; the fog was thick and heavy, a dry warm mass. I felt it resisting me and struggled for air. For a moment, I couldn't move. We clung to each other, embedded in the gray mass; I imagined it growing solid around us. Then the thick fog before me gave way, and we stumbled into the light.

I gasped for breath; Alberto was coughing. The sky above us was blue. The drugged, entranced feeling was gone, and I was beginning to notice how much my feet hurt. A two-lane road lay before us. I turned around slowly. Behind us, the wall of fog stretched to the north and south, hiding all of Chambord.

"Lois," Alberto said. "I wanted to stay."

"So did I."

"But not now."

Far to the north, on the road, I could now see what looked like roadblocks and several parked cars. One car, with a light on its roof, was coming in our direction.

It was a police car, from Orléans. The two men inside quickly motioned for us to get in. I collapsed against the seat, exhausted, while Alberto and the two men talked; during pauses in the conversation, Alberto translated for me. The authorities in Blois had requested the aid of the Orléans police in returning the residents and shopkeepers of Chambord to their establishments. They had come there to find a fog that was an impenetrable barrier, impossible to drive through and steadily increasing in height. The police had thought it best to get people farther away from the area.

We came to a stop at the intersection where the other cars were parked. All of the roads were blocked off; people stood by their cars, gazing toward Chambord. Alberto helped me out of the car, then turned to talk some more with the police. They seemed to be asking him what had happened to us. Two reporters with microphones and cameramen were moving among the crowd; another cameraman was on top of a van, his camcorder aimed in the direction of the château.

I looked south, toward Chambord. The château and its grounds were now hidden behind a vast gray dome. I thought of how the fog had held us, then yielded. Something had let us go—or perhaps hadn't wanted to keep us.

A hand clutched my elbow. "This is not the only place this has happened," Alberto murmured. "One of the policemen told me. There was news of people fleeing from Plessis-Bourré, the Chenonceau château, other places along the Loire. Now they are all behind enclosures like that one, and there is no way of knowing how many people may be trapped inside them."

"Not only here in France," a gray-haired man near us said in heavily accented English. "There is news of such happenings in Germany and Spain also."

I leaned against Alberto. A woman came to us and was thrusting a microphone in my face when a cylinder of light shot down from the sky and touched the gray dome. The fog disappeared; the pavement under my feet trembled, then shook more violently.

The ground lurched. Alberto held me up. Someone screamed behind me; the ground shook again. In the distance, the forests of Chambord were rising toward the sky. The château was a glittering, tiny crown amid the green expanse torn from the Earth. I watched its ascent until Chambord and its grounds were only a speck moving toward the sun. Where they had been, only a gaping canyon remained.

The aliens gathered up châteaux from the Loire, a couple of German castles along the Rhine, and two stone fortresses from Spain. They left deep gashes in the Earth and billions of bewildered people. Enough footage of the incomprehensible theft of these treasures had been obtained to fill news programs for weeks. Again and again, in reruns and slow motion, castles and the towns or lands around them were torn from Earth's surface and ascended to the heavens. The craters and ravines marking the places where they had once stood were filmed from different angles. There was even footage taken by the cosmonauts and astronauts in orbit. Their film showed castles on disks of land floating toward the alien ship, seemingly encased by translucent domes, small bubbles against the blackness. An opening in the metallic gray alien vessel had appeared to receive them, and then the ship vanished as mysteriously and abruptly as it had arrived.

Alberto and I spent a few weeks doing interviews, occasionally in the company of others who had managed to escape from other stolen castles. Representatives of various military establishments also had questions for us, but I suspect we didn't enlighten them much. Soon the reporters and debriefers lost interest in us. I flew back to New York, talked my friend Karen into letting me do freelance work for her in Italy, found a publisher for an account of my adventure, and then returned to Rome.

We can pretend that things will return to normal, but I doubt they ever truly will. I find myself thinking of Chambord, imagining it housed inside the alien ship, perhaps on an inner surface where one could stand on the château's terrace and see other castles in the distance. I think of the Haworths, the young Swedes, the gamekeeper Jean, and Ariane, and wonder if they're still under the spell the aliens cast. I often feel, as Alberto does, that the aliens let us go out of respect for our resistance to them, but perhaps they were only toying with us as we toy with smaller creatures, or rejecting us as unsuitable for whatever roles they wanted us to play. I tell myself that the aliens took too much trouble in collecting their castles not to care for them and preserve them, but maybe they only mean to play with them for a while, as children do with new playthings, before discarding them.

And I wonder, as everyone wonders now, if they will ever come back to collect the rest of our castles and palaces.

GETTING REAL

by Raul Cabeza de Vaca

"Raul Cabeza de Vaca" is the pen name for an Argentine writer, now residing in Tierra del Fuego, whose early work has been compared to that of his countryman, George Luis Borges. We feel he has more in common with Kilgore Trout. For all that he is remotely located, he has managed to keep up with contemporary trends, which is evident in this chronicle of a virtual future.

It was a virtual world. In the latter half of the twenty-first century, anyone who could afford to live "online," immersed in Virtual Reality twenty-four hours a day—and most people who held a steady job that involved working with, about, or on a computer could afford it—did so. (And whose job these days did not in some way involve working with, about, or on a computer? Hardly anyone's.) In another age, a decadent aristocrat had yawned: "Live? Our servants will do that for us." In this age, you hired people to take care of your "mundane," that is to say *physical,* body while your brain—wired up with implanted bioelectronic interfaces—imagined a *virtual* body that could cavort in any reality desired. You could live in any time or place, be anything or anybody, do anything you wanted to do. The master computer catered to your whims as no genie of legend had ever done before.

All the same, life on line had its vicissitudes.

Glen Arita knew his virtual life was coming to an end, but he was not concerned overmuch: at least he had not been at first. But by the time the eve of the hearing arrived, and after his lawyer warned him that the outcome was foregone, reality finally hit home.

He was to be deleted.

He spent the night at Dragonhome, his castle in the mountains. It was a huge place. He could afford it; he had a good job (financial forecast modeling for business and industry) and a wonderful services package. The effects around the castle were good: cool winds blew down from the peaks, the wind howled among the parapets, but not too loudly. Just right for atmosphere.

He lay in his sumptuous bedroom and considered whether it had all been worth it. He'd waged many bitter flame wars—but he had always stuck up for principle. At first he had nothing personal against any of his adversaries. They had started the personal attacks! Yes. And he had replied in kind. And always, the Sysops had come down on their side. The injustice of it hardened his throat.

And now, the final judgment. Deletion! Bitterness welled up inside him. He'd get back at them. Somehow.

Delete me? I'll be back, I swear. Somehow. And I'll wreak havoc on this system.

The huge clock in the east tower began bonging. And kept up for some time. He had not realized that the night was almost gone. What time was it? Six ... no, seven o'clock. The hearing was scheduled for eight.

He had the option of not attending the hearing. Abruptly, he decided not to. What was the use? He would get a chance to speak, of course, but he knew he'd simply start flaming again, and that would seal his fate, if it wasn't sealed already.

To hell with it. He would not attend. In fact, he would not stick around and be deleted. He would simply log off the system, and that would be that.

The trouble was that he had not done so in quite a long while. He had no idea what to expect.

He went to his crystal ball—his communications icon—and put in a call to Marilou Prusser, his lawyer.

Marilou's tired face appeared inside the crystal sphere.

"Yes?"

"Marilou? Glen Arita. I'm not going to wait for them to delete me. I'm logging off."

"Huh? Glen, I'm still asleep. What time is it?"

"Never mind. Just tell them I'm logging off. Permanently. No need for a hearing, right?"

"But the appeals. You have the right . . ."

"Forget it. I'll get a lawyer back in realspace and sue. Sue big. For damages."

"Good luck. I think you have a case. But I also think you're making a big mistake logging yourself off."

"I don't think so. Good-bye, Marilou. And thanks."

"Glen, you're a contentious fool. Do you know how hard it will be to get another VR service to accept you? You have an international reputation as a network troublemaker."

"Screw 'em. I'll be back, you can be sure of that. And I'll get even."

"Don't do anything rash. You're angry, you're—"

"I'm not angry. As the old saying goes, don't get mad, get even."

"I hope you enjoy life back in realspace."

"It'll be refreshing."

"To say the least," Marilou said dryly.

"It could be financially refreshing. For us on-line types, body maintenance eats up fully half our yearly income. We can never get ahead."

"Tell me about it," Marilou said with a pained expression. "Seems like I have to borrow money almost every month to meet my maintenance bill. You can't get ahead living on-line."

"Exactly. Think of the money I can save with just a few months' leave of absence. Listen, gotta run. Thanks again, and be well."

"You, too, Glen. Be careful."

The crystal went dark, a prompt told him that he had e-mail waiting. It was a text file. He brought it up.

Glen,

Well, your hearing is tomorrow, and I hope you get what you deserve, you nasty little prick. You are not fit to consort with civilized people. You are a mean-spirited, contemptable, hippocrital bully with illusions of godhead and I hope you get wasted in realspace, where you belong with the rest of the lumpen proles. Or to put it another way, eat shit and die.

Your pal, <g>
JON.PENNER [Crackerjack]

"Charming little love note," Glen muttered. "It's 'delusions,' anyway, you jerk." He got out the keyboard to compose a reply, but thought better of it. Who cared? He'd never have to deal with this semiliterate cretin again. Until he returned. And then he'd have some real fun with old "Crackerjack"

Hippocrital, indeed. Bastard was too dumb to use a spellchecker. "Contemptable." What a moron.

And too cowardly to say what he said to Glen's face. No balls. Typical of Penner and his ways. Sneaky, underhanded.

Forget it.

There was nothing left to do except lock up the castle. Might as well make it as hard on them as possible to delete it. He typed in line after line of code, throwing in every trick he could think of. It was useless, of course. They'd delete all of Dragonhome's graphic files as soon as he logged off. He sighed, hit ENTER, and got up from the console.

Slowly and sadly, he made his way up the tower stairs. The wind was whistling in through the embrasures with a plaintive song.

A bat flapped by. Nice thing about virtual bats: they don't bite, don't have rabies. Don't get tangled in your hair—if indeed realspace bats did.

He reached the top of the tower and walked out onto the parapet. He found himself on the roof of the keep. It was flat, and on it stood three dragons, all tethered to stone posts with thick rope.

They were enormous creatures, golden scales tinted with iridescent green at the tips. Their wings looked huge even folded up.

He walked past Storm, the best-looking one, all the way to Skydreamer, an old creature with ice-gray eyes and a pointed snout. Skydreamer was his ticket out. As an icon, it was empowered to log him off the system.

He untethered the beast and used a wooden ladder to mount. He sat straddling the beast's spiny back. It wasn't uncomfortable at all.

"Up, Skydreamer, away," he commanded.

Skydreamer spoke, "Sire, what is our destination?"

"The sky. All the way. To the highest reaches."

"Logging off, are we, sire?"

"Right. Up and out."

"Yes, sire."

The beast extended its huge wings and approached the edge of the parapet.

Glen tightened his legs and grabbed the reins, though he didn't have to use them to guide the beast.

"Here we go, sire," Skydreamer said, then leaped out into space.

The mammoth wings unfurled and gathered air, and the beast went into a long heart-stopping dive toward the base of the mountain before pulling up and soaring higher than the roof of Dragonhome. After making a wide circle over the valley below, Skydreamer banked and began a long upward spiral toward the clouds. In this computer-generated environment, the "sky" above was a gateway, a virtual device for making transitions from one area of cyberspace to another, and from one area of Dataspace International's services to another. The icons themselves were cutesy: cloud-borne castles with neon signs over their portcullises, each labeled with different service areas: INFORMATION, WORKSPACE, LEISURE, LIFESTYLES . . . and so forth. Dragonhome was, of course, located in the RESIDENCES area. There was another icon afloat in the blue, labeled LOG OFF. One not often used. Skydreamer was flapping slowly toward it.

Glen always enjoyed these rides. They were self-indulgent, of course, and used up premium time, but he could hardly let cost stop him now. This was his last dragon ride, or at least his last dragon ride in the virtual environment of Dataspace International.

He wondered what would be waiting for him at the Long Term Center. He'd never logged off permanently before. He'd have to find some new place to live. An apartment. The thought of it depressed him suddenly. Living in the real world again. It was going to be rough. Well, with a little legal maneuvering he'd quickly rehabilitate his fitness report and his standing in the virtual community and get back on-line in no time. Maybe he wouldn't even have to rent an apartment. He could simply hotel it for a while, and then—

"Something approaches, sire," Skydreamer said.

It was a long trail of fire reaching skyward toward them.

"A missile!" Glen yelled.

"I fear so, sire."

It was Penner, he knew it, lobbing a datamissile at him. Damn that vicious creep. A Parthian shot.

"Take evasive action!"

Skydreamer craned his neck around and gave him a strange look.

Glen understood. How could a low-tech creature like a dragon evade a high-tech thing like a missile? Although both were only computer simulations, they were true to their models.

Of course there was nothing really to fear. The missile couldn't hurt him. True, it would take out Skydreamer and let Glen fall from a great height—but the dragon wasn't real and neither was the "height." Glen could always intervene for himself—instantly summon another dragon, or this time, make it a WWII fighter plane. No, make it a twenty-first century plane, an F-25 StratoHawk, and with it he'd go strafe Crackerjack's place. Yeah. . . .

The missile hit. A green flash enveloped all of space. And time stopped.

"Wake up, dreamer. Time to awake and sing."

"Huh?"

The spinning form in front of him stopped spinning. It was the thin face of a man of about thirty-five, red-haired, a permanent sneer to his lip, and to his voice as well. He wore the white coat of a technician.

"Rise and shine. You got real. Real fast, too."

"What happened?"

"Someone bombed you out of Dataspace. You've been immersed in a Virtual Reality environment for three years, and now you're out."

Glen realized that it had been the Sysops who had

deleted him, not Penner. They must have been conferring before the hearing when they detected his leaving. And out of spite. . . .

"Yeah. Right. What're all these tubes and stuff?"

"To get you in shape for the outside, pal. You didn't give us any warning. We barely had time to pump you full of steroids before you came out of it. We popped you out of your pod and shipped you here to Recovery. How do you feel?"

"Lousy."

"And no wonder. Your body hasn't moved for three years, muscles all slack and atrophied. Fortunately we have drugs and things for that. You'll be all right. How come you came up so quick? Suddenly remember you left the bathtub running?"

"Huh? Uh, no. I just—"

"Come on, we know you're a reject. Dataspace didn't want you anymore, and you had to get real, didn't you?"

Glen snorted. "Yeah. But it's not what you—"

"Whatever. Hey, Glen, baby, it makes no never mind to me. I don't indulge. Someone has to stay awake and keep the fire going, right?"

"You've never done VR?"

"Oh, sure I have. Who hasn't? But I've never sealed myself up inside a canister and got fed through tubes so I never had to come out of it. That's only for you VR zombies. There are thousands of you. We keep fifteen hundred of you right here in this facility."

"What's your name?"

"Bim. Call me Bim."

"Bim?"

"You got a problem with that?"

"I don't like your tone. Do you work for Dataspace?"

"No, I work for TechnoMed Industries. We bought all of Dataspace's clients."

"What! When did that happen? You mean Datas-pace no longer keeps Long Term Resident facilities?"

"Nope, they got out of the zombie-nursing business and sold you to us. You're a TechnoMed client now."

"The hell I am. Let me talk to your superior."

"Sorry, Glen-person, but she's out to lunch. Like you've been for three years."

"Fuck you."

"Oh, aren't we pleasant before we've had our coffee."

"I'm getting up out of this bed."

"It isn't exactly a bed, Glen. I wouldn't advise it."

"Get me up out of here . . . Jesus."

Bim chuckled. "See? Not feeling as spiffy as you thought, are you?"

"Fuck you."

"Get that disk fixed, Glen, sweetheart. It's stuck."

"Up yours."

Bim shrugged. "At least it was different. Good boy. You'll be up and at 'em in no time. Hungry?"

It was a short convalescence. In no time he was out of bed and shuffling up and down the halls with a walker. Three days later, he was hobbling with a cane, and a day after that. . . .

"Doc says you're discharged, Glen, sweetheart."

"Quit calling me that. You have the clothes out of my storage locker?"

"Right here. They're a little out of date, hon. Whoa, Mr. Speed Demon! You've been through the program in record time, but don't jump up like that, or you might have a stroke."

"I'm fine. Gimme that."

"Please, and you're quite welcome, Mr. Arita. Say, that's Japanese, isn't it? But you don't look—"

"Father was, mother wasn't."

"You don't act Japanese. Need any help?"

"Will you please, for Christ's sake, for once in your fucking life, GET LOST?"

"Anything you say, pal. See you at the elevator. I'll take you topside."

"Topside? You mean we're ... underground?"

"Fifty meters at least. Didn't you know?"

"I was wondering. No windows, haven't seen the outside yet. Why down here?"

"You're in for a nasty shock."

"Oh?"

"It's not so safe up there any more. The war and all."

"War? Jesus."

"You haven't kept up? When was the last time you got news down there in cyberspace?"

"I read the news every day. What the hell are you talking about?"

Bim eyed him skeptically until understanding dawned. "I get it. You've been lied to, chum."

"You mean they've been feeding us false news reports?"

"Not false. Just ... how shall I say, incomplete?"

"Unbelievable."

"Not really. Why disturb the clients? They're having ever so much fun anyway in their fantasy worlds, playing knight and dragon, or whatever, and they really don't care. They all have jobs, they pay their service fees. It's been years since anyone had to go to an office or factory to work. As long as these zombie warrens aren't hit by bombs and as long as the power keeps on, why should any VR junky care what's going on in the outside world? See you at the elevator, Glen." Bim left the room.

Glen dressed as quickly as he could. There wasn't much from his locker except a wallet with some money in it. He hoped it was still good currency. There were some legal papers, insurance and such, and not much else. He pocketed the papers and walked out.

Bim was holding something in a long plastic bag with a zipper.

"This is for you."

"What?"

"A gun." Bim unzipped the top of the bag. Inside was a semiautomatic assault rifle. "And thirty rounds of ammo. You'll need every round, kid."

"The war?"

"Yeah."

"Who's fighting?"

"You'll find out."

The elevator whined and began to lift.

"Jesus. How did it start? Was there an invasion?"

"Not quite. Like I said, you'll find out real quick."

"But . . . what the hell am I supposed to do? Where do I go?"

"Your problem, Glen. But take a tip . . . there's a government refugee center about a block away. They may be able to help, get you a place to stay. But be careful of press gangs. They get you, you'll find out more about the war than you want to know."

"Jesus Christ. Bim, it can't be. They told us nothing!"

"Caveat emptor," Bim said with a shrug. "Here we are. Ground floor."

They came out into a space that had been a lobby, now a plaza surrounded by tumbled walls, littered with shattered glass, the roof blown away. The street outside was strewn with debris.

A bright flash erupted to the right, and the ground shook. Glen went to his knees. The sound of the explosion was an assault on his ears. He'd never heard anything so loud.

"What the hell was that?" Glen asked fearfully.

"Sounded like a rocket. Lots of them lately."

"For Christ's sake, this is ridiculous. I'm going to sue. I'm going to sue Dataspace for all it's got!"

"If it's got anything," Bim added. He unzipped the bag and took the rifle out. "Take this. Shoot anything that comes near you. Don't take chances."

Glen took the weapon. He had never fired anything like it in his life. At least, not in the real world.

"Where was that refugee center?"

"That way," Bim pointed.

"Thanks for the advice. So long."

"You'll be back, kid. They all come back. Even before the war. You can't handle the real world, kid. All you zombies come back eventually."

"Fuck you, asshole!"

Bim chuckled, watching Glen run down the street in a crouch with gun at the ready.

"On second thought," he said to himself, "you just might fit right in up here."

That was the last thing he said, for when the user, GLEN.ARITA [Capt. Flame], exited the immediate area, the simulacrum designated "Bim" disappeared, along with the bombed-out building and this section of the role-playing game scenario titled "City At War," of which he and it were a part.

They would no longer be needed. The user would be bared from using this icon as a gateway back to Dataspace's main program.

Permanently.

MERDINUS

by Mike Resnick and Linda Dunn

Mike Resnick, veteran science fiction writer and winner of three Hugo awards, teams up with new writer Linda Dunn to refresh us by dipping into one of the primary sources of castle lore: "The Matter of Britain," viz., that whirlpool of legend swirling about the central figure of King Arthur. This story concerns the origin of the most mysterious character in the mythos.

Merdinus tossed another shovelful of dirt into the cesspool as cold mud and human excrement splattered on his legs. He moved forward slightly, testing the firmness of the ground beneath his feet. Another cartload of dirt and the liquid pool would be mud, ready to dig out and spread on the fields.

The other servants thought him a simpleminded boy for enjoying this work, but cleaning the castle's cesspits was much easier than working in the kitchen. It was hard to remember if Cook wanted him to watch the meat or do something else. The instructions were always difficult to follow and easily forgotten.

But cleaning the cesspits in the curtain walls of the castle was easy by comparison. The task was the same every time, and easy to figure out even when his memory betrayed him.

Merdinus stood upright and stared at the mess. He was almost under the garderobe now—near the end of this cesspit.

A voice from the entrance interrupted his thoughts. "Do you enjoy working in our sewage?"

Merdinus turned to see who was talking. He didn't recognize the old man, but there was something familiar about him. He knew no one who wore such fine clothes; yet this man stood watching him carefully, the smile slightly off-center as his eyes fairly twinkled with amusement. He stood at the entrance, not stepping near the thick muck where Merdinus was standing.

Merdinus shrugged. "It's not so bad once you get used to the smell."

The old man smiled. "And the rack's not so bad once you get used to the stretching." He chuckled. "There's no future here for you, is there?" He paused thoughtfully. "In fact, there are very few positions for men of low birth that anyone would choose. What will you do when you're grown—become a soldier?"

"And die in battle? No, thank you! I'd prefer to advise others from a place of safety."

"High wishes for one of your position."

Merdinus moved toward the entrance and spoke without thinking, "It should be ability, not birth, that decides one's fate."

"This isn't a good year for radical ideas. If that came to be, there would be many lords shoveling shit."

"And intelligent commoners governing."

The smirk was gone from the man's face as he leaned against the wall. "Rare wisdom for one so young. How old are you?"

Merdinus stepped out of the tunnel under the tower wall and stood up straight. He was a good head shorter than the old man. "I'm twelve, sir."

"A little small for your age."

"But strong, sire. You have to be strong to survive around here."

There was something familiar about the old man's

eyes. Merdinus felt he should know this person, but try as he might, he couldn't stir the memory.

"Strong and adventurous, eh? And you prefer not to risk your neck to the orders of others?"

Merdinus nodded.

The man leaned forward. "Tell me true, boy—did you ever know a man named Argistes?"

Merdinus hesitated a moment before speaking, his fingers toying with the pouch around his neck. It helped him to remember, sometimes, if he touched the stone inside.

"A neighbor to my mother's family, sir. He met a most unfortunate death."

"Which you predicted."

The boy shrugged.

"And your uncle carried you away from your home in Maridunon and left you here because he feared your gift of prophecy. He heard rumors that Vortigern needed a fatherless boy to sacrifice and thought to rid himself of his sister's shame and his own fears with your death at Castle Generon."

"A fate I avoided."

"By your own quickness of mind."

Merdinus felt a chill run through his body at those words.

"Why do they call you 'Merdinus'?" continued the man. "Do you know? Or care?"

Merdinus shrugged. "I knew once, but I've forgotten."

"Merdus is Latin for 'dung.' "

"And I clean the cesspits."

"Why don't you insist upon being called by your proper name—or at least a better one?"

"And be beaten for my obstinacy?" Merdinus shook his head. "Who cares what people call me? It's just a name." *And I don't remember my birth name.* He bit back that thought. People were cruel to simpletons. This man believed him wise; it was best not to do or say anything which would change his mind.

The man stepped back and folded his arms across his chest. "When your uncle left you here and they asked your name, all you could tell them was your place of birth. The Welsh called you Myrrdin."

Merdinus nodded. He didn't remember any of these things, but if this nobleman said they were true, he wasn't about to dispute the story.

The man kicked the wall and cursed before turning back to Merdinus.

"Myrddin should have been translated to *Merlinus* even if Merdinus was more natural. A name like that may change your fate yet again."

"Sire?" Merdinus scratched his head, trying to make sense of the man's strange words.

"Never mind." He shook his head and paced for a moment, then turned and spoke slowly and softly. "I've a quest for you. Find what I've lost and bring it to me."

"What *have* you lost?"

The man turned and looked behind him before leaning forward and whispering. "A ring. It slipped off my finger as I . . . ah . . was in the garderobe. Can you find it for me?"

Merdinus sighed. The royals were forever losing things in the garderobe. A few weeks ago it had been a necklace, and he'd been sent to the cesspool to find it. They'd promised him a fine reward for that, too. Of course, he didn't receive anything. The bauble was badly discolored by then and the royal family decided they didn't want it after all. He gave it to Itonje, the kitchen maid. She didn't care that the dragon's head was tarnished and no amount of polishing could remove the stains.

"A ring is very small."

The old man nodded. "I was told you had a gift for

finding things. When you find it, slip the ring onto your finger and go into the castle proper. Then we will talk."

"How shall I find you?"

"The ring will lead you to me." He smiled and added, "We have much to discuss, you and I. If you truly wish to escape a lifetime of shoveling human excrement and being at the beck and call of others, put on the ring and come to me." He stepped back and covered his nose. "But wash up first."

"With water?"

The man winked at him. "If you can't find anything stronger."

As he walked away, the man shouted over his shoulder. "Bring me the maiden's necklace before tonight, and I'll give you a reward."

Merdinus watched him walk away. *Maiden? Necklace?* He'd asked for a ring. Was the old man daft?

He looked around, and then noticed the guard standing within hearing range. No, he was not daft: he was clever. The guard would think it was merely another lost trinket and not bother with questions or gossip.

Merdinus turned toward the cesspool and waded out into the section directly under the garderobe. It was easy to find things others had lost. If this was a rare talent, then so much the better. He had few enough advantages in life.

He concentrated for a moment, trying to see where it might be, then waded into the middle of the pool and plunged his hand into the muck. His heartbeat pounded loudly as his fingers closed on metal that fairly glowed with energy.

It *had* to be magic. But what kind?

He slid the ring onto his finger and the feeling of power vanished. Merdinus waited for something magical to happen ... but nothing did. Everything was as

it was before, and he felt nothing but the touch of
cold, slime-coated metal on his wet fingers.

Merdinus shrugged and walked back to the cart. He
shoveled the rest of the dirt into the cesspool and
went back for another load. He would return the ring
when he finished this task. If he left it undone, Cook
would beat him, and *that* was one of the few things
Merdinus had no trouble remembering.

The next cartload emptied quickly, and he began
the slow task of scooping out the area and filling the
cart with the rich muck. It would fertilize the land and
bring a good crop this year and next before they
ruined the land by planting the same crop again and
again without rest or change.

As he took the first load out to the fields, the streets
were beginning to fill with people who stopped and
pointed. He dumped the load in the east field and
turned back to fill the next—and hopefully the last—
load. By now a few people lined the streets and waited
for him to pass. That was odd. Why were they staring
and pointing? A few of them even fell into step behind
him and followed him to the wall. As he left the cart
outside and ducked into the opening, they walked forward slowly to touch the cart.

Had they all gone mad?

He checked his footing near the entrance and
started shoveling again. When the first shovelful fell
into the cart, people fell back and ran. By the time it
was half full, a guard approached and watched as he
scooped load after load of muck into the cart.

After a few moments, the guard shrugged and
turned to the crowd. "The king's sorcerer has performed tricks before. No doubt this is one of them.
Begone and attend to your duties."

Merdinus stared out at them. *Sorcerer? Tricks?*
What did that have to do with him cleaning the
cesspit?

He dumped the next load on the field and headed to the stables. He was sure he had a reason for going there, but he couldn't remember what it was. Then he pressed the stone that hung in the bag around his neck and remembered. This was the place to hide his belongings when there was something he didn't want others to know he possessed. There was a secret stash of baubles buried far back in the used straw—a place no one else ever went. The engraved stone was the only thing he carried constantly.

Merdinus shivered as he dipped his fingers into the cold water and dabbed a few spots on his neck. His hands were caked with dirt and he was reluctant to wash it off.

Finally he sighed and dunked both hands into the bucket. The water turned brown as he splashed it onto his arms and rubbed them. It was almost mud as he closed his eyes and submerged his face. He came up for air with brown scum running down his cheeks and falling to the stable floor. He plunged his face in the water again and again, rubbing furiously.

When he came up for the last time, he could feel soft skin under his fingers. His hands looked pale, and although his fingernails were still mostly black there were spots where pink showed through.

He felt naked.

He picked the bucket up and tossed the water outside. Someone screamed and he whirled around at the sound.

It was Elivri, the blacksmith.

Merdinus stared at him. "What's the matter?"

"Who said that?" Elivri looked around.

"Very funny," Merdinus said, convinced the blacksmith was mocking his new appearance. "I didn't want to wash, but one of the king's men ordered me to."

The blacksmith crossed himself. He was another one

who had abandoned the old ways and adopted the foreign god of Christians.

"Are you a demon, then, that he's sent to foul my water and ruin my work?"

"Are you crazy?" Merdinus walked closer, noting Elivri's failure to meet his eyes. "It's me—Merdinus. Don't you know me?"

"Merdinus?" The blacksmith crossed his chest again. "Are you dead and a ghost come back to haunt me?

"Dead?" repeated the boy. "Am I that pale-looking?"

"Pale? I don't see you at all."

"What?"

Merdinus looked around and grabbed one of the shields that was waiting for the blacksmith's work. He held it in front of him and turned it first right, then left. Everything around him was reflected but he himself was nowhere in sight.

Merdinus looked down at his arm. He could see it. But could anyone else see him?

He looked at the ring and realized at last what was so special about it. "I'm invisible."

"You're what?"

"Never mind."

Merdinus grinned and thought for a moment about all the things he could do now. He could steal hot buns from the baker, who would never know who took them. He could sneak into the castle proper and listen to all the private conversations. He could make his way back to his old home and torment the uncle who kicked him out—if he could just remember who his uncle was and where he lived.

But he couldn't do all this if anyone suspected what was going on.

He'd already told Elivri he was invisible and the blacksmith was certain to tell others. Merdinus had to convince Elivri that he had nothing to do with what happened here. Fortunately, those who abandoned the old gods for this new one seemed prone to superstition. Not too many years into the future, their beliefs would lead to unrest and wars which lasted for centuries.

It should be easy to trick this Christian with his own words. What were they? He touched the pouch and remembered the words. He laughed—loudly and hysterically. "Yes. I am a demon sent to trick you out of your Christian beliefs—but your faith is strong and I failed. I will leave you now."

Elivri crossed his chest again—a really annoying habit—and Merdinus tiptoed out of the stables.

He entered the courtyard and made his way to the great hall. People walked back and forth and never glanced in his direction. He felt truly free for the first time in many years.

He made his way to the kitchen and stood at the doorway for a few moments. Cook was turning the spit and complaining about what a slow boy Merdinus was and how you just couldn't find good help nowadays.

Merdinus slipped into the room and stood beside him. The cook looked up and sniffed the air. "Itonje?"

The serving girl moved forward. "Yes?"

"Did you make that smell?"

She flushed deep red and shook her head. "I thought it was you."

Merdinus backed out of the kitchen quickly. *Smell?* Did he truly stink that badly? He knew people got used to their own body odors, but could it really be *that* bad without his noticing it?

He sniffed and waited. Maybe it was the clothes. Since he was invisible, he didn't really need clothing for anything except protection from the cold—and the day was growing warmer. He could easily peel off his

clothing, but where could he hide it? Wasn't there a
special place for that?

He remembered then, and hurried back to the stables to strip off his clothes and hide them in the loft.
The stone in the pouch around his neck troubled him.
He didn't want to leave it behind, but the voice which
troubled him sometimes whispered in his ear to pull
the pouch off and remove the treasure inside.

He stared down at the stone.

He'd drawn the design himself, a simple thing to do
when one understands the ways of nature. It was the
only thing he'd kept from the time before, and it was
something he didn't trust out of his sight.

With a flip of his wrist, he popped the rock into his
mouth and swallowed hard, willing the object down
his throat.

He could feel the warmth of the castle inside him
as the etched rock slid slowly toward his windpipe.

Merdinus waited a moment for the gagging reflex
to subside as the stone fell into his stomach. It would
be safe there for the time being and he could retrieve
it later.

The cool air raised bumps on his skin as Merdinus
ventured back outside. It was a small price to pay if
passing undetected gained him what he desired.

He went back to the kitchen and slipped inside
again. This time no one seemed to notice him. He
eased close to the cook and picked up a knife. While
his back was turned, Merdinus raised the knife and
brought it down carefully, peeling a slice of meat off
the spit. It was hot and he bit back tears as he tossed
the meat back and forth from one hand to another.

The cook looked up just then and saw what probably appeared to be meat bouncing about in midair.

His mouth hung open as Merdinus tossed the meat
onto the table, then picked it up again. It was cooling
but not fast enough.

He picked it up and shoved it into his mouth, biting back tears as the hot meat burned his tongue.

It was worth it. He hadn't tasted such fine meat in years.

The cook rubbed his eyes as Merdinus swallowed the last bite of meat.

"Itonje!"

"Yes?"

"Did you see or hear anything just now?"

"Just the sound of you smacking away. Sampling your cooking again?"

"That wasn't me."

She laughed. "Sure it wasn't. It was a ghost. Right?"

"Maybe." The cook sounded dead serious. "I think it's too hot in here. I'm stepping outside for a minute."

Merdinus grinned at his success. There was just one more thing he wanted to do before moving on. As Itonje stood before the large stone sink, Merdinus sneaked up behind her.

"Do you believe in ghosts?" he asked.

She whirled around and he grabbed her. She was too surprised to struggle much as he wrapped his arms around her and kissed her firmly. She struggled a moment and then fell limp. Merdinus lowered her into a chair and picked up the knife.

That really hadn't been very satisfying. One kiss and the girl faints in fright. He sliced off another chunk of meat and blew on it to cool it off. As Itonje began to stir, he laid the knife on the table and walked out the door.

Merdinus made his way through the great hall, past the guards, and then into the actual quarters of the king himself.

He'd forgotten how luxurious the inner chambers of a castle could appear to one from humble beginnings. He slipped inside the nearest door, wanting a look at the private room of the king. The bailiff's wife was inside, mending some piece of cloth. Why would the bailiff's wife be in the king's private room?

She looked up, sniffed the air, and moved closer. Merdinus stepped back, making his way into the corner until finally he was standing on top of a chair.

The bailiff's wife looked under the chair, muttering softly. "There must be a dead mouse somewhere around here. What else could make such a foul stench?"

She turned around and walked to the door. "Here, Kitty," she called.

Merdinus jumped down and raced past her, nearly knocking the old woman over as an overgrown black cat walked inside. The cat arched its back and spat at him.

Why did the bailiff's wife notice him when the cook and Itonje did not?

Merdinus moved farther down the hall and found some women sitting near a window, laughing and talking while doing needlework. This time he stayed just within hearing range, but far enough away so that they wouldn't notice his scent.

The first girl laughed as she stabbed a piece of cloth with needle and golden thread. "They say a certain young lady was seen in the arms of a rather attractive knight."

One of the women flushed deep red. "Tongues wag foolishly about things that never happened."

Another girl giggled. "I've seen how he looks at you."

The second girl set her needlework aside and stared at the third girl. "His family does not approve. Let us not forget that."

"Many a family has changed their mind with the right kind of persuasion."

"My family is unlikely to persuade them." The girl picked up her needlework again and looked down.

"Let us discuss something else. I hear we will have entertainment tonight. . . ."

Merdinus moved down the hallway as he had no interest in women's idle gossip. So the king's quarters were *not* here as he thought. Memory was a tricky thing. He knew where he had to go now, but not how to reach the place.

He moved down hallways and up staircases, keeping an ever watchful eye out for signs of activity. At last he recognized one of the king's counselors and followed him into a large chamber where the king had gathered others.

Merdinus stood quietly at the back, far away from people who might detect his presence by his odor.

The old man he'd seen earlier was there, standing in the circle of advisers. He turned and winked in Merdinus's direction, causing him to blush and look about, wondering if others could see him as well.

"Then we are in agreement?" one of the counselors asked. Everyone nodded. "So be it. Who wishes to volunteer to present our decision to the king?"

No one volunteered and the counselor sighed. "Very well, *I* will be the bearer of bad news again. I do not like losing the kingdom of Gwyrangon to the Saxons, but Morgan Fych is right. There is no other way."

The men began to leave the room and Merdinus followed the one called Morgan Fych—the old man who had lost the magic ring.

He turned down a narrow passageway and then into one of the towers. Finally, he entered a small room where a fire was burning brightly in the fireplace.

Merdinus followed him into the room and moved close to the fire for warmth.

"You shouldn't stand so close to the fire without protection. You might singe yourself in a most painful area." The old man's voice was full of laughter.

"You can see me!"

"Of course I can. Do you think I'd give you something that would make you invisible to me? Only the untrained and untalented cannot see you. And you can see me only because I choose to be seen."

"You mean you're invisible, too?"

"No. I appear as different things to different people. The king and his men see Morgan Fych. You see me as I really am."

"I'm confused."

"And well you should be. I remember how my head hurt when it was first explained to me. But changing the telling might change something else so I had best stay with what I know."

He pointed to a chair that held clean clothing and a tall chest supporting a pitcher and bowl.

"Clean up thoroughly. Then put on those clothes. And be quick about it. It is almost time for me to go forward again and then backward."

Merdinus started toward the water, then stopped and turned. "Who are you? *What* are you?"

Morgan Fych sighed. "I knew you would ask that and I can only tell you what I was told. I have no name and many names. You may call me what you wish. The name I'm using here and now is Morgan Fych, but the name by which I'm best known is Myrrdin, for the town from which I came is Maridunon."

"That is *my* name," Merdinus said. "And Maridunon is the castle where I was born!"

Morgan nodded. "I know from whence you came better than you know yourself. I also know where you are going and what you will do if history does not unwind. I only wish I knew equally well what others are doing in the future while I am in the past."

"Can you see the future?" Merdinus asked. "Sometimes I dream of it, but the dreams never make any sense."

"Wash up." Morgan pointed toward the water. "And I will talk while you are doing so. Mind you, wash thoroughly, because it does no good to be invisible to the human eye if you can be detected by the human nose."

Merdinus picked up a cloth and began the slow task of thoroughly removing all traces of odor from his body.

"When I was a boy—your age, in fact—a great magician appeared and gave me a ring which made me invisible."

"The one I'm wearing?"

"That very one. And then he spent the day and part of the night with me, teaching me how to cast simple spells and how to read the future in the flames of a fire."

"Can you do that for me?"

"I can and I will—after you are sufficiently clean. When the magician left, I found it easy to rise from my previous position to one of trust and respect, and in time the king himself sought my advice."

"How did you accomplish that?"

"Men fear and hate what they do not understand. Call it magic and they still fear—but they do not hate it because it is something they understand. Or think they do."

Merdinus started toward the clothing.

"Not yet." Morgan winked and pointed back at the bowl. "You still smell like you've slept in a cesspool. Did you wash your hair and your feet as well as your hands and face?"

Merdinus shook his head and resumed washing.

"I let it be known that I knew some basic magic, taught to me by an old hermit named 'Blaise'."

"That name is also familiar." Merdinus thought for a moment of the stone, and the name suddenly made sense. "My first tutor? You knew him, too?"

Morgan Fych nodded. "As well as you know him yourself. Better, in fact, since I *was* him when you were an infant and thus you might say that I tutored myself."

"I don't understand."

"Let me finish. When I was a little older than you are now, I left the castle occasionally to seek out places of magic and learned much. As I aged, I learned how to walk through time. I have traveled back to my childhood and forward far into the future. Time is not monotonic. One day does not necessarily follow another, and once you understand this, it is easy to cross back and forth through one's past and future."

Merdinus turned around, looking more closely at the thin frame and the slanted eyes. He understood now why the old man looked so familiar.

"You are me!"

He nodded. "Many years from now. If the future remains unchanged."

"But if you're from the future, then I'm from your past, and hence the future is fixed and cannot be changed."

Morgan shook his head. "Those who control magic can shape the future . . . and some of us wish different things. There was a time, long ago, when you—I—walked this path alone and carved a marvelous future. But then others who had different wishes for the future started changing things, and I found it necessary to travel back to my past occasionally and insure that it remained stable. There was a time when I—you—were a boastful boy who was proud and insistent that people call him by his rightful name. That boy would never have accepted the name 'Merdinus,' and it was his forcefulness which put him in a position of power at a very young age.

"Then others began tinkering with the natural flow

of Time. They caused your father to leave without acknowledging you, and your uncle to become a drunk. In one version of the past you died as a sacrifice for Vortigern's crumbling tower at Dinas Emrys. It took some very powerful magic indeed for me to go back and set that aright."

"But if I—you—we—*died,* then how could—?"

"It takes time for the changes in the past to catch up to the future. There is a short gap during which we can set things aright. Then time flows again and we cannot return. I can meet myself, but I cannot meet the me who will meet you. Do you understand?"

Merdinus looked his puzzlement. "No."

Morgan laughed. "It *is* confusing. Listen carefully, for my time in this cycle is short. I am what you will be—but only if you put yourself forward. You must be bold if we are to guide Britain to becoming a strong kingdom upon which the sun never sets."

"Never sets? You mean the sun will always be above us?"

"No." He pointed toward the window, where the sun was sinking below the horizon. "Think outward. There are lands far beyond this one which will someday fly the flag of Britain. Ours will be a very powerful nation."

"In my lifetime?"

He shook his head. "No. But we'll walk forward to see it. We will touch the future, you and I, but only if you take chances now, while you are young."

"I am afraid," Merdinus admitted.

"Of what?"

He shrugged. "I do not know. I just feel I must be careful. Sometimes my mind doesn't seem quite right."

Morgan nodded. "That's the result of so many people trying to change your future and past. It must be confusing for you, to have so many different pasts and be unclear which one is true. Most people don't notice the changes, but you have magic and wisdom far beyond that of any magician before or since."

Me? Merdinus stared at the ring, trying to picture himself growing into the strong and capable man standing beside him.

Morgan smiled and leaned toward Merdinus. "The history of this time is unstable, and will remain so for at least another hundred years. If you don't heed my advice and grow less cautious, you may never grow up to be me, in which case this conversation will never have taken place."

Merdinus felt his head throbbing. "But we are *having* this conversation."

"Now. And when you grow into me, I hope you come back and have this conversation with your younger self. If you don't, then the future won't be as it is—and all will be lost."

Merdinus shook his head, spraying water from his wet hair against the wall. "This is too confusing."

"Put on your clothes." Morgan gestured to the floor beside him as he sat down. "Then come sit with me before the fire."

Merdinus did as ordered and stared at the flames, seeing nothing but a dying fire.

Morgan placed two more logs in the fire, stirring them carefully before sitting down beside Merdinus. "Can you see an image yet?"

Merdinus shook his head.

"Take my hand and tell me what you see now."

Merdinus did so, and gasped as images formed within the fire. "I see a large castle—several times the size of this one! Banners fly and knights joust for sport rather than in preparation for war!"

Morgan nodded. "This is the future that I live now. Legends will spring up about it and our name will travel through the centuries.

"Merdinus?"

Morgan shook his head. "No, not *that* name. You must set it aside and never allow anyone to call you that again. We shall be known as 'Merlinus' and advise the greatest king who has ever been raised by a common man. He will think *he* is ruling, but *we* shall be the true power behind the throne and enjoy all the wealth and pleasures that come with the position." He paused. "*That* is the future that awaits you if you but follow my advice."

"What is it?" Merdinus asked.

"Let everyone know about your visions and your ability to find things. Tell them you learned them from Blaise . . ."

"But Blaise—"

"—was *me*. And although I didn't teach you magic you could see, I still taught you much of the ways of magic in preparation for this day. People will believe you learned magic from another magician and cease fearing you."

"The people here are embracing the Roman god of Christianity."

"But they fear magic and will leave us alone. I will come back from time to time to guide you, and if you follow my wishes the future will be a beautiful one."

So that night, Merdinus sat at the feet of his future self and listened to the wisdom he had to offer. Then the fire grew dim as dawn approached and Morgan announced that it was time to leave.

"Never forget that you must be forceful and make your true name known."

They said good-bye and Merdinus looked down at the ring, recognizing it suddenly for all that it was now and what it would be in the future.

As the man disappeared, the stone worked its way up his throat and popped into his mouth. He removed it and whispered softly, "*Good-bye, Morgan LeFay.*

You think you have won again and changed the past, but when you return to Camelot, you will find you have lost forever."

He wrinkled his nose in disgust. She thought herself a master of magic because she could walk through time and perform a simple trick like changing her shape. *Fool!* Her lust for power and control would bring her own destruction. By sacrificing all, including his own memories, the great Merlin's dream of the future would be the one that won.

Merdinus made his way slowly back to the stables, paying careful attention to those around him as he regained his old clothes. He clutched the stone tightly, savoring the short time he could enjoy full memory. He would remember the future now and his knowledge of the past was only the dim memory of what he recalled from his future life.

No wonder the poor lad Merdinus was usually confused and seemed simpleminded.

When dawn broke, his memory of the previous day and night would be gone and only hazy memories of visions would remain. One version of himself would travel backward one day closer to his birth while another would move one year forward for each day Merdinus lost.

One step closer to Viviane and the anchor she had attached to the greatest of castles in a future time.

When Merdinus finally reached the day of his birth, Merlinus would be free to live again in the Britain he had planned.

It was a truly wondrous land filled with castles as far as the eye could see. Tall castles built of seamless rock surrounded by towers that shone with brilliance even in the darkest of nights.

Viviane had anchored his timeline to the castle that governed Britain in the future he wanted, and helped

Merlinus secure his past with this stone that carried that castle's image.

It wasn't easy to live like this: going backward without memory, becoming ever younger and more confused. At the same time, moving forward and living only a day in each year; always in a different castle and always as a lowly servant.

Twelve more years in the past, sidestepping more tricks and ploys by Morgan LeFay and those like her, and the future would be secure. He would be free to live with Viviane in a Britain that was ruled by men who came to power through their abilities rather than their inheritance.

As dawn grew near, he continued holding the stone in his hand and staring down at the castle. It glowed with warmth and he felt satisfied that his sacrifice was worthwhile. A single tear trickled down his cheek and fell upon the stone, landing on the symbol of time etched into the tower of the oddly-shaped castle that governed future Britain.

As the first rays of the sun rose above the horizon and his memory began to cascade—running first forward, then backward—he stared down at the strange lettering below the castle on the stone and wondered again at the odd name.

Parliament.

KNIGHT SQUADRON

by S. N. Dyer

S. N. Dyer is a physician and a writer of stories that elude easy classification. The following example is no different. Watch for the quick banks and sudden turns this vehicle makes as it flies toward its unseen and totally unexpected destination.

"Never in the field of human conflict was so much owed by so many to so few."

—Winston Churchill

Gone now, all were gone who had been in the unit at the start of the war, gone save for Bunny, and Fitz, and the Honorable Froggie. And Fitzhorn was in hospital with a minor wound, stretching his infirmity as long as he could, shirking his duty to family, king, country. He simply could not face a return to combat.

Fitz knew he was going to die, was willing to die, was resigned to its inevitability. It was just that he was afraid of dying. Would he be torn apart by Messerschmitt bullets like Harbour, burn alive in a fused cockpit like Dickie, or spiral down helplessly into a gaggle of watching schoolchildren like Posher? Fitz had watched all these deaths of chums, and more. His future held no lack of possibilities.

"Fitzhorn, is that you?"

Fitz looked up from his bed, surprised. Who would come to visit him at night, traveling through streets sepulchral with blackout, and with the enemy overhead?

No one from his unit had come to visit—bad luck that, and in any case most were new boys, from middling families, middling schools, middling colonies, not the sort you'd ever have expected to bunk with. And then they died so quickly, well, it was hardly worth learning their names or examining their family snapshots.

Captain Mayhew had visited—oh, yes—to ask when he'd be back. Everyone knew the captain was half-mad now, from sending out man after man to die in what must, ultimately, be futile. The enemy had swept the continent and now lay poised like a snarling Alsatian, waiting until air power exposed the island's soft underbelly to invasion. Certainly Fighter Command were putting up a wizard fight, making Jerry lose two for their one—but Jerry's planes outnumbered theirs by three to one. And this was uncomfortably like one of those maths questions which had been the despair of Fitz' schooldays.

Captain Mayhew used to hunt rabbits, in the good days of the phony war. Now during missions he wandered the airfield, mumbling. Fitz' rigger followed him once, and learned what he was saying. He was devising letters of condolence.

And so, expecting no one, Fitz looked to the doorway. The man there, in an all black uniform and the rank insignia of Flight Lieutenant, looked familiar.

"Biggy? Biggy, is that you?" Fitz limped to the door. The limp was due more to the swath of bandages than to the wound itself, but certainly looked impressive. "It's been years, old man."

Not that many years, in fact, but at least a third of his life since he'd been new boy and Biggy in the upper form, a friend of his cousin, a source of protection.

"So you're in the game, too," Fitz went on, looking curiously at the uniform. Definitely unusual. The only bits of color were a red silk scarf and a red chess knight insignia on the pocket, both such a deep scarlet, the color of dead men's blood, as to seem almost black.

"Night Squadron," answered Biggy.

"What— How do you do it?" Fitz asked, in awe. No one in his unit had ever spoken with one of those lads, just wondered from afar. The elite fighters—not that the government gave them additional glory. There was no public sanction of individual heroism, perhaps because heroes tended to die so quickly. But you could not fail to recognize a newspaper account of Night Squadron. *A junior Pilot Officer in a southern squadron made his twentieth kill last night,* reported in the same anonymous tone as the *A Flying Officer was honored for his fifth enemy kill* which celebrated Fitz' elevation to fighting ace.

Night Squadron were the top hush heroes of Flight Command, with their black planes and invincible pilots. And now Fitz discovered he knew one of them!

Biggy leaned against the door. His hand was strong and cold. "Our secret? Would you like to know?" He was still the same podgy, bread-faced, good-spirited sort as ever when he smiled, which he did now. Then all the strange, aloof mystery of his person faded, and Fitz attributed it to his not having seen the man for seven years, and now in a uniform more suited to Jerry's secret police.

He was aware of his old school friend awaiting an answer. "Naturally I would."

"Then come by our aerodrome Tuesday evening," said Biggy. "If we're not out on a sweep. Give my name at the gate."

That sunk it, then, for Fitz. He'd have to check out

of hospital, return to the game, and hope he'd still be
alive Tuesday evening to crack into this mystery.

Fitz had been in hospital not from any battle injury,
or from stunting, or from the foolish pub and sports
accidents RAF pilots were prone to. His Spitfire had
been a bit skittish that day. The crew had been fussing
over her all day to no avail. He'd watched his group
depart, then paced alongside the mumbling captain,
hearing the distant sound of guns and bombs. It
seemed so much longer, when you were waiting on
the ground, even given the way one minute of combat
could seem to stretch into hours, and leave you
breathing as if you'd run ten miles.

Finally they'd limped home, short three planes and
with the Honorable Froggie coming in afire. Fitz had
been second man to the plane and helped pull his
friend out, spraining his own ankle jumping down.
They thought they'd rescued the Honorable Froggie,
he had not seemed that badly burned—but the medi-
cos said he had something called inhalation injury to
the lungs, so that if he survived it would be as an
invalid, like the pale choking gas veterans of the
Great War.

Fitz returned to base to find his Spits was top form
now. The armorer (he had his own fitter and rigger,
but shared an armorer, electrician, and radioman with
two other planes) had painted an insignia on her, a
large horn of plenty with nine swastikas spilling out.

His men stood proudly, and he thanked them,
though the best he could say for the rather ostenta-
tious decoration was that it might draw attention from
the RAF circle, which was uncomfortably like a target.
He put his hand on the plane, and she seemed to push
toward him, purring. The planes were kept warmed
up, ready to take off with a moment's notice.

"We only painted in the certains," said Potts, the

cockney rigger who was an old man of thirty and worshiped his pilot a decade younger. "We knew you wouldn't want us to count the probables."

Fitz nodded, as if pleased. He wondered if they ought to paint in little screaming civilians, for his certains over the city, which went down causing as much damage as a bomb. But one didn't think about such things, the same way one didn't think about the fact that one would never reach one's twenty-first birthday. He went off to don his flight suit. One ate, slept, played in the thing, as ready as one's plane. He tossed away his bandage, and found his ability to walk improved, though the ankle ached when he had to sprint for his plane.

It was barely evening when they scrambled for the first time, heading north toward the city. Fitz worked his controls mechanically, staying in formation, watching his dials, while cold sweat ran down his spine and he tried to concentrate on his batman's promise of a special dinner when he returned. *If* he returned. Only it would be bad form to say that.

He had stopped by the Honorable Froggie's room before leaving hospital, only to be blocked at the door by a sister. "Is Frogmorton accepting visitors?" he'd asked. The nurse hadn't said a word, just given him such a look of sadness and pity that he'd turned straightaway and left. So now it was just him and Bunny, of the originals. Bunny who was leading the flight and constantly interupting his thoughts with messages— "N, look sharp, you're drifting. G, straighten up now."

He hoped nothing happened to Bunny, because then he'd become squad leader, and he had enough to do considering his own impending death to have to worry about the safety of the new child pilots. As young as he, actually, but these few summer months of Blitz had transformed Fitzhorn into an old man.

Bits of scenery opened up in the moonlight. Perfect bombing weather. Then he could see suburbs, tiny row houses and the occasional old church, a target thrusting up into a seemingly benevolent heaven, all under blackout but visible in the traitorous glow from the full moon. And then there was an entire enemy attack squadron before him, forty bombers—the sturdy Heinkell 111s and Junker 88s, no tiny Stuka sitting ducks—and a full hundred of Messerschmitts.

The trick was to get behind them. The M109s might outclimb and outdive a Spits, but not if you caught them quickly. They circled in behind, Bunny barking out terse orders to terrified new men while Fitz broke free, found an enemy centered in his reflector, and gave a squirt of 20 mm cannon shot.

He banked off, pressed against his seat, and emerged into a press of Junkers. Ignoring the heavy prey, he came up and got another M109 head on, while all about him bombers' gunners tried for the impossible deflection shot as he crossed their paths. He felt a couple of bullets thud into his tail assembly, didn't care. Because suddenly Fitz realized that, since he was going to die soon, perhaps it would be most manly to just do it as soon as possible and be over the suspense.

Two kills. Two minutes and two certains. He was the lucky one, the largely inexperienced pilots of his squadron were taking it hard. Then more squads arrived, Spitfires diving in to join the fray, slower Hawker Hurricanes going after the bombers.

His men fussed over him when he returned, out of ammunition, pulling him out of the cockpit and handing him over to his batman, his legs suddenly weak and unable to support him. Three more swastikas for his cornucopia.

They scrambled three more times that night, each time coming back fewer. Each time Fitz took the lead, tearing into the fighters with a suicidal glee. He slept all day, waking to another night of moonlit terror raids. Only now, when the enemy saw his insignia they seemed to veer away. He was getting a reputation. Their fear gave him more of an edge than his suicidal frenzy.

But still the Luftwaffe came, placid Junkers and Dorniers and Heinkels with their gifts of death for the land below, and the vast packs of Messerschmitts circling protectively like rabid sheepdogs. And when the RAF had begun to fail, to be unable to keep up with the press, then Night Squadron arrived. Sleek black planes from nowhere, pilots who feared nothing and never missed. Fitz watched them, shadows that seemed to appear and disappear as magic, leaving fiery debris in their wake.

Captain Mayhew met him at dawn as he deplaned. "Acting a bit excitable, I hear, Flying Officer Fitzhorn," he said.

Fitz raised an eyebrow. Was he in for a dressing down, a trip to the division headshrinker, or a Distinguished Flying Cross?

Captain Mayhew shrugged. "No letter for your family. Carry on," he said, and strode away, stepping absently over bits of debris and scarred tarmac from one of the night's crash landings.

Tuesday evening arrived, much to Fitz's surprise. It was cloudy, not a day when even the most crazed of Nazis would cross the channel. Fitz took off his flight suit for the first time in days, let his batman worry excessively over the shine of his shoes, and went to borrow a motorcar. However, before he might, a driver came for him.

He soon found out why. Night Squadron's aerodrome was every bit as unusual and top hush as the fliers themselves. He had seen the old castle from the road, even flown over it. It was poised at the limestone cliffs, slowly crumbling away into the Channel. There were ruins of Tudor manor cobbled about bits of Norman donjon added onto a Saxon fortress built over a Celtic dirt embankment covering a tumulus of Pictish origin, all surrounded by the outline of impregnable stone walls dismantled by Cromwell's Roundheads. The place was a veritable history lesson, and Fitz had always hated history. Even more so now that he felt himself becoming part of it.

From the air the place looked perfectly innocent, by day the planes would be hidden in barns, and fields of clover thick with placid sheep encroached upon the ruins. An asphalt car park doubled as runway. The dour guards, patrolling the aerodrome with Alsatians, were dressed as shepherds.

The driver pulled up beside a field of Spits painted black, with chess knights where other planes had the target. There were no swastikas or other signs of individuality, except for small coats of arms where other men painted cartoons or goddesses. He led the pilot into the castle keep, overgrown with weeds and with a few late blooms planted in a half-barrel, and pointed him into the donjon. The windows were blacked out, but inside was a large hall with a roaring fire and modern furnishings and even electric lights. But no light seemed to penetrate the gloom above, and Fitz thought the place must be unfit for habitation come winter.

Biggy came to meet Fitz, and introduced him all around. The men wore the odd black uniforms—Fitz was beginning to crave any hint of color, even thought of picking one of the scrawny petunias for his lapel— and they seemed unusually calm and quiet for RAF men, but otherwise were exactly the sort who'd filled Fitz' unit when the whole thing had begun. Men of birth, men of honor, men of purpose.

Someone was at the piano, other men were playing

chess or bridge or reading, all at a large circle of small tables pushed together. No one was smoking, though they offered Fitz a cigarette, no one was drinking, but an obsequious servant brought Fitz a Scotch and bubbly without his even asking. He sat with Biggy's friends and the men discussed battles, and drew him out about his own victories and nears and crashes. He was no closer to understanding these invincible warriors than the knowledge that they were a steadier, duller lot than his own compatriots, who were no doubt at this minute well on the way to being dead drunk, in bed with a barmaid, or both.

Then Biggy said, "Here he comes." The room fell silent and everyone rose.

A small man had entered, wearing the same black uniform but with a very nonregulation beard and hair down to his collar. He wore a sword at his waist. Not one of the lightweight ornamental sabers you wore for special occasions; no, this was a stocky, thick two-handed thing better suited to the medieval wing of a museum.

The man nodded, and everyone returned to their activities. He looked around, saw Fitz, and came over.

To Fitz' astonishment, Biggy sank to one knee. "My liege," he said.

"Rise, my friend, Sir Biggs," said the captain, with an accent that was definitely not what Fitz would have expected in this unit. It was odd, vaguely Germanic.

"This is the pilot I was telling you of, my old schoolmate Alec Fitzhorn. Fitz, this is Captain Arthur."

The captain did not shake hands or engage in small talk. "Do you know why I am here, Flying Officer Fitzhorn?"

Fitz shrugged. "Same as the rest of us, I guess—to do the job."

"And the job?"

"Well, our duty."

"And our duty?"

Fitz looked blank. Duty was duty, you didn't talk about it. His duty, he supposed, was to die.

The odd man continued for him. "My duty—my role—is to save England."

"Oh," said Fitz. "You alone?" He immediately regretted his flippancy.

"Of course not," snapped Arthur. "How could I? No, I was brought back to save England, but as I did before. With a band of knights."

The servants were coming by with wineglasses full of a deep red port. They gave one to Arthur and to Biggy, but none to Fitz.

"Flying Officer Fitzhorn," Arthur said. "Are you willing to die for your country?"

"Well, of course," said Fitz, a bit offended. "I mean, I did sign up and all." What else could he do?

"Come," Arthur said, and walked to the front of the hall, skirting the circle of tables. There, behind the piano, was a door covered by tapestry, and a passage. Arthur and Biggy both picked up candles, and led Fitz along corridors that grew narrower and moldier as they passed downward.

"Didn't know the Normans had such deep dungeons," he said nervously.

"We are past the Norman part," said Arthur, "and now even the Saxon." They had entered a cave, with stakes of limestone reaching up toward the ceiling; with better light, Fitz was sure he'd see similar stakes dripping downward.

In the center of the chamber, surrounded by candles, was a stone sepulcher, a massive ancient coffin.

"Read the inscription," said Biggy.

Fitz leaned over and read the carved message. *"HIC IACET ARTHURUS, REX QUONDAM REXQUE FUTURUS."*

"I was not dead," said Arthur. "Not truly dead. I lay only to arise again in the hour of Britain's need."

Fitz was beginning to have a very bad feeling about this.

The bearded man took a step back and, so rapidly time seemed to freeze, drew his sword. An ancient iron blade with sharp edges and a blood gutter down the center. He aimed the blunt point at Fitz.

"Will you join us?"

"It's really true," said Biggy. "He is King Arthur, Fitz old man. And you can be one of the knights of the New Round Table. You just have to die first."

Fitz felt a knot in his stomach, like the first time he'd seen combat.

"Let me think about it," he said, executing a smooth evasive maneuver and heading back upward, exiting the premises as expeditiously as possible, pausing only to look back through the open door.

The pilots of Night Squadron were holding up their wineglasses in salute. "King Arthur!" they shouted, and downed the dark liquor.

Fitz sprinted for the gate. He thought he had it bad, what with a hopeless war, a crazed captain, and a personal death wish. Now he knew that things could be worse, and he certainly now knew the phenomenal secret of the killer elite.

They were all certifiably insane.

The next evening they scrambled again, to hold back the infinite forces of evil. Fitz' fear had reasserted itself, the fear of dying, and he hung back. Only this time the fore would have been preferable, and he found himself in the sights of an M109. He tried every evasive maneuver at his command, but the bullets flew to this side and that, and he knew the next few seconds were to be his last.

And then a pitch-black plane with a red chessman

came in to his left, veering off and strafing the enemy in an almost impossible deflection shot. Hitting him directly and economically, with no more to do than you'd find at bowling practice.

The black plane circled back around, paralleling Fitz. The pilot pulled up his goggles and saluted.

It was the Honorable Froggie.

Froggie who had been an invalid, dying a slow and cruel death by inches. Froggie whom, the nurse had implied, had gone to his reward.

Fitz had been rescued by a dead man.

His Spits was wounded, not terminally but enough that he could justify returning to the airfield. He climbed out, ignoring his men's questions, and borrowed a motorbike. He rode past Captain Mayhew, hearing the man mutter. ". . . your son, who perished bravely in the line of duty . . ."

Night Squadron base was similarly empty, save for Arthur, striding the field.

"Flying Officer Fitzhorn. Have you decided?"

"Froggie was dying."

"He is dead," said Arthur. "Only the dead may join my band of brothers. Am I not dead, after all?"

"How . . ."

"We usually recruit those who are dying anyway," the captain continued. "Those who have given their lives in bravery and honor, they are my knights. But even they fall again to the enemy, and we must recruit replacements. Sir Biggs thinks you are a brave man, if only the suspense regarding your death should be ended. Then you would be able to properly get on with your job."

"You mean . . ."

"I would like you to become my knight."

Fitz gritted his teeth. "I will," he said.

Arthur was suddenly beside him. "Welcome, Sir

Knight," he said, grabbing the officer in what seemed to be an embrace.

And then his mouth was at Fitzhorn's throat, there was a sharp rending pain, and Fitz began to sink to the ground. His vision was going black, but he was looking into the night sky and only knew that the stars were disappearing.

His last thought was: "I should have known this would be how you could rise from the dead."

There was a sudden light, and Fitz awoke. He was lying in a coffin, and was dressed in a black flight suit.

His batman was leaning in, fearful, holding out a full wineglass, deep and red. It was not wine.

"Arise, Sir Alec," his batman said.

About him, Night Squadron was scrambling for action.

SWIMMING THE MOAT

by Barbara Paul

If you read mysteries, you know that Barbara Paul is the popular author of many mystery novels. If you read science fiction, you know her as a writer in that genre as well. In this piece she shrouds a bright, fanciful fairy tale in mystery and murder.

Hänsel and Philomena had opened a casement window and were leaning out staring at the moat below. "First he burns the drawbridge," Hänsel grumbled. "Then he cuts the telephone lines. Now he fills the moat with sharks."

"He doesn't want us to leave," Philomena said unnecessarily. A morning breeze ruffled the feathers of her cape.

"Whoever would have thought Eggy could be so vindictive?"

"Vindictive?" She pointed her beaklike nose at him. "He just wants us to find out who killed him. What's vindictive about that?"

"Then why didn't he just tell us to call the police?" Hänsel demanded. "Or summon up Sherlock Holmes or V. I. Warshawski, somebody like that?"

"You've met the local constable," Philomena pointed out. "He can't find his own feet, much less a murderer. As for 'summoning up' an experienced detective . . . maybe Eggy can't. He doesn't know what

260

all his new powers are yet. After all, he's never been dead before."

Hänsel stuck his hands in the pockets of his *lederhosen*. "I wish you'd stop being so damned *reasonable*."

She laughed and floated away from the window.

Hänsel turned his gaze back down toward the moat. The sharks were big, ugly brutes, more like an F/X designer's dream of monsterness than real-life *Carcharodon carcharias*. One of the sharks raised its head out of the water and snapped its teeth menacingly toward the casement window. "Yeah, I see you," Hänsel said.

Lord Eggleston, their erstwhile host and current dead person, had been stabbed in the back with a Swiss army knife. He never saw his attacker. So Eggy had appeared to them vaporously with the caveat that no one would be allowed to leave the castle until his killer was identified. Hänsel had made the mistake of announcing his intention of swimming the moat. Eggy had heard him; thus the sharks.

There were only five guests in the castle. Hänsel knew he hadn't done it, and he was as sure as he could be that Philomena wasn't in the habit of solving her problems with a Swiss army knife. It had to be one of the other three. But why would anyone want to kill the lord of the castle? He was a good, er, egg—everybody's friend and nobody's enemy.

The sound of running footsteps made Hänsel turn from the window. Mittsy came sprinting toward him, face aglow and blond curls bouncing. She stood on the tiptoes of her saddle oxfords to whisper, so the ghost of Lord Eggleston wouldn't hear: "BonBon is digging a tunnel under the moat!"

Hänsel felt a surge of hope; what a good idea! He bent down and whispered in Mittsy's ear: "Where is he?"

"In Dungeon Number Three," she whispered back.

"BonBon could use some help. All four of us. Where are Philomena and Ruby Red?"

"Phil was just here. I haven't seen Ruby for a while."

But before they could go looking for the other two, something happened. The light in the chamber disappeared, flickered back to life, then dimmed just slightly. The air shimmered in front of their eyes. The smell of cotton candy filled their nostrils.

Lord Eggleston's ghost materialized ... or tried to. One arm went stretching out in elasticized frenzy. His neck elongated so that the top of his lordly head was touching the ceiling. To add to his problems, his ghostly raiment tried to levitate while his feet never left the floor.

"He really should be better at that by now," Mittsy murmured.

The ghost finally got himself together and belatedly adopted a dignified stance. "This visitation is but to whet thy almost blunted purpose," he intoned.

Hänsel sighed. "*Hamlet,* act three, scene four. C'mon, Eggy."

"Well, you need a little whetting," the ghost said fretfully. "All you're doing is looking for ways to get out of here. You're not still thinking of swimming the moat, are you?"

"No, the sharks took care of that. But what do you expect? You're keeping us here against our wills."

"You think that's a problem? How would you like to be in *my* shoes?"

He had a point. "But Eg, nobody here knows how to investigate a murder."

"Now, now, mustn't be defeatest," the ghost scolded. "You've always been the clever one, Hänsel. Find a way."

"*He's* the clever one?" Mittsy said in irritation. "What am I, chopped liver?"

"Anything but, Mittsyluv," Lord Eggleston said soothingly. "We've always needed you. You're our cheerleader."

Mittsy perked up. "Oh. That's all right, then."

"Eg," Hänsel said hesitantly, "can't you, ah, just go back and *see* who it was poked you with that knife?"

"The spirit world does not have time travel," the lord of the castle explained patiently. "Nor do we have omniscience. Do you think I'd be going through this rigamarole if I knew any shortcuts?"

"Guess not. Okay, then. Tell us exactly what happened when you were killed."

Just then Philomena appeared in the doorway. "I thought I smelled cotton candy—oh." She broke off when she saw the ghost.

"Come on in, Phil," Hänsel said. "Eggy's about to tell us what happened when he was killed."

"Then we *are* going to try to find the killer?"

"You bet," Mittsy said enthusiastically. "And we can do it!" Living up to her role as cheerleader.

Hänsel asked, "What happened, Eg? How much did you see?"

The ghost cleared his ethereal throat. "As I was sewing in my closet—"

Hänsel waggled a finger at him. "*Hamlet* again."

"Er, right. Ahem. It happened in my bedchamber, you know. I was standing before the fireplace, watching the flames, when I felt this intense pointed pain in my back. Then I woke up dead."

There was a long silence. "Well," said Philomena, "that was helpful."

"Okay, forget that." Hänsel thought a moment. "Eg, what about motive? Nobody had it in for you. Certainly nobody here."

Lord Eggleston shuffled his feet soundlessly and refused to meet their eyes; an embarrassed ghost is a disconcerting sight under the best of circumstances.

"As a matter of fact," he said, "all five of you have a motive. You just don't know it yet."

"What are you talking about?" Mittsy sounded confused.

"You all think I invited you here for a normal, traditional, fun-filled weekend at the castle, don't you?" the ghost asked rhetorically. "Well, I had something else in mind this time."

"What?" Philomena demanded.

"Fluffy Bunny Downs."

They all stared. "You mean the rabbit race track?" Mittsy asked.

"Oh, don't play Little Miss Innocent!" the ghost said scornfully. "You're as hooked on the rabbit races as everyone else here! All five of you. And you're in deep. You owe a *lot* of money, all of you." He paused. "Well, I bought up your markers. Fifty cents on the kloznik. I asked you here to tell you I expected full payment within a week."

"Eggy!" Philomena cried plaintively. "And I thought you were one of the Good Guys!" The feathers of her cape were standing on end. "Why? Why were you doing this?"

"Why? Do you have any idea how much it costs to run a castle these days? *I needed the money,* that's why!"

"But," said Hänsel, "but if none of us knew . . ."

"It's obvious, isn't it?" Lord Eggleston asked. "One of you found out."

They digested that for a minute. Then Mittsy pointed to the floor. "Um, Eggy?"

Lord Eggleston's left foot had lengthened itself so that the toe of the boot was almost touching the opposing wall. With an effort he got it back to its normal size. "Look, it's hard for me to stay in shape," he apologized. "I'm going to have to leave for a while. But you find out who knew I held those markers, and you'll know who the killer is. Now, hop to it!" He started to disintegrate.

"Before you go completely to pieces," Hänsel asked, "who was in deepest? Who owed the most money?"

"Ruby Red!" a ghostly voice echoed in the room.

"Ruby Red," Mittsy repeated breathlessly. "She did it. She's the killer."

Philomena stared. "That must be the all-time record for jumping to conclusions."

"But who is she, really?" Mittsy persisted. "We don't know much about her."

"I don't know much about *you*," Philomena said pointedly, smoothing down the feathers of her cape.

"You've known me for years!"

"I've known you to speak to for years, that's all. I look at you and all I see is a . . . a cheerleader."

Mittsy beamed. "That's what Eggy said, too."

"This isn't getting us anywhere," Hänsel muttered.

They all lapsed into silence, trying to think what to do next. Their ruminations were interrupted by a heavy *thud* as a vibration ran through the room and the glass in the casement window rattled. Another *thud*, followed by still another.

A giant stood outside the doorway. His head sat squarely on huge neckless shoulders that were wider than the door opening, his dangling fingertips reaching halfway between knees and ankles. Tiny close-set eyes, low forehead, thrusting jaw. A tear was running down one cheek.

"BonBon!" Philomena exclaimed. "What's the matter?"

The giant turned sideways, ducked his head, and sidestepped his way into the chamber. "It would seem," BonBon said in a voice like a low rumble of thunder, "that our host had already anticipated an endeavor to excavate our way out of this unasked-for confinement. Whatever phantasmic powers he now possesses, they have enabled Lord Eggleston to implant a subterranean obstruction that all my experiments indicate to be unqualifiedly impenetrable by the only tools currently at my disposal."

"Huh?" said Mittsy.

"There's a steel wall under the moat."

"Oh, shoot."

"Never mind, BonBon," Hänsel said. "We've decided to try to figure out who Eggy's killer is." He repeated what the lord of the castle had told them about buying up their gambling markers. "So what we need to do is find out which one of us knew about it."

"And we can do it!" Mittsy said enthusiastically.

"Interesting," BonBon mused. "How does one prove the possession of *knowledge*? If it were a material object, a simple search would prove efficacious in all likelihood. But this new development does explain why the five of us *specifically* are here—I assumed I was the only one of us addicted to wagering on the rabbit races. Even you, Hänsel? I'd have thought you were too clever for that."

"Afraid so." He bent over to pull up his knee socks, hiding his discomfort at being shown to be as big a sucker as anybody.

"Ruby Red's more addicted than any of us," Mittsy offered. "Her debt is the biggest. Eggy said so."

"Where is Ruby?" Hänsel asked. "I haven't seen her for hours."

"She's in her bedchamber," Philomena replied. "Grieving. Mourning the loss of the love of her life."

"Eggy?" Mittsy said incredulously.

"So she says."

"How long did they know each other?" Hänsel asked.

"About two days, I think."

They all exchanged looks. "Something fishy there,"

Hänsel said. "Doesn't quite jibe with what Eggy told us about the markers. We ought to ask Ms. Ruby Red a few questions, methinks."

"If she deigns to talk to us," Mittsy sniffed. "Remember the entrance she made yesterday? Too busy playing the glamorous siren to speak to us common folk. She won't tell us what we want to know."

"Reluctant as I am to cater to stereotyping," the giant said, "maybe I could pound it out of her."

"That might not be necessary," Hänsel said hastily. "The situation has changed—she might be willing to talk to us now. Let's try that first."

"I'll go get her," BonBon said. He did his stoop and sideways shuffle out the door.

The others followed him out; they were in the Grand Corridor that ran the full length of the castle. They watched as the giant started groping through the air, his long arms searching the space in front of him. Finally, a small *thunk,* and BonBon carefully felt his way onto the invisible escalator. "I'll be right back," he said as he rode up into the air.

"Do you think he could have done it?" Mittsy whispered.

"Look at him," Philomena answered as the giant stepped off the escalator at the next floor. "Do you really think BonBon needs a Swiss army knife to kill someone?"

They didn't have to wait long. They heard Ruby Red before they could see her, screaming out a barrage of vituperation in a language unknown to them. They may not have understood what the words meant, but they knew cussing when they heard it.

BonBon appeared at the top of the invisible escalator carrying a red-skinned, red-haired woman under one arm. Ruby Red was kicking and fighting for all she was worth, but the giant wasn't about to let go. Cautiously he felt ahead of him with one foot and then stepped forward into seemingly empty space. "She didn't want to come," BonBon said as they rode down through the air.

"Do you think that's her natural color?" Mittsy whispered to Philomena. "I think she dyes her skin."

"Let's go in here." Hänsel led the way into the cavernous dining hall.

BonBon plunked Ruby Red down in the chair at the head of the table; the rest of them took seats on both sides of her. When she saw all the others staring at her, she burst into tears. At least she made the sounds of weeping; Hänsel couldn't actually see any tears.

"Why do you disturb me at a moment like this?" Ruby Red asked through her maybe-tears. Now that she'd finished with her screaming fit, her voice was soft and tinged with the hint of an exotic accent.

"Ruby, you knew Eggy only two days," Hänsel said. "Why all this grief?"

"I have known Lord Eggleston all my life," she said dramatically.

"You told me two days," Philomena commented, less dramatically.

"But those two days contained a lifetime of joy." Ruby dabbed daintily at the red skin under her eyes with a lace handkerchief she'd produced from somewhere. "You must understand how it was with us. There was a bond between us, a link. How do I explain?" Her accent grew stronger. "An instant understanding, from the very moment our eyes first met—"

"Where?" Hänsel asked.

"I beg your pardon?" She didn't like having her big scene interrupted.

"Where were you when your eyes first met?"

Her face softened at the memory. "At Fluffy Bunny Downs. Alas, I was in debt to these *terrible* men . . . but Lord Eggleston took care of it for me. That wonderful man actually bought my markers, out of his own pocket!"

BonBon made a noise that could have been a laugh. "And that is how Little Red Ruby Hood was eaten by the wolf. I fear, dear lady, you have been somewhat gullible."

Ruby glanced at him sharply and turned to Philomena. "What is he talking about?"

Philomena wrapped her feathered cape more closely about her and sighed. "Eggy bought your markers at a discount so he could collect on them himself. You weren't off the hook—you just had a new creditor."

"What?"

"It's true," Hänsel added. "He'd bought up all our markers. That's why we're here now ... Eggy had planned on calling in our debts. You included. He told us posthumously that you had the biggest debt of all. He wasn't paying your bills for you."

Ruby Red looked thunderstruck. "Why ... that dirty, low-down sonuvabitch!" Her voice had lost its accent. And its softness. "He was just leading me on? I gave that schmuck two of the best days of my life ... and for *nothing*? I ... I'll kill him!"

"Someone beat you to it," Mittsy said innocently.

"Someone." It was the giant who had repeated the key word. "And as distasteful as we might find the task, it behooves us to fulfill the commandment levied upon us by our somewhat-departed host and determine the identity of that 'someone.' "

"And we can," Mittsy said positively. "We put our heads together, and we figure out whodunit. We can do it!"

"We've *been* putting our heads together," Philomena remarked dryly.

"That sonuvabitch," Ruby Red muttered.

Hänsel said, "So let's proceed—"

"With alacrity," BonBon interposed.

"Him, too. How do we find out which one of us knew about the markers? I don't suppose anyone would care to confess, hm?"

The silence that followed was interrupted by the sound of a large stomach growling. The giant grinned sheepishly. "Sorry. It does that when I get hungry."

"I'm kind of hungry, too," Mittsy said. "Is it time for the noon meal?"

Philomena looked at her watch. "It's time. Well, let's start looking."

Their ghost host had a silly streak; he'd decided to take the phrase "movable feast" literally and make them go hunting for their food. They'd had exactly two meals since someone had committed Swiss army knife abuse; one had been served in the reception hall and the other in the laundry room. They started searching.

It was in the solarium this time. Five rickety TV trays had been set up; each tray held one plate, one glass, one fork.

"Oh, no!" moaned Mittsy. "Not again!"

The plates contained the same things they'd contained the other two times: cold green beans and stale chocolate cake. Philomena raised her voice and said, "Eggy, we can't subsist on fare like this! Especially BonBon. He needs red meat."

A ghostly voice reverberated through the solarium: *"I'm doing the best I can! Shut up and eat."*

Grumbling, they all sat down to their unsavory meal. Mittsy had evidently decided to make the best of things. "It keeps us alive," she declared. "We should look upon this as a test of character!"

Philomena stared down her beaklike nose at the cheerleader. "Why don't you spell your name M-i-t-z-i like everybody else?"

Mittsy giggled and blushed prettily. "I don't know."

They ate in silence for a minute.

"If we can't identify the killer," Ruby Red asked suddenly, "does that mean we spend the rest of our lives eating cold green beans and stale chocolate cake?"

They all shuddered at the thought. All but Mittsy. "But we will identify the killer!" she proclaimed cheerfully. "We can do it!"

Philomena leaned over toward Hänsel. "If Miss Bubbly-Bouncy-Perky says 'We can do it' one more time," she murmured, "there's going to be more than *one* ghost haunting this castle."

When they'd finished, Hänsel stood up and excused himself. "I've got to walk a bit, clear my mind."

The truth was, he didn't have an idea in his head; he just wanted to get away from the others for a bit. He wandered down the Grand Corridor, looking into the various rooms along the way. He passed the small chamber that Eggy had used as an office, although it was Hänsel's conviction that the lord of the castle had spent most of his time in there playing Tetris. He came to the library.

Yes: this was what he needed. A good book to get his mind off the problem for a while. He plucked one at random off the shelf—*A Brief History of Moat-Digging in Fourteenth-Century Provençe.* Just the ticket.

There was a draft in the library; he wished he'd worn his long *lederhosen* instead of his short ones. A purple-and-white afghan lay folded neatly on the leather sofa. Hänsel wrapped it around his goose-bumpy legs and settled down for a good read.

But he'd read no more than a couple of sentences when the print faded abruptly from the page. Hänsel flipped through the rest of the book: all blank pages. "Dammit, Eggy!" he yelled. "I need a little distraction . . . to help me focus. Half an hour? C'mon, Eggy!"

Print reappeared on the first three pages.

"Boy, you must think I'm one helluva slow reader."

Two more pages of print appeared—grudgingly, Hänsel thought. But no matter how much he wheedled, Lord Eggleston wouldn't give him any more. Muttering at the injustice of it all, Hänsel started to read.

He was just getting into the hot issue of seepage when he reached the end of his allotted reading matter. He closed the book and hugged it to his chest. Now he would never know how they got rid of the unwanted water during the initial digging period.

Unwanted water.

Unwanted.

Unwanted markers.

Wait a minute, wait a minute—think it through.

If someone were desperate enough to poke a hole in poor old Eggy to keep him from calling in those markers—would that person leave those very markers lying around for someone else to find? Of course not.

And would that person take only his or her own markers and leave the others behind? Maybe, maybe not.

One missing set of markers would name the killer for them ... but how could the guilty person have been aware of that ahead of time? The killer had no way of knowing that Eggy would prove so stubborn, lingering on in ghostly state and insisting his murderer be found. The killer wouldn't know that the spirit of Eggleston past would appear to announce that he held those damning markers on all of them.

A kind murderer might want to help out a few friends by getting rid of all the markers. But a distraught murderer might not even think of it.

It was worth a shot.

Where would the markers be? In Eggy's little office, clearly ... right down the Grand Corridor a few doors. But wait: what if the killer had gone back and taken the rest of the markers *after* Eg had made his startling announcement? He or she must have realized how incriminating one missing set would be.

Hänsel sat very still, concentrating, retracing all their steps since the ghost had told them. Except for the time BonBon went upstairs to fetch Ruby Red, they'd never been separated. If the markers were indeed in Eggy's office down here, neither Ruby nor the giant could have done any damage one story up. Hänsel had left all four of them together in the solarium; the killer had *not* gone back to return his/her markers or take the others ... because there had never been an opportunity to do so.

He fought down the urge to dash to Lord Eggleston's office and tear the place apart. He couldn't tell the others first; he didn't want the killer helping him look for incriminating evidence. But he needed a witness, someone who could swear Hänsel himself had not removed a set of markers in order to finger one member of their party—to convince Eggy to let the rest of them go. He needed someone he could trust.

Riding on a surge of adrenaline, Hänsel hurried back to the solarium. All four of them were still there, but the rickety TV trays had disappeared. Mittsy was dancing alone in the center of the room—eyes closed, earphones in place, Sony Walkman in hand, her flared bicolor cheerleader's skirt bouncing to music that no one else could hear.

Ruby Red and BonBon were facing each other across a small table, playing monte. Ruby's bright-red luster seemed to have faded a bit, but she gave Hänsel a tight little smile before returning to her game. The giant never looked up.

Philomena was standing by the casement window, looking down at the moat again. Hänsel eased up beside her and stood with his back to the rest of the room. "Wait about ten minutes," he said, low, "and then meet me at Eggy's office. You know where it is?"

She looked a question at him but said nothing, simply nodding.

Hänsel slipped unnoticed out of the solarium and headed for Lord Eggleston's office. He opened the door . . . and his eyes went straight to a rather elderly file cabinet standing in the corner. Hänsel didn't touch anything, postponing the search until Philomena arrived.

She didn't wait the full ten minutes. "What is it?" she asked a bit breathlessly.

He explained, and watched her face brighten at the thought of bringing this disastrous weekend to a close. Hänsel closed the heavy door behind them. He moved over to the file cabinet and gave the top drawer a good pull; it slid right open. "Didn't Eggy ever hear of security?" he complained.

Inside the file drawer was a blue fire-retardant box. Eggy had taken a Magic Marker and scrawled "Fluffy Bunny Downs" on the lid.

Carefully Hänsel lifted the box out of the drawer and carried it over to the desk. His hands were shaking as he removed the lid. Philomena crowded against him in her eagerness to see.

Inside were four standard mailing envelopes, stacked one atop the next. The topmost one had Hänsel's name on it in Eggy's scrawl. Hänsel tucked the envelope under one arm.

The next envelope was Philomena's. "Yippee!" she cried and snatched the envelope out of his hands. Hänsel grinned, relieved that his judgment of her had been right.

The third envelope had BonBon's name on it, Hänsel was surprised to see. And then he was surprised at his surprise. Had he, on some unconscious level, suspected the giant all along?

He looked at Philomena. "One envelope left. This one will tell us who the killer is."

She glared at him. "Stop milking it."

He lifted out the last envelope. The name written on the outside was that of Ruby Red.

Philomena looked stunned. "The cheerleader? *Mittsy* is the killer?"

Hänsel was a bit stunned himself. "Yeah. It's Mittsy, all right. Whaddaya know."

"Good lord. I thought it was Ruby."

Hänsel opened the envelopes to make sure they really did contain the markers. "Let's go tell the others."

Unexpectedly, Philomena burst out laughing. Hänsel glanced at her questioningly. "Sorry," she said. "I never did trust cheerleaders. And now I have an unimpeachable reason for not trusting them."

Back to the solarium. The red-skinned woman and the giant were still playing monte, but there was no sign of Mittsy. "Where's the rah-rah girl?" Hänsel asked.

"Up on the roof," said Ruby, "getting some sun. I dread sunburn myself."

Philomena raised an eyebrow. "Well, that's as good a place to play out the final scene as any. Maybe Mittsy will save us some hassle by leaping from the parapet."

"Phil!" Hänsel was shocked.

BonBon lifted his head. "Final scene?"

Hänsel handed him the envelope with "BonBon" written on it, then gave Ruby hers. "Your markers are inside. I have mine, and Phil has hers. One set was missing. Mittsy's."

A slow smile crept over the giant's face as he realized what that meant. "Very good," he nodded approvingly, "very good indeed."

Philomena smiled. "Clever Hans."

Ruby Red was at the fireplace burning her markers.

When she was satisfied they wouldn't come back to haunt her *again,* she stood up and faced the others. "To the parapet!" she cried dramatically. Back in form.

They rode the invisible elevator all the way to the top and found Mittsy dancing in the sun, still gripping her Walkman ... the very picture of the happy, wholesome young murderer.

Ruby walked over and lifted off her earphones. "The jig, as they say, is up."

"Huh?" Mittsy said.

Hänsel took a deep breath and confronted her with their evidence. "You should have taken all the envelopes. Don't try to deny it, Mittsy. We know you killed him."

She was pouting. "I didn't mean to," she mumbled.

"Excuse me?" BonBon said. "You didn't mean to stab him in the back?"

"I just meant to scare him ... you know. I took the Swiss knife that my Uncle Josiah gave me for my birthday—and I thought if I threatened him with it, he might give me back my markers. My daddy would kill me if he found out I'd been gambling again!"

"You stabbed him in the *back,*" Hänsel said. "Eggy didn't even see you!"

"Yeah, well, you know. I saw him standing there staring at his fire like he was God or something ... and, I dunno, I got *so mad* at him for doing this to me I just couldn't think straight and something came over me. I don't know what it was but all I could think of was how mad I was at him and then the next thing I know I'm sticking my knife in him."

There was a pause. "For what's it worth," Philomena said, "I think that's exactly the way it did happen. Completely mindless."

Hänsel asked, "How did you learn Eggy had your markers?"

"Oh, I just found them. You know."

"Found them? They were in a file drawer in his office!"

"Yeah, well, that's where I found them." They all stared at her. "Okay, so I'm nosy—all right? Didn't you ever look in someone else's medicine cabinet?"

"No," Ruby Red said wonderingly.

Mittsy rolled her eyes.

"Mittsy, one aspect of your current behavior is totally beyond my comprehension," BonBon said. "All along, you kept encouraging us to keep a positive attitude toward catching the killer. Why did you do that when *you* were the killer?"

"It was my cover!" the cheerleader wailed. "I thought you'd never suspect *me* if I kept urging you on all the time!"

"Double-reverse-whammy-pop-psychology?" Philomena asked.

"Yeah," Mittsy sobbed. "Like that."

There was nothing more to be said. "Well, one of us should go for the police," said Hänsel. "I assume Eggy will let us out now." No one jumped to volunter. "All right, I'll go. Keep an eye on *her*."

Three voices assured him that they would.

When Hänsel reached the main entrance of the castle, a thin streak of vapor was waiting for him there. "Well done, Hänsel," a familiar voice said. "I thank you from the bottom of my former heart."

"Eggy? Is that you? You're just a wisp of yourself."

"Yes, I seem to have lost the power to materialize. Strange."

"Well, how about letting down a drawbridge for me? Or maybe fix the phones? I have to get hold of the police."

"I can't do anything about the phones," Lord Eggleston said regretfully, "and I burned the drawbridge, if you recall."

"I remember. Can't you, er, materialize a new one for me?"

"It's odd, but I no longer have any of my special powers. Gone, every one of them. As if I no longer needed them." There was a prolonged pause, and then: "Ah. I have been summoned to a different plane. I'm afraid you're on your own, old boy—good luck, and good-bye! Remember meeeeeeee!" *Hamlet* again.

The ghost was gone.

" 'Bye, Eggy," Hänsel said softly.

He walked to the edge of the moat and looked in. The sharks were gone; Hänsel watched for ten minutes without seeing so much as a ripple. Only a few hundred yards of ditchwater keeping him from reaching the local constabulary.

Hänsel shrugged and hunkered down to unlace his shoes, preparing for his swim.

THE SOFT TERRIBLE MUSIC

by George Zebrowski

George Zebrowski, whose twenty-six books include novels, short fiction collections, anthologies, and a forthcoming book of essays, has been nominated for the Nebula Award and the Theodore Sturgeon Memorial Award. He shows himself a master of the short story in this gripping tale of love and revenge in a strange futuristic house in the Antarctic wilderness.

Each of Castle Silverstone's one hundred windows looked out on the landscape of a different country.

The iron drawbridge opened on Mars.

A stainless steel side gate led out into a neighborhood in Luna City.

A small bronze gate opened in a small public place aboard Odalisque, the largest of the Venusian floating islands drifting high above the hot, dry desert of the planet.

A sliding double door opened through the sheer face of a cliff overlooking Rio de Janiero, where one could stand before an uncrossable threshold.

There was also a door that led nowhere. It was no different in function than the other doors, except that it was not set to any destination. This castle, like any true home, was the expression of a man's insides, desolate places included.

When the castle was not powered-up for full extension, it stood on a rocky hillside in Antarctica's single warm valley, where it had been built in the early twenty-second century by Wolfgang Silverstone, who rented it out occasionally for political summits. In design it was a bouquet of tall, gleaming cylinders, topped with turrets from a variety of castle building periods. The cylinders surrounded a central courtyard, and the brief connecting walls were faced with gray stone that had been quarried from the valley.

The castle got its name as much from the flecks of fool's silver in the stone as from the name of its builder. The castle also differed from other extended homes, because it was not linked to the houses of friends and relatives, or to apartments and pieds-a-terre in major cities. The castle had its vistas, and one could step out into them, but its exits were private. Some of them even looped back into chambers within the castle.

Few homes had ever been built with as much care and attention to a human being's future needs, to his own future failings. Deep within himself, Silverstone knew what would happen, had accepted it, and had made provisions for his fate.

Halfway through construction, he altered some of the keep's plans to attract a single woman—Gailla, the woman with the perfect memory, who by age eighty had read and retained every novel written since the eighteenth century. Silverstone, in a fit of fibbing, told her that his castle had a library of one thousand previously lost and unknown works, that he found her irresistible, and that if she married him for the minimum allowable term he would give her the key to the library.

As he waited for Gailla's answer, his nights trembled with odd dreams, in which he felt that he had always known her, even though he was certain that they had never met—at least not physically. Upon waking, he would conclude that he must have seen her image somewhere; or, more simply, that he wanted her so desperately that his unconscious was inventing an unbroken history of romance, to convince him that they had always been together in their love.

What was five years of a term marriage, he told her; another century of life waited. He was not unattractive for a child of fifty, even if he said so himself. The prize of books he offered seemed to draw her curiosity. Its very existence intrigued her. But secret libraries were not unknown. The Vatican still had much of one locked away, and the history of the Middle East and North Africa was filled with stories of vanished libraries waiting under the sands along ancient, dried-up waterways. One more lost library was not an impossibility.

Fearful that she would leave him if he did not make good on his original boast, he told her that his treasure was a library of books that had been saved from the great "paper loss" of 1850–2050, when most acid paper books had crumbled to dust because there had been no money or will to preserve them; the world had been too busy dealing with global warming and rising ocean levels. He had found the books on his forays into various abandoned Antarctic bases, where the dry cold had preserved the paper. They were mostly mysteries, science fiction, adventure, suspense, bestsellers, and romance novels brought by the base personnel for amusement. Only about a thousand volumes.

As it turned out, she soon discovered that the books were a fraud. Silverstone confessed that he had found only a few; the rest were written to complete extant scraps, cover designs and jacket blurbs, by paid specialists who did not know for whom they were working or that they were part of a larger effort. But fraud or not, it was at least an echo of a newly discovered library, and given enough time, it would become interesting in itself, he assured her, and it seemed to him that she appreciated the compliment of his ploy.

He told her how paper had been made and aged, covers painted, fingerprints of the dead scattered through the volumes. Gailla seemed delighted—for about a month—until she saw how bad the books were, how trite and poorly written. Silverstone was delighted by her bedroom habits—also for about a month. She lost interest in him at about the same time she was able to prove that the books, from internal anachronisms, were fakes.

"How dare you!" she screamed, careful to put on a convincing show. "Why did you do it?"

"To attract you," he answered, astonished by her perfectly controlled bitterness, which seemed to hide another purpose. "Are you sorry? Would you have bonded with me for myself?"

"You never gave me the chance!" she sang out in a voice that began as a low grumble and ended in a high soprano.

"But you would have," he demanded, "in other circumstances?"

The question seemed to upset her greatly, and she gave no answer; but Silverstone was convinced that she was holding back a no, and he began to wonder why he had ever been attracted to her. It had seemed to him at the beginning that she would alter the course of his life, change the unknown fate that lay hidden in the back of his mind; and now it seemed to him that nothing could save him from it. It was as if she had known all along about the abyss that threatened to open before him, and was waiting for the right moment to push him into it—after she had tormented him with doubt for a sufficient period of time.

* * *

He often went to one window after another, as if looking for a landscape into which he might disappear. Autumn scenes drew him, especially mountainous ones with streams, where the leaves on the trees were turning gold and brown. Then he hungered for the sterility of desert sands; and this gave way to a need for lush jungles, and then windswept plains. He became insatiable, passing from window to window like a thief in a museum, eyeing the views greedily, feeling that there could never be enough windows.

Sometimes he liked to step out on Mars, onto his small patch of it, where he could stand and marvel at the honeycomb of habitats spreading across the planet. Five-sided, one thousand-foot-high transparent cells, immediately habitable in the Martian sunlight—they would one day roof over the red planet with an indoor-outdoors, thus solving the problem of keeping a permanent atmosphere on a low-gravity world. Here was an achievement he envied, wishing that he had been its architect. It was an accomplishment in the making that no amount of inherited wealth could buy.

There were afternoons when he would slip through the gate into Luna City and wander through the VR-game bazaars, where the miners bought their cruel distractions.

Passing into his small hotel room on Odalisque, the Venusian floating island, he would shower and dress for dinner at the Ishtar Restaurant, where huge wall-screens revealed a radar imaging of the bleak landscape fifty kilometers below, which waited for human ambitions to make a mark on it.

And at least once a month he would stand in the alcove above Rio and stare out at the city below as if it were his hometown, imagining the old streets as if he had once known them.

And again, as with the windows, there were not enough doors to satisfy him. Every *there* became a *here* when he came to it, losing the longing-magic that drew him.

On the battlements at night, as he considered his deteriorating situation with Gailla, it was—the stars! the stars!—that gave him any kind of peace. By day he felt exposed to the sky, whether a white sheet of overcast or the brilliant glare of yellow sun in a deep blue sky. In the evenings, when he took a short walk across the bare valley of stone, it was always a walk across himself, in search of something he had lost. When he stopped and looked back at the castle, he felt that he had left himself behind. Returning, he felt better, except that Gailla was still there, an intruder deep within him, and he regretted bitterly ever having let her in.

Trying to think how he might extricate himself, he would visit the castle's dungeons, where the heat exchangers drew strength from the hot springs beneath the bedrock to run the electric generators. Here, also, were the brightly lit hothouses that grew his flowers and vegetables. He did not feel exposed beneath this well-defined, contained, and nourishing daylight. Sitting there, watching the vegetables grow, he calmed himself enough to think that he would simply let the minimum term of his marriage run out. There was only a year and a half left. That would be the simplest solution. Until then, he would simply keep out of her way.

But asleep in his own room, he would often hear her moving inside him, opening doors and closing them, as if looking for something. He would wake up and hear her doing the same thing again, and he wondered what she had come into him to find. And he realized, although some part of him had known it all along, that there were two castles, that there had been two castles from the very moment he had conceived the plans for its construction in this valley—one castle outside and one within himself, and that Gailla had invaded both of them.

He began to wonder what she was looking for, and decided that he would have to spy on her to find out. Had she married him to steal something? What did he have that required so much effort? If it was so desirable, maybe he should also know about this prize, and prevent her from stealing it. What could it be? He already had everything that money could buy.

During the night of January 31st, he slept lightly, and when he heard her opening and closing doors, he got up and dressed, then went out to see what he could learn. He found her on the second level of the north turret, going from room to room down the spiral staircase, opening every door, shining a light inside, then backing away and leaving the door slightly ajar. He listened to her from behind a Freas tapestry, until she reached the bottom. There she sighed as if greatly satisfied, and went down the final curve of the stairway into the main hall below.

He crept out from his hiding place and hurried to the railing, from which he looked down and saw her pacing before the great fireplace, where the dying embers of a collapsed universe still glowed. She was dressed in her outdoor jumpsuit, but it could not conceal her tall, slender shape. At last she sat down in one of the great high chairs and closed her eyes in contentment.

It made no sense at all.

"You can come down, Wolfy," she called out suddenly. "I know you're there!"

Was she bluffing, he wondered. Had she called out like this on several nights, out of a general suspicion?

She looked up suddenly and pointed to where he stood. "I can't quite see you in this wretched light, but you're there in the shadow near the railing."

She was not bluffing. He leaned over and said, "I'll

be right with you," then came down the stairs, hoping that now he would at last learn what she was after, crossed the hall, and sat down in the high-backed chair facing hers.

Staring at her intently, he was about to ask what she was looking for.

"Be patient," she said, expecting his question.

He looked at her, puzzled. "And you bonded with me just to ... carry on some kind of search? Whatever for?"

"You'll know soon enough, Wolfy."

"Do you even know yourself?"

"I know," she said, and as the redness of the embers painted her face, it seemed that she was about to become someone else.

"So tell me," he said. "It's something I'll have to know sooner or later—right?"

She nodded grimly and said, "More than you want to know. But before I tell you, Wolfy, be advised that people know where I am."

"What do you think I'll do to you?" he asked with surprise.

"Let me tell you a story ..."

He settled back in his chair.

"During the plague deaths of the twenty-first century," she began, "a man was born in Rio. He grew up to be a thief, a murderer, a crooked politician, a mayor of more than one city, and finally the president of a country. In a depopulated world, his talents were needed, and he did well in administrative posts, although always to his own benefit. But as the century grew old and the population began to increase again, people became more jealous of political and economic power, and sought to take back from him what he had gained. He defended himself, of course, but when he saw that he would be brought down, either by assassination or by imprisonment, he decided that he had to die. So he went to a rich friend who was a recluse, killed him, and then stepped into the man's identity, through somatic changes of his own physique, which already resembled that of the victim, and finally through selective memory implants. And then he went one step further, desperate to cover his trail completely. He wiped away his own self to prevent capture, and became Wolfgang Silverstone, as completely as anyone could, short of having actually been Wolfgang Silverstone."

"What!" Silverstone cried out.

"Sit down and calm yourself, Wolfy. You can't know right now that any of this is true, but trust me, the trail is still there, because you didn't want to hide it completely."

"That's crazy. It's the same as suicide!"

"No, the man from Rio planned to come back."

"What?"

"Yes, he left a 'trigger' inside his stolen persona, so that one day it would resurrect his earlier self. I'm certain of that. This trigger is what I've been looking for. It's here in this castle, and even you don't know where it is, even though you had it built as part of your way back. The man you were was too egotistical to have allowed himself to become someone else permanently. You're not the man you were, but you will be, very soon now."

Silverstone laughed. "But how?"

"There's a pre-trigger," she said, "that will guide you to the place at the appropriate time, and there you will know how to free your true self and become again the man who killed the original Silverstone." She recited the words softly, as if she had rehearsed them a thousand times—which, of course, she had.

Silverstone stood up and lurched toward her, but she pointed a weapon at him wearily and said, "Sit down, Wolfy. Do you think I would have told you all this without some insurance?"

He stopped, then stumbled back into his chair. "Who are you?" he asked. "What is all this to you?"

She shrugged. "Police—and there's no statute of limitations on murder."

He sat back, stunned. "But surely you see ... that you have no proof beyond this story you've told me. You personally don't know that it's true. You're just putting bits and pieces together."

"You've been getting restless lately," she said, "as if you were looking for something—and you have been, constantly. You're getting close to the time you set for triggering your own return. You see, even in your persona state, your guilt remains, buried deeply, of course. Even your building this castle is part of that. You built it as a way of exploring yourself, of setting the means for your return. You'll give me all the proof I need, because you'll go to a certain prepared room at the appointed time and come out guilty of murder. It's why I'm here, and why I married you."

He laughed. "But I can't know that any of this is true!" he shouted. "Even you admit that. If I don't go to this room, you'll have no case. Even if I do go in, I don't have to say anything when I come out. Why did you bother to tell me all this? You might have done better leaving me in the dark. Mind you, that's still assuming any of this is true."

"I want you to suffer for a while."

"Did you find the room? You certainly spent enough nights annoying me with your explorations."

"Shut up, Wolfy. You're just a clever sociopath living through a dead man's memories. You set up a time for retrieving yourself, after stealing from people in troubled times. I suppose even a thug wants to be himself, to come back from, in effect, being dead."

"How long must a man lie dead," he recited, puzzled by the words that came out of him. "Forever is too long. There must be mercy somewhere."

"See, you're in there, all right," she replied, "speaking out even though you don't quite know it."

Shaken, he asked derisively, "Did you call him Wolfy? And were you his she-wolf?"

"Shut up!"

"You'll never call anyone but me Wolfy again," he said. "What can getting this other guy bring you?"

"He'll be at peace. I'll be at peace, knowing that the murderer of my beloved has been exposed."

"Oh, then you won't kill me yourself? You'll just have them take me away."

"But first you'll have to live again as the man you were."

He sat slightly forward in his chair and her hand tensed around her gun. "But don't you see," he said earnestly. "I'm not responsible. I know only what you've told me about all this. I don't know or feel anything about the crime."

"Don't worry, it'll all come back to you. That's why you did it this way, so you could say that you weren't responsible. It's part of your crime."

"Really?"

"You set it up, and I've caught you."

"Are you sure? Beware, you may not like what you find."

"Don't threaten me," she said. "You are Benito Alonso Robles, the man from Rio, who killed Wolfgang Silverstone in 2049 and downloaded the essentials of his personality into your own, overwriting yourself for a timed period in order to evade the police. Murder was only your last crime, designed to conceal all the others. We can't get you on many of those, but we will certainly get you for murder."

"How clever of me," Silverstone said. "So what now?"

She did not answer him.

"Consider," he continued, "that if I am all that is left of Silverstone, your so-called beloved, then why didn't I remember you when we met?"

"We were no longer together when you killed him," she said, "and sometime before that, in order to ease his pain, he had suppressed his experiences with me. Still, I think something in you seemed to know me."

"Ah! And then I fell in love with you again. That was why I was so earnest, so eager. But how could I know, my dear?" He held his arms out to her. "And now you want to destroy all that survives of your beloved, even after what was left of him was strong enough to come after you again!"

"No—you're only a fragment of him, and you've developed in ways he would not have, had he lived. For one thing, there's a different unconscious below the superimposed personality and its memories, and that makes you very different."

"Still, I'm all that's left of Wolfy dearest."

"But not any part that knows me very well," she said coldly. "Why did you pick him? Had he done you any wrong?"

"How do I know? If all this is true, then he was simply convenient, I suppose. Ask me later—if we get to later, and if any of this is true."

"Get up," she said. "We're going upstairs."

"Is it time, my dearest?"

"I don't know. Do you feel anything? You may have already spoken the pre-trigger."

He stood up and she motioned for him to climb the great stairs to the second level of the north tower. As he started up, she followed well below him, gun aimed at his back.

"Keep going," she said when he reached the landing.

"How do you know it's up here?" he asked.

"Where would you say, then?"

"The lower levels?" he said, laughing. "How would I know? If what you say is true, I may even be the man you say I killed—I mean physically as well as whatever identity was fed in."

"You're not," she said. "I've already had your DNA checked."

He laughed again. "Of course, the opportunity presented itself to you on more than one occasion. You simply carried a sample away in you." He turned around and faced her with open hands. "Gailla," he said, "you don't know what you're doing and neither do I, by your own claims. You don't know how the pre-trigger will kick in, or where this ... this restoration will take place. And you admit that as far as I know, I am Silverstone ..."

"You're not him," she said. "That much I know."

"Yes, yes, the DNA. But I only have your word for that too."

"Do you feel anything?" she asked. "An impulse to go somewhere, or say something to yourself?"

"Not particularly."

"Just a few moments ago you wanted to go to the lower levels below the castle."

"An idle remark."

"It might mean something."

"Well, I have lived with a vague expectation of some kind for a while now. It came to me just after we ... no longer got along."

"Really."

"Maybe your being a cop spooked me at some basic level." He turned around suddenly and watched her tense. He waited a moment, then asked, "What do you really want from me? Simple revenge, is that it?"

"No, I just want you to know again, consciously, what you did, and let the law do with you as it will. That's revenge enough."

"But what if I never remember?"

"That's what we're here for," she said. "You took him from me a long time ago, and denied us a chance of ever getting back to each other. We might have by now."

"It's pretty to think so, and sad that you do."

"You don't really care."

"Not much. You're purging me of any desire I once had for you."

"Sorry I can't say the same. It was never there."

"Are you sure?"

"Turn around and get going."

He smiled, turned, and climbed the spiral.

"Stop right there," she said suddenly. "Face the door on your right."

He obeyed. "Why here?"

"Process of elimination," she said. "You have never entered this room since we've been together. Do you recall ever entering it?"

"As a matter of fact, I don't."

"Go in."

He pressed his palm to the plate, and the door slid open. He stepped inside. She came in right behind him. The door slid shut. An overhead panel of light blinked on, filling the room with bright yellow light, and he saw another door at the end of the room.

Then he looked to his right and saw the portrait on the wall.

He turned and gazed up at a dark painting of someone sitting at a mahogany desk. It was an old man with thin white hair teased out to twice the size of his head. He was dressed in a bright red nineteenth century military tunic that seemed to be choking his wrinkled neck. There were no markings on the tunic to indicate nationality. The man's mouth was closed tightly....

And as he stared at the face, a flood of returning

memory filled his mind, and he knew that this was the trigger. And with his memories came also the remembrance of the day he had set the trigger at the portrait of Silverstone's ancestor. Then, packed away, the painting had waited for the castle to be built, where he would one day come to himself again, secure, reestablished, reawakening to himself again, slowly, secretly, safely bringing himself out of the sleepwalker's life that had been necessary for his survival.

He waited as his identity returned. It blossomed within him, realms of self and memory fitting themselves into vast empty spaces—but Silverstone stayed with him all the way, showing no sign of fading. He turned to face Gailla and said, "He's still with me . . . I can't get rid of him!"

"He'll keep you company at your trial," Gailla said joylessly.

"But you'll be killing what's left of your old love!" he cried.

"I've been prepared for some time," she said. "They'll wipe you clean and start you up as someone else. It'll be all over for both of us."

"No!" he cried, turned, and rushed to the other door. She did not fire, and he knew that she couldn't, and that he would have enough time to do what he now remembered was his last recourse, waiting for him if something went wrong.

He palmed the door, and still she had not fired. As the door slid open, he knew that she was hesitating, unable to kill the last of her lover. And he felt it also, the mountainous regret at having killed him. He could not banish it, nor the vast cloud of the man's mental remains. It refused to fade away, invading his unused regions with new patterns, and he knew that he was too weak to wipe them out. The impulse to love had infected him with weak sentiments, and he knew that she felt it also. The bodily memories of their lovemaking had softened them both. That was why she had not killed him as soon as he had regained himself. Or was she preparing him for when she would rebuild her old lover by amplifying the stubborn echoes that remained until they burgeoned and became again the personality she had known? Maybe she knew how to resurrect him and had planned it all along, and would carry out her plan after sufficient revenge had been visited on him.

Well, he would deny her that. He could still take everything from her, and achieve one last victory over a world that had opposed his every desire from the start, always forcing him to take what he wanted. There was nothing else he could do.

"Wait!" she cried as the door opened into chaos. It would have been a way to somewhere, but he had deliberately left it set to no destination—realizing that he might need its sudden exit one day.

As he tumbled into the black obscenity of existence without form, he saw her in the doorway, her mouth open wide in horror and regret, her arms reaching out to him uselessly. And as he felt himself deforming, changing, losing all sense of time and space, he knew that his death would not be quick, that no supernatural damnation could ever have equaled the slow loss of himself that was just beginning.

Gailla was shooting at him now, and he imagined that it was a gesture of pity, an effort to shorten the suffering of what was left of her lover. The third bullet opened his chest, entering slowly, as if unsure of how to obey the laws of physics in this realm. It explored his pain, telling him that he had made this final fate for himself by building the castle and its doorways, with every fleeting, trivial decision—step by inexorable step to one end, to bring him here, to this death.

"Gailla," Silverstone whispered through the pain of her bullet's dancing, failed mercy. "I'm still here."

Then Robles closed his eyes and heard the soft terrible music filtering in from behind the show of things. It was an inhuman music, with nothing of song or dance, or memory in it. It was a music of crushed glass, severed nerves, and brute rumblings, preparing the way for a theme of fear.

And as Robles knew himself in his pain, he yearned for death because Silverstone was still with him.

HELD SAFE BY MOONLIGHT AND VINES

by Charles de Lint

Charles de Lint is a Canadian writer and musician who established himself in the nineteen eighties as a prolific author of fantasy novels and stories. In this dappled tale of light and darkness he sketches the psychological castles we sometimes must build in the wilderness inside us.

Lillie's in the graveyard again, looking for ghosts. She just can't stay away.

"I'm paying my respects," she says, but it doesn't make sense.

These days All Souls Cemetery's about as forgotten as the people buried in it. The land belongs to some big company now and they're just waiting for the paperwork to go through at city hall. One day soon they'll be moving what's left of the bodies, tearing down all those old-fashioned mausoleums and crypts, and putting up something shiny and new. Who's going to miss it? Nobody goes there now except for the dealers with their little packets of oblivion and junkies looking for a fix.

The only people who care about the place are from the Crowsea Heritage Society. And Lillie. Everybody else just wants to see it go. Everybody else likes the idea of making a place gone wild safe again, never mind they don't put it quite that way. But that's what they're thinking. You can see it in the back of their eyes when they talk about it.

See, there's something that scares most people about the night, something that rises out of old memories, out of the genetic soup we all carry around inside us. Monsters in closets when we were kids and farther back still, a long way, all the way back to the things waiting out there where the fire's light can't reach. It's not something anybody talks about, but I know that's what they see in All Souls because I can see it, too.

It's got nothing to do with the drug deals going down. People know a piece of the night is biding in there, thinking about them, and they can't wait to see it go. Even the dealers. You see them hanging around by the gates, money moves from one hand to the other, packets of folded paper follow suit, everything smooth, moves like magic. They're fearless, these guys. But they don't go any farther in than they have to. Nobody does except for Lillie.

"There's been nobody buried there in fifty years," I tell her, but that just gets her back up.

"All the more reason to give those old souls some respect," she says.

But that's not it. I know she's looking for ghosts. Thing is, I don't know why.

Alex's problem is he wants an answer for everything. All he ever does is go around asking questions. Never lets a thing lie. Always has to know what's going on and why. Can't understand that some things don't have reasons. Or that some people don't feel like explaining themselves. They just do what feels right. Get an idea in their head and follow it through and don't worry about what someone else is going to think or if anybody else understands.

In Alex's world there's only right and wrong, black

and white. Me, I fall through the cracks of that world. In my head, it's all gray. In my head, it's all like walking in the twilight, a thousand shades of moonglow and dusky skies and shadow.

He thinks of me sitting here in the dark, all those old stone mausoleums standing around me, old and battered like the tenements leaning against each other on the streets where we grew up, and it spooks him. But All Souls comforts me, I don't know why. Half the trees inside are dead, the rest are dying. Most of the grass is yellow and brown and the only flowers in this place these days grow on weeds, except in one corner where a scraggly old rose bush keeps on trying, tough old bugger doesn't know enough to give up. The stone walls are crumbling down, the cast-iron gates haven't worked in years. There's a bunch of losers crowded around those gates, cutting deals, more nervous of what's here, inside, than of the man coming down and busting them. I come in over the wall and go deep, where the shadows hide me, and they never even know I'm here. Nobody does, except for Alex and he just doesn't understand.

I know what Alex sees when he looks at this place. I see it, too, at first, each time I come. But after a while, when I'm over the wall and inside, walking the narrow lanes in between the stones and tombs, uneven cobbles underfoot, the shadows lying thick everywhere I look, it gets different. I go someplace else. I don't hear the dealers, I don't see the junkies. The cemetery's gone, the city's gone, and me, I'm gone, too.

The only thing still with me are the walls, but they're different in that other place. Not so worn down. The stones have been fit together without mortar, each one cunningly placed against the other and solid. Those walls go up ten feet, and you'd have to ram them with a bulldozer before they'd come down.

Inside, it's a garden. Sort of. A wild place. A tangle

of bushes and briars, trees I've got no name for, and vines hanging everywhere. A riot of flowers haunt the ground cover, pale blossoms that catch the moonlight and hold it in their petals.

The moonlight. That moon is so big in this place it feels like it could swallow the world. When I stand there in the wild garden and look up at it, I feel small, like I'm no bigger than the space of time between one moment and the next, but not the same way I feel small anywhere else. Where I come from, there are millions of people living everywhere and each one of them's got their own world. It's so easy to lose a part of yourself in those worlds, to just find yourself getting sucked away until there's next to nothing left of who you are. But I don't have to be careful about that here. There aren't any of those millions of people here and that moon, it doesn't swallow up who I am, its golden light fills me up, reveling in what it knows me to be. I'm small in its light, sure, but the kind of small that can hold everything there is to be held. The moon's just bigger, that's all. Not more important than me, just different.

Those junkies don't know what they're missing, never getting any farther inside the gates than the first guy in a jean vest with the right price.

Trouble is, Lillie doesn't understand danger. She's never had to go through the hard times some of us did, never really seen what people can do to each other when they're feeling desperate or just plain mean. She grew up poor, like everybody else in our neighborhood, but her family loved her and she didn't get knocked around the way those of us who didn't have her kind of parents did. She was safe at home; out on the streets, I always looked after her, made sure the hard cases left her alone.

I'm working as a bouncer at Chic Cheeks the night

I hear she's been going to All Souls, so I head down
there after my shift to check things out. It's a good
thing I do. Some of the guys hanging around by the
gates have gotten bored and happened to spot her, all
alone in there and looking so pretty. Guess they decided they were going to have themselves a little fun.
Bad move. But then they didn't expect me to come
along.

I remember a teacher I had in junior high telling
me one time how wood and stone make poor conduc-
tors. Well, they conduct pain pretty good, as those
boys find out. I introduce one of them face-first to a
tombstone and kind of make a mess of his nose, knock
out a couple of teeth. His pals aren't chickenshit, I'll
give them that much. I hear the *snickt* of their blades
snapping open, so I drop the first guy. He makes some
kind of gurgling noise when he hits the ground and
rolls onto my boot. I push him away and then ignore
him. He's too busy feeling his pain to cause me any
immediate grief. I turn to his buddies, feeling a little
pissed off now, but we don't get into it.

"Oh, Christ," one of them says, recognizing me.

"We didn't mean nothing, Al," the other one says.
They're putting their knives away, backing up.

"We knew she was one of your people, we never
would've touched her. I swear it, man."

Guess I've got a bit of a rep. Nothing serious. I'm
not some big shot. What it's got to do with is my
old man.

Crazy Eddie is what they used to call him on the
streets. Started running numbers for the bosses back
when he was a kid, then moved into collections, which
is where he got his name. You don't want to think it
of your own flesh and blood, but the old man was a
psycho. He'd do any crazed thing came to mind if you
couldn't pay up. You're in for a few yards, you better
cough it up, don't matter what you've got to do to get

the money, because he'd as soon as cut your throat as collect the bread.

After a while the bosses started using him for hits, the kind where they're making a statement. Messy, crazy hits. He did that for years until he got into a situation he couldn't cut his way out of. Cops took him away in a bunch of little bags.

Man, I'll never forget that day. I was doing a short stretch in the county when I found out and I near laughed myself sick. I'd hated that old bastard for the way he'd treated ma, for what he did to my sister Juney. He used to kick the shit out of me on a regular basis, but I could deal with that. It was the things he did to them.... I knew one day I'd take him down, didn't matter he was my old man. I just hadn't got around to it yet. Hadn't figured out a way to let the bosses know it was personal, not some kind of criticism of their business.

Anyway, I'm not mean like the old man was, I'll tell you that straight-off, but I purely don't take crap from anybody. I don't have to get into it too much anymore. People take a look at me now and think, blood is blood. They see my old man's crazy eyes when they look in mine, and they find some other place to be than where I'm standing.

So I make the point with these boys that they don't want to mess with Lillie, and all it takes is a tap against a tombstone for them to get the message. I let them get their pal and take off, then I go to see what Lillie's doing.

It's the strangest thing. She's just standing there by one of those old stone mausoleums, swaying back and forth, looking off into the space between a couple of those stone crypts. I scratch my head, and take a closer look myself closer. She's mesmerized by something, but damned if I know what. I can hear her humming to herself, still doing that swaying thing,

mostly with her upper body, back and forth, smiling
that pretty smile of hers, short black hair standing up
at attention the way it always does. I'm forever trying
to talk her into growing it long, but she laughs at me
whenever I do.

I guess I watch her for about an hour that night. I
remember thinking she'd been sampling some of the
dealers' wares until she suddenly snaps out of it. I
fade back into the shadows at that point. Don't want
her to think I've been spying on her. I'm just looking
out for her, but she doesn't see it that way. She gets
seriously pissed at me, and I hate having Lillie mad
at me.

She walks right by me, still humming to herself. I
can see she's not stoned, just Lillie-strange. I watch
her climb up some vines where one of the walls is
broken and low, and then she's gone. I go out the
front way, just to remind the boys what's what, and
catch up with Lillie a few blocks away, casual-like.
Don't ask her where she's been. Just say how-do,
make sure she's okay without letting on I'm worried,
and head back to my own place.

I don't know exactly when it is I realize she's looking for ghosts in there. It just comes to me one day,
slips in sideways when I'm thinking about something
else. I try talking to her about it from time to time,
but all she does is smile, the way only she can.

"You wouldn't understand," she says.

"Try me."

She shakes her head. "It's not something *to* understand," she says. "It's just something you do. The less
you worry at it, the more it makes sense."

She's right. I don't understand.

There's a boy living in the garden. He reminds me
a little of Alex. It's not that they look the same. This
kid's all skin and bones, held together with wiry mus-

cles. Naked and scruffy, crazy tangled hair full of burrs
and twigs and stuff, peach-fuzz vying with a few actual
beard hairs, dink hanging loose when he's not holding
onto it—I guess you've got to do something with your
hands when you don't have pockets. Alex, he's like a
fridge with arms and legs. Big, strong, and loyal as all
get-out. Not school-smart, but bright. You couldn't
pick a couple of guys that looked less alike.

The reason they remind me of each other is that
they're both a little feral. Wild things. Dangerous if
you don't approach them right.

I get to the garden one night, and the trees are full
of grackles. They're feeding on berries and making a
racket like I've never heard before. I know it's a murder of ravens and a parliament of crows, but what do
you call that many grackles all together? I'm walking
around, peering up at them in the branches, smiling
at the noise, when I see the boy sitting up in one of
the trees, looking back down at me.

Neither of us say anything for a long time. There's
just the racket of the birds playing against the silence
we hold between us.

"Hey there," I say finally. "Is this your garden?"

"It's my castle."

I smile. "Doesn't look much like a castle."

"Got walls," he tells me.

"I suppose."

He looks a little put out. "It's a start."

"So when are you going to start building the rest?"
I ask.

He looks at me, the way a child looks at you when
you've said something stupid.

"Go away," he says.

I decide I can be as much of an asshole as he's
being and play the why game with him.

"Why?" I ask.

"Because I don't like you."

"Why?"

"Because you're stupid."

"Why?"

"I don't know. Guess you were born that way."

"Why?"

"Have to ask your parents that."

"Why?"

"Because I don't know."

"Why?"

He finally catches on. Pulling a twig free from the branch he's sitting on, he throws it at me. I duck and it misses. When I look back up, he's gone. The noise of the grackles sounds like laughter now.

"Guess I deserve that," I say.

I don't see the boy for a few visits after that, but the next time I do, he pops up out of the thick weeds underfoot and almost gives me a heart attack.

"I could've just snuck up on you and killed you," he tells me. "Just like that."

He leans against a tree, one hand hanging down in between his legs like he's got a piece of treasure there.

"Why would you want to do that?" I ask.

His eyes narrow. "I don't want to play the why game again."

"I'm not. I really want to know."

"It's not a thing I do or don't want to do," he tells me. "I'm just saying I could. It was a piece of information, that's all."

There's something incongruous about the way he says this—innocent and scary, all at the same time. It reminds me of when I was a little girl, how it took me the longest time to admit that I could ever like a boy, they were all such assholes. All except Alex. I wouldn't have minded so much if he'd pulled my hair or pushed me on the schoolyard, but he never did. He was always so sweet and polite to me and then after classes, he'd go out and beat up the guys that had been mean to me. I guess I was flattered, at first, but then I realized it wasn't a very nice thing to do. You have to understand, we're both still in grade school when this is going on. Things weren't the same back then the way they are for kids now. We sure never had to walk through metal detectors to get into the school.

Anyway, I asked him to stop and he did. At least so far as I know, he did. I wonder sometimes, though. Sometimes my boyfriends have the weirdest accidents—walking into doors and stuff like that.

This one time Lillie's going out with this college-type. Dave, his name is. Dave Taylor. Nice enough looking joe, I suppose, but he's not exactly the most faithful guy you'd ever meet. Happened to run into him getting a little on the side one night, so I walk up to his table and tell him I have to have a word with him, would his lady friend excuse us for a moment? He doesn't want to step outside, so I suggest to his lady friend that she go powder her nose, if she understands my meaning.

"So what the hell's this all about?" Dave asks when she's gone. He's blustering, trying to make up for the face he feels he lost in front of his girlfriend.

"I'm a friend of Lillie's," I tell him.

"Yeah? So?"

"So I don't like the idea of her getting hurt."

"Hey, what she doesn't know—"

"I'm not discussing this," I say. "I'm telling you."

The guy shakes his head. "Or what? I suppose you're going to go running to her and—"

I hit him once, a quick jab to the head that rocks him back in his seat. Doesn't even break the skin on my knuckles, but I can see he's hurting.

"I don't care who you go out with, or if you cheat on them," I say, keeping my voice conversational. "I just don't want you seeing Lillie any more."

He's holding a hand to his head where the skin's going all red. Looks a little scared like I'm going to hit him again, but I figure I've already made my point.

"Do we understand each other?" I ask him.

He gives me a quick nod. I start to leave, then pause for a moment. He gives me a worried look.

"And Dave," I say. "Let's not get stupid about this. No one's got to know we had this little talk, right?"

"What ... whatever you say...."

I wonder about Alex—worry about him, I guess you could say. He never seems to be happy or sad. He just is. It's not like he's cold, keeps it all bottled in or anything, and he's always got a smile for me, but there doesn't seem to be a whole lot of passion in his life. He doesn't talk much, and never about himself. That's another way he and the boy in the garden differ. The boy's always excited about something or other, always ready for any sort of mad escapade. And he loves to talk.

"Old castle rock," the boy tells me one time. His eyes are gleaming with excitement. "That's what these walls are made of. They were part of this castle on the other side and now they're here. There's going to be more of the castle coming, I just know there is. Towers and turrets and stables and stuff."

"When's the rest of it going to come?" I ask.

He shrugs his bony shoulders. "Dunno. Could be a long time. But I can wait."

"Where's it coming from?" I ask then.

"I told you. From the other side."

"The other side of what?"

He gives me that look again, the one that says don't you know *anything*?

"The other side of the walls," he says.

I've never looked over the walls—not from the garden. That's the first thing Alex would have done. He may not have passion in his life, but he's sure got purpose. He's always in the middle of something, always knows what's going on. Never finished high school, but he's smarter than most people I meet because he's never satisfied until he's got everything figured out. He's in the public library all the time, reading, studying stuff. Never does anything with what he knows, but he sure knows a lot.

I walk over to the nearest of those tall stone walls and the boy trails along behind me, joins me when I start to go up. It's an easier climb than you might think, plenty of finger- and toe-holds, and we scale it like a couple of monkeys, grinning at each other when we reach the top. It's flat up there, with lots of room on the rough stone to sit and look out, only there's nothing to see. Just fog, thick, the way it rolls into the city from the lake sometimes. It's like the world ends on the other side of these walls.

"It's always like this," the boy says.

I turn to look at him. My first impression was that he'd come in over the walls himself and I never learned anything to contradict it, but now I'm not so sure anymore. I mean, I knew this garden was some place else, some place magical that you could only reach the way you get to Neverneverland—you have to really want to get there. You might stumble in the first time, but after that you have to be really determined to get back in. But I also thought the real world was still out there, on the other side of the garden's magic, held back only by the walls.

"Where did you come from?" I ask him.

He gives me this look that manages to be fierce and sad, all at the same time.

"Same place as you," he says and touches a closed fist to his heart. "From the hurting world. This is the only place I can go where they can't get to me, where no one can hurt me."

I shake my head. "I didn't come here looking for sanctuary. I'm not running from anything."

"Then why are you here?"

I think of Alex and the way he's always talking about ghosts, but it's not that either. I never really think about it, I just come. Alex is the one with the need to have answers to every question. Not me. For me the experience has been enough of and by itself. But now that I think about it, now that I realize I want an answer, I find I don't have one.

"I don't know," I say.

"I thought you were like me," the boy says.

He sounds disappointed. Like I've disappointed him. He sounds angry, too. I want to say something to mollify him, but I can't find those words either. I reach out a hand, but he jerks away. He stands up, looks at me like I've turned into the enemy. I guess, in his eyes, I have. If I'm not with him, then I'm against him.

"I would never hurt you," I finally say. "I've never hurt anybody."

"That's what you think," he says.

Then he dives off the top of the wall, dives into the fog. I grab for him, but I'm not fast enough. I hold my breath, waiting to hear him hit the ground, but there's no sound. The fog swallows him and I'm alone on the top of the wall. I feel like I've missed something, something important. I feel like it was right there in front of me, all along, but now it's gone, dove off the wall with the boy and I've lost my chance to understand it.

The next time I come to the garden, everything's the same but different. The boy's not here. I've come other times, lots of times, and he hasn't been here, but this time I feel he won't be back, won't ever be back, and I miss him. I don't know why. It's not like we had a whole lot in common. It's not like we had long, meaningful conversations, or were in love with each other or anything. I mean, he was just a kid, like a little brother, not a lover. But I miss him the way I've missed a lover when the relationship ends.

I feel guilty, too. Maybe this place isn't a sanctuary for me, but it was for him. A walled, wild garden, held safe by moonlight and vines. His castle. What if I've driven him away forever? Driven him back to what he called the hurting world.

I hate that idea the most, the idea that I've stolen the one good thing he had in a life that didn't have anything else. But I don't know what to do about it, how to call him back. I'd trade my coming here for his in a moment, only how can I tell him that? I don't even know his name.

Lillie doesn't leave the graveyard this night. I watch her sitting there on the steps of one of those old mausoleums, sitting there all hunched up, sitting there all night. Finally, dawn breaks in the east, swallows the graveyard's spookiness. It's just an old forgotten place now, fallen in on itself and waiting for the wreckers' ball. The night's gone and taken the promise of danger away with it. I go over to where Lillie is and sit down beside her on the steps. I touch her arm.

"Lillie?" I say. "Are you okay?"

She turns to look at me. I'm expecting her to be mad at me for being here. She's got to know I've been following her around again. But all she does is give me a sad look.

"Did you ever lose something you never knew you had?" she asks.

"I only ever wanted one thing," I tell her, "but I never had it to lose."

"I don't even know what it is that I've lost," she says. "I just know something's gone. I had a chance to have it, to hold it and cherish it, but I let it go."

The early morning sunlight's warm on my skin, but
a shiver runs through me all the same. I think maybe
she's talking about ghosts. Maybe there really are
ghosts here. I get the crazy idea that maybe we're
ghosts, that we died and don't remember it. Or maybe
only one of us did.

"What was the one thing you wanted that you never
got?" she asks.

It's something I would never tell her. I promised
myself a long time ago that I'd never tell her because
I knew she deserved better. But that crazy idea won't
let go, that we're dead, or one of us is, and it makes
me tell her.

"It's you," I say.

Did you ever have someone tell you something you
always knew, but it never really registered until they
put it into words? That's what happens to me when
Alex tells me he loves me, that he's always loved me.

His voice trails off and I look at him, really look at
him. He almost flinches under my gaze. I can tell he
doesn't want to be here, that he wishes he'd never
spoken, that he feels a hurt swelling up inside him
that he would never have to experience if he'd kept
his feelings to himself. He reminds me of the boy, the
way the boy looked before he dove off the wall into
the fog, not the anger, but the sadness.

"Why did you never say anything about this before?" I finally ask.

"I couldn't," he says. "And anyway. Look at us,
you and me. We grew up in the same neighborhood,
sure, but. . . ." He shrugs. "You deserve better than
me."

I have to smile. This is so Alex. "Oh, right. And
who decided that?"

Alex chooses not to answer me. "You were always
different," he says instead. "You were always the first

on the block with a new sound or a new look, but you weren't following trends. It's like they followed you. And you never lost that. Anyone looks at you and they can tell there's nothing holding you back. You can do anything, go anywhere. The future's wide open for you, always was, you know what I'm saying? The streets never took their toll on you."

Then why am I still living in Foxville? I want to ask him. How come my star didn't take me to some nice uptown digs? But I know what he's talking about. It's not really about where I can go so much as where I've been.

"I was lucky," I say. "My folks treated me decently."

"And you deserved it."

"Everybody deserves to be treated decently," I tell him.

"Well, sure."

We grew up in the same building before my parents could afford a larger apartment down the block. My mom used to feel sorry for Alex's mother and we'd go over to visit when Crazy Eddie wasn't home. I'd play with Alex and his little sister, our moms would pretend our lives were normal, that none of us were dirt poor, everybody dreaming of moving to the 'burbs. Some of our neighbors did, but most of us couldn't afford it and still can't. Of course the way things are going now, you're not any safer or happier in the 'burbs than you are in the inner city. And living here, at least we've got some history.

But we never thought about that kind of thing at the time because we were just kids. Old times, simpler times. I smile, remembering how Alex always treated me so nice, right from the first.

"And then, of course, I had you looking out for me, too," I say.

"You still do."

I hadn't really got around to thinking what he was doing here in All Souls at this time of the morning, but now it makes sense. I don't know how many times I've had to ask him not to follow me around. It gives some people the creeps, but I know Alex isn't some crazed stalker, fixated on me. He means well. He really is just looking out for me. But it's a weird feeling all the same. I honestly thought I'd got him to stop.

"You really don't have to be doing this," I tell him. "I mean, it was kind of sweet when we were kids and you kept me from being bullied in the playground, but it's not the same now."

"You know the reason the dealers leave you alone?" he asks.

I glance toward the iron gates at the other end of the graveyard, but there's no one there at the moment. The drug market's closed up for the morning.

"They never knew I was here," I say.

Alex shakes his head and that's enough. He doesn't have to explain. I know the reputation he has in the neighborhood. I feel a chill and I don't know if it's from the close call I had or the fact that I live in the kind of world where a woman can't go out by herself. Probably both.

"It's still not right," I say. "I appreciate your looking out for me, really I do, but it's not right, your following me around the way you do. You've got to get a life, Alex."

He hangs his head and I feel like I've just reprimanded a puppy dog for doing something it thought was really good.

"I know," he mumbles. He won't look at me. "I . . . I'm sorry, Lillie."

He gets up and starts to walk away. I look at his broad back, and suddenly I'm thinking of the boy from the garden again. I'm seeing his sadness and anger, the way he dove off the wall into the fog and out of my life. I'm remembering what I said to him, that I would never hurt him, that I've never hurt anyone. And I remember what he said to me, just before he jumped.

That's what you think.

I'm not stupid. I know I'm not responsible for someone falling in love with me. I can't help it if they get hurt because maybe I don't love them back. But this isn't anyone. This is Alex. I've known him longer than maybe anybody I know. And if he's looked out for me, I've looked out for him, too. I stood up for him when people put him down. I visited him in the county jail when no one else did. I took him to the hospital that time the Creevy brothers left him for dead on the steps of his apartment building.

I know that for all his fierceness, he's a sweet guy. Dangerous, sure, but underneath that toughness there's no monster like his old man was. Given a different set of circumstances, a different neighborhood to grow up in, maybe, a different father, definitely, he could have made something of himself. But he didn't. And now I'm wondering if looking out for me was maybe part of what held him back. If I'd gotten myself out of the neighborhood, maybe he would have, too. Maybe we could both have been somebody.

But none of that's important right now. So maybe I'm not in love with Alex. So what? He's still my friend. He opened his heart to me and it's like I didn't even hear him.

"Alex!" I call after him.

He pauses and turns. There's nothing hopeful in the way he looks, there's not even curiosity. I get up from where I've been sitting and go to where he's standing.

"I've got to let this all sink in," I tell him. "You caught me off guard. I mean, I never even guessed you felt the way you do."

"I understand," he says.

"No, you don't. You're the best friend I ever had. I just never thought of us as a couple. Doesn't mean all of a sudden I hate you or something."

He shrugs. "I never should have said anything," he says.

I shake my head. "No. What you should have done is said something a lot sooner. The way I see it, your big problem is you keep everything all bottled up inside. You've got to let people know what you're thinking."

"That wouldn't change anything."

"How do you know? When I was a kid, I had the hugest crush on you. And later, I kept expecting you to ask me out, but you never did. Got so's I just never thought of you in terms of boyfriend material."

"So what're you saying?"

I smile. "I don't know. You could ask me to go to a movie or something."

"Do you want to go to a movie?"

"Maybe. Let me buy you breakfast and we'll talk about it."

So I'm trying to do like Lillie says, talk about stuff that means something to me, or at least I do it with her. She asks me once what I'd like to do with my life, because she can't see much future in my being a bouncer for a strip joint for the rest of my life. I tell her I've always wanted to paint and instead of laughing, she goes out and buys me a little tin of watercolors and a pad of paper. I give it a go and she tells me I'm terrible, like I don't know it, but takes the first piece I do and hangs it on her fridge.

Another time I tell her about this castle I used to dream about when I was a kid, the most useless castle you could imagine, just these walls and a garden in them that's gone all wild, but when I was there, nobody could hurt me, nobody at all.

She gives me an odd look and says, "With old castle rock for the walls."

So I guess Alex was right. I must have been looking for ghosts in All Souls—or at least I found one. Except it wasn't the ghost of someone who'd died and been buried in there. It was the ghost of a kid, a kid that was still living somewhere in an enclosed wild garden, secreted deep in his grown-up mind, a kid fooling around in trees full of grackles, hidden from the hurting world, held safe by moonlight and vines.

But you know, hiding's not always the answer. Because the more Alex talks to me, the more he opens up, the more I see him the way I did when I was a little girl, when I'd daydream about how he and I were going to spend the rest of our lives together.

I guess we were both carrying around ghosts.

FANTASY ANTHOLOGIES

☐ **ALIEN PREGNANT BY ELVIS** UE2610—$4.99
Esther M. Friesner & Martin H. Greenberg, editors
Imagination-grabbing tales that could have come straight out of the supermarket tabloid headlines. It's all the "news" that's not fit to print!

☐ **ANCIENT ENCHANTRESSES** UE2677—$5.50
Kathleen M. Massie-Ferch, Martin H. Greenberg, & Richard Gilliam, editors
Here are timeless works about those most fascinating and dangerous women—Ancient Enchantresses.

☐ **CASTLE FANTASTIC** UE2686—$5.99
John DeChancie & Martin H. Greenberg, editors
Fifteen of fantasy's finest lead us on some of the most unforgettable of castle adventures.

☐ **HEAVEN SENT** UE2656—$5.50
Peter Crowther, editor
Enjoy eighteen unforgettable encounters with those guardians of the mortal realm—the angels.

☐ **WARRIOR ENCHANTRESSES** UE2690—$5.50
Kathleen M. Massie-Ferch & Martin H. Greenberg, editors
Some of fantasy's top writers present stories of women gifted—for good or ill—with powers of both sword and spell.

☐ **WEIRD TALES FROM SHAKESPEARE** UE2605—$4.99
Katharine Kerr & Martin H. Greenberg, editors
Consider this the alternate Shakespeare, and explore both the life and works of the Bard himself.

Don't Miss These Exciting DAW Anthologies

SWORD AND SORCERESS
Marion Zimmer Bradley, editor
☐ Book XII   UE2657—$4.99
☐ Book XIII (*July '96*)   UE2703—$5.99

OTHER ORIGINAL ANTHOLOGIES
Mike Resnick & Martin H. Greenberg, editors
☐ SHERLOCK HOLMES IN ORBIT   UE2636—$5.50
☐ WITCH FANTASTIC   UE2640—$4.99

Martin H. Greenberg, editor
☐ CELEBRITY VAMPIRES   UE2667—$4.99
☐ VAMPIRE DETECTIVES   UE2626—$4.99
☐ WEREWOLVES   UE2654—$5.50

Rosalind M. & Martin H. Greenberg, editors
☐ DRAGON FANTASTIC   UE2511—$4.99
☐ HORSE FANTASTIC   UE2504—$4.50

Katharine Kerr & Martin H. Greenberg, editors
☐ ENCHANTED FORESTS   UE2672—$5.50
☐ WEIRD TALES FROM SHAKESPEARE   UE2605—$4.99

Norman Partridge & Martin H. Greenberg, editors
☐ IT CAME FROM THE DRIVE-IN   UE2680—$5.50

Cynthia Sternau & Martin H. Greenberg, editors
☐ THE SECRET PROPHECIES OF NOSTRADAMUS

                                                    UE2646—$4.99

Buy them at your local bookstore or use this convenient coupon for ordering.

PENGUIN USA P.O. Box 999—Dep. #17109, Bergenfield, New Jersey 07621

Please send me the DAW BOOKS I have checked above, for which I am enclosing
$_____ (please add $2.00 to cover postage and handling). Send check or money
order (no cash or C.O.D.'s) or charge by Mastercard or VISA (with a $15.00 minimum). Prices and
numbers are subject to change without notice.

Card #_____ Exp. Date _____
Signature_____
Name_____
Address_____
City _____ State _____ Zip Code _____

For faster service when ordering by credit card call **1-800-253-6476**

Allow a minimum of 4-6 weeks for delivery. This offer is subject to change without notice.

Welcome to DAW's Gallery of Ghoulish Delights!

☐ **DRACULA: PRINCE OF DARKNESS**
Martin H. Greenberg, editor
A blood-draining collection of all-original Dracula stories. From Dracula's traditional stalking grounds to the heart of modern-day cities, the Prince of Darkness casts his spell over his prey in a private blood drive from which there is no escape! UE2531—$4.99

☐ **FRANKENSTEIN: THE MONSTER WAKES**
Martin H. Greenberg, editor
Powerful visions of a man and monster cursed by destiny to be eternally at odds. Here are all-original stories by such well-known writers as: Rex Miller, Max Allan Collins, Brian Hodge, Rick Hautala, and Daniel Ransom. UE2584—$4.99

☐ **THE TIME OF THE VAMPIRES** May 1996
P.N. Elrod & Martin H. Greenberg, editors
From a vampire blessed by Christ to the truth about the notorious Oscar Wilde to a tale of vampirism and the Bow Street Runners, here are 18 original tales of vampires from Tanya Huff, P.N. Elrod, Lois Tilton, and others.
UE2693—$5.50

☐ **WEREWOLVES**
Martin H. Greenberg, editor
Here is a brand-new anthology of original stories about the third member of the classic horror cinema triumvirate—the werewolf, a shapeshifter who prowls the darkness, the beast within humankind unleashed to prey upon its own.
UE2654—$5.50

☐ **THE YEAR'S BEST HORROR STORIES: XXI**
Karl Edward Wagner, editor
A "bad girl" is taught a lesson no one else in her life will ever forget . . . a sketch artist takes from his model more than just her likeness . . . a Vietnam vet survives only to return to a hell worse than any he has ever known. Karl Edward Wagner once more leads readers into the heart of the horrific! UE2572—$5.50

Buy them at your local bookstore or use this convenient coupon for ordering.

PENGUIN USA P.O. Box 999—Dep. #17109, Bergenfield, New Jersey 07621

Please send me the DAW BOOKS I have checked above, for which I am enclosing
$_____ (please add $2.00 to cover postage and handling). Send check or money order (no cash or C.O.D.'s) or charge by Mastercard or VISA (with a $15.00 minimum). Prices and numbers are subject to change without notice.

Card #_____ Exp. Date _____
Signature_____
Name_____
Address_____
City _____ State _____ Zip Code _____

For faster service when ordering by credit card call 1-800-253-6476

Allow a minimum of 4-6 weeks for delivery. This offer is subject to change without notice.

Here, for your careful consideration . . .

THE TWILIGHT ZONE ANTHOLOGIES

edited by Carol Serling

☐ **JOURNEYS TO THE TWILIGHT ZONE**   UE2525—$4.99
The first of the Twilight Zone anthologies, this volume offers a wonderful array of new ventures into the unexplored territories of the imagination by such talents as Pamela Sargent, Charles de Lint, and William F. Nolan, as well as Rod Serling's chilling tale "Suggestion".

☐ **RETURN TO THE TWILIGHT ZONE**   UE2576—$4.99
Enjoy 18 new excursions into the dimension beyond our own. From a television set that is about to tune in to the future . . . to a train ride towards a destiny from which there is no turning back . . . plus "The Sole Survivor," a classic tale by Rod Serling himself!

☐ **ADVENTURES IN THE TWILIGHT ZONE**   UE2662—$4.99
Carol Serling has called upon many of today's most imaginative writers to conjure up 23 all-original tales which run the gamut from science fiction to the supernatural, the fantastical, or the truly horrific. Also included is "Lindemann's Catch," written by Rod Serling.
